# The Black Horn

# African American Cultural Theory and Heritage

## Series Editor: William C. Banfield

*The Jazz Trope: A Theory of African American Literary and Vernacular Culture*, by Alfonso W. Hawkins Jr., 2008.

*In the Heart of the Beat: The Poetry of Rap*, by Alexs D. Pate, 2009.

*George Russell: The Story of an American Composer*, by Duncan Heining, 2010.

*Cultural Codes: Makings of a Black Music Philosophy*, by William C. Banfield, 2010.

*Willie Dixon: Preacher of the Blues*, by Mitsutoshi Inaba, 2011.

*Representing Black Music Culture: Then, Now, and When Again?*, by William C. Banfield, 2011.

*The Black Church and Hip-Hop Culture: Toward Bridging the Generational Divide*, edited by Emmett G. Price III, 2012.

*The Black Horn: The Story of Classical French Hornist Robert Lee Watt*, by Robert Lee Watt, 2014

*Dean Dixon: Negro at Home, Maestro Abroad*, by Rufus Jones Jr., 2015

# The Black Horn

*The Story of Classical
French Hornist Robert Lee Watt*

Robert Lee Watt

**ROWMAN & LITTLEFIELD**
Lanham • Boulder • New York • London

Published by Rowman & Littlefield
A wholly owned subsidiary of The Rowman & Littlefield Publishing Group, Inc.
4501 Forbes Boulevard, Suite 200, Lanham, Maryland 20706
www.rowman.com

Unit A, Whitacre Mews, 26-34 Stannary Street, London SE11 4AB

British Library Cataloguing in Publication Information Available

**Library of Congress Cataloging-in-Publication Data**

The hardback edition of this book was previously catalogued by the Library of Congress
as follows:

Watt, Robert Lee.
  The black horn : the story of classical French hornist Robert Lee Watt / by Robert Lee
Watt.
     pages cm. — (African American cultural theory and heritage)
  Includes index.
  1. Watt, Robert Lee. 2. Horn players—United States—Biography. 3. African
American musicians—Biography. I. Title.
  ML419.W38A3 2014
  788.9'4092—dc23
  [B]
                                                                          2014018746
ISBN 978-1-4422-3938-8 (cloth : alk. paper)
ISBN 978-1-4422-6871-5 (pbk. : alk. paper)
ISBN 978-1-4422-3939-5 (ebook)

Printed in the United States of America

I dedicate this book to my family
and my dear friend, the late Jerome Ashby.

# Contents

# Acknowledgments

I would like to acknowledge my longtime friend Elston Carr for long ago recognizing my need to write a book, after hearing me complain so much about my orchestral life. In a phone message he said, "You need to write, Negro!"

I am also extremely grateful to my friend Marcus Eley for yelling at me to start writing my book: "There are your millions, in your book!" He also assisted me in the early stages of my manuscript preparation and in countless other ways.

I also give thanks to Euterpe (Greek Muse of Music), for helping me, via music, to call forth the emotional memories to effectively write about my past. I am also extremely grateful to that goddess of voice, Mezzo Soprano, Jessye Norman, whose recording of Richard Strauss' "Vier Letzte Lieder" (Four Last Songs) transported me there. I would like to thank writer, Mery Grey for introducing me to my first editor, Iris Schirmer (formerly with Random House), who helped me cut my book down from its formerly immense size.

I would like to thank my dear friends Todd Cochran and his wife, Hasmik, for their continued support and encouragement while writing my book.

I also wish to acknowledge many others who helped me in countless way during this process: Tina Huynh; Dr. Courtney Jones; Daisy Newman of the Young Musicians Choral Orchestra of Oakland, California; Raynor Carroll of the Los Angeles Philharmonic; and especially my family—my cousin Marjorie Nickelberry, my little brother Tony M. Watt, my big brother Ronald B. Watt, my big sister Judith Watt-Carson, and my little sister Gail D. Watt—for their helpful memories and insights.

# CHAPTER ONE

# Prelude

I was born into this world at a time when my father, after shining shoes all day at the Berkeley-Carteret Oceanfront Hotel, was not allowed to swim in the public swimming pools at the beach in Asbury Park, New Jersey. He angrily related the racist reality to us in those days:

> When I wanted to swim after work on those hot summer days I was not allowed to go into the swimming pools down at the beach, even though the sign on the building said in great big letters, "PUBLIC BATHING."
>
> Those crackers laughed as they told me, "Hey, boy, why don't you go on over to the colored beach and swim—but you might drown trying 'cause there's lots of sewer pipes in that water."
>
> When I wanted to go see a movie, black people had to sit in the balcony and the ushers didn't see you to your seat; they just directed you to the balcony and you were on your own.
>
> I went to a segregated grade school—Bangs Avenue School. There was a black principal and a white principal and all the classes were totally segregated. The entire school building was divided with blacks on one side and whites on the other. We even had separate playgrounds.
>
> Even if you wanted to take a road trip on the highway, you had to know in advance where you could stay overnight, where you could stop for gas and get served, where you could stop to eat or just get a lousy cup of coffee.
>
> There was actually a published manual, *The Negro Motorist Green Book*, that listed the places you could stay, get a haircut, get gas, or even which Chinese restaurants served colored. The book was an international travel guide for every state in America, Mexico, Bermuda, and Canada. There just wasn't much

black people could do in those days without having to first think if they would be admitted or turned away. You were just supposed to *know your place* as a black person. It was a horrible time to be black in America.

January 15, 1948, was an extremely transitional time in American history. Harry Truman was president, the Supreme Court banned religion in public schools, the Marshall Plan was enacted, the first LP records were introduced, cars had no seatbelts, there was no Civil Rights bill, there were white and black water fountains in the South, and black people were referred to as "colored," "Negro," or worse. There was a popular saying among whites *and* blacks: "I'm free, white, and 21—I can do as I please." However, the concept was only true if you were white.

A glass of beer was only a nickel, Miles Davis and Dizzy Gillespie still played normal trumpets, and the cheapest seat for a symphony orchestra concert was 60 cents.

A man could be drafted into the armed forces, go to war, and die before he was old enough to vote. Black people had fought in World War II in a seg-regated army fighting for the same freedoms as whites, but captured German soldiers who had murdered countless white Americans in battle had more rights in the United States during World War II than American black sol-diers. A black man could be lynched for interacting with a white woman. If a black person fell sick in the streets, there were only certain hospitals where treatment was available. Consequently, many black people expired before they would ever be admitted to a "white only" hospital. There were no com-puters, cell phones, or DVDs in the world in which I drew my first breath.

My father often told the story of how our great-grandfather on his side of the family was from Asia.

He was an orphan boy running errands for British missionaries on the docks of Rangoon, Burma . . . that's why you all like rice and that's why your aunt Nelly and them in New York are so yellow looking. Now, your grandmother's mama was from the so-called Gullah Geechee people, who were the last black people brought here from West Africa well after slavery was outlawed. They were left to die on those little islands off the coast of South Carolina, Georgia, and Florida, but they survived. The Geechee name came from Florida, where your grandmama's mother was married to a British ship captain who ran a steamship up and down the St. Johns River in Jacksonville, Florida.

# CHAPTER TWO

~

# Early Memories

I don't know at what age we are supposed to have our first conscious memories, but I do remember moving from one roach-infested house to an even larger one. We must have looked like a caravan of weary Bedouin carrying food, clothes, and blankets to our new house on Drummond Avenue in Neptune, New Jersey. At that age, the whole world seemed a frightening blur through my copious tears, as my family slowly pushed my rickety stroller to our new living adventure.

The new, larger, roach-infested house was in a much better neighborhood and the new house looked in great shape from the outside, but we caught holy hell in that poorly heated funhouse in winter.

There was an old wood-burning coal stove, so we had to keep a large woodpile in our backyard, which grew to more than half a story high, creating a natural temptation for us to play "King of the Woodpile."

Then there was the time Ronnie, one of my older brothers, tried to be Superman by tying a cape around his neck and jumping from the back porch roof onto that woodpile. His Superman cape flapped wildly upwards as he dropped wildly downwards with a brief scream, earning himself a broken collarbone.

The house produced many memories:

I recall one very cold evening in our new house that really stayed with me. Our mother was waiting on the front porch for Dad to take her to the supermarket. We noticed how agitated she was when she began to pace up and down. Where was my father? It was getting late, a snowstorm was starting to blow in, and we were wondering when we were going to have dinner. Suddenly our mother came back into the house and angrily threw off her coat. We heard her say under her breath, "Son of a bitch, I can never count on him."

Her lips were trembling with anger as she ordered, "Ronnie, Judy, get the large soup bowls down from the cupboard . . . and the large soupspoons." There was nothing in the house to eat. Everyone just watched as our young mother leaped onto the kitchen counter like a gazelle and pulled down an ugly green box. On the box it said, "United States Army Reconstituted Powdered Milk." She ripped it open and started spooning it into a large pot of boiling water. After a short while, the entire house smelled like Thanksgiving and Christmas and for just a brief moment we imagined that we were going to have sweet baked goodies. Mother ordered us into the kitchen to fill our bowls with the rich creamy-smelling offering. It was delicious, thick, sweet, and very warming to the stomach. She told us to "eat as much as you want and then go right to bed, because pretty soon it's going to get very cold in this house. I'll have a big breakfast waiting for you when you get up."

One by one, like marines darting from a foxhole, we made our way up the stairs to our freezing beds, screaming as our warm bodies hit the cold sheets. We fought, as usual, over which one of us got to sleep under the warm, funky, rat fur overcoat.

A few hours later, I was awakened by snow blowing through a tiny hole in the window, which had actually formed a small snowdrift in the corner of the bedroom. I wanted to get rid of it, but it was just too cold to get out of bed. Besides, I remembered that we often had snowball fights inside the house and it would be useful for the morning battles. As I was about to doze off, I heard our mother crying in her bedroom. Something told me that there would be no big breakfast waiting for us when we got up in the morning. God willing there would be some of that milky concoction left. Our father didn't come around again for nearly two weeks.

On rare occasions my father came home late at night, a little drunk, and played his trumpet with the mute stuck in the bell. He crashed out on the floor with his horn pointed towards the ceiling. He had a great sound and good musical expression, especially his jazz playing.

At seven years old, I became fascinated with his trumpet, which he kept above our defunct fireplace. It was bright and shiny and I wanted to blow it. I was too short to reach the trumpet so I put my little brother Tony on my shoulders. When he reached for the horn, I lost my balance and we both fell on the trumpet. Unfortunately we dented the horn and I came up with the bright idea of using a hammer to work out the dents. The more I tried to remove the dents the worse they became. Then I decided to take the valves out of their casings and get a really good sniff of the valve oil for myself. Valve oil, in those days was made from kerosene and little bit of whale sperm oil, giving it a most intoxicating smell. However, I innocently put the wrong valves back into the wrong valve casings. The next time my father tried to blow his horn, nothing come out. He looked at the horn and began to unscrew the valves. He held them up to his one eye looking for something small on the underside of each valve.

"What's wrong?" I asked.

He said, in a stern frightening tone, "You been messing with my horn, that's what. You replaced the valves wrong and made these dents in the bell, that's what's wrong! Come over here, boy!" he ordered, pulling me by my arm right next to him. I stood trembling in fear as he proceeded to lecture me on which valve went into which casing. "You see this little number?"

"Oh yeah, I see it. It's very tiny," I said in a scared shaky voice.

"Yeah, yeah, well, you gotta put the right-numbered valve back into the right-numbered casing, you understand?" He looked at me for a long time from behind his dark ominous glasses and said, in a calmer tone of voice, "If you were interested in the trumpet, you should've told me. I would've been glad to show you how to play it. . . . Look at this dented bell . . . damn it! You never touch a musician's instrument, never!"

Sometimes my father didn't pay the electric bill for months at a time, forcing us to use kerosene lamps and candles for light. I remember my mother carrying a kerosene lamp upstairs when we went off to bed. Ronnie carried the second lamp, Judy followed with the third, and I carried a fourth. It looked like a procession of smoking chimneys as we walked. The black smoke streamed out of the top of the lampshades, looking like the smokestacks of an ocean liner.

During those times when we didn't have lights, Ronnie often told us frightening tales of how he saw Mr. Randolph, our neighborhood warlock, turned into a man with a goat's head. He cautioned us how to safely pass by his house. "Always walk backwards while in front of his house, walk sideways for thirteen steps, and then run as fast as possible." After hearing those frightening stories, we made our way quickly past Mr. Randolph's house, executing all those silly rituals.

As we got older, Mother shopped for our Christmas toys in September. Ronnie always knew where she kept our toys hidden. His big thrill was to wait until we were all in bed on a cold winter night and then ask us if we wanted to see our Christmas toys or if we were hungry. "If anybody wants to see their Christmas toys and play with them for a little while, I can tell you where they're hidden, for a nickel. Also, if anybody's hungry, I have some sandwiches I made under the bed in a suitcase. They are Karo syrup, mayonnaise, and mustard on white bread."

~

# CHAPTER THREE

# Back to Asbury Park

In June 1958, I was ten years old. Our mother called us together and told us that our father was behind on the rent and we would have to move back to Asbury Park and live in an apartment. That was a very traumatic moment for all of us and I was especially upset by the news. It was very hard to understand why I had to move from my childhood home, with all the things I had grown up with—Mr. Randolph the warlock and the wheat field where we played and dreamed for hours on end. There was also the urban legend of the Jersey Devil, who stood eight feet tall with a horse's head, a long neck supported by batlike wings, skinny bird legs, and horse's hooves. It could fly off the ground, bite you in the face, or rip your guts out, causing you to die a horrible, bloody, death.

We went with our mother to see our new place. It was an old three-story building with a storefront just below our apartment. There was an entryway from the street that led to a dingy hallway, which smelled of wine and urine. After going up one flight of stairs, we came to the kitchen door. The floor of this hallway was warped and went uphill like a wheelchair ramp, the floorboards were black with soot, and some were sticking up and needed to be nailed down. The first thing I looked for was a gas stove, some sort of central heating, and if the place had hot water. It had none of those things. In fact, there was no kitchen stove at all. We asked the landlord if he was going to put in a gas stove. To our surprise, he said our father had a stove that he would be moving in himself. We stormed out of the liquor store downstairs and went back to continue our examination of the filthy, dreary apartment.

The walls of the kitchen were made of tin panels that had rusted out in many places, especially in the ceiling over the stove area. The bathroom was very ordinary, with a bathtub, no shower, and walls with tin panels.

Heading back through the kitchen we entered the next room, which had walls of plaster with some cracks and a chimney flue. In that room we thought perhaps we might install the kerosene stove. Moving on, we found a very large room with space for three sets of bunk beds. There were three large front windows overlooking the street below, which turned out to be great for us, because many insane things happened at night on Springwood Avenue.

I remember the day my mother got our old kitchen stove burning with a nice hot fire. She said that we were going to need some more coal so I agreed to run right out for it. Before I left, I happened to look up at the ceiling. It was covered with hundreds of large shiny roaches—the heat from the stove must have brought them out. My mother yelled, "Bob, bring some roach spray too . . . and hurry!"

When I got the blue coal home and onto the fire, we noticed that we also had mice. They were up in the ceiling and when they moved around they knocked bits of rusty debris and mouse droppings onto the stove. That night was bitter cold, but at least we had a nice warm fire going, despite our discovery of new critters.

The triple window in the large front room was a new wonder. We sat for hours just watching people and the things that happened on the street below. Once I saw the police continue to beat a handcuffed guy who still had chunks of glass in his body. At the time, there was a particular walk in vogue—we called it the "Springwood Avenue Bop"—where young men walked fast dragging one foot and on that one shoe were heel plates that caused sparks to fly.

There was one thing that happened on Springwood Avenue that I could never quite understand. The guys with the "Konk" hairstyles were the only ones who did this. Every so often we would hear a loud commotion: a guy in a Cadillac convertible would be driving down the street with a white woman sitting next to him—she usually looked more like pink pickled pig feet, wearing a dress and stuffed in a jar, compared to her black male escort—and as black women so eloquently put it, "Well, . . . she white."

Living on Springwood Avenue was fast becoming a real problem for my family, with the people loitering in the hallway entrance of our building, drinking wine, and keeping warm. One night my oldest sister, Judy, was coming home and a man decided to follow her.

She came running up the steps yelling my name. "Bobby, help!" The man had actually started up the steps after her.

When I got there, I slid down the steps, catching him in the knees with my bare feet. As he fell on top of me, I reached up and poked his eyes with my thumb and forefinger. I heard him groan. I always wondered if I'd actually damaged his eyes. He stumbled away moaning. I never found out who he was and I was glad it was too dark for him to recognize me.

# CHAPTER FOUR

~

# Left Back

My father started a new job at the West Side Community Center and lived there on the top floor by himself. He was the caretaker, janitor, athletic coach, and music director. During that time period, he tried many times to teach me trumpet. He said if I learned the trumpet, I would be joining a long line of trumpet players named "Bobby." There was my cousin Bobby Booker, or Robert Lee Booker, my namesake, a well-known jazz trumpet player in New York, and *his* Uncle Bobby who also played jazz trumpet in New York. But in spite of that great tradition, I never learned the trumpet.

The West Side Community Center in Asbury Park always had a very fine drum and bugle corps, which my father started up again. I reluctantly played soprano bugle in the corps, feeling like it was the least I could do for my father, who had taught me how to blow a brass instrument.

During that time I'd heard from my friend Stan about another drum corps called the Neptune Shoreliners. He always talked about how they played really fancy music, did very sophisticated marching maneuvers, and had really great uniforms and shiny bugles. One night I was helping my father clean up at the community center. I was going through some old 78 recordings when I found the William Tell Overture. While listening to the old recording, I asked my father what the instrument was that came in after the trumpet in the famous Lone Ranger theme.

He said, "Oh that's the *French* horn, the peck horn. It only plays the off-beats and never gets the melody. Why, you like that horn?" He asked in a surprised tone. "It's an instrument for thin-lipped white boys. Your lips are too thick for that narrow mouthpiece."

I was crushed, because that horn sounded so wonderful. I felt it in my bones, like part of my heart and soul. There was nothing in my world that beautiful.

The very next day my friend Stan invited me over to Booker's, who played baritone bugle in the Neptune Shoreliners. His bugle was completely chrome-plated. When they finally asked me to join, I told them that I could play the soprano bugle. They said what they really needed were more *French horn bugles*. I had never heard of a French horn bugle, but if it sounded anything like the French horn I heard on that 78 recording, I was in.

The first time I saw my father cry was when I got my report card telling me that I did not pass the seventh grade. I was "left back," as the kids used to say. I never thought it would happen to me. I had to take my report card to my grandmother.

She took it, looked at it, sucked her teeth in disgust, and said, "You just wait here until your father comes."

I sat around and waited for many agonizing hours. When my father showed up, he looked at my report card and just stared at me with a horrible sad look on his face.

"Why?" he asked. "You're not dumb; I know you're not."

Then to my great surprise, he began to cry right in front of me. Tears were dripping from beneath his dark glasses onto to his rough facial skin. My punishment was that I had to give up my French horn bugle and the Shoreliners until I did better in school.

The following year we were told by our black southern schoolteachers that eighth grade would be held at the high school and that we had better behave while we were there. Our homeroom was in the balcony and there were assemblies every morning where we prayed and pledged allegiance to the flag. We had some of our same black teachers at the high school teaching the black kids. The high school was half white kids and half black, which was why the black teachers were so concerned about how the black kids would behave in the presence of the white world at Asbury Park High School.

A year later I was walking through the "Old Village" when someone called out to me from one of the units.

"Hey there! Young Watt!"

I glanced around startled . . . then it came again.

"Hey, young Watt… Bobby Watt! Over here."

It was Tom Jones, a friend of the family. He asked me what year I was in high school. I told him that I was about to graduate from eighth grade and would be starting high school in the fall.

"I see, so tell me about yourself, young Watt. I don't know you as well as I know the rest of your family. I remember you as the quiet one. Just call me Jones."

Jones had a really bright-eyed expression on his face when he smiled. He was about six feet tall, dark skinned, short-cropped haircut, a square jaw line, and full lips. His neck was shaped like a bodybuilder and he was seriously buff in his torso and arms. He had played fullback on the high school football team.

"So, young Watt, what do you want to do in life? Talk to me, I've got time." It was early evening, perhaps 5:30. Jones handed me a beer and put on some music. It was jazz—Horace Silver's *Songs from My Father*. He said jazz is the music of black people. "It's our music, Watt. You must understand what it really means to be a black man in this world. If you don't, you'll wander the planet *lost* for the rest of your life. Black! To be black is cool, young Watt. It's like the night, dark and mysterious with many colorful secrets. It's one of the true wonders of the Western world. Don't ever be ashamed of being black—and don't ever let anyone *make you feel ashamed of it*. Embrace it and it will serve you forever."

We talked on many different subjects—things I had agonized over in my adolescent mind, like religion, church, Jesus (especially the white icon of Jesus), sex, black women, interracial dating—all the things no one dared talk to young people about in those days. We often sat up all night and he always ended our talks with, "To be continued, Watt."

I finally got my French horn bugle back from my grandmother and brought it home. At night, I practiced in the large unheated front room. I sat for hours playing in the dark, wearing gloves and my overcoat. I took breaks every so often and joined my family in the TV room with the kerosene stove to get warm.

The new drum corps, the Neptune Shoreliners, was my first real fascination with music. I could finally produce that French horn sound that haunted me so much. My father was not happy about my finding another drum corp. He said that it was OK if I played in that white drum corps as long as I still played with his West Side Community Center corps. "Don't leave us for them white boys."

The very last days of my eighth-grade school year, I was going into my homeroom and I noticed a girl I had never seen before. She was very cute, brown skinned with very pretty black eyes. She looked right at me and smiled. Of course, with my self-image in those days, I immediately looked behind me to see who she could be flashing such a beautiful toothy smile. I struggled to smile back as she opened her balcony door and disappeared. I was so shaken that I hit myself in the face with the door as I entered my homeroom.

From that moment on, I was a different person. It was like being awakened from a deep sleep. From that single smile, I felt so warmed and validated that I couldn't function the rest of the day. I just had to find that lovely girl. "Was she real?" I wondered. I never saw her again for the remainder of the school year.

That summer I had one the worst jobs in the world. My father used to get me up at 5:30 in the morning to drive out to Seaside Heights, New Jersey, to clean a giant seafood restaurant. There was never any time for breakfast—he woke me, waited while I dressed, and we were off. I joined my two older brothers, Edward and Ronnie, in my father's old blue-panel truck and drove to that crazy job sitting on five-gallon wax cans and holding onto his floor-waxing machines. On that trip several times a week, my mind flashed on how I was going to meet that lovely girl at school in the fall. *Who was she?*

My father always started the work with us and then left after a short while. My oldest brother, Edward, worked in the front part of the restaurant scrubbing and waxing the bar and restaurant floor with the large floor-waxing machine. Ronnie worked cleaning beneath the wooden slats in the kitchen, and I worked outside in the back of the restaurant cleaning fifteen to twenty trashcans. Since it was a seafood restaurant, I was dealing with discarded shrimp, lobster, and crab shells, rotten fish heads, and whatever else the restaurant served. When I opened the cans, the smell was nauseating. There was always something brutally sickening about smelling rotten seafood on an empty stomach early in the morning. Sometimes there were maggots and mice in the trashcans and flies that had no mercy when they bit. When my brothers heard me cursing the flies, they always yelled out to me, "Bobby, have some shrimp, I hear they're very *sweet* this time of year."

My father always showed up after the work was done eating a sandwich, but for some reason never brought any food for us. He checked everything out and said, "Good work buzzards. I might even pay you."

One day the white boss showed up. My father *jumped to* and changed his entire tone of speaking. "These are my sons, this is Edward."

"Please to greet your acreetance" came nervously out of our oldest brother's mouth.

Ronnie quickly flashed me one of his devilish smiles.

My father glared at Edward for being so nervous. I doubt the white man noticed, but my father was very embarrassed. On the way home he lectured us on how to make a proper introduction. "Always remember, when you meet someone new just say, 'How do you do?' And open your mouth wide and say it loud. Don't try to be all fancy saying, 'Please to greet your acreetance,' like your brother, sounding like a Goddamn fool!"

At the end of that crazy summer, my father finally paid us. It was just enough to buy one pair of shoes, one pair of pants, and one shirt for school. On the other hand, those were the first *new* clothes I'd ever had in my life. I always got hand-me-downs from my older brothers. But then, having *some* new clothes was going to come in handy when I got to meet that lovely girl at school.

I was always very embarrassed having to go to my grandmother's place in the projects once a week to take a bath. I recall one particularly warm evening, as I approached my grandmother's, things became quite ugly. Everyone was sitting out on the lawn: Miss Eva, Mr. Cliff and his wife, Connie, my father, my grandfather, and my grandmother. I dreaded that whole scene and tried to sneak past everyone without having a drawn-out greeting session.

My grandmother yelled out, "Don't you *dare* walk by everyone without speaking—come over here, boy, and speak!"

I was just about to speak, when my father suddenly grabbed me from behind and pushed me even closer to everyone.

"Get on over there and speak, boy!" he said under his breath.

I felt so ridiculous and humiliated that I *really* wanted to hurt somebody. Music was the only thing that calmed me down after such episodes with my father and grandmother. I sat and played my French horn bugle for hours in the dark in that large front room before I felt like myself again. I didn't know, at that time, the difference between practice and playing. I just played whatever came into my head, mostly French horn passages that I had heard on movies and television.

# CHAPTER FIVE

# First Love

My father worked part time behind the liquor counter at the Westside Drug Store, across the street from our Springwood Avenue apartment. I washed windows and swept up in the back a few times a week in that same drug store with him and he'd give me a few dollars every so often. I remember the pharmacist, a short, fat, white-haired, brown-skinned little man with thick, dry lips that clucked when he talked. He was very cruel to the customers at times and I despised him. One evening he really angered a man trying to discreetly buy condoms. The man tried with difficulty to pronounce the word "prophylactic." The mean little pharmacist pretended he didn't understand the man.

"What is it you need, sir?"

The man quietly asked, "Do you have any ah . . . prophyl . . ."

The little pharmacist pressed him, "What? Speak up, man! What do you want?"

The man finally lost it and yelled, "Do you have any rubbers, man?! Stop messin' with me, Goddamn it, and give me some rubbers!"

The petty little pharmacist laughed, along with those in line, and said, "Oh, rubbers . . . yes, we have lots of those."

At that same drugstore, there was a very priceless moment that I witnessed one evening while my father was working behind the liquor counter. One of his girlfriends came in to talk to him. She was a regular customer, six feet tall, quite brazen, and known for stealing husbands. While the woman was talking to my father, my mother happened to come in. She asked the woman to leave so she could talk to my father. The woman ignored my mother's polite request and our feisty mother picked up the wooden sign from the counter and smashed it on the side of the woman's face, nearly knocking her out. "I said move, bitch!"

I laughed out loud and my father yelled at me to go finish up my work. There was a part of my father's cruel, twisted personality that probably enjoyed the spectacle of two women fighting over him. It was a dark side of him that perhaps only I knew.

⌢

During that crazy summer of 1963, before I was to enter high school, my grandfather dropped dead while standing in line at the bank. That was my first experience with a death in the family. The death of my grandfather was very sad for me because I always felt he had a rather unfulfilling life being married to my grandmother. During the viewing of the body in the local funeral home, my grandmother took every opportunity to act out her phony, guilt-ridden, grief drama. Most people fell for it and tried to console her, but I knew better.

Besides my grandfather's funeral, the only other funeral we ever attended was that of our family doctor. My grandmother and many other black folks worshiped him, because they believed he gave them a break on their medical bills. In fact, he sold my grandmother nerve pills that we later found out were placebos.

At the doctor's funeral, we were told by my father to go up to his casket, kneel, and say, "God bless Dr. Vacarro." I dreaded the whole idea and I remember Ronnie asking, "What if we want to say more?" My father got extremely irritated and snapped at us, "Don't say *anything* else—just say what I told you and get the hell out of there." I went up with my little brother, Tony. We knelt at the casket, looked at each other, and cracked up laughing. We solemnly got back up without saying anything and no one was the wiser.

In September 1963, I entered high school. When classes began, I found out that there were three major curriculums of study at Asbury Park High School: General, Business Administration, and College Preparatory. Later I found out that, based on my GPA in grade school, I was placed in Basic Studies, separate from the three main curriculums. I was suddenly saddened with deep regret that I hadn't done better in grade school. But again, no one ever told me how one went about ending up in College Preparatory or Business Administration in high school. We were just told to go to school and do well. I must have been in a mild depression all those years without knowing it.

After the shock of entering high school wore off, I focused on trying to meet that lovely girl from eighth grade. The beginning of each high school day started with an assembly in the auditorium. We did the flag salute, the Lord's Prayer, and sang the National Anthem.

Suddenly there, in full splendor, playing the organ for the entire high school, was the girl who had smiled at me in eighth grade. She was a musician! She was adorable, so smooth, so calm and comfortable with herself. After the anthem, the entire school waited as she walked over, with her cute, stocking-covered, brown legs and her very adorable butt, and sat in with the band. She played bass clarinet too? I couldn't believe it. I was way out of my league. She looked extremely smart too—and with my being in Basic Studies, how could I even talk to her?

Arriving at school the next day, I finally found her in that same balcony with her head buried in a book. As I began to walk in her direction, I was so nervous my body began to tremble and glow with a bright yellow light. Fear churned in my gut, but I had to keep going. Suddenly, she looked up and gave me that same wonderful toothy smile from back in eighth grade. As I drew nearer, I became so locked in her gaze that I actually tripped and nearly fell on top of her. *Damn it! This couldn't be happening*, I thought.

Then she spoke, "Careful, Bob, are you OK?"

She knew *my* name?

As if she wasn't sure, she said, "Hi Bob, I'm Leslie. . . . Were you coming over to talk to me?"

I thought to myself, *How did she know my name? Me, the nobody kid, who was in Basic Studies? Come on fool, talk to her, this is your moment.* "Ah! Yes, I certainly was coming over to talk to you, Leslie. Please excuse my clumsiness." She continued to flash that wonderful smile. I couldn't believe I was actually in her presence. I told her in a very nervous manner that I enjoyed her organ and clarinet playing in assembly the previous morning. She thanked me, we said our goodbyes, and promised to meet again soon.

After meeting her a second time, I asked if I could walk her home sometime.

She smiled and said, "Of course, anytime—where do you live, Bob?"

I told her Springwood Avenue and she said she knew it well. After that I was really motivated to do *whatever I could* to come off looking good in her eyes. Yes! I washed myself every day, birdbath style, in cold water when I didn't have time to heat water on our kitchen stove. I mean, it was really cold in our flat at times and to wash up in cold soap and water in the dead of winter was bordering on insane. I ironed my own shirts, pressed my pants (when we had electricity), and wore a jacket and tie to school. I looked almost professional and hopefully smart when I left the house. For all anyone knew, I *was* in College Prep.

The way Leslie looked at me when we walked home from school together, looking right into my eyes—relating to me and me alone—was something brand new. I just couldn't believe that there were actually people in the world like her. If I had known this, I would have been an A student and passed seventh grade the first time or perhaps even *skipped* a grade. I felt betrayed somehow.

The big question on my mind then was, what did I have in my life at that moment that would put me on par with Leslie? I consulted my seventh-grade left-back companion, Bledsoe. He said he knew who Leslie was and had seen her with her family many times around town. He said to even think about going out with Leslie, I would have to pass an amazing credibility test and earn a Negro approval rating from God herself. In order to do this, he suggested that I forget the French horn bugle, join the band, and take up the *real* French horn.

I agreed with him. "You know, this could be the thing," I said as I paced up and down in front of him.

Bledsoe got right up in my face and said, "Watt, joining the band will put you *right next to her*. Take up the *real* French horn, Watt. I saw one the other night on TV, made of silver. I'm telling you, Watt, do it!"

First things first, I had to find out if I could get out of Basic Studies and end up in the College Prep curriculum. I went to the guidance counselor to talk about it. A white guidance counselor proceeded to tell me how I got where I was and why I, in so many words, belonged there. I told him what I wanted to do and he just stared at me for an uncomfortable period of time.

Finally he said, "Well, I guess you can do this? It is possible given the time you have as a freshman. You do understand, Robert, that no one has ever done such a thing before . . . but then we never had a Basic Studies curriculum before in this high school until so many of you people seemed to—" He cut himself off. "So, Mr. Watt, here's the plan, you will start changing courses of study starting in your sophomore year. You will have to take your first year of College Preparatory science next year and then in your junior year, take your first year of math and your second year of math as a senior. Now if you don't mind doing this and don't mind studying real hard for the PSATs and the SATs, you'll be ready for college."

I was thrilled! I didn't care how difficult it would be. I wanted to go to college, I wanted to be with Leslie, I wanted to be smart like Leslie, and I wanted music!

When the first edition of *Megaphone*, the high school newspaper, came out, I bought a copy and put it in my briefcase. When I got home that evening before retiring, I started to read it. Leslie's picture was in the school newspaper with the girl's hockey team. God! I couldn't believe my eyes. How could she do all those things? I put the photo of Leslie up on the wall and at night before turning off the light, I talked to the photo in a whisper: "Look at you, so grand and beautiful! Will I ever measure up to you? I can't wait until I'm in your presence once more. . . . Until then, good night."

My work was cut out for me. I had to transcend the Basic Studies program by getting the best grades possible. Meanwhile, I would keep my books covered so Leslie wouldn't know until my junior year, when I would actually be in College Prep. *And then*, I would tell her that I moved up from General to College Prep—not Basic to College Prep. That was my plan and it would be perfect.

After I had taken care of my academic future in high school, my next mission was to take up the *real* French horn. On a free period, I went down to the band room to seek out the band director. I found him napping in his office. He was a tall, elderly white man with salt and pepper hair. He had been teaching in the school district for years—he had even taught my father in high school. He played trombone and was a student of Arthur Pryor, who was trombonist for John Phillip Sousa.

"How can I help you, son?"

I told him that I wanted to take up the real French horn.

He looked up at me and said, "The what? You want to do what?"

I told him again that I wanted to start playing the French horn.

He looked at me strangely and said, "Why?"

I said in a very shy, rapid undertone, "Because I can already play the French horn bugle, but I play it by ear in a drum corps and I want to learn how to read music so I thought it was time to take up the real French horn, sir."

He tried to tell me that there was no such thing as a French horn bugle. He looked at me for a long time and said, "Well, son, I'm sorry, I don't have a French horn right now that you can start on. It's a very difficult instrument to blow. Why do you want to choose such a difficult task?" Then he clapped his hands together as if he'd thought of some great idea. "I tell ya what though, I can start you on a trombone or tuba today. I have plenty of those instruments on hand. I tell ya why I say that, son. Most of you colored fellows have the thick lips you know . . . and, well, you do better on the instruments with the larger mouthpieces. The French horn has a very small thin mouthpiece and you might have trouble blowing it."

I told him again that I already played the French horn bugle and *it* had a French horn mouthpiece and that my lips had *no* problem playing it. I told him that I didn't want to play anything else.

He glanced at me and said, "Well, you certainly are persistent, I can say that for you."

I asked him what persistent meant.

He smiled and said, "You won't take no for an answer." He paused for a while before saying, "Look son, there is an old French horn in the instrument closet. I'm not sure it even works, but you can take it home. I'll give you a method book and you see what you can do with it. How's that?"

"Yes, sir, I'll take it," I answered. I was *so* excited; I had never seen a real French horn up close. I knew it had a lot of tubing and looked very neat the way it twisted, but to have a chance to take one home was surely going to be an adventure.

In the instrument room, he dragged out an old maroon-colored leather case. "This is it," he said. He opened the case and there it was, the real French horn.

Underneath the horn, I noticed a method book, *Foundation to French Horn Playing* by Eric Hauser, French horn player for John Phillip Sousa.

He said the book would begin teaching me to read music as well as how to play the horn. I couldn't wait to get that instrument home.

As I left the band room with that horn, I instantly felt more on par with my new love and all of her advanced, accelerated, and valedictorian friends. I would become Bob Watt, French horn player, who would soon be in the College Prep curriculum, college bound, serious guy, most likely to succeed.

When I finally got that old horn home, I showed it to my mother right away and then took it into our unheated bedroom to work with it. The horn must have been sitting in that case for years. I sponged the inside of the case with soap and water and ran water through the French horn. I cleaned it up a bit with some brass polish. I took the horn in my hands, holding it the way it illustrated in the book and tried to blow it. Nothing. I couldn't believe it. What was wrong? I took my bugle and tried to play the same note. Then I noticed on the front of the French horn method book, "Horn in F." I knew that the French horn bugle was in the key of G and that was most likely the problem. I grabbed the book and started to play Lesson One. It explored whole notes and whole rests for the first five or six lessons, but the lessons kept introducing more and more notes. Next I started learning the fingering for a C scale. However, I noticed when I pushed the valve plates down, they stayed down. For a minute I tried to play a scale by pushing the valves plates down and flicking my fingers underneath them and quickly pushing them back up again. And for a moment I thought, *Could this be the way the valves worked?* I continued to play it for hours. I just couldn't get enough of that rustic-mellow sound. I couldn't wait to tell Bledsoe that I had done it.

# CHAPTER SIX

~

# Music Chose Me

I played the French horn every day for hours, just producing long tones, getting used to the instrument, and enjoying the lovely tone. When I tried to play bugle calls on the real French horn, I noticed it had a better response, a more liquid and softer feel to it.

Over the weekend, I continued to explore several lessons in the French horn book. In addition to the lessons, I worked up a fancy bugle call with lots of fast, loud notes to play for the band director because I knew he didn't believe I could play the French horn with my thick lips.

When Monday came, I was extremely anxious to get to sixth period for my first French horn lesson. That particular morning, I ran into the band director as I entered the building. He saw me, did a double take, and said hello. I was soaking wet from the rain, the horn case was wet, and I guess I looked a sight after walking all the way from the West Side in the rain.

He looked at me and asked, "You walked all the way from the West Side in this weather with that horn, son?"

I said, "Yes, I did, sir." I made an apology for the horn and nervously tried to wipe the water off the old case with my hand. I told him that I would wipe it off better as soon as I got a paper towel. "I could put some wax on the case to keep it better—"

He just looked at me and shook his head, walking away mumbling, "If I could get half the kids in the band to take their horns home I might have . . ."

I yelled after him, saying I'd see him sixth period. He just waved his hand, OK.

After a rather distracted school day, thinking about sixth period and playing the French horn for Mr. Bryan, I was finally on my way to the band room with my horn. I entered the room with many questions on my lips.

Mr. Bryan just looked at me in amazement. 'So, let's hear you play that horn, son."

I told him that I figured it out.

He said, "Figured out what, son?"

I told him that I figured-out the difference between playing the French horn bugle and the real French horn.

He scoffed again at the idea of a French horn bugle.

I told him, "The bugle was in the key of G, but the real French horn is in F. For a minute I was having a difficult time playing—"

"I told you it was difficult to blow," he interjected.

I told him that I figured out that I was playing in between the keys at first and couldn't get a clear tone.

He looked at me and said, "Just play something, son. Let me hear you blow that horn."

I took a deep breath and played the little fanfare that I prepared for him.

He snatched off his glasses and said, "Holy shit! Do that again!"

"I love the sound of this old instrument, you know," I said, after I played for him.

"Play, play that again, son, my God! Where did you learn to play like that?" he asked in amazement.

"Like I said, sir, I played French horn bugle in a drum and bugle corp. We played competitions and parades all the time. I developed quite a lip, breath control, fast tonguing, and all, but I can't read music."

Then I asked him if the valve plates should come back up on their own. I showed him how I could play a scale by pushing the valve plates back up after I pushed them down, and he looked at me, shaking his head in disbelief.

"Son, son, it's OK, of course the valve plates should return on their own. The springs are shot. Look, let's get you another instrument." Still shaking his head, he said, "How you get such a big sound out of that piece of shit I'll never know. Let's see, there's a girl who leaves her horn at school over the weekends. Yeah," he said, "you can take her horn. It works very well—and oh, it's a double horn, do you know what that is, son?"

I told him I wasn't sure, but I would read about it in the method book or perhaps he had another book on the double horn.

"OK, son, just calm down." He told me that a double horn was an F horn and a B-flat horn combined together on the same instrument. The instrument he had for me was a Conn model 6-D. He said he would get the old

F horn fixed and I could only take the girl's horn home on weekends and I would use the F horn during the week.

I spent the entire weekend reading in the French horn book about the double horn. When I played it, I noticed it had a more secure feel to it. Of course, it was a much newer instrument and the valve plates worked extremely well, popping right back up after being pushed. I played the usual exercises from the method book and tried what scales I knew. Then I noticed that the book had a fingering chart. It gave the B-flat fingerings next to the corresponding F horn fingerings.

The Eric Hauser book, *Foundation to French Horn Playing*, became the entire French horn world for me. It had famous horn parts from celebrated orchestral and opera works—the *William Tell Overture*, Wagner, and so on. I practiced so much that my mother would have to come in that cold room and tell me to take a break and go sit by the stove in the other room and get warm for a minute. She warned if I spent too much time in that cold room I'd catch a nasty cold. I always reminded her that I was wearing my overcoat and was quite comfortable.

In two months, I had finished the Eric Hauser book and started a new set of books called *Rubank Intermediate Method for French Horn*, volumes one and two. Mr. Bryan told me that I was now at the intermediate level and progressing very well. He taught me weekly and guided me somewhat, but I had my own momentum. I wasn't in the band yet, but that was my short- term goal, of course—to get in the band and be near Leslie, to be like Leslie, doing something important in the school, to be visible like she was, and to be recognized as a student of merit and achievement. With all that work cut out for me, I was happier than any time I could remember in my entire life.

I started to get more and more curious about the composers listed in the back of the Eric Hauser French horn book. Who was Wagner? Who was Mozart, who was Bach, Grieg? One cold Saturday morning, I went to have my shoes repaired. There was an old guy who lived and worked in the shoe repair shop. Leonard talked to me a lot about doing what I wanted in life. He always lectured me to keep studying and to stay in school. I liked him. He was different, very encouraging, and had great intelligence. That particular Saturday morning, he asked me to run an errand for him. He sent me over on Main Street, in the white people's section, to buy shoe repair supplies. When I returned, he gave me a fifty-cent piece. I was shocked. "Thanks!" I said, in a grateful tone. He said, "Want to earn that every Saturday?" That became my little job every Saturday morning, which earned me that half dollar, which was nice money for any young person in those days.

The following Saturday when I showed up to run my errand, Leonard had a gift for me. It was a photo collage of all the European classical composers from Bach to Ravel. There was a photo of each composer with his birth and death date. He said I should start learning music history and read up on the European masters. I put this wonderful gift on the wall of my little cubbyhole room and studied it daily trying to pronounce the names of each composer.

The following Monday morning, it was snowing quite hard and I had a rather long and difficult trek to school that morning, carrying that girl's horn and all. When I arrived at school, a big yellow school bus stopped at the intersection in front of me. After my mile-and-a-half walk *in the snow*, seeing that school bus arrive from across the lake carrying all the rich white kids from Deal, I couldn't help but feel somewhat left out in the cold. There they were, sitting together, exempt from having to walk to school. This group I called the "Beautiful People White Girls," arriving from their warm, affluent homes to a warm, comfortable school bus and then right into a warm, comfortable school building, never feeling the pain of the winter weather, dressed in the best and warmest of clothes, looking well fed, well groomed, with those peachy, cherubic "white girl" complexions. They looked so confident, so full of life, so beautiful. I actually imagined for a moment what it would be like to be with one of them. However, at that very moment, as I stood on that freezing corner, something welled up inside of me confirming the fact that *I was going to choose music for my life's work* and in doing so, I could easily have women like them in my life, if I so desired, and much more.

On entering the school building, I ran into Mr. Bryan again. I called out to him to give him the horn. I was a little worried that the girl's horn had snow all over it and I said, "I'm sorry about the snow on the horn case again, I'll wipe it off, let me get a paper towel."

"Son, son!" he interrupted. "Don't worry about it, it's all right." He looked at me again in disbelief and said, "Son, who *are* you—where do you come from?"

"Springwood Avenue—the West Side, sir," I answered nervously.

"I mean, I just find it amazing that you carry that horn home all the way over to the West Side and back every day."

I said, "Yes sir, that's where I live. Is there something wrong Mr. Bryan?"

"No, no, son—and what street do you live on over there?"

"Springwood Avenue, sir," I said proudly.

He just looked at me again, shaking his head. "And your parents don't have a car?"

"No, they don't, sir," I answered. "But I really don't mind carrying the horn home, you know. I have my books under one arm and the horn in the other so it sort of balances. But I'm really enjoying the lessons."

He just looked at me, again shaking his head as he walked away.

I added as always, "See you sixth period, Mr. Bryan!"

After school on that same day, I was walking in the new wing of the school sort of hoping I would run into Leslie so I could tell her about my progress on the horn. I found her leaning on the windowsill looking out of a giant window.

As I walked Leslie home that day, she was quiet for a long time. I told her I couldn't wait to start playing in the band and that I was "working really hard trying to figure everything out and looking forward to the day when—"

"Yeah, I know, Bob," she interrupted. "Mr. Bryan told the whole band about you today."

"What . . . told them about *me*—why?" I asked.

She said he made a big speech about how none of the band kids practice. If they'd just take their instruments home and do a little practice, the band would sound much better. And then he said, "I got a colored boy who's learning French horn who carries his horn and school books all the way over to the West Side every day *and* on weekends. Some of you live just across the lake, for God's sake, and come to school on a nice comfortable school bus and can't take your instruments home one stinking day of the week!"

She said the band people were asking what my name was and Mr. Bryan said, "Never you mind what his name is, you'll know soon enough because he's going to *really* do something on that French horn, you hear me?" She said he was really yelling and foaming at the mouth as usual. She warned me that if I came in the band room during band rehearsal that I would most likely get seriously hissed and booed. "I just wanted to tell you that," she added. Then she said warmly, while touching my hand, "But Bob, I'm glad that you are excited about music and working hard . . . and you know I would never hiss you."

Next day at school I hoped I would run into my young love gazing out her favorite window and almost like magic she appeared. She said hello to me and I asked her what she was doing.

"Oh, I'm just waiting for my parents to pick me up. How are you doing on the horn, Bob?" she asked.

I answered proudly and enthusiastically, "Just fine . . . I'm learning chromatic scales and how to transpose into E-flat horn. Of course, I know I'm a long way from being in the band where I know I'd have to have all these musical skills down perfectly before I'm ready to—"

She interrupted me. "Bob, Bob, it's not that big of a deal. It's only a matter of time and you'll have it," she said, as she caressed my back, causing a rush of adolescent blood.

I thanked her and joined her gazing out of her giant window.

Just then it began to rain as a regal black car pulled up outside. She looked at me with her large black eyes and said, "Well Bob, my parents are here. I'll see you tomorrow?" She phrased it as a question.

After she left, I felt so lonely that I started to torture myself about what she might be doing later that day. What did *she* do after school? Where did *she* go? Perhaps she had a boyfriend or a suitor, who was more together than I was academically and musically? What if they were going to meet that *very* evening and play music together—discuss their college aspirations, even attend the same college and go steady? Perhaps he was a white guy? Perhaps he would even propose marriage? I simply couldn't shake that feeling of insecurity. She just seemed so far above me and out of my reach.

A roar of thunder jolted me out of my insecure thoughts and to the realization that it was really raining and no one was coming to pick me up in a black regal sedan. I had to walk home to a house with no real heat. All I could think of to keep me warm was when I would see Leslie again.

A few days later at the same time and place, I found her gazing out the same window. "There you are again, same time, same place," I said, trying to conceal my fear of her being whisked away again by her parents to high places and more important people than myself. I asked her straight away if she was waiting for her parents again.

To my surprise she said, "Nope, actually I was waiting for you, Bob. Are you ready to walk me home?"

I got a little wobbly in the knees and that warm, yellow-white flush of light coursed through my body again. On that fine day, there was no rain and I was going to walk home with the person I most wanted to be with in the whole wide world.

# CHAPTER SEVEN

~

# Adolescent Secrets

On our walk home, Leslie asked me the most dreaded of questions: "So, Bob, what course of study are you taking? College Prep, Business, or General?"

God! I was speechless for a second. Just then, to create a distraction, I dropped everything, her books, my books, and the horn. How could she ask such a question? And to top it off, she didn't even mention Basic Studies. Perhaps she didn't know it existed. My answer was the biggest lie I'd told in years. I blurted out, "Ah! Well, you see I'm not quite sure of my course of study right now, Leslie, so I'm taking General until I decide which way I want to go."

I was sure she knew I was lying because my voice was trembling and I needed to clear my throat way too many times. Leslie was silent for a long time as we resumed our walk. She took her books back and stared straight ahead, holding her books in front of her, with both arms hanging down, as she always did, with a little grin on her face, perhaps trying to absorb my little lie.

Finally, she said, looking me right in the eyes, which I was still not used to in those days. "I see, Bob, that's a good idea. Well, I'm in College Prep and it's a *lot* of work."

I almost fell over, because I knew that already. What else would she be taking?

Then I noticed that her books were not covered, making them very difficult to carry as they slid all over the place, and I could see she was not ashamed of them or her course of study. Why would she be? Just the same, I was really excited to be with her.

Leslie turned to me and asked. "So what are your courses like, Bob? What courses did you take this first year?"

I blurted out, "Well, I'm thinking about which way I want to go, so General was the best choice for me."

Then Leslie said, "I know you're taking General, *but what courses* in General are you taking?"

God, she had me. I couldn't tell her the retarded courses I was taking. I couldn't do it! I had to lie! And worse yet, what if she saw me actually sitting in one of those Basic Studies classes? What then?

The following week, out of the blue, a person I had never seen before stepped mysteriously into my life. His name was Donald Smith, a hefty man who was the assistant superintendent of schools. I was summoned to his office for a brief meeting with him and he seemed to know my whole story. The way he talked to me was extremely uplifting and respectful. He said that he'd heard about my case and said I was very ambitious and he liked that. He knew that I had repeated seventh grade and that he could sense where I was at the present time. He told me that the plan I had worked out with the Guidance Department would work just fine if I worked hard.

That evening in great contrast to my talk with the superintendent, I had a rather ugly conversation with my father about what was OK to be or not be in life, like being a waiter.

"There's nothing wrong with being a waiter," he said. "Now, if you *do* go into music, make sure you take music education."

I asked why.

"Why?" he raised his voice, "so you'll have something to fall back on in case you don't make it as a performing musician. This way," he whispered, "at least you can live above the average nigger."

After that discouraging talk with my father, things started to get a little more interesting. I was coming along on the horn so well that Mr. Bryan let me sit in with the concert band for one piece. I was really nervous at first and then things got better and easier the more I played. I think there were two other French horns beside myself. I sat third horn. I was a little afraid that I would make a mistake in front of Leslie, who was in the row just ahead of me. But at least I was finally in the band with her, the way my crazy left-back friend Bledsoe said I should be.

Mr. Bryan started talking about an honor group called "All-Shore Band." He said he thought some of us should audition for it. Just for the experience, not that we'd make it. He said if I came to Summer Band and studied with him over the summer, I'd have a better chance if I wanted to audition. I didn't know about All-Shore Band, but I was glad to hear about the Summer

Band deal. I was planning to attend summer school anyway as part of my ascension out of Basic Studies.

I really enjoyed Summer Band because I got a chance to play all the time and it really helped my skills on the horn. I remember there was one other French horn and we played everything together. Sometimes I got lost while counting the rests in the music and some days it was really warm, but I didn't care. I was finally playing the *real* French horn, which was going to bring me closer to Leslie and not much else mattered.

After summer school band, Mr. Bryan informed me that I should try out for All-Shore Band in the coming school year. I asked him about All-Shore Band and he told me that it was an honor concert band made up of all the high schools in the shore area—some twenty high schools, he said. If I made All-Shore Band, it would be a big deal around school because in sports very few students ever made an All-Shore team. He lectured me again on how hard I had to practice.

That January I auditioned for All-Shore Band and made it. I made first chair, first stand. In those bands, they had two players on each part. First horn/first chair, first horn/second chair, and so on for all the instruments. This way it enabled them to give more students who qualified a chance to participate. It was a large group, about one hundred players. I was very surprised that I had made it. I guess I had a good audition. I learned all the scales they required and I played part of the Mozart Horn Concerto No. 3. At the All-Shore audition, I really poured my heart out in the slow movement of the concerto. I had very strong emotions in those days and I guess it came through in my music.

The band director was very impressed with my making the All-Shore Band. He said, "I always thought Watt got a sound like a man on the French horn."

All-Shore Band was very intense. The rehearsals were more serious and the level of playing was much higher than our high school band. Again, I remember the other players in the French horn section looking down the section at me every time I had something to play the way they did in my high school band. But I didn't care if they looked. It wasn't their fault that they had never seen a black person play French horn. It was actually a friendly experience once we all got a chance to talk to each other. It was just an innocent situation of curiosity between us, and of course, I had similar feelings about them. Most important it was *music* that had brought us all together at such a tender age.

# CHAPTER EIGHT

~

# A Random Blessing

Mr. Bryan conducted a professional concert band during the summer at the Arthur Pryor Band Shell at the beach in Asbury Park. He thought perhaps I might sit in with his professional band to get reading experience. One evening I walked down to the beach to hear the band. There were two French horn players who played extremely well. They were students at the Juilliard School of Music in New York. Crites, the first horn, asked me how long I had been playing and if I had a teacher. I told him just Mr. Bryan. He said if I wanted, he would help me. "Come around tomorrow to my hotel and we'll have a lesson. Don't worry about the money—just show up with your horn."

The next day I found Crites's hotel just a few blocks from the beach. I walked into the lobby with my horn and was directed to his room. On my way, I ran into an older white man, who stopped me.

"What are you doing here?" he snapped.

I fired back, "Why are you asking? Who the hell are you?"

Then he said, "And where did you get that instrument?"

I told him it was none of his damn business and I insisted again as to why was he asking.

He said he was the assistant manager of the hotel and he didn't want me wandering around.

I said, "I'm not wandering! I'm going to my friend's room. Do you have a problem with that?" I walked away from him and he actually followed me. When I got to Crites's room, he told Crites in no uncertain terms that "He didn't want this *boy* wandering around the hotel."

Crites was furious. He told the assistant manager that he had no right to hassle guests, especially for the reason he was doing it. Crites asked him if he stopped everyone he saw or just black people? The guy huffed away. Crites tried to calm me by saying, "Let's take a walk to the band shell where we can work. The walk will calm you down."

All-Shore Band took place out of town and our band director, Mr. Bryan, drove us to the rehearsal venue and left us. After the first rehearsal, we stayed with private white families for several days, which solved the transportation logistics. All of the homes were in beautiful, affluent New Jersey areas that I had never heard of or visited. When I had dinner with my host family, there was quite an elaborate table setting: There were three different forks, three different spoons, and three different knives, one with a black handle and jagged-edge blade, which was just above the dinner plate. There were two other knives on the right, a regular knife like we had at home, and a shorter round knife. Suddenly, without saying grace, the father said, "Let's eat!"

Suddenly they all looked at me to see if I knew which knife and fork to use and I didn't. I tried to cut my chicken with a knife and fork the way the father was doing and I must have looked awkward because he said, "Bob, don't bother with that knife and fork, just pick that chicken up with your hands, the way you do at home. That a boy! You can feel at home here, son."

I didn't quite like the way he talked to me, but I didn't know exactly how to respond at that moment either. I thought to myself, *How did he know how I ate at home? Was it possible that he knew the way my grandmother described our eating like heathens?* Just then, the wife illustrated, nonverbally by winking at me, as to which utensil was used for what food. I picked up on her cues and learned on the spot.

It was quite a meal—chicken, soup, salad, lobster, and baked Alaska. I really enjoyed the meal and, of course, I wanted more of everything, but I was afraid to ask—it just didn't feel right. *God!* I thought, *do people eat like this all the time?*

However, I noticed that the food had little seasoning, almost bland, and they seemed to eat as though they didn't enjoy it. There was a kind of dryness to their demeanor, a detachment, a lack of natural feeling as if they were holding their emotions back—even holding their breath.

My hosts had such opulence and comfort that it was hard for me to believe I was still in New Jersey. I had a kind of premonition that this was the beginning of a completely new life for me—a really different life that music, my horn, and my education would earn for me. Perhaps I would have a nice home like that one someday, with heat in every room, hot water, especially in the morning, and a wife to live in it with me.

I was led to a guest bedroom in the far corner of the house. It was very clean, spacious, and nicely decorated with a private bathroom just for me. After making sure my feet were clean, I climbed into the strange ultraclean bed. It took hours for me to fall asleep because the sheets were so squeaky-clean and it was so quiet. I was truly in another world—a world that, through music, would grow larger and more real for me as time went on.

Back at school, I ran into my high school oracle again, the assistant superintendent, Mr. Smith. He spoke to me with a hearty, "Good morning, Bob!"

He invited me into his office and sat me down. "So, what did I tell you? You're going to be just fine. And I heard about you and your French horn—way to go."

I tried to tell him that I made All-Shore band, but he cut me off saying, "I know, keep it up, see ya soon, now off to class with you."

How did he know all those things about me? I began to feel like I was part of some kind of academic lab experiment.

On one of my more joyful walks home with Leslie, we discussed the idea of our going to see the senior play. It was an annual high school event that everyone attended. She warned me that the only problem would be her parents. She said I should call her house and ask her mother's permission. At our usual parting place, on the corner just down the street from her house, she gave me her phone number. I took it like it was gold.

She looked at me puzzled and said, "And may I have yours, Bob?"

I froze in cold fear with Leslie's beautiful, clear black eyes still looking up at me waiting for my response. I had to fake it again, "Well, I . . . our phone is on the blink at the moment and. . . . Well, I'm not sure when it will be in service again. I'll let you know."

"Well, can I have the number anyway until your phone is repaired?"

I was speechless and tried to tell her that I didn't remember the number. I slowly started walking off saying goodbye to Leslie. It felt horrible lying to her, but we didn't have a telephone and I was just too embarrassed to tell her.

Since I was still working at the drug store, I thought I would go there and make the dreaded phone call to Leslie's mother. I took a deep breath and dialed her number. Her mother answered. I tried to be confident, but her mother took control.

"Hello!" she said, in an icy tone.

I said, in the most pitiful shaky tone of voice, "Hello my name is Bob Watt and—I, may I speak to Leslie, please?"

"And what do you wish to speak with her about young man?" she asked coldly.

I said, "Well, I . . . ah, would like to ask her out to the senior play at school—ah, well, I mean, ask you if I may take her to the play and well . . ." I just wanted to hang up and run out of that phone booth and scream. I was so nervous talking to her.

Her mother snapped back, "Oh, I see! Well, I must tell you right now young man, whomever you are, that Leslie doesn't go out with boys!" Click! She hung up!

I couldn't believe it. She just said *no*. I wasn't asking for the moon. I was just asking to take her daughter out to an innocent high school play lasting maybe two hours. I didn't have a car, so we would've walked to the play and back. I was so mad that I wished I did have a car, because I *did* want to make love to their daughter in the worst way, so they were right to be protective of her.

# CHAPTER NINE

# First Date

Back at school the next day, Leslie was in serious apology mode. She was very upset with her mother for hanging up on me. She said they had a big argument, her father jumped in, and it was pretty bad—she wanted to move out she was so angry with them. However, she must have made some headway with her parents because they agreed to let us go to the movies in the *daytime* on a Saturday! I was very surprised.

The big movie at that time was *The Sound of Music* with Julie Andrews. When I went to pick Leslie up at her home, I was invited in to meet her parents. *Oh God*, I thought, *I finally get to meet her strict, stern mother who had reduced me to a puddle on the telephone and then hung up.* As I entered their living room, I noticed the usual trappings that most black people had in their homes in those days—a photo of Martin Luther King Jr., John F. Kennedy, and the usual, white, plaster-of-paris Jesus hanging on the wall.

Leslie invited me in to sit down. Leslie's father was a really massive man with a deep scary voice. He didn't really say much to me, looked me up and down, lightly shook my hand, and then laughed at me under his breath. Leslie's mother did the talking—or should I say, interrogating. She was a rather nice-looking woman. She spoke in a very proper tone of voice, the way black folks did when suddenly in the presence of white people.

Half busy doing something else, she proceeded to grill me like a convicted criminal. "So what does your father do, Robert?"

I knew I was going to be nervous and tried to control myself, but my answers still came out all shaky.

I said, "Ah . . . he does construction work sometimes. . . . Well, most of the time he does."

The father interrupted and said, "Ha! I know what kind of work your father does and it ain't no construction work." He walked out of the room again, laughing at me under his breath.

The mother continued: "And are you a Christian, Robert, and an active member of a church?"

I did not want to talk about church. I started to get nervous and even a little scared. I told her that we attended First AME church—Saint Stevens.

"Yes, I see, but are you an *active* member in the church? Are you an usher or a choir member?"

I calmly told her that we simply attended.

She continued to press, "And do you attend Sunday school? Do you read your bible daily?"

I answered, "Yes, yes," just to get through the Gestapo-like interrogation.

Thinking the questions were done, Leslie and I stood up to escape more of her mother's private inquisition, but she continued.

"And what does your *mother* do, Robert?"

Now, she was getting into a more sensitive subject and I resented it. My entire tone and demeanor changed, and she backed off. I told her, in a very proud, matter-of-fact tone, that my mother was head chambermaid at the Howard Johnson's Motor Lodge on Highway 35.

She responded with a very cold, "I see. Well, Robert, I just want you to understand that my husband and I are very concerned about Leslie's future and don't want her to get messed-up with some no-count nigger here in Asbury Park, whomever that might be, and miss going to college. I'm sure you understand. You two have a nice time."

We walked to the movies in silence, which was about a mile or so, down to the beach. It was a nice walk and a first for us, because we had never spent any time together without our books and instruments in hand. In fact we had never walked anywhere together, except straight home from school. Yet I knew that we were both feeling that her mother's inquisition had stolen a lot of the joy from our day.

Suddenly Leslie stopped, looked me right in the eyes, touched my face in a way that caused a sudden adolescent reaction, and said, "Bob, I'm really sorry about my parents. I want to be with you regardless of what they might say. And you know what else, Bob Watt? I think you are pretty OK for putting up with all of this crazy stuff."

When we arrived at the movie theater and saw other couples filing in, we felt like our being together was finally part of the real world and not just high school dip-shitism. I paid for the tickets (a big deal for me) and we walked arm and arm into the beautiful art deco theater. It was magical, Leslie sitting right next to me, high up in the balcony, in the dark, with no one else around. It was like having our own private theater. When the movie started, Leslie snuggled up to me and we started to kiss passionately. Feeling Leslie's body made me crazy and I couldn't help putting my hand up her dress a tiny bit, touching her inner thigh. For an instant I thought we were going to lose control and get naked right there in the theater. As Julie Andrews sang "The Sound of Music," I quickly and discreetly sniffed my fingers that had briefly touched Leslie's inner thigh and rubbed them all over my face and mustache like a dog wallowing in delightfully smelly mud.

As winter settled in, there was one particularly rough morning that I named "Ugly Morning Start." On that glorious morning, there was a nasty blizzard. I sat up in bed and took a deep breath to wake myself. When I exhaled, my breath was clearly visible in the cold unheated bedroom. I could hear snow blowing against the bedroom window. It made a crackling sound as if someone were throwing sand against the glass. All the stoves had burned out during the night, leaving the entire apartment without heat. Walking to the bathroom was a shivering experience. Steam rose from the toilet when I used it, because the water had frozen into a thin sheet of ice during the night. I quickly splashed cold water on my face, combed my hair, dressed quickly, and checked the kitchen stove. There was no fire so I had to go outside in the blizzard behind the apartment and find some dry wood under a woodpile to start a fire. The snow was a dry, hard blowing type that didn't melt quickly, so most of the wood under the pile was still dry. I dragged the wood up the stairs and into the kitchen, chopped it into smaller pieces, and managed to get a nice hot fire going. Then came the blue coal on top of the red-hot burning wood. In about twenty minutes, things were getting almost comfortable.

But then, it was nothing like the comfort that Leslie had to be experiencing, in her nice home. Pausing to daydream, I imagined her getting up slowly, wearing a sheer white nightgown that flowed as she walked to the bathroom, then turning on nice hot water that steamed up to her lovely sleepy face, and perhaps going to the toilet, which didn't have frozen water in its bowl. I imagined her leisurely reading a magazine or newspaper and perhaps dozing off again. Of course, she had the time to do such idle things because she didn't have to make a fire in an antiquated wood-burning coal stove. The fire made a loud pop as the red-hot burning wood settled beneath the burning blue coal. It always took a loud noise to snap me out of my fits of daydreaming.

Finally, I had a nice hot fire to cook the ham and cheese omelet I had prepared the night before. I grabbed the omelet from the refrigerator and poured it into the heavy black frying pan that was sitting on top of the stove. When I poured my omelet into the black frying pan, I noticed scores of little black pellets in my eggs. Then, the awful smell of *mouse droppings* being cooked right along with my ham and cheese omelet reached me. In anger, I tossed the whole mess into the kitchen sink, grabbed my books and horn, and stormed out the door. I would have given anything for a ride on that morning.

Suddenly there was a large gust of wind that whipped up a blast of snow, nearly knocking me down. A whiteout! I couldn't see where I was. I lost track of the streets I had crossed. Then I heard the late bell ring. If I wasn't in class by *that* bell, I was considered late. I panicked and took off in a run. I slipped on some ice hidden under the snow and my horn and books went flying in every direction, and I ripped my pants, which really angered me. As I got up from my fall, I could barely see the high school through the swirling snow. The whiteout had really led me astray. I was in the middle of the street and didn't realize it. I knew I was already late, so I ceased trying to hurry. As I entered the school building, my footsteps echoed in the empty hallways mocking my tardiness. All the other students were comfortably in their seats. They were warm and dry, well fed, and not freezing from walking to school in a blizzard. I hated them all.

I burst into class and walked angrily to my seat, slamming my books on the floor. The teacher stopped everything, "And just why are we late this morning, Mr. Watt? Please tell the class, we're waiting."

I snapped, "You don't want to know."

The teacher yelled back, "I'll see you after school, young man, you hear me!"

I told him, "Yeah . . . and I'll see you in hell!"

The class went crazy with chatter. The teacher grabbed my coat collar and shook me. When I pushed him away, he said, "OK, young man, I'll take the matter up with the principal."

After calming the class, he went back to the lesson. I slouched into my seat and escaped into a serious daydreaming state. My eyes drifted out the window to the beautiful lake next to the high school. I let my mind wander out to the ocean. I imagined heading south on the ocean all the way down to the Bahamas. I was there with Leslie in ecstasy, when suddenly, "Mr. Watt! The answer, Mr. Watt!"

I snapped back at him viciously. "What, what? I don't know the answer so get out of my face!"

He threw me out of the class. I walked down to the band room area where I usually met Leslie after school. I stared out of her favorite window and tried to calm myself. When I finally saw Leslie later that day, she sensed I was upset and quietly took my hand. I instantly exhaled all my tension from the day and inhaled her Shalimar perfume.

Silently probing my face with her warm compassionate black eyes, Leslie tenderly touched my face and asked, "Are you OK, Bob?"

In an instant, just hearing her voice and being in her presence healed my wounds.

# CHAPTER TEN

~

# Pleasure and Pain

That summer my father found me a most unpleasant job. His old friend Harry, who was headwaiter at a fancy seafood restaurant, said at sixteen I was old enough to work as a busboy at the restaurant where he waited tables. He said I could make a decent salary and earn really good tips. My father agreed on my behalf and told Harry that I would do it. I was not happy. A busboy followed the waiters around doing things like pouring water, putting bread and butter on the tables, removing the dishes after meals, and any other flunky jobs the waiters needed. I hated it and I hated my father's friend Harry.

When I started to work with him, he told me that he had heard from my father that I played the French horn and wanted to be a musician. He said he couldn't understand why I wanted to play the French horn when my father played trumpet. "You niggers from Asbury Park tickle me. Who do you think you are, boy? Ain't nobody ever heard a no nigger playing no French horn, so get off that bullshit and find you a tenor sax to bite on and get real. A French horn—what's that look like anyway?"

"What, you don't know what it looks like?" I angrily snapped back.

He looked at me with his hostile bloodshot eyes and said in a nasty threatening tone, "Don't you even think about talking to me like that, boy." He continued, "Oh, is that the horn you put your hand inside the bell or something? Oh yeah, yeah, boy, you know what? You better be careful or one day a snake is going to crawl up inside that horn and bite your hand." He told me to come to my senses and think about pursuing a job like his. Perhaps one

43

day I *too* could become a waiter and make a real living like he and the other men had done for years.

The next day Harry picked me up as usual and again on the way to the job he started in on his lectures. "Now, Bobby, one thing you gotta learn on this new job is how to move when you're told. When I tell you to do something you gotta *move*, boy. And if the 'Man' tells you to do something, you better move even faster, you hear me?"

I asked him who the Man was and he *yelled* back, "The white man, boy—who pays your salary!"

My first day on the job, I found myself talking to the people as I was serving them. Harry overheard me and quickly pulled me in the back. "Let me tell you something, boy. You don't say shit to those people! They ain't hardly interested in no nigger like you. You are a servant and you are not on their level! Can you please remember that?"

It was always a relief to get back to music after dealing with that busboy job. I continued to learn more and more about music, especially French horn music, since I had met Crites. The first recording I bought was the Tchaikovsky 5th Symphony with the Boston Symphony. This was the symphony with a big French horn solo in the second movement. I knew about the solo because it was in the back of my French horn method book, but I had never heard it. I wanted to hear it played by a top symphony horn player. Crites told me to buy the recording of the Boston Symphony with James Stagliano playing the horn solo. I found the recording, but we didn't have a stereo at home, so in order to hear it I had to use the stereo of one of my father's girlfriends. The way I overheard my father ask his girlfriend was very revealing of his true feelings about my wanting to be involved with classical music.

He said, "Listen, my son he wants to listen to some of that long hair symphony music of his. Would it bother you too much if he used your stereo for a while?"

I felt a little strange using someone's stereo, but I just had to hear that music. They left me alone.

The first movement of the Tchaikovsky 5th Symphony was absolutely beautiful, starting with the clarinets playing a very dark, melancholy tune with just the right emotion that I had felt many times myself. The ending of the first movement ended in such a way as to totally set up the mood for the second movement. *Andante cantabile con alcuna licenza:* in a walking-singing manner with some license. When the French horn began to play, I held my breath and became a little dizzy after hearing how amazing it sounded.

I wondered if I could ever play it that way. I was thrilled with the idea that I was going into a world where I could possibly have a chance to play that beautiful solo with an orchestra one day. I could use the power of music to express all those feelings that I had when walking to high school in freezing weather with no breakfast, or the times I wanted so desperately to be with Leslie and couldn't. After my private session with Tchaikovsky, I was useless for the rest of the day.

After that experience, I went out and bought another recording, the Choral Fantasy by Beethoven. I loved the sound of his music—it really touched me. Of course, I had a nice photo of him on the collage of composers on my bedroom wall. Somehow I got hold of a small record player, which I could hide under my bed. It didn't have a cover, just a turntable that worked and a good stylus. When I was home alone, I listened to the Beethoven Choral Fantasy with the volume turned up.

Once, for the experience, Crites invited me to play a concert with the Cosmopolitan Youth Orchestra of New York City, led by the assistant conductor of the New York Philharmonic. It was a large orchestra with lots of beautiful New York women. God! They were Italian, Jewish, Asian, and Puerto Rican—but no black women. I was in awe and a bit intimidated because playing in an orchestra was still quite new to me.

Crites needed me to assist him in the Rachmaninoff Symphony No. 2. It was a very long symphony with lots of notes for French horn. I had to transpose mentally—on the spot—to horn in E. That is, every note on the page had to be played one half-step lower. Everything went by so fast and everyone seemed to know the music, except me. I felt so behind the eight-ball. I couldn't believe how well Crites played. It was a beautiful work and I thought, *Here I am right where I want to be sitting in an orchestra, not watching one on TV, but sitting and playing my horn in a real French horn section.* However, I must say I didn't have a good experience at that particular rehearsal. I was having a hard time keeping up. I suddenly had the frightening feeling that I had chosen the wrong profession. All the other musicians were just playing away and I was lost most of the time. I felt sick to my stomach. When the rehearsal was over, I was still on the first page of the music it seemed. People were saying their goodbyes and I felt like I was spinning around and getting bumped by everyone as they left.

As we were leaving the rehearsal, Crites said, "You're so quiet, what's wrong?"

Reaching the subway station, I told Crites that I was going to throw my horn in front of the train when it came.

Crites was shocked. "What the hell is wrong with you?" he asked.

I told him that I was going to quit playing the horn and maybe throw myself in front of the train too.

He grabbed me and slammed me hard against the wall and said, "I'll kick your ass before I let you do that." He shook me and said, "You're not going to quit!" He said these feelings were all part of the process and that I would just have to get through it and a lot of other insane stuff before it was all over. Crites kept a hold of me until my train came. He dragged me on board by my collar, sat me in a seat, and yelled at me to go home and think about what I'd just said. As he walked away, he yelled back at me, "And stay out of New York for a while."

Summer came again and Crites was back in Asbury Park playing in the Summer Band on the boardwalk. That summer I was asked to sit in with them. It was a real thrill trying to keep up with those players, but I loved it. Once I started playing with those pros I felt a lot better about my playing and my wounds had healed from feeling like I wanted to quit playing and jump in front of that train in New York.

That same summer, my high school mentor Jones and I started to talk a lot more about women and life. He said since I was getting older and maturing that girls at school would start to notice me. "But, young Watt, not only the girls—the female teachers are going to start looking at you in a sexual way too."

He added, "Look, there's a myth about black men that you should know about. That myth is that black men are well endowed and good in the sack. This myth will follow you for the rest of your life, so get used to it. But remember, it's only a myth and regardless of its truth, women are still fascinated by it."

About two weeks later, we had a substitute teacher from out of town for a couple of weeks in English class. She had alabaster white skin with a flawless complexion, shiny black hair, tall, a healthy bust line, and good posture. Everyone liked her because she gave all of us a chance to speak our minds in class. I did notice that when I stood to speak in class she looked me over exactly the way Jones described. It was thrilling! If I hadn't talked to him, I would have missed out on such carnal knowledge, perhaps for years.

One day after class, the substitute teacher told me that she really enjoyed what I had to say in class and if I ever just wanted to talk sometime I could come back after school.

One day after school I happened to walk by her class and, sure enough, I found her reading over her lesson plans. I stopped in to tell her that I really enjoyed her class. I then excused myself, telling her that I had a long walk home.

She replied, "You walk home in this cold weather, Bob? What about the school bus?"

I told her that the school buses were for the rich kids across the lake. There had never been a bus for the black kids from the West Side.

She was appalled and said she would be glad to drive me if I didn't mind walking her to her car.

As we walked, she was looking at me in that magical way that tells a man she's attracted to him. It was brand new to me and it *was* like magic—but was it the same magic I felt with Leslie or was it just the magic of women in general?

"Gee, you're nice and tall, Bob," she said. "How tall are you?"

"Almost six foot," I bragged.

When we got to her car, she looked me up and down again, smiled, and touched my face. She said she'd heard from the other teachers that most of the black kids lived on the West Side, but she didn't know where it was exactly since she was from out of town. I showed her the way to my house and she couldn't believe it.

"You walk this far every day . . . and you live in *this* place?"

I told her this was home and thanks for the ride.

"Why are most of the streetlights broken out, Bob? It's frighteningly dark too." She suddenly became quiet and began to stare at me with a curious expression. "You have a girl, Bob?"

I told her yes, as I felt her hand rubbing the inside of my thigh.

"Is this all right, Bob? I'll stop if it makes you uncomfortable."

"No, it feels very nice," I said, with a dry mouth.

She looked at me in silence for a long time before saying, "Bob, you're so young and beautiful" as she kissed my lips and started to undress me.

From the light on her car dash I could see that she had opened her blouse. However, there were a few carnal details that I had never counted on when being with a white woman for the first time. Her skin was much whiter under her garments and large blue-green veins were visible on her breasts, along with several hairy moles. My teenage mind defaulted to the local vernacular, *that shit looked nasty and I didn't want to touch it.*

At that point, I got ahold of myself and told her that I just couldn't do this with a teacher. It would seriously interfere with my concentration in her class and that I was really in love with my girlfriend and it was with *her* that I really wanted to have sex. I quickly jumped out of her car and ran home.

When I told Jones about the substitute teacher, he shook my hand and laughed like crazy. "I told you, I told you!" He started pacing up and down again as he lectured me, "Man, this is just the beginning, wait until college. The white bitches will be all over your black ass. So from this moment on, you will never look at women in the same light anymore or put them on a pedestal, like you do your high school sweetheart, Leslie.

I asked him what he meant, that I put Leslie on a pedestal? I told him to be careful what he said about her.

He got right in my face and yelled, "Yes, you put her on a pedestal! You worship her, don't you? You want her so bad your nuts ache—right? Right?"

I grabbed Jones and told him not to talk about Leslie that way. "She's my—"

Jones began really laughing loudly at me. "She's your what? Ha! Your what?" Then he slammed me against the refrigerator, knocking the wind out of me. Jones was a football player and was much heavier than I was. He just held me by the collar and told me in loud, booming tones right up in my face, "Listen motherfucker, you don't have to put anyone on a pedestal. You are a 'Watt' and that really means something in this town. I mean, look at you. You're successful in your music already and you almost got laid by a white school teacher at age sixteen? Come on,  give yourself some credit here. This Leslie is no better than you, Watt. Oh yeah, yeah, she may have had an easier upbringing than you and perhaps she did well in grade school due to a more comfortable home environment, but that's all. Remember who you are and who your family is!"

# CHAPTER ELEVEN

## Lessons in Life

The next big event in my busy high school life was the Junior Prom. Talking with some of my male friends, we were discussing our choice of the women we wanted ask. Crazy Bledsoe asked me if I had the guts to ask one of the "Beautiful People" white girls. He enjoyed toying with the idea of actually asking one of those women to the prom just to see what would happen. How surprised would they be if a black guy that they barely knew seriously asked them to the high school event of the year? What kind of experience would it have been if she had accepted? What would it have been like for her parents? What would they have said to me when I came to pick up their daughter in their affluent neighborhood without a car? There was not one interracial couple at our high school that I can remember. Unbeknownst to Bledsoe, I had already seriously entertained such an idea with a white woman from All-State Regional band earlier in the year. However, I came to the realization that it was something that would surely happen later in my life, in college perhaps, and to forget about doing such a worldly thing in the small racist town of Asbury Park, New Jersey.

Besides, in my heart of hearts, I already knew I was going to ask Leslie. Sure enough, one day on the way home from school, I popped the question to Leslie. She gave me that shy smile that said, "I'm glad you asked, I was hoping you would—you'll be glad you did." So I rented a tuxedo and walked over to Leslie's house where her parents took pictures of us together. Leslie looked wonderful in her prom dress and I was very proud to have her by my side.

Leslie's parents drove us to the prom in their regal black sedan. The prom was held in the high school gymnasium and everything seemed perfect. We all sat at assigned tables and I remember dreading the moment when Leslie would ask me to dance. Instead of waiting, I asked her myself. I shivered inside as she graciously took me up on my offer. As she rose, her beautiful prom dress made a wonderful rustling sound that just thrilled me because it was so feminine, so sexy, so Leslie. As we embraced to dance, I fumbled to find her hand and couldn't remember if I should hold the right hand in the air or at her side.

Leslie told me to relax and just move with the music.

*Music, move to the music? I could relate to that.* I took a quick glance around the room to see if people were watching us . . . or watching me.

Leslie asked me what I was looking at.

I said, "Nothing, I'm just a little nervous," as I stepped all over her feet. "Oh! Sorry—God! Don't tell anybody," I pleaded.

She chuckled and whispered back into my ear, "Don't worry, Bob. Just hold me close and move to the music."

The Junior Prom was like a prelude to the Senior Prom. At the Junior Prom, we didn't get to do very much afterwards, except go back home. But everyone boasted of big plans for the Senior Prom. Leslie and I decided that we were going to finally get it on after the Senior Prom. I couldn't wait. What actually happened at the Senior Prom was a nightmare. Someone's parents got wind of our ambitious plans and ruined the whole evening. Everyone was whisked back home right after the Senior Prom. But that was later.

After Junior Prom, the next logical thing to do was to start applying for colleges. I talked with Jones about it and he said I should go where I felt like going. There was something about the city of Boston that captivated me. Perhaps I felt that I could study better there than in New York. Perhaps it was because I had watched the *Boston Symphony* on CBS Sunday nights for years?

In the final analysis, the New England Conservatory of Music was my first and final choice. I had already sent for the applications and that would be my focus. At that point, my very life was contingent on my getting into college and leaving Asbury Park, New Jersey. I asked Crites if I went to the New England Conservatory of Music, was it possible I could study with one of the horn players of the Boston Symphony?

He said, "For sure, it will be either James Stagliano or Harry Shapiro. They both teach at the conservatory and you will be in good hands with either one of them."

I knew then that I had to audition for the New England Conservatory.

I checked my grade point average at school the next day. I had about an 87.60 GPA. Jones said that was excellent.

I asked Crites what the audition for the conservatory would be like.

"Well, it will be a fairly short audition. They will have you play a concerto of your choice and stop you when they've heard enough and that will be it. Then they will decide your acceptance based on what they heard at your audition, your SAT scores, your general application, and your GPA from high school."

When I finally applied to the conservatory, the first phase of acceptance was to be invited to audition. The auditions were held in New York City at the Biltmore Hotel. When the correspondence came in the mail, I got a little nervous because I knew that this audition would be more important than any that I had done so far.

Crites assured me that it was not such a big deal. "Just play a concerto—or just part of one. Just stand up there and play your ass off, regardless of what music you're playing. They will hear what you are about as a player. Just dump all of your emotions into the music and let *it* talk for you and you'll be fine."

I took the short cab ride uptown to the Biltmore Hotel and learned that the audition was being held in one of the ballrooms. It was a dark room filled with lots of empty chairs and wall-to-wall carpet. I played for about ten minutes and it was over. An elderly white-haired man came out of the shadows and said, "That will be just fine, Bob. Thank you, we'll be in touch." Next thing I knew, I was back in a taxi headed to Port Authority bus terminal and I hadn't even gotten into the music. I was ready to play more.

In one of my last discussions with Jones, he said it annoyed him that black people were referred to as "Negros." He admitted that he had used the term himself, but there was always something about it that irritated him. He said it was insane for black folks to allow themselves to be named by whites or any other group. "NEGRO!!" he yelled, "What a fucked-up label! What a sorry-ass concept. Watt. I hate it!" Jones began to pace up and down, gesturing upwards with his index finger:

"In the saddest sense, Watt, 'The Negro' was a black person who, for the most part, believed everything white folks said about black people. For example, black people had ugly thick lips. Therefore many children, especially little black girls, were told to roll their lips back into their mouth until they appeared as thin as any white person's. 'The Negro' had bad hair. Instead of being straight, it curled up into itself to keep his head cool in his native Africa. To the Negro, *hair* was supposed to be straight. Jesus had long straight hair, at least according to the white icon of Jesus that the 'Negro' prayed to every Sunday. The 'Negro' couldn't imagine that his hair was just as whole, complete, and perfect as any hair on the planet. Much less that man, *homo sapiens*, and all of its evolutionary stages took place in Africa and that *his* type of hair was the first hair."

He went on at length. The "Negro" woman had a "nigger ass," instead of the sexiest female form that ever existed, that would cause even God to do a double-take on her creation. Therefore, the Negro woman was taught from a very young age to tone down her sexuality. She was told to "Pull in that butt, girl," wear loose-fitting clothes instead of any form-fitting garment that would dare to expose her godly figure and cause men and women to swoon at the sight of her sexual glory. She was taught that she had to have her hair straightened at all times. This would prevent it from *going back* to its perfectly natural state, which could be so awesome if allowed to grow and be itself. But no, they feared its *wild splendor* would frighten white folks, so it had to be *relaxed* to put them at *their* ease. She was taught to straighten her hair so much that it finally gave up growing and receded so far back on her head that she had to resort to a wig. And then, as a man, you dare not touch it, not that you'd want to—you just watched her wear it in all her misery and fear, that it might be discovered or, worse yet, fall off.

The Negro woman had to be a churchgoing woman and sex, especially *her* exalted sex, was depicted as savage. She was supposed to be prone to wild animal-like, sexual gyrations and therefore a double sinner. She therefore was compelled to tone it down in the name of good Christian values and the "Word."

The Negro male was taught to tie his maleness to his leg, least he sexually excite some white woman or threaten a white male and be lynched (figuratively or literally) by a pathologically jealous white societal mob. His Negro wife kept him in sexual check by constantly holding him up in critical comparison to the white icon of Jesus. He was constantly told that he should pray to Jesus for his improvement—that is, to the white icon of Jesus to whom he was constantly compared but would never quite measure up.

"Those are the modern-day shackles of the black man. The most effective brainwashing job ever imposed on a people—ain't it fucked up, Watt?"

Jones went on talking to me like that until morning, and as the sun rose we enjoyed a *Negro breakfast* of slab bacon, cheese grits, and scrambled eggs.

# CHAPTER TWELVE

~

# My Great Escape

My final musical achievement in high school was being accepted to All-Eastern Band, a symphonic band made up of students from the entire Eastern Seaboard. The concert was to be held in Boston, Massachusetts. I was chosen as one of the principal horns. I was extremely excited about going to Boston and having a chance to visit the New England Conservatory while still waiting to be accepted there.

The first sights I wanted to see were the New England Conservatory and Symphony Hall. I couldn't believe how old the conservatory building looked and how close it was to Symphony Hall where the Boston Symphony played. I thought if I got accepted to the conservatory, I would be living in a musical paradise having the conservatory and Symphony Hall so close to each other. I thought about all the live concerts of the Boston Symphony I could attend.

All-Eastern Band was truly a sensation, and the players were better than all the other honor bands and orchestras. We had two rehearsals per day and performed one concert. After All-Eastern Band and the trip to Boston, it was very difficult to return home.

After returning from Boston, I found Leslie gazing out of her favorite window. I joined her and told her how much fun I had at All-Eastern Band. I also confided in her that I was very nervous and tense thinking about my future.

She said I should try and relax. She suggested I let her give me a massage.

We went into one of the practice rooms and she slowly started to work me over. It felt great. While she was massaging me, she told me that when a reply from the conservatory comes, a small envelope means you didn't get in, because it takes very little paper to say no. On the other hand, a large envelope means you got in because it will include paperwork and other information. After my massage, I felt like making love to Leslie right then and there. Instead we embraced and kissed deeply.

One fine day, as life would have it, a *large* brown envelope did show up. I opened it and there was a letter along with lots of other papers. I read the crumpled-up letter as my heart pounded.

Dear Mr. Watt,
    We are pleased to inform you that you have been chosen to join the class of 1970 of the New England Conservatory of Music with a full four-year scholarship. Congratulations!

I threw the entire envelope up in the air and screamed, "Yeah, shit!" A few people came out of their apartments to see if I had lost my mind. My mother ran out of the apartment, gave me a big hug, and dragged me inside. We spent the rest of the evening filling out the application. I let her fill out the forms because she had such fine penmanship. We were laughing and joking about silly stuff like who was going to make me garlic-fried chicken or collard greens in Boston? Before retiring, my mother told me that I would be the first person in our family history to attend college and that she was extremely proud of me.

From my seat in the band, I had always dreamed of being that first couple leading the graduating class into the high school commencement ceremony. The next time I saw Leslie, I still had a tinge of guilt in my heart about the white substitute teacher, but I just had to, ask, "Ah, Leslie who are the first two people who lead the class into commencement ceremonies? Is it the student council president or the highest grade point average valedictorian?"

She looked at me smiling with a very suspicious look on her face and said, "Well Bob, everybody knows that the first person walking down the aisle, leading the class in, is the student council president . . . walking with whomever he or she chooses, followed by the valedictorians with the highest grade point average in the school. So why are you asking this question, Bob?"

Leslie had been elected student council president and I was really nervous about asking her for fear she had already had something arranged with one of the valedictorians since she was, after all, student council president with a higher GPA than mine. For that reason, I didn't think I had a chance on the far side of hell of leading the class in, walking next to her with my 87.60 GPA, against the "Beautiful People White Girls" who had 98.89 averages and higher. So the next time I saw Leslie, I just knew I had to ask her who she was walking with at commencement.

The next day I found her waiting at her favorite spot, "Hi Leslie, ah, how are you today—ah, how are you feeling—you look great . . . ah, well you always look great."

Leslie looked at me and asked, almost laughing, "Why are you so nervous, Bob? Are you all right?"

I just said outright, with a very dry mouth, "Leslie, is it at all possible for *me* to walk with *you* in the commencement, down the aisle, you know—in front, I mean—the first couple, with you—ah, I mean next to you—please? But I understand if you have to walk with someone of a higher GPA than mine—and well that would be OK."

She looked at me laughing and said, "Is *that* why you're so nervous? Why, of course you can walk with me in commencement, Bob."

I was so happy that I almost cried right in front of her. I took her hand, hugged her, and said, "Thank you, Leslie—you have *no idea* what this means to me."

She looked at me, cocked her head to one side as she wiped my tears away, and said in a very serious tone, "Oh, Bob, but I *do* know what this means to you. I know how hard you've worked and where you started out. Pulling yourself up from *Basic Studies*."

What? She knew? I was mortified.

Then, with all the reassurance one human being could give another, she said, "But, Bob, I've always known—and you should never have been ashamed. I knew you would transform yourself. You deserve to lead this class into the commencement ceremony more than anyone. Especially more than those spoiled rich little white girls you so admired from afar—thinking they were somehow better than you. Remember I told you about them when I did a sleepover at one of their homes. They are *way* overrated, Bob. Well, they will be behind us when we march into the convention hall as the first couple, leading the class of '67 into its future."

# CHAPTER THIRTEEN

~

# First Sweet Victory

Graduation night was overwhelming. As we got dressed in our long blue robes and mortarboards I felt so content, so fulfilled, with the sweet taste of academic victory on my lips. I was going to lead the class of '67 down the aisle with Leslie on my arm. The class of '67, our class, had been the backdrop of my love affair with Leslie and the Armageddon of my self-discovery and ascension—me, the nobody kid, who got left back in seventh grade and slept in his socks until black crust formed on his ankles, who carried twenty-five-pound bags of coal to make a fire for cooking, when most people had gas ranges. The poor black kid from the West Side, who started out in Basic Studies and ended up in College Prep. All sparked by a single solitary smile from a precious young black girl.

I became very emotional when the band started playing the graduation march, "Pomp and Circumstance."

Leslie looked at me and flashed that same toothy smile that grabbed my attention in eighth grade. And with a very proud expression on her face, she said, "Well, Bob, this is it." She took my arm with such delight and confidence that I found it difficult to hold back the tears. We took our place at the front of the line—head of the class of '67.

When we began to walk, Leslie squeezed my arm even tighter as we stepped in time to the music. We almost lost our footing for a second because of the many flashing cameras. I couldn't believe it. All of the "Beautiful People White Girls" were behind us and at that very moment it dawned on me that I had never actually met or even talked to any of them.

The exciting evening continued with an after-party. My parents were there, my aunts and uncles, friends, and Mr. Smith, the high school assistant superintendent, who watched me go through my curriculum ascension and who was so helpful and encouraging during those years of pure striving and stretching. My mother gave me a big hug and kiss, because she was *always* there at the beginning of everything I ever tried to achieve in my life.

My last battle with my father regarding my career was a shouting match. "Remember what I said about music education." I walked away from him when he started in on that again and he yelled after me, "You're out of your Goddamn mind if you think those crackers are going to let a nigger into one of them symphony orchestras, boy!" I told him once and for all, that I was not a nigger. "You'll see, son, you'll see."

After my father calmed down, he told me that he had auditioned for Julliard School of Music. "Ah, they wanted me to play part of the Bach Brandenburg Concerto No. 2 BWV 1047, using a D trumpet. I didn't have a D trumpet—never even heard of a D trumpet. They wanted to hear that lily-white classical style—ah! I got flustered and ran out of the damn audition." I could see he was deeply hurt by that incident.

Those final weeks at home allowed a few long walks on the beach with Leslie, talking about our futures in college, wondering what it would be like. She talked about how sorry she was for the way her parents had treated me when I was trying to court her. She said she wished it could have been different—"more normal, like the white kids. You know, having a cherry Coke after school at the Sunset Landing restaurant, with the rest of the kids—simple stuff like that. Or perhaps seeing you after school—or even on a Sunday. It could've been *so* different—*so* much better." I was feeling her pain and my own since of defeat that I wouldn't get to make love to her before we left for our respective collegiate adventures.

After my last night playing with the band at the beach, I was invited out to dinner by my high school band director, Mr. Bryan, and his brother, who also played French horn in the band. They wanted me to meet the famous tuba player Bill Bell, who was at the concert. I walked into the famous Italian restaurant that I had always admired because it looked so expensive and exclusive.

As I entered, still wearing my white tuxedo jacket, the maître d' stopped me and said, "What do you want here, boy?"

I looked at him like he was crazy and said, "I'm meeting some people here for dinner—what else would I want here?"

He laughed in disbelief, raising his voice, "You what?"

Just then my band director came out from the back of the restaurant and called to me, "Bob, we're back here, come on back."

The maître d' looked at me with a very stupid, confused expression on his face.

I just had to ask, "So are you going to show me to my table or what?"

When I reached the table, there were a dozen people seated. At the head of the table was a four-hundred-pound man sitting very still. He glanced up at me briefly, saying nothing. My band director's brother introduced us.

"Mr. Bell, we'd like you to meet Bob Watt, a very talented French horn player who will be attending the New England Conservatory next fall."

He squeezed my hand so hard I almost died.

He looked at me for an uncomfortable amount of time and said, "We have a *boy* up at Indiana who plays baritone horn."

Just then my band director's brother whispered in my ear, "When he says *boy* he means black, the boy at Indiana is black."

I snapped back and said, "Yes, yes, I know *exactly* what he means!"

As September neared, I was getting more and more excited about leaving Asbury Park even though I didn't know how I was going to travel to Boston. But to my great surprise, my father offered to *fly* me. That was another side of my father that was pretentious and proud. "Yes, my son's flying up to Boston to attend the New England Conservatory of Music." I could hear him bragging to his friends.

I was a little nervous since I had never flown on an airplane. My little brother Tony said, "Don't worry, big brother, you always wanted to fly. The way you used to look at those little airplanes when we were playing in the wheat field as kids. Have a good trip, we'll miss you."

Of course, Jones had the most positive things to say. His advice carried the most weight with me because he had actually been to college for a year. He congratulated me with a big hug and a punch in the chest, which was a little local male bonding ritual we had. He said loudly, "Enjoy the white bitches, Watt!" Letting out one of his loud screeching laughs, he hugged me and patted me on the back. "Go pack your bags, Watt. You're outta here."

# CHAPTER FOURTEEN

# Tension

I finally had enough clothes and everything else I needed for school. The last person I talked to from home was my uncle Joe, who drove his own taxi and offered to take me to Newark Airport. On the way, he talked to me like never before, telling me about all of his female exploits.

Next thing I knew, I was sitting on a DC-9 jet with lots of apprehension about my first time flying. After the doors closed, I could feel the tightness of pressurization in the cabin. There was no one seated next to me, but I could see that one of the flight attendants had already spotted me as a first-time flyer. The second the plane began to move along the ground to the taxiway, I knew I was going to be uncomfortable. When the jet lifted off, I held my breath.

The flight attendant rushed over to me and said, "Sir, don't hold your breath, relax and breathe, everything's going to be all right. First time flying?"

I looked at her between glances out the window because of the light turbulence climbing out and said, "Yeah, my first time ever."

She brought me some water and sat down in the empty seat beside me and told me to take off my shoes and try to relax. "Just flow with the motion of the aircraft." she coached.

She was a young attractive, clean-cut brunette and I thought, *If I live through this flight, I'm going to meet me a white woman like her in Boston, fall deeply in love, and have a great experience at the conservatory.*

Walking to the baggage claim area, I was amazed at how much busier Boston's Logan Airport was than Newark's Liberty. I was feeling the excitement of being in Boston, where the Boston Symphony played—my new town, my new life! I would soon meet the horn player that I had watched for so long on TV. I would be seeing him every week for years to come. God!

When I left the terminal, I noticed Boston's weather was indeed a bit cooler. There was a steady breeze giving me that chilling feeling that I had truly left home. A van was waiting to pick up arriving students for Freshman Orientation. On arriving at the conservatory dormitory, we were told that Freshman Orientation would be at the castle. The castle? There was a castle on an island just off the coast of Boston. This was the traditional venue where conservatory freshmen had their welcoming dinner during orientation. I had never been in such surroundings. A castle, with multiple bedrooms, stables, moats, chains, and dungeons—it was already a welcome change from my hometown. I had to get used to the fact that I was in a totally different environment. There would always be heat and hot water, enough food, and most places would be free of mice and roaches. I was surprised to be thinking of such things, but I guess couldn't help it.

During the orientation boat trip, the first person to say hello in a friendly and normal way was a horn player named Dick. He was from rural Connecticut and had a rugged, country look about him. He introduced me to Janice, another horn player, a really cute brunette with a twinkle in her eye and freckles. She had a great personality and looked a bit like a cowgirl.

The three of us talked about ourselves, our excitement about being in music, and what it was going to be like attending the conservatory. Most of the other people were quite nice, but somewhat stiff. It was obvious that they, as Jones always said, "Never knew any Negroes."

There were various parts to the orientation. The dean, the same white-haired man I had met briefly at my audition in New York, welcomed the freshman class of 1970. He told us that he too was a musician: "I played the oboe." Many others spoke and then they served dinner. The castle was just beautiful, like a large country mansion in Cheshire, England, where people went fox hunting and had servants and footmen.

The first day at the dormitory was like moving into an apartment. About an hour later, my roommate arrived. His name was Grossman. He introduced me to his father, who addressed me as "son."

"You can put that over there, son, or is this your stuff, son?"

His son chided him for being so bossy. I could see right away that Grossman was going to be a great roommate. They invited me to the "Bulkie" for dinner.

After dinner Grossman and I went back to the dormitory to try out the practice rooms. Later back in the room, Grossman told me about something he'd overheard in the dormitory lounge. He said, "Watts,"—that's what he always called me—"there was a horn player with a strong Southern accent talking about you to someone. He was saying, 'Aw suck! Ya shoulda' heard this colored boy play French horn over there in the dormitory practice rooms. I mean it was unreal; he was just all over the horn, garl . . . darn! I didn't know colored could play no French horn, I swear I didn't.' The guy's name was Verne and he was from Alabama."

When classes started, I was excited and apprehensive wondering if the college preparatory curriculum in my high school that I had so coveted had *really* prepared me. The classes moved at a much quicker pace than high school. I even felt overwhelmed at times, but I didn't care. I just wallowed in all that musical knowledge.

After two weeks into the semester, I was informed by the dean's office that my horn teacher was ready to begin my horn lessons. I had chosen Harry Shapiro, second horn of the Boston Symphony. I called him and arranged my first lesson. That evening I practiced like mad to have a good lip for my first lesson. I wondered what Mr. Shapiro would think of my playing. Would he like me? Would he talk down to me like tuba player Bill Bell did, referring to me as boy? Would I be too nervous to play well and be placed in the "Basic Studies French horn class?"

I told Grossman I was really nervous but excited too. Grossman told me to relax and everything would be fine. "If his name is Shapiro, Bob, everything will be OK."

I asked him what he meant.

"He's Jewish, Bob, it'll be fine."

Then he gave me that crazy wink again. He said he would explain the whole "wink" concept to me later. I loved Grossman.

My first horn lesson finally came and I met Harry Shapiro at the famed "Beethoven Statue" in the hallway of the main building. We showed up at the same time, he looked me right in the eye, and he said, "Mr. Watt?"

I said, "Yes, sir."

We shook hands and he said, "I have a room already picked out, let's go upstairs." As we walked he told me that he'd heard a lot about me and was looking forward to working with me.

When we started the lesson, he asked me to just play a few things for him so he could hear me. After I played, he showed me a new tonguing concept. He had me start a note without using my tongue, using the syllable "whooo"—just blowing air through the horn and then adding the tongue slowly like a valve, making breaks in the tone—fascinating. He told me that I had very good tone production, a beautiful sound, and that I was very big talent. He continued by telling me that although I had a lot of talent, I was still going to have to work my tail off to become a good horn player.

"What we will do mostly in the first year is break down for you all the components of playing. Even the things you do well will have to be examined and taken apart so you'll understand how you do the things you do. This way, Bob, if you ever have any problems playing later in life, you will know how to fix things—and you will also know how to teach these things to others. What I noticed here today about your playing is that your middle-low register needs some work, but everybody has this problem. It's the most difficult register on the horn, see?"

He gave me a list of books to order. They were all Paris Conservatory method books. The most interesting one was a transposing method that taught transposing using beautiful melodies of French composers. The exercises were broken up into different transposing keys and they fit together like a puzzle and sounded great if one played the correct transpositions.

Harry was very paternal and even concerned about my personal comforts. I liked him not only as a horn teacher but as a human being as well. He reassured me that "Everything will be fine, Bob, if you work hard. Don't worry I'll explain everything about the horn even to the point where you'll be able to get up at 3:00 in the morning and play. This is how it has to be, Bob, if you want to make a living on the horn."

A crazy thing happened that proved even more who my horn teacher was and how he regarded me. For a brief period of time, I was into smoking pipes, in particular, the Sherlock Holmes calabash type. I even found a Sherlock Holmes hat and caped coat. One day I ran into my horn teacher on the street. I spoke to him with great confidence, "Hi Harry." Now, in my nineteen-year-old mind, I actually thought he would be impressed by my fancy pipe and Sherlock Holmes getup. He was not.

He just stared at me with a very stern expression and said, "You get rid of that Goddamn pipe or I'll never teach you another horn lesson." Poking me in my chest he added, "And you don't call me *Harry* until you get a good job playing your horn." He walked away.

I stood there on that corner for half an hour in shock. When I was finally able to move again, I went home and threw out all my stupid pipes, and gave my silly hat to a little kid, but I kept the coat.

Even though I was working very hard, I still didn't grasp all that Harry expected of me. My first bad lesson happened because I was two minutes late. Harry lectured me for ten minutes about how I couldn't show up two minutes late on a professional job.

He said sternly, "If I can be here on time, so can you." He left the room.

I thought, *God! I made him walk away again.* I sat there for a long time thinking about how I couldn't afford to mess up with him again. I was very depressed and went to look for Grossman. I told him what happened with the pipe and how Harry walked away again at my lesson, because I was two minutes late.

Grossman said that I should see it for what it really was. "This guy loves your ass, Watts. He wants you to understand that if he's going to help you, you have to meet him at least half way. He cares, Watts, that's why he walked out of the lesson and left you standing on the street."

# CHAPTER FIFTEEN

~

# Welcome to the World

Christmas was my first trip back home since I'd left in September. However, once I arrived back home I realized that I had made a definite transition. I was part of the greater world and, as the saying goes, "You can't go home again."

Back at school, spring arrived with its usual fever. Headed down to practice, I ran into Janice, one of my favorite horn players at the conservatory, sitting on the floor downstairs in front of the Coke machine. As I approached her, I noticed she had her head in her hands. I greeted her, "Hey, Janice, you OK?

She said "Hey, Bob, you know what?"

"Yeah, tell me, Janice?" I asked.

"I want sex."

I looked at her, surprised, and said, "You don't say . . . and by any chance is it *me* you want, Janice?"

"Yeah, of course it's you I want, silly, who else?" Placing her foot firmly in my crotch, she said, "I need it bad, Bob. How can we fix this?"

I told her it would not be a problem.

Thirty minutes later, we were standing in the middle of my friend's bedroom holding hands and looking into each other's eyes. I told Janice I was really flattered that she wanted me in this way.

She pulled me close and whispered in my ear, "Hey, Bob, I've always wanted you in this way, but you never seemed very interested in me—anyway, let's really take our time with this."

We slowly removed each other's clothes, talking and laughing. Finally Janice asked, "Are you excited yet, Bob? Oh, I see that you are, sorry I asked, God!"

It was really great to be finally having sex, especially since Jones told me it would help me study better. I'd been looking at women all year at the conservatory and around Boston, yearning to be intimate with a nice woman, but I guess I just didn't really know how to "pull any bitches," as Jones would say. I guess I was still being haunted by the fact I never made love to my high school sweetheart, Leslie.

Janice and I rested for a long time in each other's arms, talking about school, our teachers, other players, and our futures as musicians.

She said that she'd overheard Verne, the horn player from Alabama, trying to get me into trouble on many occasions by saying I was supposed to be playing in ensembles even when I wasn't scheduled. "He's really trying to smear you, why? You know, Bob, I think, and don't take this the wrong way, but—because you're not a cute little white boy from a good all-American home, you might run into some resistance trying to become a horn player in this world, you know that?"

Toward the end of the second semester, I got tired of walking around campus with no money in my pockets so I found a part-time job. I did call home for money just once and somehow my mother got the idea that I didn't have money for food and she panicked. It was the dead of winter and my mother wanted to send me a postal money order. My sister Judy said our mother was willing to brave a brutal blizzard to send me that money order but didn't have the proper snowshoes. My older sister tried to calm our mother, who was in a worried frenzy that I was actually walking around Boston hungry. She said my mother then proceeded to wrap newspaper around her regular shoes using black electrical tape to form a pair of *newspaper boots*. She then walked almost a mile in that blizzard to the post office just to mail me a $20.00 postal money order.

The part-time job I found at Brigham's Ice Cream Parlor paid more than enough for my needs as a student.

I became famous for the size of ice cream cones that I scooped. They always said, "Let him make my cone." Consequently I made several dates with women from other colleges but got in trouble for making the cones too large. "Damn, Watt, no wonder my profits are off! You're making the cones too big, son. And also, Watt, by and by I'll expect a little more speed from you. Your lines are way too long—ah, maybe a little less chit-chat with the girlies, OK?"

I'll always remember the very next day at work, while I was clocking in, I heard the news that Robert Kennedy had been shot in Los Angeles. It was the spring of 1968 and the second political assassination that year. First Dr. Martin Luther King Jr., whose wife had also attended the New England Conservatory—in fact, Coretta and Martin met in Boston and married there.

One of the trumpet players of the Boston Symphony coached a repertoire class, Brass Rep., for the brass players. We read all the standard orchestral music on a weekly basis. One particular week, he brought in Igor Stravinsky's *Petruska*. The parts were difficult for me since I had never played some of those changing complex time signatures before.

I was surprised at my next lesson that Harry knew all about it. The repertoire coach told him everything. Then Harry said to me, "You can't read as well as you should. You can't think quickly enough in musical situations, I heard about it from Rodger. He said you couldn't read the *Petruska* parts. Don't worry, Bob, I know exactly what to do. We will work on it, that's all."

And how we worked on it. He must have dragged every horn part in the Boston Symphony library to my lesson. Every week he had new music for me to read at sight, all sorts of odd time signatures and rhythms. To top this off, Harry found me a community orchestra where I could play first horn.

It was the Newton Symphony, conducted by a violinist from the Boston Symphony. The orchestra was quite good and the best thing in the world for my playing. Right away, I learned that I had to project my sound more in that group. It was bigger and better than the conservatory orchestra with many very strong string players. My reading training with Harry really paid off. I could read most anything the first time we played it.

Just when the Newton Symphony was getting comfortable for me, Harry came up with another offer. For the summer, especially after my difficult first year, he thought I should be at a music camp. A cello player from the Boston Symphony ran a music camp in the Berkshire Mountains, Red Fox Music Camp. Harry asked me if I had an interest in being in the country for the summer. I told him I had never heard of a music camp. He told me basically that it was an orchestra that rehearsed and played concerts. The conductor was superb and I would benefit from the entire experience. My next question was, how much did it cost?

Harry said, "Now you don't worry about that, Bob. There are always ways around these things, see." He said that I would go to the camp on a work scholarship—which meant I would go to the camp early and help set up the place. In exchange for this, I could attend the camp cost free all summer as his first horn.

I got really excited about the offer, which sounded almost too good to be true. Besides, I had not given one thought about what I was going to do for the summer. Like my mother, Harry was always a step ahead of me.

At my next lesson, Harry had John S., the director of the music camp there to hear me play. He asked me a few questions about my health and if I could do a little hard work. Then he wanted to see if I could take direction from a conductor so he had me play a few orchestra parts in different ways. That was my audition. He said, "Fine, you can be my first horn and you're going to have a wonderful summer." I almost cried.

When I told Grossman, he said that he'd never heard of a teacher doing so much for a student. "What's next, Watts, a solo with the Boston Pops? Bob, he really likes you, you must be playing your ass off in the lessons."

Oddly enough, Harry seemed to be working me extra hard on the Strauss Concerto No. 1. One day after I had played through the concerto, he told me to put my horn down. I had a feeling something amazing was about to happen. He looked at me and said that I was really doing well and sounded very good in general and that my sound had really opened up since he'd been working with me. He even said that he really enjoyed working with me. I had a lot to learn in the beginning and still had a lot more to learn. Then, to my amazement, he said that he thought I should play the Strauss Concerto with the Boston Pops. At first I thought I had heard him wrong. He said we would talk more about it later, but that I should practice the piece like mad for the next lesson.

I couldn't wait to find Grossman and tell him. I saw him making his way across Gainsborough Street to the dorm. I met him in the lobby and yelled, "Grossman! Holy shit! We gotta talk!"

"Watts, what's up, you look so excited—let's go to the Bulkie for dinner."

As we walked through the cold windy streets of Boston, I told him what Harry said. I reminded Grossman about how he mused just some weeks earlier about my "playing a solo with the Boston Pops, we were joking then, right? But now, Grossman, now it's really going to happen."

Grossman's eyes lit up through his glasses. "Goddamn, Watts, that's unbelievable, congratulations! This guy loves your ass, Watts—you are so lucky. What are you going to play?"

I told him the whole story about how Harry felt that I was playing the Strauss Concerto No.1 very well and that I should play it with the Boston Pops. I would have to audition for the Boston Pops conductor, Arthur Fiedler. At my next lesson, Harry told me to come to Symphony Hall that next day with my horn and the music to the Strauss concerto. He said when the Pops rehearsal was over, I was to go stand next to the piano on the stage and wait for his cue. "When I point at you, start playing the Strauss." I started to ask a question and Harry told me not to ask any questions, just be there and do what he said and everything would be all right.

The next day I showed up at Symphony Hall and took my place on the stage next to the orchestra pianist. He had the piano part to the concerto in front of him. I was a little nervous because I still didn't know exactly how things were going play out, except that I was supposed to start playing when the rehearsal ended. It all happened very fast. Arthur Fiedler tapped the podium with his large baton and said, "Thank you, orchestra," as they all stood up to leave. Harry came from out of nowhere and pointed at me to play. As I played the opening of the Strauss, the entire Boston Pops orchestra turned in surprise and politely sat back down and listened while I played through the entire first movement of the concerto. It was brilliant! It was frightening, but it worked. Harry had orchestrated that whole amazing scene.

When I finished, the orchestra applauded and Arthur Fiedler said, "Very good, Harry, very good, he's a very talented boy. Maybe we could have him play this in Plumber Park, in the colored area—this summer, yeah . . . that might work. See me in my office, Harry." Arthur Fiedler came over to me and shook my hand, "Thank you, son, you play very well."

Harry told me later that everything went very well and not to worry, because now "Fiedler thinks it's his idea, so you'll be playing this concerto with the Boston Pops this summer for sure." The problem then was how to live with the idea that I was actually going to be a soloist with the Boston Pops.

~

# CHAPTER SIXTEEN

# Music Camp and the Boston Pops

The next thing I knew, I was in the Berkshire Mountains at Red Fox Music Camp assembling prefabricated practice rooms and painting flower boxes. The camp was like something out of a New England novel: acres of rolling hills, an old New England barn, trees, a stream, and of course, lots of meadows and dense woods. In the distance, the higher Berkshire Mountains created a stunning visual backdrop.

When the music camp started, word got around quickly that I was going to play a solo with the Boston Pops. It was my ID tag for the summer, but I can't remember a happier time in my life. I had a great musical opportunity to improve my playing over the summer, I had a solo engagement with the Boston Pops under Arthur Fiedler, and I had a great teacher who made all of it possible. I was extremely blessed.

Sometimes I was so full of excitement that I had to just sit for a while and be quiet. I found a beautiful spot far out in the woods where I went to meditate. In that place, I could reflect on all the things that had happened in my short musical life. It all seemed so unbelievable at times. All because one very cute black girl happened to smile at me in eighth grade and in that magical moment, that single stroke of human tenderness, jump-started my entire life. I had often wondered how her college life was going, but I didn't hear from her until late that summer. She had done very well her first year in college and I heard she was majoring in sociology. I missed her and often thought about her during my first year at conservatory.

As my mind slowly drifted from thoughts of my high school, Leslie, I couldn't help wondering what the other campers would be like. Would the orchestra be good? Would the conductor be good? Would he "mess with me" because I was black? Would the horn section be good? So many questions flashed through my mind as I went about my work-scholarship duties.

Playing the horn was such a pleasure after a year studying with Harry. I knew so many new techniques. I had become a totally different player. It gave me real confidence to meet the other students who would be coming to the camp.

Finally opening day of the music camp arrived and for the entire weekend, scores of very nice cars pulled into the parking lot. I was getting very curious to see with whom I'd be spending my summer making music. By that Sunday, everyone was settled in and John S. the camp director, called an orientation meeting in "The Barn," which was also the concert hall. He gave everyone a warm welcome and some general camp guidelines.

At the opening reception, I saw two really attractive women with dark shiny, parted hair—what Grossman and I called "that dark parted look," our favorite look for Jewish women in our student years. As I made my way over to talk to them, I felt a little nervous, but then I was suddenly empowered remembering what Jones always told me: "And don't be afraid to do shit, Watt."

The first woman I approached was Lydia. She was the swimming coach who also played violin. I introduced myself and welcomed her to Red Fox Music Camp.

She turned, looking me straight in the eyes, and said, "Oh, thank you, and what instrument do you play, Bob?"

I told her I was a horn player from the New England Conservatory. I asked who was going to be her swimming students and she said anyone who needed lessons. She was still looking at me through squinted eyes, as if wondering about me.

The very next day I went to the barn for my mail and noticed a woman walking toward me. She had a classy, regal look about her. She was tall, with long legs, wearing loafers and cut-off Levis. When I got closer, I remembered her from the opening night party. She was the other dark-haired woman I noticed but never got to meet. We introduced ourselves. Her name was Rachel-Marie and instantly I felt an affinity well up between us. She sensed it too and we agreed to meet later at dinner and perhaps take a walk in the meadows.

My walk with Rachel-Marie was like a dream. A beautiful moonlit night, with fireflies and a million stars closer than I ever thought possible. We conversed for hours, and it turned out she was also from New Jersey—a place I'd never heard of that sounded rich and affluent, like "Upper Crustic Heights" or "Brior-Bane Brisby," New Jersey. I loved the way she talked, always running her words together. Because of her sensitivity, her eyelashes fluttered nervously when she was making a point. I was stunned by the manner in which she so confidently took my hand as we started to walk. It was just like Jones said it would be. "You will meet all kinds of bitches from all walks of life, even the rich ones, Watt." Rachel-Marie insisted on holding my hand as we sat in the tall grass. God! She was with me, the poor, nobody kid from a cold-water flat on Springwood Avenue, who slept in his socks and fought mice and roaches all his life.

Suddenly with great poise and style, Rachel-Marie quietly asked if it was all right if she snuggled up closer to me to keep warm. My entire face glowed, as if someone had suddenly turned a heat lamp onto it. I couldn't talk, I just felt. She smelled so wonderful and looked so beautiful in the moonlight cuddled up next to me with her shiny wavy hair with its classic "Watt–Grossman dark parted look," reflecting the lunar rays. The look on her face was so sincere and tender as she gazed deeply into my soul. Just the thought that she needed something from me that I could so readily offer was overwhelmingly gratifying. We held each other very close with our eyes locked together in breathtaking silence.

After our long basking in the warmth of each other, we ever so slowly stood up, never breaking the locked gaze between us, and kissed deeply. As we started towards the road still holding hands, we spotted at least a dozen deer that were also enjoying the moonlight. That was pure magic for me. I walked Rachel-Marie back to her cabin and we embraced once more followed by another deep kiss. I walked back to my cabin very slowly with lots of emotion in my heart, looking up at the dark sky full of stars, and for the first time in my life I could feel myself walking on the planet as a tiny being, looking right into the face of God.

The Red Fox Music Camp orchestra was about sixty players, all conservatory level, with a really creative and talented conductor, James Paul. I played mostly first horn and a really great guy named B. G. Moran played third. The horn section got along very well and we had all kinds of insane fun. We even played horn quartets when not rehearsing with the orchestra.

There was also chamber music. We performed a fantastic work by Benjamin Britten, Canticles III for Horn, Piano, and Tenor. Our music director and conductor, James Paul, was also a fine tenor. The piece was about the World War II raids over London. The text was from scripture and other great literature. The horn part supplied the sound effects of the air raids over London as John Paul delivered the text with delightfully tasteful diction.

In spite of all that was happening musically at Red Fox, I still had to go back into Boston and perform the Strauss Horn Concerto No. 1 with the Boston Pops. I was constantly reminded and ribbed about it by all the camp musicians. I almost started to dread it because I knew it was going to be a lonely experience. Most of my friends were at home on summer vacation and no one was coming with me from Red Fox Music Camp. Still, it was an enormous opportunity and I had to pull it off and do well, especially since it was going to be in Plummer Park, in the black community of Boston, in an area called Roxbury.

I stayed at a friend's apartment for one night. The next day the Boston Pops sent a car and drove me to Arthur Fiedler's house in Brookline for a run-through of the concerto with a pianist.

The famous Boston Pops maestro conducted and coached me throughout the concerto. He told me to look up at him every so often for communication and all would be fine.

"OK, good, now let's have some beer!" he said.

We retired to his enormous porch.

"God, it's hot! You drink beer, son?" His servant rolled out a small beer machine and filled up two glasses. "Let me see you toss that back, son," he said, chuckling.

I drank the entire glass of very cold beer right down and Fiedler said, "*Prost!* Good thirst you have there."

He took a beer in hand, kicked off his shoes, and said, "Good luck tomorrow night—just remember to have a little nip of whisky beforehand."

I really enjoyed hanging with Arthur Fiedler.

On the day of the performance, I met my parents in Boston on the steps of Symphony Hall. My mother came with my namesake, Robert Lee Booker or Bobby Booker, a well-known jazz trumpet player from Brooklyn. My father, on the other hand, came with another woman. It was rather awkward, with lots of vitriolic glares of disgust from my mother thrown at my father. After that ugly moment passed, we all went our separate ways. My mother and I went with Bobby Booker to a relative's house to have dinner and my father went to a motel with his woman.

During dinner my mother asked me how I felt before playing a concert. I told her that it was like having a little entity in the stomach that remains there until I perform. She said she was nervous for me, especially remembering when I first started and how I struggled sometimes trying to make things work on the horn.

I could see it was going to be a hot steamy August night in Boston and I was ready to get on with the show. After dinner we walked over to Plummer

Park and found the Boston Pops orchestra warming up. Arthur Fiedler was in his private trailer.

He called me in to say hello. "Want some whisky, son?" he bellowed, offering me a swig from a small silver flask in his jacket pocket.

I told him it would make my lips numb. Then I introduced him to my mother, someone took photos, and he went out to conduct the overture. When he came back it was my turn. My mind started racing. I was about to play a concerto with the Boston Pops. I wished Rachel-Marie or Lydia could've been there and many of my other friends from school, like Grossman or Janice. I flashed on where my high school love, Leslie, was and what she would have thought of the amazing opportunity I was about to have.

I walked out ahead of Fiedler to the stage and right away the audience applauded. It was an all-black audience for sure. Most people were sitting on benches, some on the grass, some were standing, and some of the young people were in trees with binoculars. The most amusing part of the audience was that front row of outspoken black men, who yelled, "Yes, my brother, we are glad to see you! We are here for *you*! Now ah know, we gone hear something. Show 'um whatcha got, brother!" they yelled.

It all happened so fast, the next thing I knew I was playing the famous opening of the concerto that I knew so well. When the last movement came, things got off for a split second. I started a half beat late but caught up and it all ended well. The crowd roared. I was soaking wet with perspiration. It was intermission and everybody *poured* backstage to see me. It was a little scary at first having so many people physically rush me in such an excited manner. I just stayed calm, held onto my mother's arm, smiled, and shook hands.

In the back of my mind, perhaps because he had rejected the French horn and my classical music passions, I was still waiting for my father to appear. I guess it still mattered to me what he thought about my being a classical musician, but he didn't appear. Bobby Booker was there, as always, very supportive.

He shook my hand and hugged me, saying, "Way to go, Cuz."

Finally, when I did see my father, he looked real strange.

I asked him if he liked it and he said, "Yeah, well, ya know, Jesus Christ, I don't know what happened—Ah! Sorry, I just got here, son."

He had missed the concert! I couldn't believe it! My mother was visibly disgusted and said in my ear, "How could he come all the way up to Boston, some 300 miles, and miss the whole damn concert?" Apparently he had overslept at the motel with his woman.

# CHAPTER SEVENTEEN

~

# Best Summer

It was back at Red Fox for two more weeks of camp. I'd only been gone for three days, but it seemed like a week. I guess I was getting really attached to the country air and to Rachel-Marie. When I arrived back at camp, she greeted me with open arms.

"So, how did it go?" she asked.

"Just fine," I said. We hugged for a good while and she whispered in my ear that she missed me. She put her arm low around my waist as we walked to my cabin. I told her that there were some family problems. She was very concerned and said if I wanted to talk about it she would be a good listener. I thanked her and told her that I was falling in love with her.

She said, "I know that, Bob, and I feel the same.

I took her face in my hands and kissed her. Rachel-Marie's reply—that she felt the same about me—just made my young body flush with hot blood again. In that same moment, I also realized that my father's sleeping through my concert had hurt me deeply and I needed to talk about it.

One night after dinner, we found an empty car and started to kiss wildly and passionately. It felt like we were going to go all the way when suddenly Rachel-Marie slammed on the brakes, sat upright, and said, "Sorry, sorry, Bob, I don't want to continue."

I was shocked out of my state of passion, but I must say, she looked quite beautiful in that moment of bliss and despair with her top off. Her beautiful dark crinkly hair hung in my face as she sat on top of me.

"It's too soon, Bob—and it's not the place I imagined it with you. I'm sorry, can we just talk—will you forgive me?" she pleaded.

"It's OK, Rachel-Marie, I'm just glad to be with you again . . . holding you, looking at you."

I began to talk about what happened with my father at the Boston Pops concert.

When I told her that he missed my performance, she said, "My God, Bob, that's unfathomable to me how such a thing could happen. What kind of father would do such a thing?"

I started to explain the situation with my father and I ended up bursting into tears. I had a very deep cry as Rachel-Marie held me.

In a few weeks, it was all over at Red Fox Music Camp. I had truly enjoyed the entire summer. The solo engagement with the Boston Pops, meeting Rachel-Marie, the music at Red Fox, my great horn section, and the mind-opening lessons with Harry all summer. It was all like a well-scripted dream, except that it really happened.

Rachel-Marie and I corresponded for quite some time, but I never got to see her again and that pained me immensely. I heard sometime later that she moved to the San Francisco area.

Back in Boston for my second year at the conservatory, I rented an apartment. I was lucky to find a place across the street from school. It was a nice old brownstone owned by an eccentric Mr. Coleman, who was always walking around talking to himself. He rented me a studio apartment for $90.00 a month.

When school started, I felt a lot better having my own place. I was quite busy working part time and doing my schoolwork, practicing, and so on. I got used to the schedule. My classes were actually more difficult my second year, but I was better prepared mentally. I had more confidence in myself after Red Fox and appearing as a soloist with the Boston Pops. I also felt well established as a player at the conservatory. People knew who I was since I had played as a soloist with the Pops. All of a sudden, I got more chances to play in all of the ensembles at school.

In spite of my new player status at school, I was very excited about my position in the Newton Symphony that Harry helped me acquire. There was one woman in particular who played in the string section who constantly stared at me during rehearsals. Monica was in her late thirties, divorced, no children, and lonely. She said she was going into Boston and heard that I was at the conservatory and that I could ride with her if I wanted. I thanked her and took her up on her offer. She smiled at me warmly as I loaded my horn into her station wagon. She said her ex used to play the horn and that it was one of her favorite instruments. As we drove she began to talk, looking me up and down physically, the way Jones described.

She smiled at me and said, "I want to tell you, Bob, you play very well and I do so enjoy listening to you in the orchestra."

I thanked her graciously. Monica was brunette, well built, about five foot eight, but she seemed somewhat on edge while talking to me. I knew there would be a passionate explosion if we ever got close together in a room alone.

When we arrived at my apartment, she turned and looked at me in silence. I broke the silence by saying thanks for the ride and perhaps we could do this again and perhaps next time stop for coffee or a drink.

I was just about to say good night and climb out of her car when she asked, "Do you mind if I come up and see your place tonight, Bob?"

I said it wasn't much to see, just a place to operate from for school.

Then she said, "Oh please don't be modest, I'm sure it's lovely."

Once we were in my apartment, we spontaneously embraced. She looked me right in the eyes and said, "You know, Bob, I was somewhat shy and didn't quite know how to approach you at rehearsals." She said she was hopelessly attracted to me and would I mind if she kissed my lips? We kissed and she got so worked up from the one kiss she didn't want to let me go. She started by taking off my shirt and got more aggressive with her hands, which gradually broke into a slapping pattern. Then she really started to hit me on the sides of my face with an open hand, harder and faster until I stopped her,

"Hey, hey, what are you doing?"

Then she caught herself, "Oh my God! I'm so sorry, I'm so sorry! I forgot! I forgot!" She was crying as she rubbed my face, asking if I was OK. Then she started to explain. "Please forgive me, it was my ex-husband who needed this kind of—" We passionately christened my cheap, new red carpet.

One day Harry called and told me to meet him at the Beethoven statue. I was very curious because it was midweek and we didn't have a lesson scheduled. He was waiting there with a little envelope when I arrived. He greeted me warmly and asked how I was doing in school so far that year. I told him that school was still difficult, but I was doing a lot better.

He looked at me in that familiar deadpan manner, which told me that something amazing was about to happen. He handed me the envelope. "Now this is a little job, Bob. All the information is enclosed."

Curious, I opened the envelope.

"Now, whatever you do, don't be late for this job, Bob. You only get one chance in this business." He had just hired me for the Boston Ballet playing *The Nutcracker* ballet with Arthur Fiedler conducting.

On the paper it said something about Musicians Union Local 9. In addition to the little piece of paper, there was a check from Harry for $80.00 to join the union. I looked at him puzzled and said, "This is a check from you—I don't understand what to—"

He cut me off, "Don't say anything, Bob. Remember, this check is just a little loan. When you get your paycheck, you pay me back." I smiled and thanked him again. I ran and joined the Musician's Union. That was the day I became a professional musician.

Finally the first rehearsal for the Boston Ballet job came. I went to the music hall with my horn and lots of extra time to get there. The music hall was quite large and I made my way to the pit with the other musicians. I was playing fourth horn, a heavy-set guy was on third, a middle-aged woman was on second, and Dave Ohanian was first horn.

I felt really special being there, so young, still in school, and having worked with Arthur Fiedler the past summer. The other players told me to concentrate, even worry, about keeping my place in the music. The music was busy with lots of notes, but easy to read at sight. I found out right away what Harry meant when he said I had to learn to think fast in music. There were lots of stops and starts during the rehearsal. There were six rehearsals and three performances and I couldn't help sitting there enjoying the lovely female dancers of the Boston Ballet.

# CHAPTER EIGHTEEN

~

# Turning Pro

Going home to my family for Christmas that year was much better than the year before. I reminded my mother that I was going to stay in Boston one week longer after school ended, because I had that job with the Boston Ballet.

My father always managed to slip in unnoticed and just lurk in the distance and stare at me. I found him a little creepy.

He loved to constantly ask me about school and what I was doing up there. He suddenly tossed his head back to its usual condescending position and started interrogating me, "Do you know all your scales?"

My answer was always a wry "Yes, by now, I do, Dad. In fact, I know a lot of scales."

Back in Boston, I was determined to work very hard. I practically lived in the conservatory library. All the wonderful books on music were there and the listening room was just the best. I couldn't think of a better place for me to be on Earth than at school, even though I was in a big city like Boston with all it had to offer me as a young professional musician. I was extremely happy.

Once I was hired to play a job outside the city limits of Boston. It was an orchestra job with the New Bedford Symphony. In fact, several conservatory students were hired to play that job. I borrowed Grossman's car and took three other players with me. It was a nasty rainy night in Massachusetts, which had many three-lane highways. I was driving along when suddenly, from out of nowhere, red lights appeared in my rearview mirror. It was the highway patrol.

"Pull over," I heard over a loudspeaker.

The officer told me that I was "hanging in that left lane." He wanted to see my driver's license. Unfortunately, it had expired, it was a New Jersey license, and I was driving Grossman's car with an Illinois plate. The officer told me to step out of the car, he handcuffed me, and walked me to his patrol car. He asked one of my friends to drive and follow him to the station.

When we arrived in the little hick town of Bridgewater, Massachusetts, the station captain said they had to book me on driving without a license. That was a serious offense in the state of Massachusetts plus the traffic violation of driving in the passing lane. If I could produce the bail on the spot, I was free to go. However, I was not allowed to drive the car with my expired license. Either way I had to be in court the next morning at 9:00 a.m. for the judge to rule on my case. If I didn't arrive on time for my trial, I would forfeit the bail, which was $109.00.

My friends were all violin students of Joseph Silverstein, concertmaster of the Boston Symphony. Meanwhile, they had already locked me in a cell downstairs and it took me a minute to get used to being locked up. I closed my eyes, perhaps hoping I'd wake up and it all would have been a bad dream. I must have dozed off for a minute when an officer came down to tell me that my teacher was upstairs.

Harry was upstairs? If that were true, I was safer in the cell.

The officer said, "Yes, your teacher, Mr. Silverstein—from the Boston Symphony? Who are you people, anyway?"

I was really embarrassed.

When I got upstairs, there he stood, the concertmaster of the Boston Symphony, holding a check for my bail, and he didn't look happy. Then the officer on duty had the nerve to question the validity of the check.

Mr. Silverstein said in a loud annoyed voice, "You're damn right the check is good, I'm the concertmaster of the Boston Symphony!"

They took the check and reminded me that I still had to be back in the Bridgewater courthouse at 9:00 a.m. or I would forfeit the bail money.

I thought I would rather spend a night in jail than to risk blowing Mr. Silverstein's money. I thanked him and hobbled back to my jail cell holding up my pants. I got off with a $25.00 fine.

A week later, my get out of jail bonus was that I got a call from the Boston Symphony asking if I could play a week with them as assistant first horn. I said yes, with pleasure. The music was Bruckner Symphony No. 8, which called for eight French horns and four Wagnerian *Tubens*, which are small tubas that composer Richard Wagner invented to reinforce the viola and cello voices in his opera orchestra, which are played by French horn players.

The Boston Symphony Orchestra music library called and told me that I could have the music any time I wanted. It was all very exciting and a little bit scary too.

At my next lesson, I tried to tell Harry, but he knew all about it. Of course he knew—he was the one who spoke up for me. He told me that it would be a snap for me. He suggested I go to the conservatory library and listen to the piece so I would have an idea of what it sounded like before the first rehearsal. He had also arranged for me to take one of the Wagnerian *Tubens* home and learn to play it, since this was the first time I'd played in a piece that used them. I wasn't going to play *Tuben*, but he said perhaps next time. I went to pick up the *Tuben*.

About a week later I got a check in the mail from the Boston Symphony. I had forgotten that they were so organized that they often paid in advance.

The day of the first rehearsal with the Boston Symphony, I went over to Symphony Hall early, because I didn't even want to even think about how Harry would chew me out if I even *looked* like I was going to be late. I entered the backstage area, took out my horn, and went to feel out the stage. There were only a few people on stage. I was a little nervous, but my lip felt so good from preparing for that moment that I relaxed after a few minutes.

# CHAPTER NINETEEN

## Musical Adventures

A few minutes before the rehearsal started, the personnel manager came to me on stage and said that the conservatory president, Gunther Schuller, was very upset that I was not at school playing in the wind ensemble and that he was coming over to the Boston Symphony rehearsal to drag me back across the street where I belonged. He didn't care that I had been hired by the Boston Symphony—I had an obligation to the conservatory. It turned out that I wasn't scheduled to be playing in the conservatory wind ensemble, someone had made a grave mistake.

Suddenly, Erich Leinsdorf, the conductor that I had watched conduct the Boston Symphony on CBS Sunday evenings for years, came floating out on stage like a god. He was holding his conducting baton between his hands in prayer position. He started the symphony right away. I forgot about everything else when the music started and became totally engrossed in what I was doing. The first horn, James Stagliano, whom I had also watched play for many years, seemed so relaxed when he played. Nothing seemed to bother him. He just leaned back and played the many solos in the symphony with a beautiful style and tone. When it came my time to relieve him, I could feel Harry glancing over at me from his second horn position. I felt quick but fleeting bits of nerves when he did that, but after a short while I relaxed. The real shock came for me when the full brass section played together on the loud *tutti* passages. It made the floor under my chair vibrate and I felt goosebumps on top of my head when I was playing with them. It was hard to believe, that I was actually on that stage playing with those guys.

On the morning of the dress rehearsal, the principal horn didn't show up. It was already 10:05 a.m. and Leinsdorf was ready to start the rehearsal. When he looked back at the horn section and saw that there was no principal horn, he went ballistic. "Bill, Bill!" he yelled for the personnel manager. "Where is Jimmy? It's five past ten and we are ready to start—and no Jimmy. I mean, we must have a solo horn for this symphony! What are we supposed to do?"

The personnel manager slithered out on stage with a sweaty grin on his face and told Leinsdorf, "Ah, Jimmy said he was not able to walk this morning because of his gout condition so he won't be coming to rehearsal this morning."

Leinsdorf threw up his hands in disgust and then, the unthinkable, the unimaginable happened. He looked into the horn section and said, "So now what shall we do?"

At that moment, the associate principal horn player stood up and said, "Well, Erich, I don't mind filling in for the rehearsal."

Leinsdorf told him no, that he needed him to play first *Tuben*. Then to my great surprise he looked right at me and said, "So we'll have the conservatory boy play first. I mean, what else can we do?"

I felt this cold fear at first, but it all vanished when he told me, "Move over, son, and play first horn for us this morning, will you?"

The entire orchestra turned around and looked at me.

I must have looked at Harry with an expression of complete surprise, because I heard him say, "It's all right, Bob. Just play everything with a nice big tone and don't worry about a thing."

*Holy shit*! Before I knew it, we had started the symphony and all the notes that the first horn was playing that seemed so daring to me when I first heard them, I was suddenly playing. It was magic. Here I was playing solo horn with the Boston Symphony Orchestra. Wait until Grossman hears this! *I just have to pull it off*, I thought.

Once we got going into the first movement, I got so deep into the music that I didn't have nerves any longer. Harry jumped in a few times when he feared I might not make my entrance. He seemed more nervous for me than I was. I was amazed that my sound matched with the section as much as it did. I could feel the brass players behind me watching and listening. It was my trial by fire—my life on the line. It was one of those experiences that I didn't think I would live through; that there could actually be life after such an ordeal was beyond comprehension at that moment. I knew I had to do well and I concentrated like never before and tried to ace every important passage. Sometimes Harry would lean over to me and say, "Bob, you don't have an assistant so rest your lips here."

Then when a big juicy solo passage was coming up he'd say, "Play out on this, Bob, sing out with a great big beautiful tone." It was just like being in a lesson, but with the entire Boston Symphony Orchestra playing with me. Finally the big horn quartet passage at the end of the slow movement came. My lips were getting tired and I suddenly understood why the principal horn needed an assistant. I took a deep breath and really poured out my best tone possible. I loved that part and had played through it by myself many times at home. I got into it so much that people were turning around looking at me.

Harry noticed that it was distracting me and said, "Don't worry about them, Bob, just keep playing, you're doing great."

I almost fell over when I heard him say that. He was so encouraging, especially during that amazing moment in my life.

At the end of the slow movement, Leinsdorf paused for a moment and looked at me. "Are your lips tired, son?"

The entire orchestra turned again and looked back at me again. I told the maestro in a very nervous tone of voice that my lips were not tired and that I was having a great time. He briskly raised his arms and started the finale.

The finale movement was extremely exciting with lots of loud fanfares for the entire brass section. Once again I felt goosebumps because of all the great parts I had to play with that brass section.

When the symphony was over, Leinsdorf said to the orchestra, "I would like to thank the boy from the conservatory, whatever his name is, for filling in for us this morning. He has done very well." The entire orchestra applauded me.

A string player with a strong French accent turned around to me and said, "From where do you come, my boy? You play beautiful, you are an artist."

People were smiling and patting me on the back. I didn't know what to do or say. I was numb. I looked at Harry and shook my head in disbelief.

Harry made one of his classic remarks "Ya see, Bob, you were terrific! Congratulations."

As if that weren't enough, Leinsdorf told Michael Tilson Thomas, the assistant conductor at the time, to take me in a room and review the tempi with me just in case I had to play first on the concert that night. I looked at Harry again in disbelief.

He looked me square in the eyes and said, "If you have to do it, you'll do it. Now go rehearse with Michael, Bob."

There didn't seem to be an end to that incredible day. After working with Michael, I walked home in a daze. How could I tell Grossman what had happened? *He won't believe it.* I found Grossman and we had lunch. I looked at him and I said "Grossman, are you ready for this?

"Now what, Watts? How'd it go this morning at the dress rehearsal?"

"You won't believe what happened this morning." I told him how Stagliano didn't show up and I had to play principal horn for the whole rehearsal.

"My God, Watts, that's unbelievable! How did you do?"

I told him everything. "I'm still not sure that I won't have to play first horn tonight."

"Wow! You might play the concert? Watts, that's great!"

"They told me if they haven't called me by 3:00 that I would be playing the concert on first."

Grossman said, "My God, Watts, you must be so nervous. How can you stand it?"

After leaving Grossman, I fell asleep and later received a call around 4:00 p.m. from the Boston Symphony telling me that the principal horn would be coming to the concert and I would not have to play principal horn on the concert. They thanked me for stepping in as principal at rehearsal and that it would reflect on my paycheck.

That night at the concert, I wondered how I would have played under that pressure. Harry said I would've done just fine, but it would've been scary.

# CHAPTER TWENTY

# Tanglewood

At my next lesson, Harry told me that it was time for me to audition for the Berkshire Music Festival at Tanglewood. I was a little surprised because I thought I was going back to Red Fox Music Camp. Soon after that, Harry sent me over to Symphony Hall to audition for Armando Ghitalla, principal trumpet of the Boston Symphony Orchestra. I felt a little nervous, but after a few seconds' playing I was just fine. I was in very good playing condition for the audition and all went well.

Ghitalla complimented me, "Harry said you could blow the hell out of that thing and he was right. Congratulations, son. We'll see you this summer at the Berkshire Music Festival at Tanglewood."

I found Grossman at the market.

He could tell I was excited. "Watts, what's happening? You look excited again."

I told him that I had just auditioned for Tanglewood and was accepted.

Grossman's eyes opened wide as always when he was excited. "You auditioned today and they already told you that you got it?"

"Yeah, can you believe it?"

Before my next lesson, I received my acceptance letter from Tanglewood. I took it to show Harry. I walked into the lesson with a big smile on my face and showed him the letter, but he knew already.

"Well, congratulations, Bob! That's terrific! I heard about it this morning from Ghitalla. He said you played great. I'm glad to hear that."

Then Harry got real quiet. "Now, Bob, let me talk to you a little bit. Many great things are happening for you and that's how it should be. You deserve it, but you must remember that even when everything's going great and you think you can do no wrong, you still have to keep your nose to the grindstone. Don't get cocky! You still have a long way to go and you'll make it, but you have to keep your wits about you. It's not over yet. Remember that."

It was a strong lecture, but I really knew he was in my corner. I looked him straight in the eyes and said, "I understand completely. Thank you." I had a really good lesson that day.

Things had really gone well that school year; I had played with the Boston Symphony and I had my own apartment.

The Tanglewood Institute consisted of fellowship orchestra players, fellowship conductors, and fellowship composers. My favorite conductor that summer was Michael Tilson Thomas, assistant conductor of the Boston Symphony. He had a skilled conducting technique and a great musical ear. I worked with him on several difficult contemporary compositions and I must say, he really knew how to work through the difficult problems of a piece and give it polish.

The Fellowship Orchestra was a great challenge also. There were many chances to perform lots of standard orchestral repertoire as well as contemporary works by the fellowship composers. The orchestral playing was politic free and evenly distributed among the orchestra fellowship students.

I was honored to meet other black artists who were at Tanglewood that year. There was one really great black tenor who sang in one of the opera productions, James Wagner, and the celebrated composer David Baker, a professor of jazz at Indiana University. Harry introduced me to the celebrated black maestro Henry Lewis, who was there conducting the Boston Symphony. I had a very nice talk with him about many musical topics. He was music director of the New Jersey Symphony at the time.

Some weeks later I was attending a Boston Symphony rehearsal where pianist André Watts was performing. I was completely awestruck listening to him. He was simply amazing, so deeply into the music. I had read about how he filled in at the last minute for an ailing Glenn Gould on a concert with Leonard Bernstein and the New York Philharmonic, playing the Brahms 2nd Piano Concerto.

After the rehearsal I just had to meet him somehow. Again, it was my horn teacher, Harry Shapiro, who came through for me. He introduced us as "Mr. Watt, meet Mr. Watts." André was very charmed by our similar names. He said something like, "I bet you received a lot of my checks too." We shook hands and talked a little before he had to leave. Tanglewood was certainly the place to be.

One could *never* say that there wasn't enough playing to go around at Tanglewood. My most memorable experience was performing the Brahms Horn Trio for Violin, Horn, and Piano. We were coached by the principal horn of the Boston Symphony, James Stagliano. He coached us for two rehearsals and then we had two rehearsals with the celebrated pianist Lilian Kallir.

Just before I left for Tanglewood, I had purchased a new Alexander model-103 from James Stagliano. He often ordered several from Germany at one time and those he didn't like he sold to students. I paid $500.00 for that wonderful instrument and I broke it in at Tanglewood playing that Brahms Horn Trio.

My saddest time at Tanglewood was at lunchtime. After a long morning of hard playing, there were days when I was hungry and didn't have any money for lunch. I had to somehow manage until dinner. It was kind of hard because I needed a midday meal more than an evening meal. That was the only drawback about Tanglewood. I couldn't work and make pocket money like I did in Boston. After buying the horn, my bank account was pretty low. At the same time, I had to leave some money in my bank account for my apartment and for school in the fall.

One day I ran into Harry around lunchtime at the Tanglewood cafeteria. I tried to pretend that I wasn't hungry, but I was starving. He went up for his lunch and I was just going to sit there and talk to him drinking a cup of water. I was fully prepared to skip lunch, which I had done many times before, but he caught me.

"You're not having lunch, Bob?"

I said, "No sir, I'll be fine."

Harry got right up in my face and said, "You're working very hard up here, Bob—you gotta eat, for Christ's sake."

I tried to tell him that I would eat dinner later at the school.

"Dinner?" he yelled. "You're going to wait until dinner?"

I told him point blank, "Mr. Shapiro, I never eat lunch here at Tanglewood because I don't have the money. I eat at breakfast and I come here and play, hoping that I'll get so involved with the music that I won't think about food and it kind of works most of the time."

He fired back at me, "You're crazy, you know that? Ya gotta eat, Bob, or you'll pass out."

He reached in his pocket and gave me $20.00. I was filled with emotions, embarrassed, angry, and so damn hungry that my hands were trembling. I looked him in the eyes and took the money. Walking up to the cafeteria, I broke into tears so bad that I couldn't read the menu. I thought, *My God, who is this guy? I can't keep taking from him.* Of course my pride was a little bruised because I was used to feeding myself, especially when I was in Boston. I went back and sat with Harry. He was really upset. We ate in silence.

Leonard Bernstein was chosen to direct the Berkshire Music Festival at Tanglewood the following summer. It was rumored that he was going to be walking around the grounds looking the place over and talking to students. I had read Bernstein's book, *The Joy of Music*, in high school and I was well aware of who he was. It was going to be an interesting week if he actually showed up.

One day several of us were sitting on the grass near the orchestra shed and off in the distance we could see what appeared at first to be a cloud of dust rising. It looked like a being from another world approaching, and for a split second, it looked like a half-dozen elephants. After a short while, we could see that it was actually a group of about sixteen people following one man, who had his jacket thrown over his shoulders, smoking a cigarette, and talking to those on either side of him. Closer and closer they came until we could clearly see that it was indeed Leonard Bernstein. We all stood up quickly and became very quiet as the pack of followers passed us by looking as if they were all in a trance while listening to Bernstein talk.

They followed him whichever way he turned. He looked magnificent, but they all looked like extras in a movie, hired to make him look good. In fact, one got the impression that the whole spectacle *was* being filmed.

Mr. Bernstein was about five foot eight—not the tallest in the group by any measure—but he was the only one talking. I caught a bit of his passing conversation: "Well, Jack told him that it was just out of the question, didn't he, Jack? And of course we all know the outcome to that story. And where are we going now? Where are the students? I want to hear some students playing, for God's sake, this is Tanglewood!" He was larger than life and everyone followed him, catered to him, and loved him. We were thrilled to see him just the same. He was a musical giant.

The next day, I had a rehearsal with Michael Tilson Thomas. The music was a modern work with a very difficult and flashy French horn part. I was so wrapped up in the music that I never noticed that Leonard Bernstein sat through the entire rehearsal. People told me later that he was there, but I didn't believe them.

After Tanglewood, I returned to Boston for my third year at the conservatory. The president, Gunther Schuller, summoned me into his office. He told me about a situation that had developed that past summer at Tanglewood. He said Leonard Bernstein sat in on a rehearsal of mine. He really liked my playing and wanted me as a player in the New York Philharmonic.

That summer while I had been at Tanglewood two black classical musicians claiming racial discrimination were suing the New York Philharmonic. The argument was that the New York Philharmonic never invited black players to its auditions and that, in fact, it didn't even know of any black classical musicians. Consequently, the New York Philharmonic engaged itself in a mad dash to find black classical musicians. See Appendix.

President Schuller went on to tell me that he was sure they would be contacting me soon, since they were in such a mad desperate rush to find qualified black classical musicians. He said that they would most likely invite me to the audition that was coming up for fourth French horn. He was concerned that the audition committee would then perhaps try and spoon me into the position, for the sake of argument in their lawsuit or, at least, say they did in fact know a black classical musician who was qualified.

Gunther Schuller's position was that he didn't like that they would try using me in that way. He warned me not to correspond with them in writing, lest it be used in their court case argument. I was amazed to hear such a thing and agreed to follow his advice.

After a short while, a letter did come in the mail from the New York Philharmonic inviting me to the fourth horn audition. I called the personnel manager who was listed on the letter and declined the invitation. He argued with me a little bit, saying that I was throwing away a lifetime opportunity. I thanked him and hung up the phone. This gave me quite a sense of foreboding about the politics that might lie ahead for me as a black French horn player in any symphony orchestra in these United States. I thanked Gunther Schuller for speaking up. I told Harry about it and he didn't like the sound of it at all. He said Gunther was right to warn me.

# CHAPTER TWENTY-ONE

~

# The Musical Mountain

Several months later, news about the New England Conservatory's financial problems hit all the newspapers and was even on the nightly news. The conservatory even hung a banner on the side of the school building asking for funds and donations.

In light of that situation, Harry informed me at my next lesson that I wasn't going to be attending school next year because all scholarships were canceled. He said it was time for me to look for a job. And what did I say? "A job doing what?"

Harry fired back, "Playing your horn, dummy—it's time for you to take a few auditions for a symphony orchestra position. Is that clear enough for you?"

Raising his voice, he started to pace around the room. "There are a half-dozen openings around the country and you should try for at least two of them. I want you to be in a very good orchestra, as close to the top as possible."

I was still a little shaken by his words and took a moment to speak. I invoked the fears from my father and my thoughts about the charges of racial discrimination during the New York Philharmonic court case. I asked Harry point blank if he thought I really had a chance of getting hired by an orchestra, regardless of how well I played.

He looked me deeply in the eyes and said, "Bob, you just go to these damn auditions and play your ass off and you'll cross that bridge when you come to it."

I managed to ask Harry which orchestra he thought I should consider.

He said, "Yeah . . . good question. You should probably take the Los Angeles audition—they play with a nice big sound and you'd be fine in that orchestra, and then on your way back from LA you should stop in Chicago, which would be perfect for you, see? We'll talk about this later, but the most important thing you need to learn now is the 'audition profile.'"

Every lesson from that point on was about auditioning.

He explained, "Anything that would be on these auditions you've studied with me in the last three years or you've played it somewhere. So don't worry, Bob, you're very close to being ready for any audition.

"Now, here's what happens at these auditions: You go out on the stage and there will be a music stand with a large black folder full of music. They will welcome you and then tell you to proceed with your solo first. You play part of a concerto, everybody plays the same concerto, so don't worry. After they've heard enough of your concerto, they stop you and tell you to play the preselected excerpts that are on a list next to the black excerpt book. The list is nothing more than the page numbers in the large black excerpt book. You turn to the excerpt and play it. When you finish playing the list, you're done, they thank you, and they go on to the next person.

"In these auditions, Bob, you gotta make a big impression right away, see? If you start screwing up, they'll stop you and say thank you. Then you've had it. You don't want this to happen. So for the next several months, we will review all the major excerpts for the horn. From now on, your lessons will start with a mock audition. We will repeat the audition profile over and over until it's second nature to you. After that, your audition will be a snap. Let's get started."

We played the excerpts (important French horn parts, solos, and major passages from the standard symphony orchestra repertoire) by music periods.

In my daily practice, I thought back to the feeling I always had after an audition in high school, for example. After an audition, I always had the feeling that I could have prepared better for what one *actually* does in an audition.

That idea was haunting me from the past. After several weeks of playing the excerpts over and over, never knowing when I had practiced enough, one evening it finally hit me. In my own practice, I had to prepare mentally for what I was actually going to do in that audition. In that small window of time, I had to make a strong impression on the audition committee. Now that Harry explained the process, I understood exactly what had to be done. I had to practice for accuracy for each excerpt. I had to prepare my mind to concentrate on playing—not only musically but with extreme accuracy.

I came up with a little game that really helped me. First I played my concerto. I played it three times. If there were any missed notes or anything that I didn't like, I would add another repetition to the set of three until I could play the concerto three times perfectly. This really forced me into extreme concentration. I did the same procedure with each excerpt. If all three times were perfect, I went on to the next excerpt.

Every night after dinner I played for hours. This was in addition to hours put in during the day with the French horn étude books, the Maxime-Alphonse method books from the Paris Conservatory School of playing. After several months of that routine, I could sit in a practice room with the lights off and go through the excerpts almost from memory. It got to be a real fun game.

Harry said I couldn't just play the excerpt from a sheet of music, especially if I had never heard or never played the entire work. I had to go to the music library and listen to the entire work to understand how the excerpt fit in and how it was supposed to sound in the context of the entire piece.

I became almost obsessed with my audition project—a one-shot deal in a small window of time with all the pressure imaginable to play well. My underlying personal curiosity was to see how I rated as a French horn player on a national level. I was extremely motivated.

I created a resume and cover letter requesting an invitation to the audition. Harry said he would have a bassoonist from the Boston Symphony, who was in the army with the personnel manager of the Los Angeles Philharmonic call and ask if the audition was on the level, to find out if they already had someone in mind and not just holding an audition for appearances, which Harry said was done on occasion.

I soon received an invitation to the auditions for the Los Angeles Philharmonic and the Chicago Symphony. I bought my tickets and I was off to Los Angeles. I practiced right up until one hour before I had to leave for the airport in order to get as much practice in before taking the long flight. The flight to Los Angeles was six hours. I feared that by the time I got there my lip would be out of shape and I would play poorly. I was very wrong.

# CHAPTER TWENTY-TWO

~

# First Auditions

The morning after my flight to Los Angeles, I went outside to have a look at the town. It was stunning! I couldn't believe how green everything was in March, when Boston was still ugly and gray with winter. I marveled at the palm trees, so tall and stately as they blew gently in the balmy West Coast breeze. I felt a kinship with Los Angeles right away. There were so many different types of people speaking so many different languages, so many different types of restaurants, and the streets were so wide. I stayed at the Mayflower Hotel (now Checkers) just down the street from the Los Angeles Music Center.

I also remember a serious hill to climb up to the concert hall. The auditions were to be held in the Ahmanson Theatre, which was part of the music center. The music center made me think of Lincoln Center in New York City. I was always thrilled by the idea of a center just for music. I was becoming extremely excited about my audition.

I walked up the steep hill to the Ahmanson Theatre to warm up. On entering I met a middle-aged man with a face full of skin sores. He looked me straight in the eyes and said, "Hello, Mr. Watt, I'm the personnel manager of the Los Angeles Philharmonic. Welcome—I have a warm-up room for you." This was the friend of the bassoonist in the Boston Symphony whom Harry had mentioned.

After a long careful warm-up, I was ready to take the stage and play my first audition for a major symphony orchestra. I was pulsing with anticipation and ready to play music, ready to put to use all the months of preparation—test out the ideas I had discovered about relaxation and focusing on the exact thing at hand, that of playing orchestral excerpts accurately and musically.

Finally my time to play arrived. The personnel manager pointed me in the right direction and said, "Good luck, Mr. Watt."

As I walked onstage, I noticed that it was set up for a play of some kind. There was a sofa, a coffee table, lamps, and so on. Looking further downstage, I saw the music stand with a chair. I looked out into the house to see who was going to audition me and there was no one in sight. The lights onstage were so bright that they made it almost impossible to see out into the house. If there were people out there, surely they would have said something. I waited for a while and then left.

As I exited the stage, the personnel manager came running up to me. "Where are you going? What's wrong?"

I told him that there was no one out there. He looked at me incredulously and snapped back, "What do you mean, there's no one out there? Please go back onstage!"

"Look, I've come a long way for this, I went out there and no one said anything and I didn't see anyone. Can you please tell me for whom or what am I supposed to be playing?"

He cut me off. "I'm sorry, I'll take care of this." He went out to see for himself and then he came back and said it would take only a minute while he called someone. I reentered the stage and this time I could barely make out six or eight people sitting in distant dark shadows. I couldn't help but wonder, Had they been there all the time? If so, how strange that they let me come onstage and not greet me or say anything. Were they examining me like a specimen under a microscope? Now I was really ready to play almost with a vengeance. I had no nerves, just a sudden strong driving desire to play extremely well.

Finally someone, still not fully visible, greeted me and said with an accent, "Can you please start with the Wagner?" He wanted to hear the Siegfried long call from the opera, where the brash young Siegfried blows on his horn to imitate sounds in nature and inadvertently wakes a dragon that he is forced to slay.

I was totally fascinated with the operas of Wagner and was very knowledgeable about the opera *Siegfried*. I had really prepared the long call and I guess with my interest in the story it helped me bring some drama to the music. I really got into it and all my little musical nuances worked—the echo horn, the big crescendo up to the high C, it all worked.

After the long call, I heard the same voice with the accent say, "You play that like you know something about this opera, yes?"

I told him that it was one of my favorite operas. In fact, I had fallen in love with the entire trilogy. I especially liked the fact that the long call was developed from the sword motive all the way back in Rheingold, the first opera.

The voice abruptly cut me off, saying, "Yes, yes, I know the story. Now can you play the Tchaikovsky 5th Symphony solo, please?"

I sat down for that one. I closed my eyes to give myself the feeling that I was in my dark practice room back at the conservatory. I just transformed myself mentally and the solo came out just the way I wanted. I couldn't believe how well my lips were responding. I had all the endurance I needed.

After the Tchaikovsky 5th solo, the voice asked me if I would mind playing the two previous excerpts on another instrument. Another make of instrument? It was the make of instrument they played in the Los Angeles Philharmonic.

He said he realized it was an extremely unusual request, but nonetheless, he would like to hear me play on that instrument.

I shrugged my shoulders and said, "Sure, a horn's a horn."

The voice snapped back, "Don't shrug your shoulders—don't be too confident, just play. Thank you."

I was beginning not to like "the voice," or perhaps he didn't like me, but whatever was happening I was not going to let it bother me.

I played the previous two excerpts on the other instrument, a Conn 8-D, which I recognized when they brought it up to me. My street-kid instincts kicked in and told me it was best not to tell them up front that I previously owned two Conn 8-Ds and had just sold one a year earlier. If I said nothing about owning or playing one, it would certainly win me points.

The voice was very impressed. He fired back with, "It's amazing, Mr. Watt, how easily you can switch instruments. This is the brand of instrument we use here in the LA Philharmonic, it's called the Conn 8-D."

I said, "Yes, I believe I've heard of such an instrument." I forgot and shrugged my shoulders again and answered, "But like I said, a horn's a horn."

The voice fired back, "Yes, yes, you told me."

He clapped his hands together and said, "Come, come, now let's continue with The Midsummer Night's Dream solo and go back to your own instrument now, Mr. Watt."

Next he wanted to hear Strauss's Ein Heldenleben, and then Till Eulenspiegel, Symphonia Domestica, and Also Sprach Zarathustra. When I was finished, I dropped myself onto the sofa behind me in exhaustion.

The voice then asked, "Are you tired?"

"Not really," I answered.

He replied, "OK, then will you come back this afternoon and play some more for us?"

I sat up quickly and asked, "Does this mean I've made the finals?"

The voice came once more, this time seemingly annoyed, and said, "Yes, yes, please go now and come back at 2:30."

The time then was 11:00 a.m. I was elated. I walked back down the hill to my hotel, dropped off my horn, and went for lunch on the town.

Such a beautiful day it was—and what an amazing city. *What a wonderful life I could have here if I got this job*, I thought. I was still wondering in the back of my mind what they would ask me at the final part of the audition. I had lunch at Grand Central Market on Hill Street and went back to the hotel for a nap.

After a good sleep, I walked back up the hill to play some more. When I arrived onstage, there were other horn players there. It was the entire Los Angeles Philharmonic French horn section. They were going to play with me? I was overjoyed because that part of the audition was going to be fun— that was my best type of playing. I felt then that I had a true advantage. The voice asked me to play first horn on *Semiramide*. I was really happy that he chose that excerpt, because I knew it well and liked it.

Next the voice said, "Let's take now the *Der Freischütz* overture, followed by Les Preludes."

This time I was asked to play fourth horn, using the Conn 8-D again. Finally, I played first horn on the famous horn trio from the Dvořák Cello Concerto and it was over. The voice thanked me and I was told to wait backstage while they heard two other players. I thought for sure when I left Los Angeles I would know if I had the job or not. At the end of the audition, they thanked everyone and said they would let us know soon.

That evening the personnel manager and one of the philharmonic horn players invited me to dinner. The horn player and the personnel manager said that I had a good chance because the music director really liked my playing. The only holdup was that they wanted to hear from a horn player in the New York Philharmonic.

The next day I flew to Chicago to take the horn audition for the Chicago Symphony. I arrived midafternoon, found a hotel, showered, and went directly to the hall to practice. There were many other horn players hanging around, practicing and trying to impress each other. I quietly found a room, warmed up, and went through my practice routine. I was exhausted so I returned to my hotel and fell asleep in my clothes until morning.

# CHAPTER TWENTY-THREE

~

# Madness!

The next day I walked to the hall, which was just down the street from my hotel. I had never been to Chicago before. It had a coldness that was unlike New York and was a great contrast to the sunshine and warmth of Los Angeles.

Orchestra Hall was a very imposing-looking building with brass-trimmed doors and a doorman wearing a dark green uniform. I took the elevator down to the basement and joined the many horn players. There were a few horn players from the New England Conservatory, including my not-so-favorite Alabaman, Verne. They simultaneously flashed me a vapid surprised look from across the room that said, "What are *you* doing here? I thought I was the only one on the level to audition for the Chicago Symphony. How could you (black boy) think that *you* would have a chance?"

After my warm-up, I did something that really worked at the Los Angeles audition. Instead of standing around with all the other horn players ripping through excerpts, I sat in a chair and went into a quiet zone, a kind of meditation, to conserve my energy. When it came close to my time to play, I got up, grabbed my horn, touched my lips to the mouthpiece to confirm that I was still warmed up, and went up to the stage.

The personnel manager of the Chicago Symphony was the proctor for the actual playing part of the audition. He sent each applicant onstage, gave them the proper directives, said good luck, and closed the stage door behind them. He didn't listen to any of them play. When it was my turn, he gave me the same information and sent me out to the stage. As I walked onstage,

I noticed that they had dropped a curtain down as a screen to hide the applicants from the audition committee to supposedly prevent any kind of discrimination. However, I could clearly see the audition committee quite easily because the curtain was not nearly tall enough to hide me. I looked over the curtain and greeted the committee as I sat down to play. Suddenly I could hear someone on the committee saying how stupid that whole arrangement was. "Oh, for Christ sake, Jack, you can see he's colored—I ask you. What good is this Goddamn curtain?"

Once the committee calmed down, a voice—this time with a southern accent—told me to go ahead and play the numbers that were written on the sheet. I was to play them in order. The first number corresponded to Tchaikovsky's 5th Symphony. I did the same thing that I did when I played the excerpt in Los Angeles. I closed my eyes and pretended to be in the practice room at the conservatory. However, the sound of the horn in Orchestra Hall was so breathtaking that it helped me play even better.

As I was searching in the book for the next excerpt, I noticed someone standing behind me. It was the personnel manager. He was outside the stage door listening to me with a most curious look on his face, a look of utter curiosity and disbelief. I glanced at him quickly and continued my audition.

After I had completed the list, I heard someone from the audition committee say, "Thank you." As I got up to leave, I noticed that my curious observer had left.

When I got back downstairs with the other players, they asked me how it went. I told them fine and sat down to relax before heading to the airport. My favorite Alabaman from the New England Conservatory came down from the stage after me and was upset. The player after him threw his horn against the wall, crunching it up in a ball. I ignored them.

Soon a secretary came down to thank us and announced that I was the only one from the group who had advanced to the finals. Everyone looked in my direction to see my reaction.

Verne showed marked anger and stormed out of the room. "What? Shee-it! Shee-it!"

I joined the others and headed for the door when the secretary called out to me, "Mr. Watt—don't leave, they want to hear you play again."

*Play again?* I was very surprised.

She said, "Actually we need you to stay until Friday to play with the other finalists."

I told the secretary that I couldn't possibly do that. I admitted to her that I simply didn't have the money to stay in Chicago until Friday.

"Oh! Is that all?" She asked if I could wait for five minutes while she made a phone call.

I wondered just who in the world she was going to call. A few minutes later, a man wearing a gray three-piece business suit stepped off the elevator. He announced that he was the controller of the Chicago Symphony and would I please hold out my hand. I held out my right hand and he said, "Both hands, please." He proceeded to pile hundred dollar bills in my hands and told me to tell him when to stop. I held my breath and lost count after $600.00. He must have given me $1,200.00. He called my hotel and told them that I would be staying until Friday and that my hotel tab would be picked up by the Chicago Symphony.

The next day was Tuesday and another group of young conservatory players like myself gathered into the hall to audition. I was there just practicing, preparing for the finals on Friday. All the players kept asking me when my time was to play. I told them that I had already played on Monday, made the finals, and had to wait until Friday. Some were very polite and said congratulations. Others got that oh-so-familiar attitude of white curiosity: "Oh, really? I see—well, who do you study with? Where do you go to school? How did you . . . ?"

The next day there was a rehearsal for the Chicago Symphony and some of the celebrated brass players were there warming up for a rehearsal. I was almost finished with my routine when the principal horn, whose voice I recognized from the audition committee, came in and started listening to me play.

He said that my horn, an Alexander model 103, would sound good in their section.

I thanked him and told him I had bought it from James Stagliano and really enjoyed playing it. I was working on Richard Strauss's Der Rozenkavalier.

He quickly turned and checked with the principal trumpet if it was all right that he coached me, since I was still in the running for the job and the auditions were not over.

The principal trumpet said, "Shouldn't be a problem."

The principal horn started telling me how to approach the pickup to the opening. "Just git it and don't worry about the notes in between the glissando, just git it, that's right, like that, just rip up to it."

I played through the entire excerpt and everyone said, "Very nice." Then I had to stop and think for whom I had just played. That was the brass section of the Chicago Symphony.

Then out of the blue, the principal horn asked me, "Play any jazz?"

I was a little surprised and responded, "Not yet, why?"

He said, "Well I thought surely being Negro you played jazz?"

I told him I was sorry that I didn't but planned to get into it later in my career.

He wished me good luck in the finals and went on stage.

That evening, I called my former roommate Grossman, who had moved back to Chicago after only two years at the New England Conservatory. He invited me over for dinner or to stay there if I liked. I told him perhaps I would consider it after the audition.

Grossman and I hadn't seen each other for over a year, so it was going to be a great evening of catching up. When I arrived at his house in Skokie, his parents greeted me warmly. I could see that Grossman's mother was still a little embarrassed about the way she had acted when Grossman wanted share an apartment with me in Boston. She was afraid that if we shared an apartment that I would have Gentile women around and he might not marry a Jewish woman.

Nonetheless, we had a pleasant dinner. I couldn't wait to tell Grossman all about my audition experiences. He was very happy to hear how things had gone in Los Angeles. He asked if I was nervous being in the finals for the Chicago Symphony. I told him that I was all nerved-out at that point and nothing bothered me anymore. We had so much to talk about.

At long last it was Friday. I had practiced all week to prepare for the finals. That morning when I woke up I was sick from the horrible weather in Chicago. I knew that it would affect my playing somewhat, but I went ahead and played anyway. There were two other finalists. One from Boston, David Ohanian, whom I knew well, had arrived with interesting news. He said that Verne, the horn player from Alabama who had auditioned with me that Monday, was spreading rumors that I made it to the finals *just* because I was black. As it turned out, Ohanian got the job.

The music director, Georg Solti, spoke briefly to me as he walked by, "You're a very talented boy, but we cannot teach you rhythm." He said this because I took liberties in the Tchaikovsky 5th Symphony solo, even though it clearly states in the music that one should take license.

I was glad to leave Chicago and go back to school. The audition process was such a pressure cooker that I was relieved it was over, even though I wasn't coming home with a job.

Once back in Boston, I got right back into my school routine. People at the conservatory knew that I had taken two major orchestra auditions. Many asked, "You didn't expect to get one of those the big jobs on your first try, did you?" or "Well, now do you see how hard it is and how much further you have to go?"

Two months later, after a long day of playing with the Boston Ballet, I returned home very late. It was after 1:30 a.m. I found a note under my door to call the personnel manager of the Los Angeles Philharmonic. I called, since it was still early in Los Angeles.

When I got him on the line, he raised his voice, saying, "I've been trying to reach you all day!"

My reply was, "Well I'm sorry, I've been out working all day. What can I do for you?"

"The music director wants to know if you still want this job?" I was really surprised because it had been over two months since my audition and I had heard absolutely nothing from them regarding the position.

My natural reply was, "You mean the job is still available?"

The voice on the line was getting impatient. "Yes, yes, do you want it?" he pressed.

"Well, I don't know. When does it start?" I asked.

"He would like you to start in June, if possible."

"No, I can't start in June, I've been invited back to Tanglewood—"

He really blew his stack and yelled, "Tanglewood? What the hell do you want to do, stay a student all your life? We're offering you a job in a major symphony orchestra, a major position, don't you realize that?"

I said, "Of course I realize that." I asked what it paid.

"Three hundred dollars per week."

"Every week?" I asked him.

"Yes! Yes! Of course, every week, now come on, damn it, give me an answer!"

I thought about it for a few seconds. "Yes! I'll take it, sir."

He thanked me in a very sarcastic tone and hung up.

I sat back in my rocking chair and collected my thoughts. *Now I have a job, a big job, in a major orchestra, that I wasn't supposed to get the first time out. What now?* I had to tell Grossman first, but wait . . . it was 1:30 in the morning. Who could I call at that hour?

I finally gathered my wits and called my oldest brother, Edward. He was awake and said it was good to hear from me. I told him I had won the audition for the Los Angeles Philharmonic and they just offered me the job. He congratulated me and said he thought it was great that I got a major position so soon—and so young. He asked me what a job like that paid.

I told him $300.00 per week.

"Every week?" he asked.

I said yes and he said, "Take it! Wow!" He said he'd tell everyone at home in the morning and that I should try to get some sleep.

Sleep? No way! My mind was racing from one thing to another until morning, when I called home to talk to my mother. When I told her the news, she was very happy. She said she would tell my father as soon as she could. She wanted to know if I was coming home before I went to Los Angeles. I told her I didn't think I'd have time. She said she was very proud of me.

The next day at school I went to see the dean of students. When I entered his office, he said he was glad I came in because he had some great news for me.

"This just came in, Bob—the Atlanta Symphony is now accepting colored people. When I heard that great news, Bob, I immediately thought of you."

"Me?" I asked.

"Yes, you, Bob. Isn't this wonderful news?"

"I don't know, Dean Williams. Do they have any openings for French horn?" I added, "I'm glad to hear about the Atlanta Symphony and I truly hope that they find some colored people, but I came in to tell you that I will not be attending school next year, not only because my scholarship was canceled, but because I've been hired by the Los Angeles Philharmonic."

The dean looked at me with that typical surprised, wide-eyed, and trembling lips look that older white people typically give a black person when said black person significantly exceeds their expectations.

With his trembling lips, he managed to say, "Oh my God, Bob, why that's wonderful! When did you find out?"

I told him that I had found out late last night. He proceeded to congratulate me and said how wonderful this was for me and for the conservatory. "Well, have you told anyone?"

I told him that I hadn't told anyone at school.

"Well let's call the president right now, he'll be thrilled!" He picked up the phone and called Gunther Schuller, who asked me to come to his office immediately.

He called me in and said he'd heard the news and congratulations. "But, are you really going to take that job, Bob?"

I told the president, "Yes, since my scholarship was cancelled and I won't be in school next year, I intend to take the job. Otherwise I'd be here in Boston freelancing and trying to make it somehow."

Gunther said he understood my position, but he thought the Los Angeles Philharmonic was kind of a bombastic orchestra in its playing style. He said he conducted them once and they gave him a difficult time. He basically didn't like their overall sound. He said the style of horn playing was very heavy, unmusical, and uncharacteristic—more of a studio sound concept. He thought that I might not like it. Then he shook my hand and said, "Well, it's a job and we all have to do something in life. Good luck, Bob."

# CHAPTER TWENTY-FOUR

~

# The Los Angeles Philharmonic

Several weeks later, I happily left the city of my conservatory years and boarded a one-way flight to Los Angeles. The flight didn't seem so long the second time. I couldn't help but feel somehow vindicated and content that I had made it through a lot of crazy drama during my school years in Boston. I had finally earned something substantial in my life, in spite of all the naysayers back at the conservatory, and most of all, in spite of my father's doubts.

I was truly closing a chapter of my life. It was a sweet victory and yet somehow sad, leaving some of my best friends behind.

I don't ever remember feeling so alone in my entire life. The idea of being on an airplane leaving a life behind that I knew for one of newness and uncertainty was daunting. Perhaps that was the sweet pain of growth. In the long run and in a very short while, things in my life would be better than ever; I wondered if my entire life would be that way if I kept striving.

When the aircraft touched down, a feeling of great excitement rushed through my young body. I was back in the city that had so impressed me just a few months earlier. I had a job that would enable me, through the glory of music, to fully experience the amazing city of Los Angeles. I briefly mused about all the great things that would happen: With all the great weather, I would enjoy all the beautiful women, get in really great physical shape by running for miles on the beach enjoying the Pacific Ocean, play film scores in the studios of Los Angeles—it was all looking fantastically surreal.

The next morning, after staying in the same hotel, I walked up that same steep hill again, this time to go to the offices of the Los Angeles Philharmonic and report in. They gave me a warm welcome and sent me to the office of the executive director. He said that the first thing I should do was to transfer my Boston Local 9 musician's union membership to LA's Local 47. There was a rental car available and they lent it to me. The first freeway I used was the Hollywood Freeway—a most beautiful highway lined with palm trees and green ice plants dotted with pink flowers covering the hillsides. Already, I was enjoying my beautiful new city.

The Los Angeles Musician's Union Local 47 was an entire complex of buildings compared to the small, hole-in-the-wall Local 9 in Boston. The hallways were lined with photos of famous musicians and most interesting was a photo commemorating the merger of the black and white musicians' unions from the days when labor unions in these United States were segregated—two completely separate unions, with two completely separate memberships. There was the white union, Local 47, and its black counterpart, Local 767, as well as Boston's Local 9-535.

I proudly walked into the main office, which looked more like a large bank with teller windows and numerous people waiting in line. Each window was marked with a placard naming its function: Work Dues, Record Dates, Residuals, Pick Up Checks, Lost Checks, Jingles, Television, Motion Picture Residuals. These were all the indications that Los Angeles was the entertainment capital of the world. I located my window marked "Membership" and made the transfer from Local 9-535 to Local 47-737. It cost $140.00. I couldn't help wondering what it might have been like less than twenty years earlier, when I couldn't have joined Local 47.

When I returned the car to the philharmonic office, they asked me where I was staying. I told them the Mayflower Hotel and they said that one of the philharmonic players said I could stay at his house until I found a place. The player had a nice home in the suburbs with a swimming pool. It seemed all right until his homely wife started parading around me in her bathing suit. It was a nightmare in the making.

Sure enough, the very next day that orchestra player came to me and said, "Ya know, you can't stay around here forever. You gotta find yourself a place."

That very day I found a place near the Hollywood Bowl called the Highland Avenue Hotel, at the intersection of Highland and Franklin Avenues. There was a grocery store and dry cleaners right on that busy corner so I thought it was a pretty good find. The hotel had a room up in the hills with a balcony, which had a rather nice view of Hollywood. I lived in that hotel room for my first summer in Los Angeles. There was no air conditioning, but it was in a cool spot surrounded by trees and ivy. Living there enabled me to walk to the Hollywood Bowl for rehearsals, concerts, and for my own personal practice sessions.

The first rehearsal of the 1970 Hollywood Bowl season was at 9:30 a.m. I walked early to the amphitheater from my Highland Avenue Hotel abode, found a room, and did a really good warm-up. I had already met the horn section at my audition, but it was the rest of the group that I was concerned about. What would they be like? Would they be like the players in the Boston Symphony? Would I feel welcomed with open arms? Would they be listening to me only to see if I could play? All of those thoughts flashed through my young mind in a nanosecond.

Finally at 9:30 a.m. on the last day of June 1970, I played with the Los Angeles Philharmonic as assistant first French horn for the first time. The music was Beethoven's 5th Symphony, a very familiar symphony even to me as a young professional. I said good morning to the first horn in a hearty manner.

He turned and looked at me somewhat taken aback and said, "Heh!"

I responded, "Not good morning then," and he said nothing. He just stared straight ahead.

When I started to play, he motioned to me "not to drag." It was a little difficult reading off of the same music stand and trying to see the conductor at the same time. Perhaps I was dragging, but only the conductor would know that for sure. I found out later that some principal horns accused their assistant of dragging because they so desperately wanted to have something to say, to appear in control, or to appear knowledgeable. Some might say you're dragging just to put you on the defensive. A lot of the problem was caused by the proximity of the assistant horn to the principal horn. The assistant horn didn't have a music stand and had to look over onto the principal's music stand to see the music. This created an awkward twisted position, which pointed my bell away from the section. A rather stupid arrangement, I thought.

When I played assistant horn with the Boston Symphony, they had a separate part and a separate music stand with the music already marked where the first horn wanted to rest and have the assistant take over. The Los Angeles Philharmonic had *never* had a full-time assistant first horn. For that reason, they didn't have the extra parts and the music librarian wasn't at all interested in copying extra parts for me. In fact, he yelled at me, "Just read off the first horn's music."

Somewhere in the middle of the first rehearsal, I realized that any apprehensions I had about the other players in the orchestra had vanished.

Most people were very friendly—in fact, my most memorable encounter that morning was with a Chinese violinist named TK.

He approached me in a very friendly manner and said, "Welcome to the orchestra, Bob. Now that you're here, try to get as many black people where you are as possible. That's the way to change things, you see."

He became my first friend in the orchestra.

However, there was definitely friction between the horn section and the trombone section that morning. They were making threats to each other throughout the rehearsal.

During the break, one of the clarinet players came over to me and said, "So—how do ya like it so far?" He shook my hand and said, "Welcome." Other people approached me, saying welcome. "We could use some new blood in this horn section." I felt quite comfortable for the remainder of the rehearsal.

# CHAPTER TWENTY-FIVE

~

# The Dream

My first performance with the Los Angeles Philharmonic was for the most part uneventful. I remember the principal horn telling me to just keep tapping my foot the way I did in rehearsal (I didn't realize I was doing it) because it helped him in certain places during the music. I guess I wasn't dragging after all.

At the intermission of my uneventful first concert, I was paged to the stage door. It was the moment I had been waiting for with great excitement: After playing for 18,000 people at the Hollywood Bowl, there just *had* to be scores of Los Angeles women waiting and wanting to talk to me at intermission.

My twenty-two-year-old mind started racing feverishly from one delicious type of woman to the next: perhaps a tall brown-skinned black or perhaps a regal Scandinavian blonde with freckles and fuzzy blonde hair on her arms and thighs, or an Asian woman with shiny, jet-black hair, shoulder length, with the most gorgeous eyes in the world, described by racists as slanted, but that I find so awesomely beautiful. Perhaps these women would want to get together and play chamber music. Oh, the things my young male mind conjured up in those fleeting moments!

Instead, waiting for me were three of the strangest looking black men I had ever seen anywhere. One was five feet tall with a dark complexion and a horrible greasy hairdo that looked like it had been soaked in old motor oil and then rolled in dirt. His eyes were bloodshot, he was sweating profusely and fanning himself with his program. Pseudo-intellectual horn-rimmed glasses hung around his neck and he had a flat greasy nose and thin black lips that were in constant chatter with the other two men. He had on a white outfit made of shiny silk along with white shoes. As I casually looked out for my many imagined female admirers, his bloodshot eyes strained upward at me and then back to his program to find my name.

In a flirtatious tone he said, "Good evening, Mr. Watt, it's nice to see you in the orchestra."

His two partners, with their eyes bugged out, looked like two baboonish goons or oversized trolls. The fearless black dwarf threw his shoulders back and proudly announced, "I am Dr. D. Franklin Jr., composer and musicologist, and on behalf of Black Los Angeles, we would like to welcome you to our great city. It is an honor and pleasure to see you in our fine orchestra. So tell me, Mr. Watt, with your handsome self, are you married? Oh my, isn't he handsome, gentlemen?"

The two trolls nodded in gleeful agreement, "Uh huh, yes, oh yes."

Frozen in disbelief and disappointment—and still looking out for my backstage women to appear—I managed to say to the strange trio, "Surely there must be more than three black people in Los Angeles."

I had to step back slightly as the pompous musicologist tried to touch me on the side of my leg. "Oh! And a sense of humor too—you are just too much, aren't you?"

I asked him if he was the person who had paged me.

"Oh yes, I confess, it was I."

I was extremely disappointed and asked him, "Just where *is* the black community in Los Angeles?"

His eyes bugged out with excitement and he said, "Well, I'll tell you what—why don't you attend my church tomorrow morning and I'll introduce you to the black community firsthand? We'll tell you where everything is, even where you can get a haircut."

I thanked the man and told him that I didn't go to church and certainly not to meet a group of people called "Black Los Angeles."

He got quite disturbed with me and said, "But Mr. Watt, that's where all of Los Angeles's black people go—that's where you'll find them, at church. Oh! You must come to church to meet black Los Angeles, that's how it's done here."

I told him that I would meet black Los Angeles in my own time and I sincerely hoped that all of black Los Angeles didn't fit into one church.

He shook his head and said I was missing out on a great opportunity.

Perhaps I was.

As the black greasy short man left, he tried again to pat me on the side of my leg, as he said, "And don't be so tall next time."

Intermission was over, no women showed up, and I walked back onstage mildly depressed.

As my first summer in the orchestra progressed, it didn't take me long to find out that my position as assistant first horn wasn't nearly demanding enough for the type of player that I was. I was just twenty-two, with some very good orchestral experience working with the Boston Symphony and Boston Pops. On the other hand, I was totally aware that I simply needed to spend time in a symphony orchestra just playing and learning the music, but my position of assistant first horn didn't allow me to play enough of the notes to really *get into* the music. Thank God part of my job was to fill in on other positions in the horn section.

On the bright side, some of the younger players in the orchestra invited me to play chamber music in their homes, which I really enjoyed. It gave me a chance to really show what I could do as a player.

My official title in the Los Angeles Philharmonic was assistant first horn. A French horn section is made up of four positions: principal or first horn, second horn, third horn, and fourth horn. All major orchestras have six French horns, consisting of two principals, assistant principal, second, third, and fourth.

Assistant first French horn is also referred to as utility and in Europe they call it "bumper horn"—that is, to bump up the principal horn when needed in loud parts of the music so the principal horn can rest his or her lips. Utility means moving up and down in the section, playing some first horn, usually those works the principal horns don't want to play. I had to play a certain amount of second horn, which is a very busy position, some third and fourth horn. Therefore the player for assistant first horn position has to be quite flexible, playing well in all registers of the horn, high and low notes.

That was why they had given me such a grueling audition. Moving around in the horn section was the part of the job I liked the most. It gave me so many different musical perspectives. It helped to further train my ear and taught me to listen in context. I learned how composers used the different French horn parts with other instruments of the orchestra—like third horn with the cellos, second horn with the violas, and fourth horn with the basses. It was also a challenge just to read another part for the sheer joy of doing a different task and playing in a different register or just expanding the mind. I especially enjoyed it when I had to play someone's part in an emergency at a concert when I didn't rehearse that part, making me the only one in the orchestra playing the concert without a rehearsal.

~

# CHAPTER TWENTY-SIX

# Black Los Angeles

Without help from the greasy black dwarf and his two troll companions, I began meeting black people in my own natural way.

A young black horn student was referred to me by one of the principal horns. The story was that the student's lips didn't quite fit into the thin mouthpiece of the French horn and that particular principal claimed he didn't know what to do or how to make it work. He approached me and asked if I wanted a student.

"He's a black boy with thick lips and I just can't figure out how to help him, so would you like to take him off my hands?"

One fine day a black French horn student showed up at rehearsal and began to study horn with me. I fixed his problem easily. It wasn't the student's problem: It was his teacher's, who had a problem of perception. He was trying to get that poor kid to fit both of his lips, which were somewhat full, into the mouthpiece the way his thin white-folks lips fit. Even a person with thin lips never puts both lips totally into the French horn mouthpiece, it just appears that way. The way it works is the rim of both lips are placed on the edge of the mouthpiece, buzzing only in the very center of the lips (similar to the way one blows bubbles) and whatever is left over is rolled back into the mouth.

It was that black French horn student who actually jump-started my foray into the black community of Los Angeles. He invited me to someone's home for a dinner party and they in turn invited me to other events and so it went. I met scores of black mothers who were dying to introduce me to their young, unmarried Nubian daughters. Of course, the entire ordeal of meeting the black community of Los Angeles was very new, bordering on amusing to me, since the only real black community I knew was still back in Asbury Park, New Jersey, with my family, the black barbershop, and the Jersey Devil.

I should mention that most of the black folks were at least upper-middle class or what E. Franklin Frazier[1] called the "black bourgeoisie." They were all totally into what *he* called "second-class white citizenshipism." That is, they did all they could to emulate the lifestyles and values of whites in America but without ever really interacting with them—while still remaining as black as possible.

Consequently, a black person like me, in a high-profile position with white folks, was highly regarded and respected by such "upper-crustic" black folks. Whenever I was introduced, as soon as the "Los Angeles Philharmonic" was mentioned, their faces glowed and eyes bugged out. To them, I was a black man operating in the "real white world," and not the white world they had superimposed onto themselves. I had instant cachet—instant class—and they sucked up and kissed my ass something awful.

However, I thought the black bourgeoisie of Los Angeles were wonderful folks, all part of the larger diversity of black folks in general, in these United States. I continued to meet and enjoy the women of black, upper-crustic Los Angeles. I especially delighted in the ones with the *beautiful* dark skin. They always stood out to me, but I had a feeling that they were not high in the pecking order of their group. Nonetheless, the dark ones were the ones I always pursued.

They had it all, as far as I was concerned: the most beautiful black skin that almost glistened, coupled with natural, short-cropped hair. And to top it off, they also had the amazing black female body, with the *sacred butt* to go with it. It seemed quite remarkable, that one female being could have all those quality human traits. To take it further, women—and people, in general—with that dark skin color are said by anthropologists to have the most promising genetic future on the planet.

Regardless of their skin color, those lovely black women invited me everywhere—to their homes, their parties, and to their church functions. They talked funny, a strange combination of trying to stay connected with what little blackness was left in them and at the same time trying to show me that they could talk white as well, in the event we ever happened to be in a white social situation together, they wouldn't embarrass me like those other black women, who were, after all, as they put it, "just too black."

My new beautiful black women friends had all kinds of odd hang-ups. As I suspected, they believed and talked about skin color as though it really made a difference in the world. They had a color code—or should I say a color gradient?—that they used to decide who they would date or even talk to. They honestly believed in the "brown paper bag concept"—that is, if a black person was darker than the bag, they were denied entry to parties and certain black social functions. But even more bizarre, if one couldn't run a comb (designed for straight hair) through their normal African hair, it was a deal breaker for entry into said circles. Until they told me, I had no idea that they, or anyone, considered me to be "light-skinned." Little did they know I always wished I were darker, to give me a more striking presence.

There was one bizarre conversation where one of their treasured "high-yellow" friends explained how she had to use sunblock in the summer months. The others, the less-yellow ones, listened in awe and high praise, it seemed, as the high-yellow girl went on to say, "Well yes, you see—I peel in the summer so I have to use sunblock lotion, 70+ SPF" as she threw her head back swishing her long crinkly-frizzy quasi-red hair, as if basking in some kind of sick glory of being better than most blacks by having to do something that was associated with whites. The others all gave tacit approval.

When making love to those women, many of them were actually ashamed of their beautiful sexy black bodies. I'm not referring to the usual female doubts but to something purely racial.

For example, after giving them a breathless compliment on their bodies, they would always say things like, "Thank you, but I wished my butt were different—I wish it didn't have that extra hump. It causes my clothes to fit funny."

I always answered as best I could in the heat of passion, "Yes, but remember, the clothes you speak of were not designed for your beautiful butt . . . and that funny fit you speak of looks as if your sexy butt is just busting out of a 'flat-ass paradigm,' which makes you look all the more sexy."

It seemed they were never satisfied with themselves, never able to embrace their unique blackness and sexiness, always desiring something that was leaning more toward sexless. They wanted their butts to be flatter and less sexually inflammatory. I always argued and told them that a black woman's butt had to be the most beautiful sight in the world, but they would always disagree.

One day, they actually ganged up on me. "Now tell us the truth, Bob. Wouldn't you, as would other black men of your pedigree, *really* prefer the figure of a white woman, with that thin waistline, trim butt, and *good hair*? I mean, you've got to admit they have the *best hair*."

My mind started to race. There it was again, the *hair thing*—always a taboo subject with black women, it's like a room one dare not enter, a room full of 246-year-old, stinky farts and lies inherited from slavery that have never seen the light of air, a room that would violently explode at the strike of any self-respecting inquiry. And of all the lies ever told about black people, this was the one that struck the deepest, working its poison deep into the souls of black folk, that our hair is bad and cursed.

One day, for the sake of argument, I asked the woman I was seeing to do me a favor: "Let's make love and afterwards take a shower together and let *me* wash your hair, rinse it, dry it with a towel, and you just shake it, letting it dry on its own. I bet your hair will be the most wonderful sexy sight this world has ever seen." She took me up on it and afterwards she looked magnificent, so natural, so free, so exclusively African, so sexy, but she just couldn't see it.

I continued to date and fall in love with many of those stunning black women, who deep down inside didn't really believe that they were truly beautiful or that I, given my "pedigree," could truly love them: that a black guy like me, in my, so to speak, high-profile white position, would surely rather jump sky-high at the coveted, once-in-a-lifetime opportunity to have a white woman; that *she* is supposedly the ultimate merit badge to every successful black man, in these United States. Many times I just wanted to *scream* in frustration, but I only looked at them thinking my private thoughts: *No, no, it's not true. I've been with white women and they are not a prize to every black man . . . and once and for all, there's nothing wrong with your hair and nothing wrong with your butt. The glory of your sacred butt was stolen from you by a Latina woman from the Bronx. Because for so long, you let them make you ashamed of it. Always trying to cover it up, hiding its sexual splendor, when they knew all along that it was awesome, so they kept hiding the mirror from you, until they found a way to steal your precious butt. That's your butt and you deserve its glory. And now you admire its splendor on another, as if it were something brand new.* My mind continued to race with private thoughts: *These strokes of God's grace are as beautiful on you today as they were when you were running through the green, vine-covered paths of West Africa. As they were when you were stolen and stuffed aboard slave ships and their sexual splendor ravaged over and over as you lay in squalor across the oceans of the world. And in these United States, where they were just as beautiful to sick ravaging eyes as you were displayed on the auction block for sale. And finally, just as beautiful under the slave master's whip, as they were in his savage raping hands. And now, finally that I have you safely in my arms, our wonderful dark colors meeting and kissing, you deny that beauty?*

As if my beautiful black women hadn't mangled my head enough, I was at a newspaper stand one night in Westwood near UCLA, when two groups of students passed in front of me. One group was all blonde women, with bone-straight hairstyles. The other group was all black women with the typical, hot-comb-straightened hairstyles.

As the two groups passed each other, I heard one of the black women say, "Girl, that's how I'm going to have my hair one day."

Another woman scolded, "Girl, don't even be thinking about that 'cause you won't ever have no hair like that so don't be dreaming, OK?"

That scene affected me so deeply that I went home and wrote a poem about black women:

> "Original Woman"
> How grand you are as you,
> How close to God you seem.
> I feel such oneness when I behold,
> The closest one to me:
> Your bright smile
> Your dark presence
> Your smooth skin
> Your coarse hair.
> These rich qualities convince me that
> Only you could have been "Mother of Humanity."
> How lost I feel when I see you strain to be some other.
> For it was your bodily form, that begot the likeness of all.
> It was your full sweet lips that defined and created the kiss.
> Were it not for your regal hair . . . then there would be no hair:
> Long, short, straight, blonde, wavy—none!
> How far I stray when not at your side.
> How often my mind conjures up your sacred image.
> How grand it is when we unite,
> How the universe yearns for this.
> You are the foundation, the beginning, black woman,
> "Original Woman"

## Note

1. E. Franklin Frazier. *Black Bourgeoisie*, New York: Simon and Schuster, 1957.

# CHAPTER TWENTY-SEVEN

~

# Deeper into the Dream

It was the last few weeks of the Hollywood Bowl and there were still a few orchestra members I hadn't met. One of the brass players who had been on leave showed up for the last week. At one of the rehearsals, I approached him and introduced myself, giving him regards from people back East that I knew we had in common. I extended my hand for a normal handshake, but he wouldn't shake my hand and didn't utter a word.

He just looked at me as if to say, "What are you going to do now? I don't *want* to meet you." I looked him square in the eyes and said, "OK, I'll remember this." I walked away.

After the Hollywood Bowl season ended, we started our Fall Season at the Dorothy Chandler Pavilion. It was the hall I'd seen in a photo, the hall with all the people that I thought would be so frightening. In fact, the orchestra sounded much better in that hall than at the Hollywood Bowl.

The music director wanted me to play principal horn on the Bartok Concerto for Orchestra. He said it was going to be on a TV broadcast and asked me if I was comfortable with that. I told him that I was very comfortable. In fact, I was quite comfortable in general playing in the orchestra and thanked him for considering me for the position. I could see that he really liked hearing that.

On the other hand, the Primo principal horn was really annoyed. I could see him standing in wings of the stage while we were rehearsing the Bartok, watching, listening, pacing up and down, stalking me, like some rabid animal.

He complimented me, but it was always laced with a distinct tone of condescension. I noticed too that he only gave me such compliments in front of the music director. Of course, the music director always chimed in, in agreement: "And remember to always watch me, Watt. I must see your eyes, you know."

I knew that the music director was constantly testing me to see how I performed under pressure and I loved it. I knew that every new player was on two years' probation and had a tenure review after each year. Only after passing the second tenure review is the player allowed to remain in the orchestra as a staff musician. Therefore, I just practiced and played as much as I could to stay in top condition.

Once the philharmonic winter season was underway, we finally taped the television show on which I played principal horn on the Bartók Concerto for Orchestra. I enjoyed the TV taping process, playing things over and over. I welcomed that kind of challenge just to see if I could do it right every time. There was again a little feeling of pressure from the other players, especially the brass players, looking, watching, and listening, but I actually got energy from that.

The music director called me to his room after the TV taping and said he was very pleased and that I was playing very well. Then he called in the Primo principal horn. They wanted to talk to me about the older retiring principal horn.

The music director let the Primo principal horn talk. He talked down to me as usual, but this didn't seem to bother the music director. He wanted to tell me that it was just a matter of time before the old man was going to leave the orchestra and, well, "Do you know what we mean when we say you have to play a little politics? Ya know, you just have to be patient and things can begin to happen for you here, if you play ball with me. You know what I mean?"

I looked at him in disbelief and said, "Yes, yes, of course I know what it means to play politics, I see it all around me every day, so what is your point?"

He said we'd talk about it later and not to worry. The music director said nothing and nothing further came of it. Perhaps I didn't come off as the right kind of political animal that the Primo principal horn and the music director had in mind.

Later I found out from orchestra audition committee members that this particular principal had actually threatened to quit if they hired me and was asked to put it in writing by the music director. Knowing that really put things in perspective. I never made a big deal about it, but it was just good to know. Actually the Primo principal was a good player—the music director claimed he was "God on the French horn"—but I thought he played out of tune sometimes, especially when he sustained a note and tried to make it softer, the note went flat. I was surprised that the music director didn't hear it. In fact, a few of the trumpet players used to playfully imitate it.

Some players actually came out and told me that he was jealous of me and didn't like me getting so many opportunities to play principal horn so soon after being hired.

One morning before rehearsal I was in the dressing room warming up. I was wearing jeans and in those days jeans were mostly bell-bottoms with large belt loops to accommodate the large thick leather belts everyone wore.

There were a few other players in the room warming up when this particular Primo principal horn player entered and said, "Good morning! How you doin', ma boy—everything OK?" Suddenly he glanced downwards.

I thought he was reaching for something on my horn, but instead he grabbed my belt buckle and actually started rustling my crotch up and down, saying, "Gee, look at this guy."

I quickly stood up, slamming him hard against the dressing room mirror and I told him never to put his hands on me like that again.

He rushed out of the room shaking his head, "I'm sorry. . . . God! I didn't mean anything."

Everyone was shocked.

My mind quickly went back to what Jones had said to me in high school about the black male phallus and how white males had a fascination with black male sexuality. Jones often said that in the South, black men were lynched and often castrated as a form of intimidation and humiliation. I had just experienced a most blatant example of sexual-racial assault. None of the orchestra players present really perceived what had *actually* happened, nor would they or management have understood or believed its deep racial-pathological implications had I tried to report it.

There was one other issue that always caused trouble and that was the insistence of some of the older men in the orchestra trying to pat me on my ass as a greeting. As a relatively new person in the orchestra, I always thought that unspoken social slight was way out of line to actually think that it was OK to pat *me* on my ass, especially since I clearly observed that they didn't greet others that way. It was as if they were still hanging on to some deep racially pathological yearning that had to be expressed when they encountered me, as if they just couldn't give me the full consideration that they gave others. It was like their own personal Jim Crow that they just couldn't relinquish. I always protested by grabbing their hand, twisting their wrists very hard, and looking them deeply into their eyes asking, "What the hell are you doing?" One of the older players took issue with my grabbing his wrist and twisting it. We almost went to blows.

One of the woodwind players, an extremely nice older man, apparently wanted to say something nice to me in regards to black people. He pulled me aside one day and said, "Bob, I've been meaning to say this to you ever since we met. You know I believe some of the most beautiful music ever produced on this God's green Earth was sung by your ancestors the slaves, do you know that? When I hear that music it makes me want to weep every time. I just wanted you to know that."

I thanked him for his gesture of good will but just had to ask him how in the world he would have been on hand to hear such music so long ago?

My question went over his head and he answered by patting me on my shoulder, "I just know."

At one of the main concerts we played at the Dorothy Chandler Pavilion, the second horn player became ill just hours before the concert. I was called at 5:30 that evening and told that I would have to play second horn on the evening concert. The big piece for the evening was Beethoven Symphony No. 7, which has a nice second horn part in the *scherzo* movement. The message from the music director was, "Play out with a big tone and be sure to watch me carefully all the time." During the big second horn solo, I could hear my low notes bouncing off of the back wall of the concert hall. The music director was smiling and nodded his head at me with reassurance. I had saved the day.

Then the fourth horn next to me, who was doubling, said, "You're *in now*, boy!"

All the other horn players and some of the clarinet players shuffled their feet on the floor (an orchestra's subtle signal of approval, a silent applause during performance).

After my second horn triumph, the music director summoned me to his office. He wanted to know if I would play a private fund-raiser for César Chávez, the Mexican American labor activist who founded what was later the United Farm Workers. He was the lone voice for migrant workers all over the American Southwest. The music director conducted a small chamber group played at a private home in the San Fernando Valley. César Chávez spoke briefly about the struggle, which was followed by a reception where I had the honor and pleasure of meeting him. He was an imposing figure yet still a humble man, who seemed to look right into your soul. We spoke only of the struggle and the future of the United Farm Workers (UFW). I remember everyone boycotting grapes for years in support of the farmworkers. After that exciting event, I was forced to look at the music director with different eyes. I was truly honored to be part of such an event.

# CHAPTER TWENTY-EIGHT

~

# Emotional Highs and Lows

In the fall of 1970, the orchestra went on an East Coast tour. I was still uncomfortable with flying so I stayed strapped in with sweaty palms while other orchestra members were walking around talking to each other, drinking, and playing cards.

The first stop on the East Coast tour was Indiana University. We were welcomed with fall weather, which I always loved so much about the East Coast. So we played touch football. One by one, more of the orchestra men joined in the game. We played for about two hours and then used the campus facilities to shower like a football team.

That night at the concert I had to play first horn on a Mozart symphony (*The Paris*). In the slow movement, there are several high-note entrances for the first horn.

Since I was so out of shape from not doing any regular exercise, that football game really shocked my body and made my arms a little muscle-bound, making it difficult to steady my instrument. Consequently, it caused my tone to shake a little on my high notes.

After the performance, the Primo principal approached me and said, "Ya know, you don't have to sweat those high notes on first horn in the Mozart. Why don't you give the part to one of us, you know, the real first horns. Besides, they're not really paying you to play first horn and I don't think you should do it."

I told him that I wasn't sweating anything in this band.

He got real nasty and said point blank, "OK, so then, your high Ds in the Mozart sounded shaky tonight. I mean, you can keep playing the part if you want, I don't care, but if you 'psyche-out' it will look real bad for you, I'm telling you."

I told him no such thing was going to happen and that he shouldn't worry about it. "The music director gave me the part to play and I'm not going to give it up." I could see then that he was the type of person who was *not* used to taking no for an answer.

After the concert, there was a party for the brass players hosted by the Indiana University Music Department, where I had the pleasure of meeting Phillip Farkas, the celebrated teacher and former principal French horn of the Chicago Symphony. I thanked him for writing his first book, *The Art of French Horn Playing*, because it really helped me when I was just starting out in high school.

While in Boston, I looked up Edwin, a friend from conservatory days. He was still living in my old apartment building and working in Boston as a freelance horn player. We had a great time talking and catching up. I had been lonely in Los Angeles and didn't realize it until I came back to familiar territory.

The big work on the Boston concert was Symphony Domestica by Richard Strauss. It had fantastic horn parts, which were very technically demanding. I enjoyed rehearsing the piece because I had a good part to play and the music director was constantly watching and listening to me.

There was, however, one particular rehearsal of the Symphony Domestica before the Boston performance that really troubled me. The music director was rehearsing the horn section separately and I was truly engaged and excited to play my best and learn everything possible. During that rehearsal, I was instructed to bring out certain parts and certain motifs in the music that were in my fifth horn part. The music director made a point of asking me if I had any questions about anything and that I sounded good and to keep it up.

He said, "In these inner parts, Watt, I need your strength to bring out these horn voices, OK?"

I complied with great enthusiasm, but I also made a suggestion. Apparently I broke some vague rule in protocol, because suddenly the entire horn section became very quiet and looked at me as if to say, "What are doing? You don't make musical suggestions."

It was a most emphatic, clear, nonverbal message that my status in the orchestra and horn section was not what I thought it was. I never forgot how that felt. It was so obvious that the horn section, regarded me in a certain way and it was certainly not on par with everyone else. Yes, I was new on the scene, but this was something beyond that. They were not interested in my musical opinions or enthusiasm and there was a particular place that they had in mind for me and I had yet to find it.

That was a big wake-up call for me. I realized then that the enthusiasm the music director was expressing to me about the music was totally wasted on the rest of the horn section. It was not really about the music for them. It was not about art. It was simply survival—just work, getting by, and I was blowing their cover with my artistic enthusiasm. The harshest truth of that moment was, although I had yet to find my place, they had long ago found theirs.

The overall performance went well that afternoon and it was very exciting to be playing in Boston again. However, the spoiler for the Strauss Symphony Domestica was the older first horn. He had a rough time playing one of the beautiful slow solos in the Strauss, visibly trembling throughout his body as he performed it.

It was not fun to watch by any means. When something like that happens, all the other players on stage should pray it never happens to them. It reminded me of how horses behave when one of them is being led out to the glue factory. Every horse in that stable retreats to the back of its stall and freezes.

After the performance, I overheard the Primo principal discussing the incident with the music director. "Oh, he was beside himself, it was awful . . ."

On a happier note, there was a big party hosted by the Boston Symphony for the Los Angeles Philharmonic at the Amalfi restaurant behind Symphony Hall. That restaurant held sweet memories for me because it was the place I took my special dates after a performance, when I was a student. I remember taking Karen Tzo, a math major at Massachusetts Institute of Technology (MIT). That was my very first time dating an Asian woman. I always thought she was so lovely, so beautiful, while everyone else only remarked on how "Chinese" she looked. I remember that Karen wore a beautiful blue, traditional Chinese jacket with her hair in that wonderful traditional Chinese style. My stomach was full of butterflies that evening, as I walked into Amalfi restaurant for dinner with her on my arm.

After Boston we flew to New York, where some of my family attended the concert. My mother was sitting in the balcony of Carnegie Hall with my older sister, Judy. She was constantly looking at me while I was on stage. She even waved and winked like a teenager. My father came as usual with his girlfriend and sat nearby. He was still wearing those ominous dark glasses that always made him appear distant and cold, as if he didn't want people to see into his soul.

After the Carnegie Hall concert, my family came backstage to see me.

My father never showed open warm affection; he was always awkward and critical instead. "Why don't you polish your horn, boy, like all the others? Jesus-Christ! Your horn stands out like a sore thumb! Don't they have any brass polish in Los Angeles?"

I had no other option, besides telling him to go to hell, than to ignore his criticisms and speak to him in a normal manner.

Conversely, my mother always warmed up the situation, "Bob, the music was so nice, so beautiful."

It was nice to get back to Los Angeles after the tour and just be home again. I reflected greatly on my first tour with the philharmonic. So many rich experiences, meeting new people like Phillip Farkas and seeing old friends like Ed. It gave me a sense that I had truly arrived in the music world.

When I checked my large pile of mail after being gone for several weeks, I found a notice from the United States Army Draft Board. I had forgotten that once I left school I automatically became 1-A and would be eligible for the draft. The army had developed a draft lottery, and the higher the number, the less likely you were to be called. My number was 17. The lottery concept played right into the prevailing political belief at the time, that an inordinate number of black men were being steered to Viet Nam, by way of the draft.

In 1970 the Viet Nam War was still raging. President Nixon, for military expedience, invaded neighboring Cambodia, and all hell had broken loose on the college campuses. That decision by Nixon intensified the antiwar movement, with student strikes and even more demonstrations. It was common knowledge by then that the military needed men—bodies, anyone to fill the ranks—and I was ripe meat at age twenty-two, just out of school, except I had a career, a career I had worked very hard for and didn't want to give up. I didn't want to go into the army, even for a few years. I could only imagine what would have happened to my playing after two years in the military. I had a talk with the music director about being drafted.

He was very upset, saying, "You can't leave here, you know?" He told me he wished he could help but he didn't have any influence with the military here in the United States.

I thanked him and told him that I would have to take my chances and report to the draft board. He said, "Watt, take all the time off that you need, but be sure to tell them who you are and what you do."

# CHAPTER TWENTY-NINE

~

# To Viet Nam?

During the entire evening before draft day, I kept running over in my mind about any physical ailments that might keep me out of the army. I remembered the letter that a psychiatrist wrote for me while I was still a student in Boston. A professional horn player in Boston referred me to him, saying, "Hey, man, this guy will get you out of the army, trust me." The letter the psychiatrist wrote for me said, "I couldn't be separated from my French horn or I would suffer severe mental trauma."

I was surprised to find out that many of the players in the philharmonic thought I *should* just go into the military, not resist the draft and serve my country like so many of the other musicians had done in town.

Once again the Primo principal horn player tried to make amends by offering to buy me a drink. He apologized for his actions and said he wanted to talk to me about some things of importance. He brought along the second horn player for support, I guess. They were both in agreement about my going into the military. He was trying to tell me how many great things this country had to offer young people like me and that I should go into the military without question. In fact, I should be glad to serve.

The second horn gave a nod of tacit agreement. "Let me tell you something, my boy, you're no longer in college with those radical freaks who want to destroy this country. You're in the big time now, with real top-notch people."

I looked at them both and told them that "I certainly didn't have to listen to this top-notch bullshit." I walked out before the drinks came.

Not long after that confrontation, I received my orders to report to the Army Draft Board with a specific date and time. I dreaded the whole ordeal. I showed up at the U.S. Army Selective Service Mid-Wilshire office. The first order of business was to take a written exam, which took two hours. It was extremely elementary material and quite boring.

After the exam, we were told to undress and hit the showers. On entering the showers, it reminded me of high school gym class for a moment, and then an army sergeant started yelling at us as if we were already in the military.

"All right, soldiers, get your asses dried off and line up wearing only your drawers and the paper sandals! Hold your clothes bag in your right hand and your paperwork in your left hand. Give your paperwork to the attendant as you approach each station! See you in eight hours, now move, soldiers!" he yelled.

The line dragged on for hours and there were many outbursts between the men in line and the army personnel working at each station. The first incident was a jet of blood shooting up and splattering on the ceiling. The army person taking the blood samples snatched a guy's arm while the needle was still in his vein. This made me really angry and perhaps deep down inside I had it in for that soldier and wanted to hurt him. When it was my turn with the out-of-order soldier, I was fuming inside. Apparently I had my paperwork in the wrong hand so he reached across my body, grabbing my right hand with the paperwork, causing me to spin around really hard.

"Hold your paperwork in your left hand! Can't you follow orders, soldier?" he snapped.

I reached across the table and yanked him out of his seat as the military police moved in yelling, "Stand down, soldier!"

They used their batons to force us apart. They pulled me off the soldier with the baton pressed hard into my stomach.

As they took him away, I heard one of them say to him, "I think you need to be relieved, soldier."

They told me to back off, calm down, and move on in the line, pushing me in my back with the baton. I was furious. The U.S. Army never got any of my blood that day.

The next interesting station was where we were told to remove our underwear and stand facing each other with our toes on a white line, which formed a large rectangle. There were about six such rectangles. There were all sorts of body types, overweight white men with red sagging behinds covered in red pimples and even guys wearing colostomy bags.

Toward the end of the day, I reached the final two stations, the EKG and the psychiatrist. The EKG test was very interesting with all the wires, electrodes, and electronic scopes. However, the technician was vocalizing and obviously had a trained voice so I asked him if he sang professionally.

"Yes, I do, sir." Then he glanced at my paperwork and said with great surprise, "Los Angeles Philharmonic? You're a member of the L.A. Philharmonic?"

"Yes, I am," I replied.

"My God, then what in heaven's name are you doing in here, sir? Oh this is not right—oh no, I'll be right back."

The technician raced out of the room and down the hall, still vocalizing. He returned talking extremely fast and agitated. "OK, Mr. Philharmonic, let's get you out of this mess, wires, petroleum jelly, and all. The doctor will see you now, go right in, sir."

My New Jersey "street sense" told me that something was up and it was going to go down hard and fast. I put my clothes on and walked into the final station of the U.S. Army Draft Board physical—the army psychiatrist.

When I slowly entered the semi-dark room, I found myself standing before a very dark-skinned black man with processed hair and the classic psychiatrist's white coat. He just stared at me, saying nothing. He had the coldest expression I'd ever seen on a black man in my life. He ordered me to sit down.

I complied and quickly he ordered me to stand up, "On your feet, sol . . . dier!" he yelled.

"Now sit down!"

I looked at him with disdain and was about to tell him where to go when he snapped back quickly, "You don't talk, soldier, just listen! Is that clear, boy? Do they call you boy down at the philharmonic?"

I was about to reply when he silenced me again. "You say one Goddamn word and I'll have your black ass shipped off to Fort Ord—tonight! Is that clear, soldier?" he shouted. Suddenly his voiced softened to a more normal tone. "Say, Mr. Philharmonic, do your lips quiver when you play your, what is it, French horn, in front of all those white folks? I know them white women just loves your black ass, don't they, boy? And I know you loves them white women too—all you uppity niggers do."

I glared at him, biting my tongue until I could taste blood.

Banging on his desk, he yelled, "Do you really play in the Los Angeles Philharmonic, because I ain't never seen no niggers like you in that orchestra, now come on, tell me the truth, boy?" He continued to stare right into my face as if he was trying to break me military style.

I closed my eyes for a moment trying to block out the madness, but he was all over me.

"Look at me soldier! Eyes front, stand up! Now march in place, hut-two-three-four and hut-two three-four!" He opened the letter from my files and began to read it out loud. "'Dear U.S. Army, Mr. Watt cannot be separated from his French horn or he will suffer severe traumatic. . . .' What is this bullshit, boy? Do you want out or do you want in this man's army? 'Cause this bullshit letter right here will get you in, for sure."

I began to speak and again he brutally cut me off. "Ah, ah! Not a word, sol . . . dier! Sit . . . down!" he ordered.

The next thing that came out of his mouth was truly amazing. He said, "Now you listen to me, boy. I'm not part of this 'Eccstablishment'"—a word he had trouble pronouncing, but he made it clear that if I wanted out of this man's army *he* would tell me what to do.

"Now, here's what you do, Mr. Philharmonic: First of all let me introduce myself, I'm Dr. Evan Woodson, and you may speak now."

I looked at him in disbelief and he laughed very loud. "I was just messing with you, Mr. Watt, but you know I had to see what kind of nigger you was before telling you anything about me and what we're going to do.

"My goodness, you look so uptight, as well you should, but here's the deal. I'll tear up this letter that you got from a Dr. David Vis . . . from Boston. This was the type of letter that might have worked back when it was written a few years ago, but these days, son, they'll laugh this shit right out the door, so allow me."

He tore up the letter that had been my trump card for several years of avoiding the military draft. He continued to tell me that he would disqualify me for one year so that he could observe me in his weekly therapy group. "It will cost you $12.00 a week. Can you afford that Mr. Philharmonic . . . stiff-ass. Oops, sorry, I mean, Mr. Watt? Come on, you can speak now."

I remained silent as he explained, "The people in my weekly group have serious problems, way beyond your being a little uptight about the draft. You just come every week and after one year along with a letter from another psychiatrist concurring the things I'm going to write about you—which you will never see, by the way—in my letter to the draft board after observing you for one year. Then you will bring that letter back to the draft board in one year and go through the entire examination again like you did today. . . . Oh, and please, don't be grabbing these soldiers, I heard about you. What kinda street nigger are you, boy? Damn! Now, when you come back to me with letter in hand together with your year of observation by me, I'll have you disqualified with a 4-F—how's that, Mr. Watt? Are you willing to do that? Can I trust you? You won't tell Nixon, will you?"

The therapy group was more than interesting. It was a weekly showcase of people and their personal neurotic extremes. The group consisted mostly of spoiled pampered brats of politicians and Hollywood celebrities. Dr. Woodson openly admitted that he loved money and wealth. He drove a white Cadillac with white interior, and he wore white all the time. He even admitted that he loved white everything. He loved white people, white culture, and all that it had to offer.

Dr. Woodson introduced me to the group, told them my profession, and then proceeded to tell them that I was a little uptight and that they were going to loosen me up. "Ain't that right, group?"

The group answered in a loud resounding "Yes!"

It almost frightened me. I admitted I was uptight down at the draft board walking around in my underwear for eight hours, but there was something else they were after. I got very defensive and I noticed that Dr. Woodson seemed to enjoy that. He had a smug look on his face as he invited each group member to take a bite out of me. I even got a little ticked off. There were a few black men who seemed to take special pleasure in saying, "But you're still uptight, but you're still uptight, we can see it."

Towards the end of the year, Dr. Woodson told me to take a sealed envelope to another psychiatrist. I was told not to open the envelope. The other doctor would respond to Dr. Woodson about whatever was in the letter and after a session with me give me another sealed envelope for Dr. Woodson. The next step was for me to return to the draft board, go through the entire physical again, ending up in Dr. Woodson's office. He would then report to the draft board that after a year's observation—and whatever was in the secret envelope—that I was unfit for military service and he recommended a classification of 4-F for me.

The next thing I knew, I was sitting on a bench daydreaming when I heard a loud voice say, "Hey, soldier! What the hell are you waiting for, get your ass on the bus, now move!"

I looked up at the loudmouth sergeant and said, "I'm not going anywhere! What are you talking about?"

"This is the last call for the bus to Fort Ord. Now come on, boy, move your ass!"

Dr. Woodson was watching that whole scene and let out one of his whooping laughs again. "He's not one of yours, sergeant. He stays here," Doctor Woodson said. "After all you've been through you just had to go and sit on the wrong bench, didn't you? Now please go home, Bob . . . and have a drink."

# CHAPTER THIRTY

~

# On with Life

As time passed, I began meeting more of the freelance musicians in Los Angeles. There were well over two hundred and fifty who played in the motion picture, TV, theater, and recording industries. In years past, each movie studio had its own orchestra under contract year round. When I arrived in Los Angeles, that era had passed. Some of the players I met in the studios wanted to play chamber music. I ended up playing at different homes of movie producers and film composers. That was how a new player in town got hired for work in the studios back then.

However, my first call was from legendary jazz musician/composer/arranger, trumpet and sax player Benny Carter. He just called me up and asked if I had time to play a series of recording sessions at Capitol Records. I nervously replied, "Of course, sir—I'm not really a jazz player—."

He cut me off, saying, "Don't worry about *that*, son, you'll be fine on these sessions—otherwise you wouldn't be where you are." He hung up.

That was my first real studio job in Los Angeles. I was very excited

The Benny Carter recording session at Capitol Records was an assembly of jazz greats. I couldn't believe I was there with such legends as Cat Anderson, the screech trumpet player known for his nosebleed high notes; Harry Sweets Edison, trumpet; the legendary Clark Terry, trumpet; George Bohanon, trombone; Louie Bellson, drums, woodwinds; Buddy Collette, Bud Shank, Marshall Royal, and Shelly Manne, drums; Roger Kellaway, piano; Quincy Jones, conductor and arranger; and with singers Carmen McRae, Sue Raney, Joe Williams, Ernestine Anderson, Tommy Mercer, Ray Brown on bass, Joe Pass on guitar, and many others.

After my maiden studio sessions at Capitol Records, several established black freelance musicians told me that there were black contractors in Los Angeles who were ready and willing to hire me. I only needed to call a few of them. Thus I began to get calls to record with giants like Barry White and Jerry Peters. Isaac Hayes even hired me to record and play concerts, and I was part of the original Wattstax Festival in the Los Angeles Coliseum (of which a film, *Wattstax*, was produced about that legendary concert as a healing truce after the Watts riots). Ernie Fields of Jade Sound booked players for all the black pop groups that came through town and needed an orchestra.

I discovered that there was an entire group of black instrumentalists who played record dates, except for major motion picture and TV, which was still an almost exclusively white clique, unless the writers were black, in which case the black players would be hired for that one time and then things would go back to normal.

Interestingly enough, I also began to get work in the all-white clique.

A contractor from a major movie studio called me one Easter morning. He had a heavy German accent and asked, "Are you Robert Watt?"

"Yes," I replied. "And whom might you be?"

He then asked without responding to me, "Are you the horn player in the Los Angeles Philharmonic?"

"Yes, yes," I said.

"Are you the Negro horn player of the LA Philharmonic?"

I cautioned him not to call me that, but I was a black man since he just had to know.

He told me his name and that he was the music contractor for a major movie studio and that he had several days' work for me. I always believed that was my unofficial audition for the white freelance clique. I ended up playing with one of the top freelance horn players in Los Angeles.

On that session, it was just the two of us for an entire week. I could see right away that he wanted to feel me out as a person, which I didn't mind at all. The thing I noticed most about his playing was how relaxed his technique was. He never tensed up, especially for the high notes. He seemed to relax even more when he played high.

When he wasn't talking to me, he was engaged in a conversation with the other players. They all seemed to be carefully and profoundly kowtowing to him. Sometimes they talked on the same topic all day. It was like a club with a definite pecking order and everyone seemed to know their place. When each person spoke, they seemed ever so careful to say the right thing, lest they lose their standing in that feudalistic structure.

The horn player was definitely the leader of the group and therefore the only one comfortable enough to say what he wanted. For me, the outsider, it never crossed my mind to make any attempt to join in conversation with such an established clique. I just listened and smiled.

In extreme contrast to everything else I was playing in Los Angeles, there was, as I said, a definite cadre of black freelance musicians who played all the session work for the major black recording artists. I was warmly welcomed into that fold and I loved it. Some of the players were the legendary trumpet player Harry "Sweets" Edison; George Bohanon, trombone; Oscar Brashear and Bobby Bryant, trumpets; Buddy Colette, flute-woodwinds; Fred Jackson, woodwinds; Ernie Fields, music contractor; Charles Veal, violin; Earl Madison, cello; Nolan Rasheed Smith, trumpet; Sidney Muldrow and Emily Booth, French horn; Janice Gower, viola; Patrice Rushen, composer-producer; Ron Clark, violin; Lesa Terry, violin; and Ndugu Chancler, drums.

On many occasions, some of those individuals ended up saving many a recording session, when the leaders and producers became chemically over-relaxed. George Bohanon, trombone, was well known for getting us through the night by taking over, so to speak. "Straight ahead and strive for tone" was his motto. It was all such a totally black experience. Charles Veal, freelance violinist, was also known for such impromptu skills of saving the day in those crazy, pop music recording sessions. Some of the black freelancers called me "Symphony Bob" because I used to show up on the late-night record dates still dressed in my tails after playing a philharmonic concert. They even lifted the tails on my full-dress coat and joked, "Look! This brother has wings!" I enjoyed that teasing as much as I enjoyed the late-night recording sessions. There was never anything really difficult to play, but there was always plenty to eat and drink and lots of beautiful women just hanging around the control booth looking very excited about the music and creating a warm party-like atmosphere.

# CHAPTER THIRTY-ONE

~

# Fear of Flying

Right about that time, 1973, I took stock of my life. I was twenty-five years old, I had moved to the part of town I liked, had a great job, great salary, had my own car, and I was beginning to meet women and got around socially to some extent. Still, I felt that I needed a balance to the tremendous musical weight that had dominated my life so far.

On the way back to Los Angeles from a tour of the western states, I was still a little uncomfortable flying. One of the percussion players picked up on it and sat with me.

"Notice you're a little tense. You don't like flying?"

I told him that I hated it.

He smiled and said, "Well, I'm going to suggest something that might help you get over that fear."

I looked at him with great curiosity. "What? Please tell me."

He said, "Well, I'm a private pilot, you know, the 'Cessna' type?"

"Yeah," I said. "I used to watch those when I was a kid."

The percussion player suggested I go take an introductory flight at a Cessna flight center. It intrigued me so much that one day I actually did it.

I went to the local airport in Santa Monica and asked about the Cessna introductory flight.

The guy said, "How about going up right now?"

I was afraid, but I went anyway. The take-off was interesting and smooth until we reached the shoreline and got some turbulence. Then he gave me the airplane to fly. When we got back, the pilot asked me how I liked it. I didn't.

One year later, I was back at the Cessna pilot center to try another ride in the tiny airplane. The weather on that day was perfect.

"All right, you've got the airplane," yelled the instructor. "Turn right at the shoreline."

The shoreline was a word that had been with me all my life: The Shoreliners drum and bugle corps, the Jersey Shore, All-Shore Band from high school.

The instructor said, "OK, level off here and keep her at 3500 feet." He showed me the trim tab, which took pressure off the stick, and I could then fly hands-free.

We were now over the Santa Monica bay, where I want my ashes scattered when I die. I began to realize that there was an art and beauty to flying that really appealed to my artistic temperament. I noticed when I had control of the aircraft, all my fear of flying vanished. I never expected to experience such comfort. I got hooked on flying. It was hard to believe the fear was gone.

My neighbor was a pilot and had trained through the Cessna program and he recommended a flight instructor over at the school. By the third lesson, I knew that I wasn't going to keep my neighbor's instructor. He had an overly curious and envious attitude about me. He was constantly asking how I got to play in the philharmonic so early in life. On my third flight lesson, we both had a real scare. We were climbing out from Santa Monica airport to our usual air-work altitude when the plane dropped one hundred feet straight down like a free-falling elevator. It happened so fast that I couldn't speak for a moment. Apparently we were caught under some wake turbulence from a 747 jumbo jet that had passed through the area before us and had blown in our direction. Although I was scared, the instructor continued on as though nothing happened.

The following week, the philharmonic was scheduled for a tour of Japan. I was very excited because I had never been anywhere, across any ocean. We flew from Los Angeles to Tokyo via Honolulu on a Boeing 707, stopping only to refuel and continue on to Tokyo. After those few hours flying the Cessna aircraft, the jet plane felt so comfortable. I was so relaxed. I got up, walked around—I was cured of my fear of flying!

On the second flight, Honolulu to Tokyo, I had my first romance with a Japanese woman. Her name was Alga, chief flight attendant. She kept coming to my seat, giving me special attention. Before the end of the flight I asked for Alga's phone number in Tokyo. She offered to take me out on the town and introduce me to the art of eating sushi.

# CHAPTER THIRTY-TWO

~

# Japan

In October 1972, as the plane made its approach to Tokyo Narita Airport, I felt a great sense of excitement. I already had a date with Alga, the chief flight attendant on the second Japan Airlines flight out of Hawaii. Just before we were to land, she passed by my seat one more time and whispered, "Bob San, please call me tomorrow, yes?"

The next day I was up early to exercise in the hotel gym and afterwards had a steam bath, but I could still feel the effects of the two long flights. I went down to have breakfast and to my great surprise, I found several orchestra members sitting around the lobby complaining about how they didn't know what to do for fun and recreation. "Yeah, they've got us *way* over here in the middle of nowhere to play concerts, but what are we supposed to do in the meantime?"

After hearing their complaining, I feared if I had told them that I had a date with a beautiful Japanese woman in a few hours they would've ostracized me for sure.

I took a table and sat alone with my thoughts, which kept drifting to my meeting with Alga. I decided to order a Japanese breakfast only to find out that there was no such thing. The waitress recommended other things on the menu, all of which came under the category of a "real American breakfast."

When Alga arrived at my hotel, she was wearing a traditional Japanese kimono, looked me right in the eyes, and bowed. "Good morning, Bob-San."

As she took her bow, the material of her kimono made a sensuous rustling sound. She looked magnificent, her hair was done in a ball showing the

145

lovely, feminine skin on her neck, and she wore just a touch of makeup. Her eyes were shiny black with an innocent sparkle. The kimono was navy blue that tastefully twisted down her body. Her obi was silver and gold, wrapping her waist, nicely setting off her lovely figure. I bowed back to her and she shuffled over to me in her wooden slippers with feet clad in pure white silk socks, took my arm, and we were off.

We went to the heart of the Ginza district, which was actually a lot smoggier than Los Angeles, and I noticed many people were wearing masks. However, unlike Los Angeles, after about 11:30 a.m. a light wind rushed through and cleared the air.

We went to a restaurant where we sat on the floor. Our waitress greeted us and proceeded to serve sake and an assortment of sushi. Alga demonstrated nonverbally the correct way to eat the fishy delights. First, she mixed the wasabi in the shoyu together and stirred it with the chopsticks, all the time smiling at me with her sparkling beautiful black eyes as she educated me. Then she picked up the sushi with her hands, dipped it in the tasty solution, and ate the whole thing, giggling, as she opened her mouth—never taking her eyes off me.

The music part of the tour was quite exciting. The Japanese audience liked everything we did and applauded for long periods, showing great politeness. During the concerts, between the movements of the music, they had a very tight routine of coughing and stopping on a dime. There was another phenomenon that perhaps only I could see. When I looked out at the Japanese audience, which had no empty seats, I saw for the first time the effect of color. An entire audience with people of color created a different visual sensation to my eyes, which were used to seeing only a sea of white faces.

The tour jumped all around Japan, going to the west coast along the Sea of Japan traveling on the famous "bullet train." I remember one very funny incident that happened on the bullet train. One of the orchestra members, Miles, ordered a cheeseburger, but in 1973, Japan had not been introduced to American fast food. The waiter returned with what he thought Miles had ordered, a cheese sandwich next to a hamburger sandwich.

Miles was very patient with the waiter as he took the cheese from the cheese sandwich and placed it inside the hamburger sandwich, pointed, and said, "Now that is a cheeseburger, OK pal?"

Then all of the other waiters came over, the chef came out of the kitchen, and they all began to take notes while chattering to each other, "Ah, cheese–burger, ah so, cheese–burger, hai!"

When I resumed my flying lessons, the first thing I did was change flight instructors. I confronted my former instructor with the fact that I had come to flying being afraid to be on *any* airplane, much less a two-seat trainer with an impatient flight instructor yelling in my ear.

We went on to talk about his racial remarks, his out-and-out envy of the fact that I was college educated, and at times trying to browbeat me over a simple flight calculation, saying that if he had gone to college like I had, he would have no problem figuring out such easy problems.

I was assigned a new flight instructor, with whom I did my first solo flight, a milestone in every pilot's life. One day, in the middle of a lesson, you are told to land the plane, come to a full stop, and to your amazement the instructor gets out and tells you to take the plane up by yourself for three full-stop landings.

I had my first solo flight at eight-thirty in the morning on the day of a concert. As the instructor walked away, I felt an amazing sense of loneliness. The plane seemed much larger and the voice from the control tower echoed much louder in the half-empty cockpit, which until that moment had been filled with the instructor's body. I was scared. Then suddenly I heard, "Cessna 94 Golf cleared for takeoff, caution wake turbulence on liftoff. Have a good flight." Wake turbulence? I remember that term. Would I drop a hundred feet, panic, and crash?

As I climbed out, I was so nervous that my knees were shaking. The plane felt super light and climbed faster than ever. However, after my first turn, I was suddenly more relaxed. I settled back into the seat and just *flew* the airplane as I'd done so many times before—but this time, there was no doubt that *I* was flying the aircraft.

"OK, Cessna 94 Golf, you're looking good. You are number three to land just behind the blue and white 150 turning base, altimeter two niner niner three, wind 218 at fifteen knots." With a slight crosswind blowing, I crossed Bundy Boulevard and added ten degrees of flaps. I kept the right wing down with a little left rudder for the crosswind, and I was home free.

By 1975, flying had become a new hobby or perhaps even a compensatory activity—compensatory because I had been in the orchestra for almost five years and the job had become routine. Something was missing. The excitement that I once thought I would get from being in an orchestra and playing my horn was slipping away. The job, my particular position, was nowhere near challenging enough for me. I was *not* principal horn, so my duties were almost too light at times.

On the brighter side, I was glad that perhaps I had reconnected to a childhood love, a fascination for airplanes. Perhaps this was also one of the many joys that music brought to me, one that I surely never imagined: a rich new and exciting experience, a new love, a new world as a licensed airplane pilot.

Perhaps in a way flying an airplane *was* a type of performance. Once started, like music, it had to be ended with all its movements played and with a landing that just had to be successful—successful because an airplane has to land for life to go on, just as a piece of music must be played to its end for life to be enriched and fulfilling. These performances—these daring, soaring feats of art—were a type of lifeblood vital to my soul. I was glad that I had overcome my fear of flying. It was an obstacle worth clearing to reach the level of happiness and fulfillment I was beginning to feel. I had many rich and exciting experiences flying to concerts and flying my friends around California.

~

# CHAPTER THIRTY-THREE

# A New Black Player and the Ark

In the fall of 1975, the orchestra traveled to New York City for a week of concerts in Carnegie Hall. I always looked forward to that concert series because I could so easily go home to New Jersey to visit my family. Also I loved playing in Carnegie Hall because it just sounded good.

While crossing the street one night, I ran into one of the players on the auditions committee for the Los Angeles Philharmonic. He informed me that the philharmonic had just hired another black player. He made such a big deal out of telling me how well the guy played, that he was indeed the best player, and how he looked like a real serious guy. Of course, I was thrilled and couldn't wait to meet him and find out what kind of black man he was for myself.

At least with just *one* other black person I could share the occasional awkwardness of the situation—those times when only another black person would understand.

I contacted the office to get the new player's phone number. Surprisingly they gave up his name and phone number quite readily, as if they knew that I wanted and needed another black person in the orchestra as much as they apparently needed the image of diversity.

When I finally called him, he was very pleasant and glad to talk to me. He said he'd heard my name and knew for a long time that I was in the orchestra and wanted to know how many *other* black folks were in the philharmonic. I told him, "I'm the only one and could you hurry up and join me out here?"

He was very surprised and yelled through the phone, "What, you're the only one in the *whole* orchestra? Goddamn, boy, how'd you manage that?

And for how many years? Damn! I'm coming—I'm coming, OK, bye." I was no longer completely alone.

～

Horace Tapscott—a freelance pianist, trombonist, and composer—jumped off the bus that was bound for a nationwide tour with Lionel Hampton's orchestra to start a revolutionary community movement, the Pan African Peoples ARKestra, and its foundation, the Union of God's Musicians and Artists Ascension (or UGMA). He called me to play on a film score titled "Sweet Jesus, Preacher Man." He said it would be a two- or three-day session.

I arrived at the session thinking I would see the usual freelance musicians and usual studio setup. Instead there were scores of black folks sitting on the floor in robes.

Horace said, grinning, "There ain't none of them folks here, Bob. This is *your* ARKestra."

I noticed that he used the word "Ark." I sat on the floor and joined in on the *ostinato* (repeated melodic pattern or rhythm) everyone else was playing. Soon, on top of the ostinato, I heard a flute player enter playing some real slick lines. Everyone took a solo in turn. It was like a seminar in improvisation. It was all so seamless and effortless the way Tapscott just looked at each player without pointing or conducting. I had the harmonic structure in my ear by the time my turn came. I had never really played an improvised solo like they were doing, but I loved what I heard and tried to get into that style. They all gave me approving looks after my short solo.

After the piece was over, Horace looked at me, laughed, and said, "What you thinkin', Bob? That wasn't the music for the movie! We was just warming up."

After playing for the movie, I was asked to play with the Ark on a regular basis. I played many live concerts and even played on one of their recordings. Horace wrote a tune that featured the French horn titled "Mother Ship." All the concerts took place in South Central Los Angeles, usually in churches, playing to capacity crowds.

The rehearsals were long, but I formed a great friendship with trombonist Lester Robertson. He kept me awake by constantly going out to buy pinch pints (half-pints) of cheap wine.

After drinking that cheap wine, Lester could still take a solo and play his ass off. Then he would sit down and almost pass out.

There was one concert I'll never forget. It took place at what Horace called "The Big House," an old Craftsman house on Western Avenue owned by a supporter of the foundation. The concert was in high gear and everybody had played solos, except me. I thought Horace was going to skip over me since I was new in the group. Next thing I knew, the entire ARK was shouting my name. This was a plural request for me to go up front and take a solo. My knees were shaking, and when I looked at Horace he was laughing.

"Just play, Bob! Your 'ancestral echoes' will see you through."

I closed my eyes and started to play. I don't remember what came out, but it felt good.

Then to my amazement a man in a wheelchair started waving his hands, yelling, "That's my music, mother Africa, that's my music!"

The music was so strong and moving at that point that the man in the wheelchair actually got up and walked six or eight steps before falling, still waving and yelling. I saw people in the audience just sitting in a trance with tears streaming down their cheeks.

The music had a wailing and healing quality to it. Horace said he didn't want it perfectly in tune. He wanted chaos of intonation and anarchy of tonality, an African sound.

However, to me, the most amazing thing about Horace Tapscott was his playing. He transcended the piano; he went so far in his expression that when he was done I remember people saying, after a long silent pause, "DAAAAMMMN!!"

In those days, I was still flying airplanes and had just earned my instrument rating when Horace called me one day and asked if I would take him flying sometime. He said he had a few other brothers who wanted to go. I asked him where he wanted to go.

He said, "Shit—as long as we can fly over Crenshaw and South Central that would be cool. I'd like to see the 'hood from up there—can we do that?"

I told him that if we flew over that area we would have to go above 5,000 feet.

He said, "Let's just go up. How about tomorrow afternoon?"

As we taxied out to the runway the next day, Horace leaned back to the other two brothers and said, "Ain't this a bitch? A brother is taking us flying."

There was a twin engine ahead of us. When the twin was airborne, the tower cleared us for takeoff. "42 Golf, cleared for takeoff, caution wake turbulence from the departing twin. Have a good day."

Horace quickly glanced at me, "Is that us, Bob?"

I said, "Yeah, that's us." As we began our takeoff roll, Horace leaned back in his seat and I heard a loud sucking sound as we rotated off the ground. When I glanced over at him, he had a big fat joint in his mouth and was taking really long drags on it.

Smiling, he looked at me and said, "I always wanted to do that, but couldn't on a commercial jet. It's cool, ain't it, Bob?"

I said, "You know I'll get high too, Horace, don't you?"

As we turned right at the shoreline heading for my favorite spot in Los Angeles, Horace said, "Yeah, let's fly over the water. You ever flown while you was high, Bob?" Then he let out his big laugh.

I told him that the higher we go, the higher we all get.

Horace looked at me concerned and said, "No shit, that's right, I forgot—you all right, Bob?"

~

# CHAPTER THIRTY-FOUR

# Leave the LA Philharmonic?

The old principal horn finally retired, creating a principal horn opening, and the music director told me in no uncertain terms that he wanted me to audition for principal horn. I thought about what I would sound like at an audition, since I had already played full time with the orchestra, playing a different make of instrument and surrounded by a style of horn playing that I didn't really like. Then it hit me: I was certainly going to audition for the Los Angeles Philharmonic principal horn opening, but I could also go to take other auditions for other orchestras if there were any vacancies.

Everyone agreed that I played a really fine audition, but the music director wanted to talk to me. I always hated going into his room, because I always felt that he talked down to me. When I finally got in front of him, he said I played even better than my first audition. I thanked him and waited for the "but."

He closed his eyes, made a solemn face, and said, "However, I must tell you that at this time—as much as I feel that your playing is in top form—I also feel that your sound is *not yet thick enough* to be chosen as principal horn of the Los Angeles Philharmonic. We therefore chose a player that has the sound I want."

I just had to ask him what he meant by not thick enough. How does a person play very well, yet not thick enough? And what does "thick enough" have to do with music?

He said that when I get a chance to hear the other player that he chose for the job I would understand.

He said that he thought for sure that by being in the orchestra and playing in the horn section for a few years I would have picked up the sound from the other players in the section and adjusted to what they were doing. He explained:

"A first horn player must allow his sound concept to be molded and shaped into what the music director wants and feels is good for the music the orchestra will play. You play very well in the orchestra, no doubt, but you don't sound like the others. You don't have that *air around your sound* that I like, especially when you have a solo or exposed part to play. Your sound is crystal clear and very well in tune, but I don't hear the things in your sound that I hear in the others. I mean, a horn section should sound like a unit with the same concept of sound, whether playing alone, as a soloist, or together as a section—it must always be the same sound regardless."

I thanked him and walked out of his room. If he thought I was going to actually spend my time working at sounding like those guys, he was really mistaken, I thought. *If they knew what they really sounded like—such ugly, fuzzy, tubby sounds.*

I think the most disturbing part of my conversation with the music director was that it was clear at that moment that, yes, he did see me as a strong player. I *had* to remember that, above all, he *did* hire me. But what was really hard to swallow was the fact that he saw me as having the *potential* of becoming the kind of player who was in the horn section at that time. That was a total deal breaker and a big disappointment.

I stayed ready to audition on the horn for many weeks, almost angrily searching for openings in other orchestras around the country. There were two openings: the Boston Symphony and the New York Philharmonic. Well, actually the New York Philharmonic was a stretch because I knew that they had the same horn-playing style as Los Angeles, but I took the audition anyway because they were back-to-back time wise and the New York Philharmonic audition would warm me up for Boston.

As I approached Lincoln Center and entered Avery Fischer Hall, I noticed a young black man who was dressed in an usher's uniform sporting a nice Afro hairstyle. Apparently there was to be a performance that day. The young man fixed his eyes on me with growing interest, no words were exchanged, but we made definite eye contact. He was nodding his head up and down with a definite approving grin on his face. I wondered at the time if he was perhaps a musician. There was just something about him that stuck in my mind.

As I entered the room, the audition committee was seated on risers like a chorus. There was no screen or any pretense of a screen.

I played through the material with a vengeance. I missed nothing. I felt like a mad man at times. I was so deeply angry it was a wonder that I could play at all. Then it came, my first and only mistake. It was on the Ravel piano concerto, the beautiful solo in the slow movement, which goes up to a high C. I wanted to nail it so badly and play it so full and perfect that I pushed too hard and clipped the note. It almost felt as if someone had jerked my chair causing me to clip that juicy high note.

To my amazement, one of the men on the audition committee actually *laughed out loud* with a nasty sarcasm. Then it was over, someone said, "Thank you." As I left the room, I looked angrily into the eyes of the one who had laughed, transmitting an ugly thought to him.

I thought I had played very well except for the one high C that I nicked, but the personnel manager found me later and told me that I had not advanced to the finals.

He went on to say, "You understand that for the New York Philharmonic you have to play really, really solid and that's what we're looking for."

I told him thanks for inviting me and of course I understood what kind of horn player they were looking for. We shook hands and I turned to walk away when suddenly, as if he had been hypnotized or programmed by shock therapy, he stopped me and started to rattle off some sort of proclamation: "By order of the New York Human Rights Commission I am required to inform you that as a minority, you can, if you so choose, request to be advanced to the finals and be heard by the music director of the New York Philharmonic, clearing said organization of any accusation of discrimination based on race, creed, gender, or—"

I yelled at him, "Stop, stop! What the hell are you saying?"

He looked at me as if I had slapped him to his senses.

I said, "No, thank you, I'm going to the next audition which is in Boston. Goodbye."

Then I remembered that lawsuit against the New York Philharmonic by two black string players when I was attending the Berkshire Music Festival at Tanglewood. I recalled how the New York Philharmonic tried to involve me in that trial as part of their defense. Even though the two black musicians lost the suit, there had obviously been some sort of agreement made with the New York Philharmonic and the New York Human Rights Commission regarding auditions.

I was glad to be going back to Boston, if only for a short time. At least there, I was once respected as a good player with a big enough sound that didn't need to be "thickened" like some kind of bizarre, musical chicken soup, just to please some misguided faux pas school of horn playing. I played a pretty good audition in Boston, but didn't advance to the finals there either. It was nice to see Harry, my horn teacher from conservatory, who was the adjudicator. I had dinner with him and flew back to New Jersey for Christmas with my family.

As I rode home on the New York–New Jersey transit bus, the same bus that I had ridden on my very first visit to New York as a high school kid, I thought, looking at the cold stark reality of the streets of New York and New Jersey, *at least I still had a job somewhere and was not out there on those streets with nothing.* Such thoughts only a New Jersey street kid, who had grown up as I did, could ponder.

When I returned to Los Angeles to continue the winter concert season, a member of management approached me, rather smugly, asking how I did on my auditions.

I said, "Why didn't you *ask* them while you had them on the phone?"

He blankly stared at me and said, "Well, we're sorry you want to leave here, but we're glad you're still with us for now."

*Mother, age 35*

*Father, age 40*

*Grandmother, age 30*

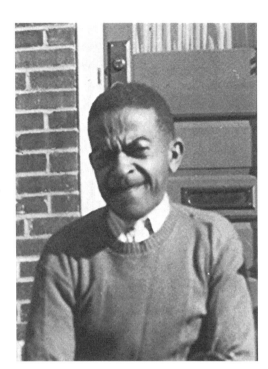

*Grandfather*

*My father, trumpet, age 20, "Cuba's Bar," Asbury Park, N.J.*

*My father at 8th grade graduation (segregated), Bangs Ave. School*

*The Watt Family 1985 Family Reunion*

*Me, age 5, with big sister*

*Me, age 8*

*Me, age 10, school photo*

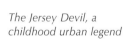

*The Jersey Devil, a childhood urban legend*

*New Jersey All-State Band-Paramus, High School (1966)*

*The Projects—my last residence
before going to conservatory (1967)*

*With my mother and Arthur Fiedler after performing concerto with Boston Pops orchestra (August 1968)*

*On tour with Los Angeles Philharmonic (1970)*

*Zubin Mehta. He hired me as assistant principal french horn of the Los Angeles Philharmonic*

*Bob Watt at L.A. Philharmonic rehearsal (1975)*

I. UNITED STATES OF AMERICA

Department of Transportation — FEDERAL AVIATION ADMINISTRATION

THIS CERTIFIES
THAT
IV. ROBERT LEE WATT
V. 317 OCEAN PARK BOULEVARD
SANTA MONICA    CA    90405

| DATE OF BIRTH | HEIGHT IN. | WEIGHT | HAIR | EYES | SEX | NATIONALITY |
|---|---|---|---|---|---|---|
| 01-15-48 | 76 | 195 | BROWN | BROWN | M | USA |

X. HAS BEEN FOUND TO BE PROPERLY QUALIFIED TO EXERCISE THE PRIVILEGES OF

I. PRIVATE PILOT    III. CERT. NO. ▨▨▨▨▨
RATINGS AND LIMITATIONS
XII. AIRPLANE SINGLE ENGINE LAND
INSTRUMENT AIRPLANE▨

XIII.

II. *Robert L. Watt*
SIGNATURE OF HOLDER    X. *Alexander P. Butterfield*
DATE OF ISSUE 10-27-75    VIII.    ADMINISTRATOR

*My pilot's license*

*Performing at Hollywood Bowl (1972)*

*Me jumping "Beauregard" (1979)*

*Carlo Maria Giulini, one of my favorite maestros (1980)*

*Duets with dad, at the 1985 family reunion*

*With my godchildren at Disneyland*

*Learning to kayak with Maarit in Finland 1989*

*In Munich, Germany (1987)*

*Riding my dressage horse, Mandela*

*Mounting my dressage horse, Mandela*

*Performing Mozart Horn concerto No. 1, with Esa-Pekka Salonen conducting (Finland, 1987)*

*New Brass Ensemble, Lieksa Brass Week (Finland, 1988)*

*Hiking in the Alps, "Sue Bolen Tours" (June 1988)*

*In-house concert, Avanti Festival (1987)*

*Limbering up before a concert at UCLA*

*With Anne-Sofie Mutter in Nantalie, Finland (1987)*

*On Dressage horse "Crocket" in Malibu, California*

*Drawing my saber in Bel-Air, California*

*Chewing on a cigar with André Watts*

*Riding my Hannoverana "Othello," in Malibu, California*

*My dear friend and only true peer, Jerome Ashby, associate principal french horn of the New York Philharmonic*

*At the Great Wall of China 2003 International French Horn Symposium*

*Playing on the Great Wall of China*

*With Barbara, who introduced me to Miles Davis; she was his dear friend*

*My favorite two violinists in Los Angeles*

~

# CHAPTER THIRTY-FIVE

# What We Fear the Most

During a rehearsal scheduled to audition assistant conductors, the new black player and I were forced to witness an ethnic nightmare: that throwback from the bygone, dehumanizing minstrel era when black folks performed on stage in self-deprecating ways. The black candidate dashed on stage as a candidate for assistant conductor of the Los Angeles Philharmonic. He looked as though he were in a constant state of fright the way his large eyes protruded (apparently part of his act) from his head. He wore a short-cropped Afro hairstyle, which was his only redeeming feature in that moment of ethnic horror.

The most disturbing and unsettling part of that scene was the orchestra's reaction to the black man's peculiar coon act. Before he was even introduced, it was obvious by the immediate change in countenance of the entire orchestra that he had their deep, racially stereotypical approval.

In one sense, it was hard to tell whether he was auditioning for the assistant conductor position or for permission to be in front of the orchestra as a black man.

Before he even opened his mouth, the new black player and I simultaneously, as if on some arcane signal (I swear, sometimes I think blacks folks are psychic!) covered our ears and closed our eyes. When he spoke, many of the orchestra players laughed outright at his high-pitched castrato voice.

As I opened my eyes, the apologizing maestro was ready to start the music. He raised his arms to conduct and in a split-second before he gave the down beat he squeezed in one more twitch of skillful cooning, by rolling out his lips and dropping his arms as if to say, "You folks don't *really* take me seriously, do you?"

The new black player quickly glanced back at me from across the orchestra with an expression of pure disgust. The orchestra's reaction continued to unsettle me as they shuffled their feet with grade-school-like approval. Before he conducted one note of music, I knew he had passed his audition, at least as a black man.

Just as I feared, the clowning maestro was hired as assistant conductor. Some of the orchestra players were so condescendingly pleased with the new maestro that they gave him the nickname of "Skeeter."

The new black player was appalled with that name so he asked one of the players what a name like Skeeter meant.

One of the players responded, "Well, we thought since he was such a *cute* guy that this was a good name for him. Why, is something wrong with that name?"

There was a British composer who was guest conductor for the week and the assistant conductor's job in that case was to serve as a kind of second set of ears for the principal conductor. This half-dead, half-blind relic from the Rudyard Kipling era could barely see all the players in the orchestra. "Trombones, I can't quite see you, but wherever you are, you're too loud."

The work we were performing was one of his own, an oratorio of some kind, very British, dry, snooty, and bland. About halfway through the rehearsal, the new bright Uncle Tom genius came up on stage to speak with the guest conductor about the balance in the chorus.

The British Empire maestro shooed him away like so many annoying flies. "No, no, not now, not now!" getting louder and more annoyed. "You never interrupt a senior conductor, stupid boy. Now where were we?"

There was a strange silence throughout the orchestra followed by an undertone of "Awwww—poor thing," as the clowning maestro swished himself off the stage with his tail between his legs.

I didn't even have to look at the new black player, who was already turned in my direction from across the orchestra with a look of deep anger.

Of course, the British Empire maestro, in all his imperialistic glory, carried on with the rehearsal as though nothing had happened and so did the orchestra. Not one of his "approving fans" appeared the least bit incensed by that insulting incident.

It seems when it comes to a black person being insulted by a white person, most other whites are sadly more than willing to tacitly approve, as if said black person weren't human or somehow deserved the put-down—a throwback to the slave owner mentality of "They don't really matter. It's not as if it were one of us." Or like what Huck Finn's friend said when a black boy they knew drowned: "He was just a nigger."

Nonetheless, the orchestra loved him, the management loved him, all the worst reactionaries in the orchestra loved him, even those who barely spoke to me or the other black player loved that "high-tech" Uncle Tom. Delighted with the nickname they gave him, he gleefully became their mascot.

After experiencing the reception of the young, gifted, and black maestro-mascot Skeeter, I was forced to ask myself: "If there *had* to be black men in symphony orchestras in these United States, was *he* the type of black man that they *really* wanted? Was there *still* a deep yearning for the self-deprecating minstrel-type black man?"

Frederick Douglass said it best in a speech, September 25, 1883, 130 years ago:

> Though the colored man is no longer subject to barter and sale, he is surrounded by an adverse settlement which fetters all his movements. In his downward course, he meets with no resistance, but his course upward is resented and resisted at every step of his progress.
>
> If he comes in ignorance, rags and wretchedness . . . he conforms to the popular belief of his character, and in that character he is welcome; but if he shall come as a gentleman, a scholar and a statesman, he is hailed as a contradiction to the national faith concerning his race, and his coming is resented as impudence. In one case he may provoke contempt and derision, but in the other he is an affront to pride and provokes malice.

As New York music critic Stanley Crouch said, classical music and symphony orchestras were never of great interest to black people. And perhaps for that reason there had never been, in all of my three-plus decades in the orchestra, more than a handful of black folks regularly attending the Los Angeles Philharmonic concerts. Out of 3,800 patrons, maybe twenty black folks were present at any given concert. Those who did attend were what E. Franklin Frazier called "second-class white citizens" in that they looked at themselves as not being cultured at all in comparison to whites. To them *culture in total* was white, European, and *far* above them. They tiptoed into the concert hall as if hoping not to be discovered. After all, they were attending an event that, as they always said to me, "not many of *us* are into."

I had the distinct pleasure on several occasions of meeting some of those uncomfortable black patrons at concert intermissions. They always approached me with great caution and what annoyed me most about them was that they constantly whispered.

The most common exchange from them was (whispering), "Hello there, so nice to see you in the orchestra. You look *good* up there among all those . . . you know? I mean, you blend in nicely—you're not too dark—that's a good thing. Keep up the good work—and the fact that you're the *only one* makes you *all the more special,* keep it that way. Nice talking to you."

I always held my breath watching them, as they tiptoed back to their seats as if being watched by some sort of invisible, white, cultural God.

In 1983, there was still only one other black player in the Los Angeles Philharmonic other than myself. To my delight, a black woman violinist, a graduate of USC whom I had met a few years earlier through friends, and a young black percussion player, who had played as an extra many times with the orchestra and won the co-principal timpani audition, were introduced as new members of the Los Angeles Philharmonic at the same time. I distinctly remember hearing two principal players openly making negative comments.

One in particular blurted out, as he sheepishly buried his head in his chest, speaking to the floor, "The standards are going down—the standards are going down!"

Then another principal, sitting right next to me, said something about using screens at the auditions. The comment from the second principal was especially appalling, since during that *very* rehearsal he had trouble playing some of the simple meter changes in Stravinsky's Petruska.

Some weeks later, the new co-principal timpani began to play with the orchestra. I was very happy to see him there. I could see he *loved* playing timpani. It was *in him* somehow. It was part of his African manhood—his ancestral echoes. *The drums.*

That young black man had a wonderful sound and touch on the instrument. During his first months as co-principal timpani, the orchestra played a few difficult works for timpani. One piece I remember in particular was Bartok's Piano Concerto No. 2. It had tricky rhythms that were hard to play on time. That is, when they reached the conductor's ears, they could easily sound late. The conductor for the week was the legendary Erich Leinsdorf. Adding to the problem, our concert hall at the time had a large gap at least eight feet wide between the percussion section and the rest of the orchestra. Leinsdorf kept hounding the young man, "*Pauken! Pauken!* [Timpani!] It's late . . . it's late!"

There were some rumbles of criticism about the new timpani player by some of the same kingpin principals that I believed were double agents. That is, some of them were on the orchestra committee, even the auditions committee, but at the same time informants with some factions of management. Therefore, in a dark and sick kind of way, they had a modicum of influence.

There seemed to be an entire culture of lackeys and double agents, who often threatened people during an argument: "I'll take care of you upstairs"—that is, report them to management.

A year passed and I began hearing talk about the young black man *not* getting tenure as co-principal timpani, but instead was given tenure as principal percussion. That was strange, since there were two more auditions held for co-principal timpani and the young black man auditioned each time and no one outplayed him, yet they still wouldn't offer him that position.

In between his two tenure review years, the orchestra changed music directors. That meant that a totally different music director would be responsible for granting tenure for those players who were hired before the change in music directors. So the new timpani player, in a sense, got caught in between the cracks.

The new interim music director was quite spineless about the whole ordeal when the new timpani player asked about his tenure status. He was told, "This all started before I got here—this all came from upstairs" (referring to management).

I had to wonder, *why had this happened?* Why would management interfere with the hiring of an orchestra player? Were some of the double agent, lackey, kingpin principals uncomfortable with a young black man in such a strong dominant position in the orchestra, since the timpani is one of the most prominent positions and certainly one of the highest paid? The rest of the mosaic was, not only did the young black man win the audition, he was handsome and self-assured. He carried himself in a manner that, in that environment and at that time, actually worked *against* him. He remains principal percussion to this day.

~

# CHAPTER THIRTY-SIX

# Conversations with Jerome Ashby

1983, our new Italian music director had been with us for a year and wanted to add another solo horn to the section. After a short search, a rather well-known principal horn was hired. He did a very nice job, even though he was just that, a solo horn. He only played the solos and not much else in the horn part. He kept me very busy when I was assisting him, so we got on quite well.

Soon after he was hired, during conversation one day, he told me that the New York Philharmonic had just hired a young black associate principal horn player. "He was a student of James Chambers—he's not the player you are, but just the same he plays great."

I always wondered why he felt he had to compare us. Anyway, I thanked him for the news and asked the man's name.

I thought about that black horn player for days until one day I decided I just had to call him. By the time I got around to calling him, there was a tour coming up that took the Los Angeles Philharmonic to New York.

I called the new black horn player and in our brief phone conversation we made plans to meet in New York. He said he had known about me since high school and couldn't wait to meet and talk. His name was Jerome Ashby. I hung up the phone and thought how great it was to finally have a *true peer* in the world of symphony orchestra French horn players.

When the tour to New York finally came, I called Jerome as soon as I got to my hotel. I was really looking forward to meeting him—a person playing the French horn in a major symphony orchestra who looked like me!

We agreed to meet at the Carnegie Tavern at 5:00 for a drink. When I walked in, Jerome was already seated at the bar. He quickly stood up and vigorously shook my hand. He was a tall, dark, thin man with a short-cropped haircut and squinty eyes that clenched half-closed and looked warm and sincere when he smiled. He had somewhat of a cocky swashbuckling swagger to his walk, but I didn't care. We were two black men playing French horns in major symphony orchestras in these United States and we had things to talk about. Jerome started the conversation:

Ashby: So, what happened out there in Los Angeles? I heard guys didn't like you. Is that true? I've been waiting for *years* to hear *your* side of these rumors, because I didn't get *any* flack here in New York, to be honest with you.

Watt: Well, let's see—to begin with, I had heard several times that many of the freelance musicians around Los Angeles referred to me as "Boston Blackie."

Ashby: Oh, really? Did anyone actually address you that way?

Watt: Oh no, but just the same it did give me a sense of the general attitude some players had about a black guy being hired by the LA Philharmonic.

Ashby: I'm sorry to hear that, because I didn't get anything close to that kind of reception here—then too, I *am* in my home environment.

Watt: Yeah, true, and I'm really glad to hear things were better for you, but do you think your experience would have been different for you in your home environment had you come along when I did, some ten years ago?

Ashby: (after looking at me for a long time in silence) My God, I don't know, never thought about that.

Watt: I'm sure by now you realize that no black man or woman in these United States had been hired by a major symphony orchestra playing French horn before I came along. And of course, it wasn't the kind of thing I thought about until I had already arrived on the scene and one day it suddenly dawned on me. I was a pioneer, some might say. And I know, in a sad sense, it was the fulfillment of a dream that famed jazz horn player Julius Watkins, for example, and many others were never allowed to pursue in their day. And I think you know that not so long ago in *your* orchestra there was a black violinist who had a rather rough experience at times, perhaps you know him?

Ashby: Yes, of course, Sanford Allen—I know him, a great human being.

Watt: I agree. You know, I used to see him on the subway after the New York Philharmonic concerts when I was in high school. I always wanted to talk to him, but he looked so intense and deep in thought that I was too shy to approach him.

Ashby: So now, Robert Lee, give me a few examples of the things that happened to you out there in LA.

Watt: Well, let's see, I believe in all honesty that the music director—who hired us both, by the way—liked and respected me as a strong player and saw me as having the most *potential* of playing like that horn section out there. I believe that's why he chose me over the other two finalists at the audition. I also believe it earned the orchestra political brownie points in those days for hiring a black guy.

Ashby: Right, I'm with you. So how *do* those guys play out there? I don't know much about the playing style in the Los Angeles Philharmonic. I've only heard rumors about the players in the studios.

Watt: (taking a deep breath and trying to be as honest as I could) Ah, well—they play, you know, that heavy Conn 8-D style. A misconception of how the horn should sound—somewhat tubby with fuzzy tones, sounding more like trombones sometimes."

Ashby: (his face lit up like a Christmas tree) "Ah ha! Let me stop you there, Robert Lee Watt! Hmmm, I don't think we're going see eye to eye on horn playing, because what you just described is pretty much the way I was taught and it is *indeed* the New York Philharmonic's horn-playing style, so continue at your own risk."

Watt: Oh, sorry, of course I forgot, forgive me if I was inconsiderate, but you know what? It's all right with me if we don't see eye to eye on horn playing. I'm just glad you exist. The fact that someone else who *looks like me* decided to take up this wonderful instrument and win a major symphony position is more important than anything else. And now that you're on the scene, perhaps I wasn't totally crazy for wanting to play French horn in a symphony orchestra in these United States and still be black.

Ashby: (laughing loudly, with a look of deep understanding in his eyes) I'll order another round of drinks and then you can tell me how you got along with the music director. I can't *wait* to hear that.

After the drinks arrived, I continued.

Watt: I must honestly say it was not always comfortable between us.

Ashby: Really? Interesting, because I had some uncomfortable times with him too. Ya know, he often accused me of sassing him, but basically we were OK, and well, at least he likes my horn sound.

Watt: Right, a sound that's thick enough.

Ashby: What? He said your sound wasn't thick enough?

Ashby: (sharing another big laugh) So what about conductors, Watt? Let's talk a little about conductors while we're on the subject. What do you think of them in general—besides our mutual music director? Go for it, Watt—tell me a story.

Watt: Well, now that I'm in the classical music world, I must say honestly that they have never been my main focus by any means. It was always the music first for me. But I'd have to go back to my experience with Alsatian conductor Charles Münch, who was music director of the Boston Symphony from 1949 to 1962. In 1967, my first year at conservatory, I was an usher at Symphony Hall. When all the people were seated, I would step inside the hall, find a seat, and listen to the Boston Symphony concerts.

It must have been one of his last concerts before his death in 1968. I heard him conduct the Brahms Symphony No. 1.

And you know that wonderful brass chorale in the last movement? I've never heard it played in such a musically sensitive manner. I never knew it could be so magical—so warm and tender. It was as if he dared to transcend its instrumental bounds of brass and take it to another level. I was stunned and never forgot the way it sounded.

Then, in the early seventies, my first few years with the Los Angeles Philharmonic, there was a world-renowned Hungarian orchestral and operatic conductor István Kertész. The musical experience I had with him was of a different point of view—far beyond his being a good or bad conductor. His stylish musical ideas made me feel that I had not wasted my time developing my own musical standards. I was hoping that he would be a principal guest conductor and would be around on a regular basis. It was the most devastating news to hear that he drowned while swimming off the coast of Israel.

Ashby: Well, Robert Lee, you are way before my time in all of this. Sounds like *you* had definite musical ideas in your early days though.

Watt: For sure, but sometimes I think I was a bit too serious for my age. You know, I just wasn't impressed with the musical ideas and standards of the musicians in the LA Philharmonic at the time, especially after being around the Boston Symphony.

Ashby: So what other maestro suited your fancy, Robert Lee?

Watt: I had an interesting experience with Eugene Ormandy. It was another one of those mornings when the principal horn didn't show up. The personnel manager came over to me and told me that the principal horn was detained at the airport and wouldn't be at rehearsal. I moved over and played first horn on the Stravinsky, Firebird Suite.

Ashby: Hey, nice, the Firebird—a great opportunity for you. How did it go?

Watt: I had a great time playing it. Nothing difficult for me in that piece—I nailed it.

Ashby: What did Ormandy say?

Watt: Funny you should ask. He had lots to say. He called me into his room after the rehearsal and said, "I didn't know you were principal. You play great. I hope you're playing the concert."

I had to tell him that I was assistant principal and I was just filling in for the rehearsal and would not be playing the concert. Then he said, to my surprise, "I think you should play the concert—you sound great—why not?"

I knew that was going to cause a problem. The next morning at rehearsal, the Primo principal showed up screaming bloody murder. He was yelling at the personnel manager. "How could you let this happen? I only missed one rehearsal and I am still the principal horn of this orchestra, Goddamn it! You fix this, now!"

Ashby: Damn, Robert Lee, that is pretty bad stuff. How that principal could get away with such behavior—and that was not his first time doing such things? Sounds like you have very poor orchestra management out there. We could never get away with that here in New York. So which one of you ended up playing the concert?

Watt: Ha! I had a good chuckle while assisting the principal, who had a rather rough evening playing the Firebird Suite. Ormandy was very upset.

~

# CHAPTER THIRTY-SEVEN

# Challenged by a Peer

Ashby: Quite a story about Ormandy. I never had the pleasure of playing under him. So now, Robert Lee—Robert Lee Watt, how do you *really* feel about our mutual music director—our mutual maestro, who hired us both?

Watt: Zubin Mehta? OK, well, I must say I had never met anyone quite like him in my musical career until he hired me. I often wondered where he got his knowledge about how the French horn should sound. The fact that he had conducted so many European orchestras and experienced so many authentic and truly characteristic horn styles and sounds, I just don't understand how he ended up favoring the Conn 8-D style of horn playing.

Ashby: (grabbing a butter knife from the table) Feel that sharp object in your stomach, Watt?

Watt: What? What are you doing?

Ashby: That's a knife that will be pushed into your gut if you keep talking about my style of horn playing—the New York Philharmonic's style of horn playing—in such a negative manner.

Watt: OK, OK, sorry! Don't kill me until I'm finished telling you about Zubin Mehta. I think he saw me as a very strong player, but I don't think he realized that it threatened the other principals when he referred to me that way. For example, during rehearsals he would say, "Watt, you should double on that part with the principal, I need your strength there."

On the other hand, I'm sure in those instances he was all about the music and not thinking about horn section politics and personalities. He had to know that there would be some resistance to my being in the horn section, if it was true what the philharmonic auditions and renewals committee people told me about the primo principal threatening to quit if I was hired. However, I'm forever grateful to Zubin for standing his ground and hiring me.

Now despite all the stuff that happened between us regarding those token black concerts and his not hiring me as Primo principal because he felt my horn sound was not yet thick enough to match the section, I would have to say he had the most profound musical feeling and expression I've ever seen in any conductor. He felt the damn music and was a good liaison between what the music was saying and his audience.

Ashby: Come on, Watt, there must be more you can say about him—give it up, Robert Lee.

Watt: Yeah, Ashby, but I hate talking about conductors . . . well, OK, we did have kind of a fun moment once on tour in the southwestern United States, when he dragged me from the hotel lobby to a waiting car, thinking I was propositioning a prostitute.

Ashby: Were you doing that, Robert Lee?

Watt: Oh hell no, Ashby, but he thought I was. He wanted me to come to dinner with him and a group of musicians. We went over the border into Mexico to a very special restaurant that specialized in spicy food. At dinner he asked me if I liked hot food. My twenty-two-year-old ego told him that I would eat anything spicy that he would. Big mistake—big mistake—he killed me. He started putting hot sauce on these very dark green chilies that he carried in his pocket. He was just popping them into his mouth and offering them to me—to warm up the pallet, he said. I suffered with a burning mouth for days trying to keep up with him.

Ashby: Yeah, see, that was a great story, Watt. You two did all right. Still, I think it was just uncomfortable chemistry between you two that was just an unavoidable reality about big-headed men in general. Say yes, Watt. Come on—say it!

Watt: Oh hell, Ashby—all right, all right—yes! (Lots of laughter)

Ashby: Oh! I just love it when you give in. So who's next on your list of conductors?

Watt: Well, after Zubin left the LA Philharmonic, Carlo Maria Giulini was hired in 1982. It was the beginning of a whole new era for the orchestra. He was the first conductor who reminded me of the sensitivity and musical style of Charles Münch. Now, Giulini was not a conductor in the strictest sense of the word. He once told the orchestra, "*Mi scuzzi*, but I know not what I do with my hands, so please forgive me, but it is the music that I do."

He was indeed all about the music. His entire body exuded what the music was about to him. To cue certain parts of the music he often used bone-chilling facial expressions and powerful glares, with all the meaning of a particular passage showing in his eyes. There was never any doubt about what he wanted from the musicians. I always looked forward to playing principal horn when he was conducting. I just loved being in his musical presence.

He used extremely sensitive musical terms when referring to the percussion section like *dolce forte* (sweetly strong). He got the most fantastic colors and sounds from the percussion I had ever heard. The music was deeply in him and it was a true pleasure to be on the same stage with him.

Once while on a tour of the East Coast, I played principal horn on the Maurice Ravel Scheherazade in Carnegie Hall. You know the piece, I'm sure.

Ashby: Oh yes, played it many times.

Watt: You know that soft pianissimo muted solo at the end? I played it with ease never giving it a second thought. After the Carnegie Hall concert, which seemed to be very important to the maestro, the orchestra flew to Washington, D.C., the next day. After landing in Washington, as the orchestra was walking through the airport, I heard someone call out to me. "Mr. Watt! *Aspetta!* [Wait!]" I turned around to find Carlo Maria Giulini trying to catch up to me. I stopped immediately and warmly greeted the out-of-breath maestro. (He smoked.)

After catching his breath, he said in front of all the orchestra members in an earshot, "Mr. Watt, I just want to say that I really enjoyed your beautiful pianissimo solo playing at the end of the Scheherazade last night. It was very beautiful. Thank you."

Ashby: Wow, fantastic! He said that in front of everyone? Now that must have prompted quite a barrage of envious, snide comments from orchestra members.

Watt: Boy, did it ever—comments like, "Hey Bob, now you get to keep your job, bravo! Looks like you might also be our new principal horn. Way to go." I'll say this about Giulini, he was never what some conductors often became—the ruthless Greek gods who ruled absolutely over the hearts and minds of their musicians. He was an absolute gentleman.

Ashby: So who else can we talk about, Watt? I'm about to fall over—I'm so ripped. How many of those things did we have, Watt, of those damn grappas?

Watt: I believe we had three, sir.

I continued.

Watt: Most conductors of symphony orchestras in these United States always seem to be European or foreign, except in a few cases, given the many American-born conductors: Leonard Bernstein, Leonard Slatkin, Herbert

Blomstedt, Antal Doráti, James Levine, James DePreist, Henry Lewis, Michael Tilson Thomas, Dean Dixon, and others.

In spite of the ample existence of highly qualified American maestros, American orchestras, regardless of their size—major, regional, or metropolitan—the European maestros always get the nod as their music director. It's as if they were somehow inherently the better deal, as if there existed some sort of cultural inferiority complex in the American symphony orchestras or in the American classical music psyche that deems European or as close to European as possible, the superior entity.

Ashby: I agree. Are we done, Watt? Have we forgotten anyone?

Watt: Of course—let's not forget our own people, at least the ones I worked with—two major African American maestros, James DePreist and Henry Lewis. I played under DePreist several times. I shall never forget his Tchaikovsky 6th Symphony. He had such passion in his heart when he conducted and I felt connected to him instantly. He actually did land a post with an American symphony orchestra in Portland, Oregon. He brought the orchestra to prominence, really making a name for himself there as well as abroad. Finally, there was Henry Lewis, who was from Los Angeles and whom I knew well, having done a concerto with him when he was music director of the New Jersey Symphony. In conversation with him over drinks, he lamented, "You know, for all of the major American orchestras I've conducted and with all the experience I've had with European opera orchestras, you would think I'd be a bargain for some American orchestra somewhere in this country as music director." I could feel his pain, because underneath all of his huff and fluff, he was a great guy who loved to conduct and this was most evident when he walked off stage. He was the happiest person in the world. It was like he had been in shock therapy. I always loved talking to him in that state of mind.

The maestro and I went on to discuss the fact that if American orchestras don't perceive a white American conductor as European-ish enough for their music director—then sadly it would follow that an African American maestro would be perceived as even less culturally viable. So there's your answer to why so few African American maestros are conducting *any* orchestra in these United States, much less a major orchestra, not that you asked.

Ashby: Now—I have one more really good question for you. In your opinion, why don't they want black classical musicians in symphony orchestras in this country? I mean really, what's that all about, Watt?

Watt: Oh hell, Ashby! Do you really want me to answer that question in my condition?

Ashby: Absolutely—go ahead, you haven't had *that* much to drink.

Watt: OK, OK. I'll try, oh boy— Why don't they want us in symphony orchestras? . . . Well don't you know? . . . Because you're frightening!

Ashby: Frightening?

Watt: Yeah . . . you're too scary, too much of a confrontation.

Ashby: A confrontation? What kind of confrontation? Where are you going with this?

Watt: Well, the color confrontation—skin color. Something they spend billions on every year, you have naturally—and then it's your stature, you're too big, with your classic African build, muscular arms, muscular ass, and thunder thighs that might bust open your tuxedo pants and destroy the formal look. And besides, you'd be in dangerously close proximity to the many lovely white female violinists—and with the sexual reputation that they've assigned to you . . . it would be way too scary. And again, with your beautiful striking skin color, you'd break up the mosaic flow of whiteness in the orchestra. So yes, you're too frightening.

Ashby: What the hell! . . . Are you serious, Watt? Sorry, go on . . . preach!

Watt: Yes, well that's just the basic stuff. Now imagine after all the obstacles they've thrown at you to keep you down in this country and you have the nerve to take up the French horn, with your full African lips, despite the fact that your African soup-coolers are supposed to be too thick for that thin, white-boy mouthpiece—and still you end up in a major symphony orchestra—on their sacred cultural turf? Frightening? Yes! *Your* success is *their* worst nightmare, because it destroys all the lies they've told and ingested about you.

Ashby: Stop, stop . . . soup-coolers, Robert Lee?

Watt: Yeah . . . don't you know that term for full lips?

Ashby: OK, I see . . . go on, God! (laughter) Come on, Watt, stop it now—focus!

Watt: OK, I'm focused.

Ashby: And be serious, too.

Watt: OK, I'm serious. . . . Let's see, to answer your question, how far should I go back? So, if you choose to enslave a people, by definition you never intend to make them a part of your enterprise after they've done your dirty work. That is to say, in this county they never intended to include black people in *any* aspect of normal American life. I mean, it's not like they had visions of integration or affirmative action in their long-term plans. There were no visions of your sitting around a campfire at summer camp holding hands with whites and especially white women singing "Kumbayah."

Ashby: Holy shit, Robert Lee . . . of course not, but go on, finish your sermon—your answer, sorry.

Watt: What, what—am I preaching?

Ashby: Well, sometimes, but you're good at it. Did you ever want to be a preacher?

Watt: What? Hell no, Ashby! So come on, you know this stuff . . . so then why didn't they want us in *most* American institutions that were, at one time, exclusively all white? The *white only* concept goes back to early America, when founding fathers like Jefferson, Madison, and even honest Abe Lincoln ultimately perceived these United States as a white utopia. In fact, Lincoln's true concept of emancipation was to deport all blacks, slave and free, out of the country.[1] The white-only concept persisted in nearly all American institutions, especially in things considered All American, which I always felt was a euphemism for "All White," like baseball, hockey, football, basketball, and of course, the symphony orchestra. In fact the concept of whiteness was born in these United States. Then honestly, Ashby, I believe it all boils down to a very primal element in all people: identity.

Ashby: Identity—really?

Watt: Oh yeah, an extremely precious turf that people cling to for dear life. *Who* they are—or in too many cases—who they'd *like to think* they are.

Ashby: How do you mean? Give me an example.

Watt: Well, you know: "I'm white, therefore I am entitled. I am the dominant culture." Or my favorite, "I'm a Christian."

Ashby: Now wait a minute, Watt! Don't be talking about religion . . . Nothing—go on.

Watt: What? What'd I say now?

Ashby: Nothing—just be careful or I might have to perform a New York ass-whipping on you, Watt.

Watt: What? Aw, come on Ashby, I'm trying to do what you asked. OK, let me finish and you can kick my ass later.

Ashby: Absolutely, Robert Lee, I've got my nigger stick right here.

Watt: No, no, you didn't say that! . . . So this identity is a powerful element and is most lethal when manipulated by governments or political powers, like it was in Nazi Germany. The "Aryan superior race" concept worked very well, because people love to feel superior.

In the case of classical music in these United States—i.e., white classical musicians—I noticed that they had a strong tendency to cling to—even be on their knees to—Europe as their cultural touchstone. So when we show up on the scene as black classical musicians, playing French horns in major symphony orchestras, which in their cultural conscience is exclusively reserved for them, this challenges their cultural identity. And in some cases we're treading on their cultural fantasy. Sadly, part of that cultural fantasy is that they believe they are better suited to play classical music than we are.

So again, when encountering you as a black classical musician, coupled with all the unconscious fears they may have absorbed from an American society with a rather comprehensive racist mosaic about you, it would be damn near impossible for them *not to say or do* something patronizing or off-color, when meeting you initially. I'm sure you've experienced this yourself.

Ashby: Absolutely, Robert Lee—way too many times.

Watt: Indeed—and you know for many years they claimed black people couldn't play classical music—couldn't read the music or depart from the jazz feel. But even when we show absolute competence in classical music, as we have, some still don't really *want* to accept it, because it crushes their deeply ingrained belief that we are not capable of achieving such a white-only artistic level. That is, they want you to be what they say you are. Yes, they are actually more comfortable with the lie.

Even after my being in the philharmonic for these past years there were those who were still in denial about my competence—and ever vigilant, hoping to discover some chicken-shit evidence that, in their mind, would prove my incompetence.

So, my dear friend, Jerome Ashby, in the not-so-distant past, in these United States, the classical music world was strongly compelled to keep black folks out of symphony orchestras completely. So—that's the short version, in my opinion.

Ashby: God! Brutal—hard to hear, but I like your answer, Watt. Can I give you an A-men? Good night.

## Note

1. Lerone Bennett Jr. *Forced into Glory: Abraham Lincoln's White Dream.* Chicago: Johnson Publishing, 2000.

~

# CHAPTER THIRTY-EIGHT

# Give It Up

The next morning at breakfast:

Ashby: So, tell me how do you like your position—your actual job? I mean what's it like for a player like you to play assistant horn most of the time?

Watt: (after thinking for a moment) First, let me say good morning, Ashby, and that it's way too early for such a question, but OK—I'll tell you this, as hard as I try, I can't help but feel that it's kind of a flunky job except for the times I'm playing other positions in the section.

Ashby: No—really—a flunky job?

Watt: Yeah . . . the type of job that perhaps a British imperialist would've invented for a person in one of their conquered colonies. A sort of Rudyard Kipling, "take up the white man's burden" type job, especially if the principal horn you're assisting has a sort of imperialist outlook in that he believes it's ordained by God that *you* take up *his* burden.

Ashby: (looking puzzled, raising his voice) Wait, Rudyard Kipling— Rudyard Kipling? You mean the guy who wrote "Little Black Sambo?"

Watt: Oh God! Jerome, it really is way too early for this stuff! No, no, actually that was Helen Bannerman, a Scottish woman.

Ashby: OK right, so tell me about the "take up the white man's burden" part. That creeps me out, Watt.

I told him about the famous poem alluding to white supremacy and British imperialism and he was still in a state of disbelief.

Ashby: So you *really* feel that way? And you *really* work with people who have such attitudes? God! All of a sudden I feel very fortunate to have *my* situation.

Watt: Well, it's more about the way it feels when actually doing the assistant part of the the job. There is something very musically disconnected about it—like you're not really playing or part of the *real action*. Kind of like those TV commercials where they insert a token black person, but said black person is always in the background and never part of the *real* action. They show the black person perhaps in one or two frames, but no more—after that it's always the white actors who get the yummy gravy.

So maybe one could also say assistant horn is kind of like being *water boy*, especially when you have principal horns who don't want to tell you where to assist them, that the assistant should read their mnds. So I'm always a little haunted by the fact that my white colleagues and management will become way too comfortable having *me* in such a position.

Ashby: (looking surprised) I don't know if that's true, Robert Lee—water boy? My God! So please tell me more about what it's like with your horn section. It's starting to sound dreadful.

Watt: To tell you the truth, it's a little bit of a crazy existence for me because I never get enough of the right kind of playing, even though I do play *some* first horn. It's the type of situation where the principal horns don't really want me to get *too* comfortable playing first horn for fear of making them look bad and not that I would, but they seemed to possess that degree of pathological paranoia.

Ashby: (interrupting) Ah ha, now that concept I want to tell you about later—sorry, go on, keep talking.

Watt: Well, for example, when I play first, they make it as difficult as possible by only offering me one little piece to play spaced over long periods of time, like one little piece per month or even less. They know quite well, from playing principal horn themselves, that the less principal horn one plays, the more difficult it is. Of course, if I get any type of accolades about my principal horn playing from the other brass players, then the principals freeze me out of principal horn playing altogether, for even longer periods.

Another example of the lunacy is having a principal horn wanting me to play a piece but never telling me—actually keeping it a secret until the last possible minute, hoping *that* will put me at a disadvantage.

Ashby: Amazing that they consciously do that, but in a way I understand their fears—so keep going, Robert Lee, tell me more.

Watt: One of the principal horns wanted me to play first horn on a Mozart piano concerto but never told me. The day the piece was to be rehearsed, I overheard him telling the second horn that I would be playing first horn on the concerto. Said principal turned and walked right by me saying nothing. I decided to let it ride on purpose just to see how it would play out. I went home for lunch between the two rehearsals. I waited at home to see what would happen. When the second rehearsal started, I didn't get a call so I thought perhaps the part was covered. Not so.

*Thirty minutes* into the rehearsal of the piano concerto, my phone rang. It was the personnel manager yelling over the phone. "I can't have a horn section that doesn't communicate. You're supposed to be playing first horn on the Mozart piano concerto, so where are you?"

I laughed and told him that I knew of no such thing and why would he be calling me thirty minutes into the rehearsal and ultimately, who's responsible for the horn section and why aren't you calling him? The concerto was actually being rehearsed without a first horn while the personnel manager sat in the audience for thirty minutes before noticing.

Then the personnel manager had the gall to tell me that it was my job as well to make sure the parts were covered. I told him that he was not helping the situation by telling me such a thing. I asked him why he was so afraid to put the blame and responsibility where it belonged, on the principal horn— the alleged leader of the section. Then I asked him point blank, why is it that personnel managers always favor the principals? That type of thing happened time and time again over the years.

Ashby: (shaking his head in disbelief) That would never happen in our section or in our orchestra. We plan all the playing out far in advance. But you know, I can't say based on *my* experience that the personnel manager *always* favors the principals. But God, your section sounds so ass backwards, I would think that the leaders of a section would want everyone to play well and sound good.

Watt: You know, Ashby, you would think so, but when one or both of the principals are shaky and insecure enough about their own playing, the concept of everyone in the horn section sounding good would not be to their advantage. To purposely put the other principal, the assistant principal, or anyone in the section at a disadvantage, *hoping* they will have trouble, just so they could say someone else is having playing problems, jeopardizes the horn section's performance level, or the entire orchestra for that matter, and would be expendable to them—sort of collateral damage in their fearful minds.

Ashby: (smiling, but looking somewhat guilty) Look, I don't mean to laugh at what you just told me and please don't take offense to this, Watt, but—if you were in *my* section I wouldn't let you play either, because you play too well, that is truly the principal horn player's creed of irrational insecurity, to be honest with you.

Watt: You're a dead man, Ashby.

Ashby: No, honestly, your principals out there really *don't* want you to sound good. They would prefer you sound like you're barely making it but that they were merciful in giving you a chance to play and at the same time hoping the orchestra will condescend to compliment you for your herculean effort. That's what they would like to happen if you ask me. But no, you play the hell out of whatever they offer you, making them look bad.

After dinner, Jerome and I went to the basement of Lincoln Center and played duets. When we started playing, I could hear that he was totally into that heavy Conn 8-D style of playing, especially the way he tongued his scales. We played and talked for several hours. He said he thought I had a lot of endurance. We laughed, packed up, and went out for another drink.

It was about 2:00 a.m. and it seemed Jerome and I just couldn't get enough of each other. We had so much to share, so much to learn about each other and our experiences.

When I returned to my hotel room, I couldn't sleep thinking about my meeting with him. How much better his playing situation was than mine . . . and that his horn section got along better and that he fortunately had a better position than I did. He was associate principal horn where he played only first horn, but all the time and not one piece per month and he didn't have to play assistant horn. I was truly happy for him—happy to see that the second black French horn player to play in a major symphony orchestra in these United States was doing better.

Several days later, Jerome and I met again in Chinatown. We ordered Chinese beer and started talking shop again.

Ashby: All right, Watt, I have a real sick racist story to tell you. Are you ready? Take a swig of beer and a deep breath.

Watt: What, somebody call you nigger . . . or "New York Blackie"?

Ashby: (putting a chopstick to my throat) Watt, I'm gonna kill you yet—give me a break! Ashby: (laughing) OK, where was I? About a year ago the New York Philharmonic did a run-out concert upstate one evening. When the bus arrived at the concert hall, I needed to warm up so I went right onstage without changing into my concert dress. As I began to warm up, I realized that I should probably use a mute because several other people were warming up. So I stepped offstage to get a mute from my horn case and was rushed by backstage security.

"Can I help you? What are you doing in here?" I told him that I was with the New York Philharmonic and I started to walk away. The guy actually grabbed my arm and said, "Yeah . . . and I'm Rip Van Winkle, now you get the hell outta here."

I was really outraged, because here I was in the middle of my warm-up and that idiot was holding me up and about to physically throw me out. I called for our personnel manager to help me and what *he* said really blew my mind. "Well, Jerome, this is what happens when you go onstage without dressing first. I've told you time and time again that you should." Now I had two people barking up the wrong tree. I wanted to scream, but when the personnel manager realized later what had *actually* happened, he apologized profusely to me. Have you ever had such a thing happen to you?

Watt: (taking a deep breath) Oh yes, these are classic, "little white" situations that writer James Baldwin referred to as "innocent and ignorant at the same time, a conundrum." It's the utter confusion that some white people experience when they suddenly can't fathom the presence of a black person in their midst.

I recall a much more subtle incident that happened in the early seventies, while the orchestra was checking into a hotel in Ann Arbor.

As the orchestra filed off the buses and entered the hotel, we were told by the staff to form two lines, give our names to the clerk, and they would give us our room key.

All was going smoothly until I reached the desk. Before I could say my name, the clerk froze looking really confused, and said, "Ah, can I help you? Do you have a reservation?" I looked into her empty confused eyes and pointed to my name on the list. The poor clerk snapped out of her "innocent and ignorant" prejudice trance and gave me my room key.

Ah! And then there was a similar incident involving a hotel room key that happened in Glasgow, Scotland. You know how in most European hotels they give you a key identification card and you leave your room key with the front desk? Well, I went to dinner with one of the other black players in the philharmonic after a concert. We handed our keys to the front desk and were off to have some haggis and whiskey. On returning later that evening, we walked into the hotel lobby along with several other orchestra members. As we approached the front desk, several of the orchestra members started yelling out their room numbers and the clerk just handed them their keys without even thinking about asking for their key identification cards. When *we* got up to the front desk and tried the same thing, by just giving our room number and holding out our hand the clerk suddenly wanted to see our key identification cards. We refused and he said he couldn't issue us a key without it. Several of the orchestra members yelled out, "Wow! Discrimination in action!" Just then, some idiot orchestra member yelled out, "They're OK, they're with us."

The next morning I met the same black player at breakfast. We weren't really upset or angry, but still somewhat annoyed, so we decided to go see the hotel manager.

We presented our story, which really put him on the defensive. "Oh no, lads, we don't have a discrimination policy at our hotel. Please don't think that of us. It's not like the United States here, I assure you." We told the manager that it was quite an embarrassment for us in front of our colleagues. I think he offered us free meals for the remainder of our stay.

Ashby: Ridiculous, Watt, just ridiculous. Looks like you have one more story in you. Come on . . . tell me a story.

(Ashby leaned across the table and put his head in his hands like a little kid. It was very funny.)

Watt: OK, OK. Now, this one is so deeply insulting that I wanted to truly slap the person involved. It happened after one of the principal horn auditions I played for the Los Angeles Philharmonic during Giulini's time, when the orchestra politics were somewhat out of control—so much so that I went to Giulini to be sure he was going to be at the finals. He assured me that he would be there and that he was looking forward to my audition. In fact, when I walked out on stage to play, I remember him waving his hand to let me know that he was present. I had worked very hard for that audition and it went quite well as I remember.

After the audition, I was waiting anxiously for the results like everyone else. As I remember, the results were—they didn't choose anyone. As I was leaving the building, one of the executive secretaries, who had heard my audition, walked up to me and said, "Bob, I just want you to know that a lot of us were *very proud* to see you up there auditioning." That remark came so far out of left field—I was speechless.

There I was waiting to see if I got the job and she came up with that lame condescending shit. I continued walking away to keep from going off on her.

Ashby: Really? Unbelievable, Watt. Did she pat you on your head too? I mean . . . it must have been very hard not to slap her. OK, I've heard enough of these condescending stories, let's go play our horns.

# CHAPTER THIRTY-NINE

~

# My Sandbox Buddy

After dinner, Jerome and I went to the hall to play again. That night we read the celebrated Mozart horn duets. We got more into talking about missed notes and pitch—what was considered a miss to me was nothing to him. We clearly had very different approaches and sensitivities about playing in general. However, spending those moments with him were some of the most life-affirming times in my career.

Watt: So did anyone ever tell you that your lips were too thick to play the French horn mouthpiece?

Ashby: Absolutely, Robert Lee—a classic remark and just as classically ridiculous too.

We fell out laughing for a long time about that. We played another duet. In that last duet, there were some very low notes for the second horn.

Ashby: You have really clear low notes, Watt. Ya know, I wish I had more opportunities to play low horn, because I really enjoy it.

I explained how one of our principal horns always came off as if he never ventured below middle C.

Watt: Oh, whenever there were a lot of low notes or bass clef in the music, this principal would always ask, "What are those notes down there, Bob? I never play down that low."

Ashby: That's hard to believe that a horn player in a major symphony orchestra claiming he can't read notes in the bass clef—very expensive arrogance. Please tell me more, Robert Lee. It sounds like you have a crazy section out there.

183

Watt: (after thinking for a moment) Oh, would you like to hear the Mahler Fifth story?

Ashby: There's a Mahler Fifth story? Sure, sure, tell me.

Watt: Well, the two principals, one I'm sure you know, were enemies from the start. They were always fighting over parts or almost anything imaginable between two extreme rivals. So get this, the Mahler Fifth story happened during a performance.

Ashby: *During* a performance? God! I don't believe it, go on.

Watt: The philharmonic was well into the symphony and doing a fine job at playing that day. When the big *scherzo* movement came, with the big horn obbligato solo, the principal playing first on that concert was upstaged from the fifth horn position by the other principal. When the principal playing first horn started to play the beautiful obbligato part, the other principal doubled his solo, blasting, fortissimo, trying to obliterate the first horn with his enormous sound. You can imagine it was a jolting shock to everyone in the horn section. People from other sections of the orchestra begin to turn around as the violent assault was taking place.

The upstaging insanity continued as the two exchanged profane insults until the movement was over. I've never seen the horn section so angry and why the conductor didn't notice, I'll never know.

Ashby: So tell me this, how did the other principal get to play the solo horn part? That solo is not in any of the other horn parts, or is it?

Watt: Well, some of it is in the third horn part and even in the fifth horn. The other principal went to the conductor and asked if he could double up with the third horn and that gave him most of the notes in the obbligato part and the rest he could fill in, giving him a clear shot to savagely blast the solo, upstaging his rival principal horn.

Ashby: Ridiculous, Watt, just ridiculous, for two grown men to carry on that way—and during a performance too. So what was the fallout from that—did the other principal get fired? Did they go to blows, or what?

Watt: You know, Ashby . . . absolutely nothing happened. Management did nothing as far as I know. The conductor, as far as I know, said nothing. There was a kind of half-assed meeting with the brass players, but it was such a whitewash that it caused me to lose respect for those guys forever.

Ashby: My God, Robert Lee, that *that* would happen in any orchestra—and during a performance!

# CHAPTER FORTY

~

# Where Had He Been All My Life?

Watt: So, Ashby, what happens here in New York, in *your* section? Hopefully nothing like we have.

Ashby: Well, we are just fine as a whole. What you just described is really extreme for any horn section. However, I must say this—and I admit this only to you. When the other principal has a big solo part like the Tchaikovsky Fifth Symphony, I sometimes feel a little envious and I'm usually totally out of the building after I've played the first half of the concert.

Watt: Really—and why is that?

Ashby: So I won't have to listen to the other principal play his solo. Now, I'm not saying this is right or even the most mature attitude, but I have to admit that I feel that way sometimes, even though I'm the best of friends with the principal horn.

Ashby and I continued to talk. He wanted to hear more. So we went to his favorite watering hole across the street from Lincoln Center. I think it was called O'Neal's.

He could outdrink me on any day. I think it was also an East Coast thing of having a colder climate and a more intense lifestyle in general. We ordered grappa, which I liked, because it didn't affect me very much. I could still remain lucid and talk for hours, which is exactly what we did.

Watt: Now this next little tale happened around my second or third year in the philharmonic, involving a substitute horn player. I was playing one of the extra horn parts in Bruckner Symphony No. 8. During one of the many rehearsals, one of the substitute horn players sitting next to me kept looking at my part as if something were wrong. When the music started again, I saw the problem. He was reading the clef incorrectly and I told him he should be playing a D-flat and his response was, "Oh yeah?" I said, "Yes, I'm sure of it." He said, "Well, if it *is* wrong, I don't want to hear it from *you*. I'll check with the principal." I responded, "Well, *somebody* ought to tell you something, because you've been playing it wrong all week." He said, "We'll take this up with the principal. Let's go talk to him right now." I said, "I'm not talking to anyone." He turned beet red and said, "Ya know, I don't like your attitude."

Ashby: If it *is* wrong? That is just the most disrespectful thing to say—and *your* attitude? That is just so insulting, Watt. Sorry, go on.

Watt: The real drag about that incident was having that same substitute horn player on tour with the orchestra some weeks after that. We were in Italy and I had made a date with a lovely Italian flight attendant on the flight over. Now, Ashby, you can imagine *that* was uppermost in my mind. After a rehearsal, that same substitute horn player came up to me and said he wanted to buy me a drink and then talk to me. I reluctantly agreed as we walked to the Duomo in Florence, Italy. We found a bar right in front of the concert hall.

He began: "You need to learn how to get along with people, ya know that? You've got a really bad attitude." I told him that my attitude was none of his business and who in hell was he to come into *this* orchestra as a substitute musician and tell me *anything*?

He said that he deserved more respect from me, because he had been in the music business before I was born and if I was smart I would take his advice. I reminded him that I barely knew him and that respect was something earned and so far he had earned nothing from me. He said that he was a good friend of the principal horn and that should mean something. I told him it meant nothing to me. He continued, "Let me tell you something, boy, this is *our* music, white European art music, you're playing. This is the top of the music business. This is not jazz or rhythm and blues or any of that black stuff. If you want to make it in this music, you'd better shape up." I lost my temper a little and angrily told him that this was *not* his music. "Yes, it's white, but European white, not American white." "Now you wait a minute, don't you lecture me, sonny," he snapped back. I continued. "Oh, I'm gonna lecture you. Even your European ancestors can't claim this music, because most of them were prisoners, religious outcasts, or serfs, working under a feudal system and surely not writing music or attending symphony concerts, so let's get things straight."

He just stared at me, trembling in silent anger for a long time and finally said, "I wish I could get through to you, ya know that? You could be such a nice fellow if you tried."

I told him that I was done talking to him and to keep his drink, because I had a date soon and had to go. He angrily fired back, "A date? Who do *you* know over here, for Christ's sake?" I told him it was none of his damn business as I began to walk away. He said he had one more suggestion. I told him I couldn't wait to hear it. He said, raising his voice, "You know the other colored fellow, who's on tour with us?" He was yelling now. "I mean, Jesus, why can't you act more like *him?*" As I continued to walk away from him, he tried one more desperate measure, "Tell me then, are you a Christian? Maybe I can reach you that way." "That won't work either," I said. I left him sitting at the bar. As I walked out, to my great surprise, I ran into the rest of the horn section. They had been there all the time, off in the distance, *watching* and *listening* to our conversation.

Ashby: What, Robert Lee—colored fellow? Did he actually say that? That is the most outrageous of all your stories. And the entire horn section was listening? So they were *all* in on it?

Watt: Well, I guess so . . . that was so strange that whole scene. OK, let's see, as time went on I began to get calls from various contractors for freelance work in the Los Angeles studios. I took it when I was free from the orchestra. On the other hand, many players, when they got a call, say on the morning of a philharmonic service, they would accept the studio job and then immediately call in sick for the philharmonic service—usually a rehearsal—and then go play the studio job hoping not to be discovered.

A common scenario would be for me to get a call in the morning of a philharmonic rehearsal from a contractor at Fox Studios, for example. I would turn down the job and then when I arrived at the philharmonic rehearsal, one of the principal horns would have called in sick because he had taken the job I had turned down. The personnel manager would then ask *me* to fill in for the principal horn for the morning rehearsal.

Ashby: No shit! The personnel manager was in on the whole thing?

Watt: Yes, absolutely.

Ashby: My God, Watt, no wonder you think personnel managers always favor principals. Amazing! Go on.

Watt: Yeah—the whole extra job thing got worse. One morning arriving at work, I ran into the third horn in the parking lot. He said hello, but was acting a little strange. Next I saw one of the principal horns approach and he spoke in his usual manner. The two of them walked ahead of me, hurrying into the building. When I reached the stage, the personnel manager appeared to be waiting for me.

He walked right up to me and said the third horn would not be at rehearsal today and would I please fill in for him?

I just froze and looked at him. Then he said, "Didn't you hear me?" I said, "Of course I heard you, but I think *you* should hear this. I just saw the third horn coming into the building with everyone else. I saw him, did you hear *me*? He's here," I yelled. The personnel manager yelled back at me saying, "Yeah, yeah, I heard you. Now please go on stage and play third horn and don't ask any more questions." I refused to move. I stood and demanded he tell me what was going on. He continued to stonewall me. He just kept yelling, "Go on stage, please, go on stage!"

When I reached the stage and sat in the third horn chair, the second horn, who for amusement always liked to stir things up a little, said, "Hmmm? Interesting—I guess the third horn is on the same job as the principal horn this morning."

I looked to find the other principal playing first horn, quietly covering for his colleague. I later found out that the two horn players were right upstairs on the fourth floor playing with the Glendale Symphony, a regional orchestra from a nearby town that paid well. That kind of thing went on for many years. As new personnel managers were hired, it changed somewhat, but never completely.

Ashby: Unbelievable, just unbelievable. How have you put up with that for so long?

Watt: Actually I didn't. I went to management and asked for a change in my contract, that when I played principal horn I would get paid extra and they agreed. On the other hand, nothing was done about the double-dipping of the principal horns. They pushed it until one day they actually went too far.

Ashby: What happened—how far was too far?

Watt: It finally came to a head one fall when the orchestra splits into two separate A and B orchestras and each performs three short concerts in high schools.

On one of those days my orchestra, orchestra B, performed only two school concerts and I had already arrived back home when I got a call from the personnel manager, who was so angry he could barely speak. I asked him what was wrong and he said,"I'll pay you double if you can go play principal horn on the third concert of orchestra A for me. I asked him what had happened and he said something about the principal leaving the concert early to play another job and that he had just suspended him.

Ashby: My God, Watt. How did it turn out?

Watt: It was like a bad dream when I showed up to play that third orchestra A concert. The other players started cheering me on, making "Saving the day" jokes. "And—it's Watt to the rescue once again, folks! Hurray!" But you know what, Jerome? As amazing as it sounds, *the other principal* at the time tried a similar stunt and got the same seven months' suspension—almost back to back, they were suspended. On the other hand, it was quite a windfall for me, nearly fourteen months of filling in on principal horn.

Ashby: Quite an ironic windfall, Robert Lee.

~

# CHAPTER FORTY-ONE

# Who Was He, Really?

Ashby: So—let's talk about something else for a while. Something nicer, something interesting. This horn section stuff is just too dark and ugly, Watt.

Watt: OK, good idea. Let's take a break. You go first, Ashby. Ask me about something warm and wonderful.

Ashby: Let's see . . . aha! When are you having the best time playing your horn? Despite your crazy horn section out there, you must have a favorite musical situation.

Watt: Oh, for sure—when I'm playing principal horn, with my favorite person on second horn, who happens to be a lovely female friend. It usually takes place during a slow movement of a Beethoven piano concerto. There's something about his slow movements that really touch me. In those moments, I feel so content and satisfied that I pursued music and the French horn, and the fact that I'm able to make a living playing Beethoven's music and enjoy it as I'm performing it. It's almost like being onstage and in the audience at the same time. During that music, I also fantasize about beautiful women, holding them, talking about deep, beautiful ideas, and of course that includes making love to them.

So OK, next nice topic. Let's see, how did you grow up, Jerome Ashby? Do you have brothers and sisters?

Ashby: I was an only child, raised by a single mother—pretty simple. And you?

Watt: Ah! There were seven of us.

Ashby: Seven? What was that like growing up?

Watt: Looking back, it was a rather rich experience, although we were not rich by any means. We were quite poor actually, but it was always fun having brothers and sisters to share the good and bad experiences.

Ashby: Give me an example of a rich, shared experience, Robert Lee.

Watt: I remember a very early experience when I was fishing with my father and my two older brothers. It was at one of the lakes in our town. They were all standing in shallow water, but they placed me on a rock to keep me dry, I guess. My father was out further in the lake wearing hip boots and my two brothers were fishing behind me in their rolled-up pants. It was just about sunset and very quiet. I closed my eyes for a second just enjoying the cool calm breeze on my face. Suddenly I felt a tug on my line. I started to reel in the fish and just as he came out of the water, I heard my father yell, "Get Bobby!" Instantly, one of my brothers lifted me off that rock and high above the water, with my little fish still dangling on my line. The tide had risen suddenly and I would have been washed off that rock with my little fish.

The whole thing felt so magical. I felt so warm, protected, and insulated from danger by my family. I never forgot that little incident.

Ashby: (breaking into tears) God! I wish—sorry, getting emotional, I guess.

Watt: What's the matter . . . did I—?

Ashby: No, nothing—I just wish I had your upbringing, poor or not, that's all. I mean, when I was a kid, it was lonely. I had to *find* other kids to play with and share things. I was just thinking when you said "Sharing that warm experience with family," it really sounded beautiful—I guess it struck a nerve with me. But I tell you this, Watt. I always vowed that when I grew up I would have a wonderful wife and a house full of kids. And look at me now—that's exactly what I have and I love it. I truly, truly love my wonderful wife and wonderful children. It's a real feeling of completeness, ya know? What about you, did you ever want to get married?

Watt: Well, I suppose it was floating around in my head somewhere, but to tell you the truth, after growing up with seven siblings, it seemed all I wanted was space. I can't say that I ever had a strong inclination towards marriage. Perhaps it's a fallout from my experience with my parents. They fought pretty fiercely, you know—and I think it deeply undermined my attitude about marriage.

Ashby: But Robert Lee, are you not somewhat of a playboy? I mean, forgive me if I'm wrong, but I've always heard that—or thought that.

Watt: (sharing a good, long laugh) Seriously, though, to answer your question, I think playing in a major symphony orchestra in these United States, being a young black man, and not following a conventional line of behavior—like getting married and having children right away—makes it hard to avoid that stereotype. Actually I'm more of a romantic than a lady-killer type. In fact, I was very touched by what you said about loving your wife and kids. To tell you the truth, single men like me tire of listening to married guys complain about their family life and how they always want to tell me about some honey they have on the side. They think that's what I want to talk about, because I'm single and perhaps they can get me to tell them about the fifteen women I'm supposed to have as a single man.

Ashby: OK, then, that makes me more comfortable telling you my story: First of all, I've never had a serious relationship with an American black woman, like so many black men. I actually married my first love. Now please understand that I was a little nervous telling you this for fear you'd judge me. But now that I understand you are not that way—I'm glad to share this with you.

Watt: Fantastic—so you married your first love? Nothing wrong with that, Jerome, sir. Now, see—to me, *that's* romantic. That's the real thing, rich, bold, and pure. I commend you. How did you meet her?

Ashby: As you know, I played in an orchestra in Mexico before the philharmonic. I met her while I was playing down there and the rest is history. I now have my house full of beautiful kids—all girls, mind you, and a wonderful wife.

Watt: So life is good for you then? A wife and kids and a good situation in your horn section.

Ashby: Ah, ah, Robert Lee, don't start with that horn section stuff again. Give it a rest. Well, if we must talk about that stuff, let's talk about what you enjoy about playing the horn, the good stuff, the stuff you love, the stuff that got you playing so well—so early in life.

Watt: Like most musicians, I fell in love with the sound of the French horn. I tell you, Jerome, there was absolutely nothing so beautiful in my environment growing up in New Jersey. I felt that if there was a music world out there that I could be a part of *and* play this beautiful instrument *and* make a living, I was going to do it. I knew there just had to be more out there in the world than most people were telling me in my hometown.

I also think my emotional setup as a young man connected with the sound of the French horn. It had a deeply rich and, yes, romantic quality that at that time in my young life was indescribable.

People thought I was crazy to play an instrument different than my father, who played trumpet. No one in my world really knew what a French horn was—yet I was deeply drawn to it. By the way, it was a lonely vigil—loving something that no one else around you understood or could relate to. Did you have similar feelings about the horn when you were growing up?

Ashby: Absolutely, Robert Lee . . . I was a fiend, totally into playing. I practiced like crazy all the time. I listened to all the recordings I could get my hands on. I played in groups, read books about the horn, and I was always at New York Philharmonic concerts whenever I could afford it. I became an usher there so I could attend the concerts for free. Then living in New York did make it a lot easier to be exposed to what I needed musically and culturally.

Now, don't let your big swollen juicy water head take this the wrong way, but I must admit, Robert Lee, that *you* made it a lot easier for me to believe I could pursue a career playing the French horn. When I saw you playing on TV with the Los Angeles Philharmonic, I was captivated. You were *so* young and all my other black French horn friends in New York were thrilled to see you. It was a very exciting moment in history for all of us.

Now, here's something I've always wanted to ask you. What was happening in your world during that time? Did you realize you were making history?

Watt: Not exactly, not right away—actually I was feeling that the philharmonic was just showcasing me. You know, "Hey, look, we have a black person in our orchestra! Aren't we open-minded and liberal?"

I felt that way because—well, remember, I was the only black person in that entire organization and they did a lot of showcasing of me in other ways during that time. But I tell you this, when I realized how many people would see me on those TV broadcasts I came to my senses, and thought of all the young future black French horn players and other up-and-coming young classical musicians of all instruments and all colors. I suddenly felt very honored to be in such a position.

Ashby: Amazing, Robert Lee, just amazing, how different our experiences have been in all of this. So what else can I pick your brain about?

Watt: Whatever, OK, as long as it's not about French horn sections and principal horns. So, let's see, what about an amusing story of the black opera singer auditioning at the Juilliard School of Music?

Ashby: I'm all ears.

Watt: As the story goes, a talented tenor was bringing a famous Italian opera aria to a fantastic musical climax, which brought great applause from the Juilliard jury. But one of the judges wasn't having it. He jumped up, irate, and yelled, "Just what makes *you people* think you can just *bust in here* and sing *our* music?" The very surprised and deeply insulted tenor knocked the judge out cold with one swift blow.

Ashby: Ah, ah, I've heard this story before, so it must be true.

Watt: I got it from a very reliable source in Europe. Oh, what about the story of the legendary bassist Stanley Clarke, when asked by his teacher at Philadelphia Music Academy, "So, Stanley, what do you intend to do when you graduate from the academy?" Stanley replied, "Well, I think I'll audition for a position in one of the major orchestras." The teacher replied, "That's all well and good, Stanley, but you've got to be realistic. You know that a lot of people will be against your doing such a thing?" The young Stanley replied, "I understand that might be the case, but nevertheless I want to try." The teacher replied, "You don't understand Stanley, even *I* would be against your auditioning for a position in a major symphony orchestra."

Jerome and I had drunk ourselves into feeling pretty fine and mellow by then.

Ashby: But, Robert Lee, aren't we lucky in another sense, that Stanley Clarke didn't end up in a symphony orchestra as one of twelve basses, where they might have condescended to accept him as a member? And, and . . . where they would most likely have thought of him as a talented black musician who *might* have a ghost of a chance on the far side of hell of one day being on par with them, instead of the legend he became?

Watt: Yes, Jerome, absolutely, you're right, never thought about it that way. Then there was the amazing story of classic American racial prejudice that took place with a Canadian orchestra. A young and extremely talented black tuba player whom we both know auditioned for a well-known Canadian symphony orchestra and beat out more than two dozen candidates.

He won the audition hands down. He was congratulated by the orchestra's audition committee and told that in about a week he would be invited to play with the orchestra as part of his audition. After arriving back home, the winning candidate was told by the audition committee that there would be another tuba player brought in to play with the orchestra as well, so he would have someone to play against. The playing with the orchestra never happened and time dragged on. Then he was told that the player vacating the tuba position was suing the orchestra and therefore, there was going to be a completely new audition for tuba.

Then the winning candidate was called by one of the brass players on the audition committee saying that there was a certain American trumpet player from Texas on the audition committee who had a problem with said Canadian symphony hiring a black American—mainly because the symphony didn't know or couldn't really know about black Americans the way *he* knew them—that they were lazy, shiftless, and temperamental. Therefore, *he* didn't think the orchestra should hire that type of person.

The amazing part of that story was that the audition committee believed that racist Texan and started a telephone inquiry. They actually questioned people as to whether the candidate was lazy, shiftless, and temperamental. Later the symphony had another audition, hired another white tuba from Jacksonville, and never contacted the winning young black candidate again.

Ashby: Yup, heard some of that story, too. Pretty insane, Robert Lee.

# CHAPTER FORTY-TWO

~

# Tales from the Symphony

Watt: So tell me, Ashby, about some of the clashes you had with the music director.

Ashby: Actually, I was generally all right with him. That is, we didn't have any real clashes. Remember, I had a horn sound that was thick enough.

Watt: (laughing) Well, for me the major clash I had with him was over an ongoing debate about the way they were presenting themselves to the black community in general, and the music director was not happy about my attitude. Tell me, did you do those token black concerts here in New York as well?

Ashby: Yes, Robert Lee, we did those same token black concerts at the Abyssinian Baptist Church in Harlem.

Watt: You know, I became so sick of those pandering, token concerts that I actually boycotted one of them.

Ashby: Come on, Robert Lee, how does one boycott a philharmonic concert?

Watt: Well—it wasn't that difficult really. I just planned ahead. I just put in for a vacation week and they gave it to me. It was all standard orchestra bureaucracy and I did it so far in advance that no one noticed. The music director was very upset with me for doing that, because I was still the only black person in the Los Angeles Philharmonic—so I could render them "lily white" anytime I chose.

Ashby: God, my God—how you dealt with it all, I'll never know. Now— on another note, Robert Lee, how do we end up with such players like the

197

ones you've described? How do they end up with these top-level positions and then turn out to be so laden with playing problems once they arrive on the job? Who are these people?

Watt: Ah! Here we go—back to the horn section stuff—OK. They are an interesting group indeed. They usually have superior playing abilities when young and were always the big fish in their respective ponds. For example, they may be able to play super loud, super fast, and super high. These three technical attributes happen to be all they have or will ever have as players. They get over because when a player is young the expectation is that they will someday develop into well-rounded musicians like most musicians. However, many of them never develop beyond loud, fast, and high. They often move on into higher and higher playing positions because of their raw techniques. When they attend institutes of higher learning, their technique still helps them get over, even though they are seldom interested in learning any advanced musical knowledge and are therefore very poor and undeveloped musicians, but still manage to get all the playing opportunities.

In fact, many of them lose interest in music altogether. Music to them becomes a series of political/power moves. They have been spoiled by a musical system and culture that favors and rewards their limited superficial techniques of loud, fast, and high. They become desperately insecure, because little by little they start to realize that they are actually substandard and therefore develop enormous defense mechanisms. This usually manifests itself in the form of clever ways to attack other players about their playing—for fear such players will attack them first or discover their flaws. They tend to despise anyone who plays their same instrument, especially if said player is exceptional—in which case, they do all they can to destroy such players. They go on to higher positions until one day some conductor, who is partial to their particular musical superficialities, offers them a major position and then they are set.

For example, they may be hired for some aspect of their playing that sounded great in the audition but in reality is not sustainable for any reasonable length of time—like being able to play extremely loud—that after a few years breaks them down as a player and they start having problems playing. They don't have a clue about how to fix it. And I'm sorry to say that in white society, they are often protected—even coddled.

Ashby: Damn, Watt, give me a minute to absorb all that. Are you sure you shouldn't have been a Baptist preacher? Sorry, sorry—just couldn't help that, go on.

Watt: They are, at best, imitators who usually get their musical values and styles from recordings. They don't relate to the reality of live sound.

In fact, in a live situation, they try to produce the sound they've heard on recordings and they get led astray. They end up trying to produce a sound that only causes them playing problems. Like trying to play with a sound that resembles an entire horn section. As we all know, such a sound was never intended to come from one player. When they try to play Mozart, Beethoven, and Schubert with such a heavy sound, they simply can't do it. They end up using mutes and stopped horn and all sorts of tricks to play these works, because they simply can't play soft enough.

Jerome and I were pretty drunk by then.

From that day on, whenever I was in New York City for any reason, Jerome Ashby was the person I most looked forward to seeing and hanging out with in the world. He gave me so much comfort and at times a bit of a swollen head, especially when he told me that I was his idol from the time he first saw me playing on TV when he was in high school. I told him that whatever difficulties I might have encountered, it was all worth it seeing him show up on the French horn scene the way he did, winning such a prestigious position in the French horn world.

The next time we met was when I made a trip home to see my family in New Jersey. We met at his favorite watering hole and restaurant, O'Neal's. We ordered the first drink, looked at each other, and just started laughing:

Ashby: What's so funny, Robert Lee?

Watt: Nothing, what's so funny to you? I'm kind of remembering what we talked about the last time and perhaps tickled about what I'm about to ask you.

Ashby: What? Come on, ask me.

Watt: So, Ashby, did you get into classical music just because it was white?

Ashby: What? Oh hell, screw you, Watt—OK, I know what this is about. I know what you're working up to here.

Watt: You do?

Ashby: Yup, it's your roundabout way of seeing if I like white women, right?

Watt: (laughing) Oh God, no!

Ashby: You are just asking for a cold drink poured over your head, aren't you, Watt?

Watt: No, seriously, this is a big issue with some black classical musicians. It was the whiteness of classical music that was their attraction. A distinction, in their minds, of high culture—high above the uncultured, "average nigger," so to speak. Yet somewhere inside that person is supposed to be a love for their instrument and a passion for music. I mean, I've heard black classical musicians say the most ridiculous, racist, self-loathing things. I'm not kidding.

Ashby: OK, Robert Lee, where are you going with this now?

Watt: All right, for example, a black trombone player that I went to conservatory with had *this* to say,

"You know my friends back where I grew up thought I should become a jazz musician. I told them that I was not in any way, shape, or form a jazz musician. I was instead a *classical* musician who will one day play in a symphony orchestra with *the white people*."

Then the black trombone player moved so close to me that I could smell his breath, squinted his eyes half-closed and whispered, "You know, my parents wanted me to marry some . . . some black bitch, but I told them in no uncertain terms that I . . . I was going to marry a *white girl*."

And when he said "white girl," he threw his head back in a proud haughty gesture.

Ashby: My God, Robert Lee, he sounds sadly interesting, but with a lot of hang-ups. It's not that big a deal to be with a white woman, God! I mean, well since we're on the topic, I like white women, but not because I have disdain for black women. The truth is I can't honestly say that I ever met enough black women who could relate to what I was doing in music. So I think in my case I sort of defaulted to white women before I got married.

I mean, let's be honest, Robert Lee. How many black women did *you* meet who were involved in classical music the way you were—the way white women were? How many black women were on the music scene for you to choose from for dating or as a girlfriend when you were coming up?

Watt: I guess what I'm really asking is, did you or did we both get into classical music because we thought it would make us appear better than other black people? See, that's where my conservatory friend and all the other black folks who were driven crazy by this European culture were coming from—and it's frightening.

Ashby: OK, I see, I see, and that's too bad for them, but no, I didn't get into classical music for those reasons. But I tell you this, Watt, for me it was always the white women who were on hand, always the white women who were in my face ready to rock 'n' roll. And you know what else? To tell you the truth, Watt, after a while, after so many years of this same situation, I just didn't care anymore.

And you should know this about me. I was always the easygoing guy, often yielding to the path of least resistance. Robert Lee, like I told you before and unlike most of the black guys I knew, I never had a serious relationship with a black woman.

Watt: Really? I remember your telling me this. Still, I'm a little surprised.

Ashby: Why?

Watt: You mean you've never had the pleasure of the sacred black butt—and the sexy lips? My God!

Ashby: Come on, Robert Lee . . . I'm being very honest and serious here.

Watt: OK, OK, I don't mean to judge you.

Ashby: Well now, remember I told you that I married my first love and you know she's not a black woman. On the other hand, I'm not afraid to say that I did enjoy the white women I experienced and that's just the way it was. Nothing I can do to change that. However, having said all that (and he starts raising his voice) does not mean I would *not* have had a relationship with a black woman.

Watt: Come on, Ashby, calm down. Of course I understand you didn't have contempt for black women the way my conservatory buddy did, who actually hated black women.

Ashby: Can you give me any more examples of this black madness? Come on, Watt, tell me a story.

Watt: Sure, I knew a black symphony conductor who worshiped white women and white folks in general. He was the most demented black person I had ever encountered regarding this. He once told me that I needed to go to Europe, specifically Scandinavia, where the *real* white people and *real* white women were.

Once I was riding with him in his car in Beverly Hills, stopped at a traffic light. As the people walked by us in the crosswalk, he made a very bizarre statement. "I just can't get over these people's hair. Look at these beautiful white bitches." Then he turned to me and yelled at the top of his voice, "Man, let me tell you something, there is no better woman in the world suited for the successful black man than the white woman!"

He actually pronounced the word white in two syllables. I then asked him while he was in the middle of his madness why he excluded black women. Then he really started ranting and raving. "Black women? Black women?" he yelled. "Are you serious? I . . . I don't like 'em. . . . They, they are ignorant black bitches who have no class and I have no use for them in my life—ever!" The boy was seriously sick.

Ashby: What else ya got, Watt?

Watt: Oh, God! There was a black woman that I was totally in love with and thought I would marry. She was a movie producer. I wanted her in my life so bad, but there was something about my being a classical musician that *really* bothered her. I had just picked her up for a date one night when she started to interrogate me: "May I ask you a question? What kind of music do you listen to when you're not playing with the philharmonic, not playing record dates or movie calls?"

I told her, "As a musician, who plays live music all the time that I didn't listen to music like most people—in fact I don't just listen—I hear music. To answer your question, I listen to almost every kind of music: I listen to jazz, especially the old classic jazz, some classical, of course—I'm not crazy about rock, but some of the love ballads are good."

She explained her concerns: "Well I just can't hang with you if it's gonna be like—these parties with corny-assed white guys with curly hair, wearing horn-rimmed glasses, argyle sweaters, and corduroy pants, listening to Mozart, Beethoven, and Bach—talking about developments, recapitulations, first and second subjects of the last movement of the Schubert Great C Major, and then listening to examples of it—discussing it for hours ad infinitum. I mean if that's the way your life is going to be, count me out."

# CHAPTER FORTY-THREE

~

# Final Revelations

On that same New York trip, I met up with Jerome one last time. We had lunch at an Italian restaurant in midtown Manhattan and the topic came up of just how many black French horn players actually existed in the world. After a few drinks, Jerome started naming those he knew: Marshall Sealy, freelance player and master repairman in New York City; Greg Williams, freelance player on Broadway; Vincent Chancey, jazz hornist and freelance player in New York City; Jeff Scott, freelance hornist, Imani Winds, New York City; Willie Ruff, jazz hornist, orchestral hornist, and professor at Yale University.

There was Julius Watkins, celebrated Broadway player and fabulous jazz musician who was totally qualified to play in any symphony orchestra but was never allowed to audition in his day because of his race—he's deceased; Linda Blacken, orchestral and freelance horn player in New York City, a student of Jerome Ashby; David Byrd-Marrow, freelance horn player in New York City; Deborah Sandoval Thurlow, freelance horn player, composer, and teacher in New York City and New Jersey; Donna Blaninger, New York City; Nicole Cash Saks, associate principal, San Francisco Symphony; Deryck Clarke, jazz hornist, freelance musician in Brooklyn, New York; Maurice Grice, freelance hornist, Chicago, Illinois; Nelson Lawson, freelance hornist, Richmond, Virginia; Joe Lovinsky, Presidents Own Army band, principal horn, Washington, D.C.; Robert Northern (Brother Ah), Washington, D.C.; James Rose; Ursula Stewart; Chrystal Swepson; Mark Taylor, jazz hornist; Mark Williams and Larry Williams, Baltimore, Maryland; Rodger Whitworth; and David Dickerson, Washington, D.C.

In Los Angeles, I listed Emily Booth, freelance professional; Sid Muldrow, freelance hornist; Fundi Legohn, jazz hornist, Pan African Peoples Arkestra, band director, Oxnard High school; and Johnny Malone, freelance horn player. And—with a nice grappa—we toasted all black horn players, even those who played during the Civil War.

At the end of our Italian dinner, I asked Jerome if he was ever an usher at Lincoln Center.

Ashby: Yes, I was. What made you ask that?

Watt: I don't know, I just remembered your saying that earlier and I suddenly remembered a young man eyeing me when I came to Lincoln Center to audition for the New York Philharmonic years ago. Did you have an Afro?

Ashby: Yeah, everyone did in those days, Robert Lee. OK, OK, yes—I remember seeing you carrying your horn case, and I knew exactly who you were then, but you looked so intense and frightening that I was afraid to approach you, honestly. Remember, you were way up there to me. I was barely in high school then and to me you were "ROBERT WATT!" in lights, French horn player with the Los Angeles Philharmonic—I was intimidated, so I just watched you walk by.

Watt: So that was *you*—my God—did I really appear that stiff and unapproachable?

Ashby: Yes, you did my friend—you looked *real* scary. (We laughed wildly.)

Ashby: So, Robert Lee, what's your horn concept? I know we're going to fight over this, so let's get on with it.

Watt: Well, now, I always thought, and I'm sure you feel the same, that the French horn has a special sound and quality of tone like no other instrument. The most important aspect of this instrument is that it must sound authentic—like the great outdoors or from the French hunting field, where it actually originated.

Ashby: I'm with you, Robert Lee, and you must realize that I know all of this stuff—so anyway . . . keep talking.

Watt: I'm good for now—so OK, Ashby, what turned you on about the French horn?

Ashby: Well, to be honest with you, I would have to say the robust sound. There was something extremely masculine about it that I could seriously identify with as a young man. I mean, well, I didn't really get into the French hunting field stuff, but I guess I was mostly influenced by just being around certain players, like my high school horn teacher, Brooks Tillotson.

He had a son, Christopher, who also played horn and we both took lessons with him. After our lessons, Chris and I would go in a room and play together for hours.

Now I want to tell you, my first horn teacher, Brooks Tillotson, had a really big sound and *that* was a major influence, besides the New York Philharmonic Conn 8-D concept.

Watt: OK, I don't mean to sound pedantic or boring, but that 8-D, big, dark, heavy sound concept has an interesting history, starting right here in New York.

Ashby: What, how do you mean?

Watt: When Lincoln Center was finished, Philharmonic Hall was not the same hall it is now. It was especially bad for French horns. To improve the horn projection, the players adopted this 8-D, bored-out mouthpiece, dark sound without any high frequencies in the sound, expecting it to project better.

Ashby: Now wait a minute, Robert Lee, this is the sound I've always known and loved. God! I knew this was going to happen, so go on, keep talking—but watch your back, buddy.

Watt: All right—I know this is your sound. My point is that there were always horns that were built to project. The great German horn makers made really top-quality horns, which included the technology to solve the problem they had at Lincoln Center. But as you know, the problems at the hall were not just about the type of instruments they played. There were other more serious acoustical issues that I understand were later corrected.

Still, this idea of a horn that made an enormous sound without getting brassy was born out of that situation, of trying to improve the horn sound in that hall.

Originally, the Conn Company tried to copy the silver Kruspe and somehow came up with what we know as the Conn 8-D. This 8-D was also designed as a band instrument so it didn't *need* the projecting qualities that a German orchestral horn would have, hence the dark sound quality of the instrument. In fact, the Conn 8-D doesn't really sound like a French horn until you muscle it and then—

Ashby: Stop, stop, Robert Lee—those are fightin' words—especially here in New York. Be careful, my friend, you are in 8-D land—so if you see stars on the ceiling of this fine restaurant, that means I've knocked you out cold.

Watt: Oh my God, OK, I'm sorry, but I'm just trying to tell a story here, Jerome. Don't shoot the messenger—I'll try to be careful. So when—

Ashby: No, no, I'm not sure I want to hear any more of this stuff.

Watt: So, shall I continue?

Ashby: I don't know, Robert Lee, I might have to kick your ass right here and now—tonight, but I think instead I'll order another round of drinks. Go ahead, continue.

Watt: Damn, Ashby, are you sure? OK, as I was saying, the reason you and many other players ended up with an 8-D as a sound concept is because the New York Philharmonic horn section chose the Conn 8-D to help fix the horn problem in the new hall. It worked OK, but they still had to play plenty loud to be heard so they began using bored-out mouthpieces, creating an enormous sound, which needed a sort of puffy percussive attack to move such a big, wide, tubby sound. Hence the tonguing style taught here at Juilliard—

Suddenly, I felt two hands around my neck. It was Ashby about to choke me if I didn't shut up.

Ashby: Come on, Robert Lee, enough! It's not a tubby sound—it's a big sound, a robust sound! It's the New York Philharmonic style of horn playing! Get over it! I tell you this. In the rest of New York, the freelancers, the guys on Broadway and everywhere else in New York, they don't play like we do here in the New York Philharmonic. Bet you didn't know that, did you?

Watt: Well, I was getting around to—

I felt a cold drink being poured over my head as Jerome roared with laughter.

Ashby: OK! Robert Lee, I've had it with your story, but you may continue with your narrative—your lecture—at great risk.

Watt: Oh thank you for that, sir! Damn, that was cold, Ashby! So, because of the way the players in your orchestra felt they had to play for that hall, their style of playing developed into an *actual school* of playing—the Conn 8-D style—centered on a single make of instrument, the Conn 8-D.

Ashby: So how come you don't play that way, Robert Lee? Gotcha!

Watt: Oh, shut up, Jerome! OK, when I was with my first teacher I did head in that direction. I was in high school then and the first horn I owned was a Conn 8-D.

Ashby: No, I don't believe it—of course, I knew that.

Watt: Yes, it's true, but I sold it in my second year at conservatory. So I guess that was my departure from that whole concept. Some people might call it growth and some might say it was just a change in taste—a change from bad taste to good taste.

Ashby: That's it, Robert Lee, that remark calls for a penalty punch to the stomach. Stand up!

We were quite wasted by then. Ashby grabbed my shoulder and tried to punch me in my stomach, but he lost his balance and fell on me.

On my next visit to New York, I met up again with Jerome. As we approached each other, he said something like, "Hello, Robert Lee, so where were we? Oh, I remember."

He lunged towards me trying to punch me in the stomach again, which turned into a manly hug and greeting.

Ashby: So, Watt, I hope you like our Chinatown here. This place has great food. I imagine you have some really fine Chinese restaurants in LA, with such a large Asian population?

Watt: Absolutely the best.

Ashby: So tell me, Robert Lee, what vintage 8-D do you play out there?

Watt: I bought a very good Elkhart M-Series from one of my students who soaked me for it, but it really plays great and has an amazing high and low register. But—

Ashby: Stop, stop, but what? Come on, spit it out, Watt.

Watt: Well—it's an 8-D, which actually has a "burr" in its sound.

Ashby: A burr? I'm gonna have to slap you yet, Robert Lee.

Watt: Ah, sorry, sorry, that's what I was told. Now let me explain what a burr is. It's an unpure—

Ashby: I know what a burr is! See, now you're making me raise my voice—God! Ridiculous, Watt.

Watt: Shall I go on or are you going to kick my ass right here in the restaurant?

Ashby: You're getting close, Robert Lee, real close. So seriously, continue, I can take it—and if I can't, I'll let you have it in the face.

Watt: Oh hell, Ashby—OK, I'll continue in fear of my life. Unless the 8-D is muscled a little, it really doesn't have a characteristic French horn sound.

Ashby: Bullshit, Watt, but keep talking.

Watt: Well, sometimes it sounds like a baritone.

Ashby: A what?

Watt: A baritone horn, way too dark for the sound to project and way too uncharacteristic for my taste. Granted, it sounds enormously powerful standing in close proximity to it, but that sound with the burr and the darkness or the lack of high frequencies in the tone will not project like the German horns, which were designed just for that. The technology existed back at the turn of the century, when Ed Kruspe was first making horns.

Ashby: That far back? Look, Robert Lee, you need to understand this. I like to play loud and as far as I know I've never had a problem being heard. I mean, Phil and I get together and *really* pump up the volume.

Watt: You mean you practice playing loud together?

Ashby: Yeah, we also go for matching our pitch exactly and try to get the most volume possible and still stay in tune. It feels good, to tell you the truth. Haven't you ever done that?

Watt: No, not with my horn section in LA.

Ashby: OK, go on, I can't wait to hear more. (Laughing)

Watt: Holy shit, Ashby, stop laughing. You know, part of the reason this style of playing caught on was through the recording studio. Having a mike placed right behind the horn in a studio was one way to capture the sound the 8-D was making in close proximity. Many horn students heard that studio sound from LA on TV and films and thought they could produce it in real life, in an orchestra, for example. It does not sound the same.

Ashby: Your days are numbered, Robert Lee.

Watt: No, honestly—many horn players actually think that.

Ashby: Well, like I said, no one ever asked me to play out more. It was always, "Horns play less, please," or "Jerry, too loud," which kind of became my nickname in music circles. Hey, didn't you also have a nickname, Robert Lee? Oh yeah, I forgot, "Boston Blackie." (Really laughing now)

Watt: You're a dead man, Ashby.

Ashby: Are you done, Robert Lee?

Watt: Yes—well done, sir.

# CHAPTER FORTY-FOUR

~

# The New Brass Ensemble and Adventures with Madame

In the late 1980s, I got a call from a college roommate who wanted to start an all-black brass quintet. We lived in different cities but managed to meet in the most strategic one to rehearse. It worked.

The brass quintet idea was a perfect supplement for the dangerously small amount of playing I was doing in the philharmonic. It was also a project I could be absorbed in throughout the year until I could get back to Europe, which I had done for the past few years, playing music. This was the perfect opportunity to get in some first-rate playing exposure *and* with all black men—superb.

I had already made European connections for playing in summer festivals and now had an all-black brass quintet to play with me. I'll never forget the first rehearsal.

The first comment made was from the lead trumpet, "Don't tune, just play in tune."

I liked that approach and the feeling it gave the group, and consequently everyone played amazingly well in tune.

After the reading of the first piece, we all looked at each other and said, "Damn, you brothers can play," followed by great laughter.

Next the leader said, "Since that was so easy, let's try this." The rehearsal continued in that manner for hours.

After that maiden rehearsal, the group—The New Brass Ensemble— became a major item in my life. I can't say I remember how we came up with that name, but the group was great. We formed a partnership and began to set up concerts.

When the group came to Los Angeles to rehearse, I hosted them in my West Los Angeles home. They slept in sleeping bags and on sofas, we cooked our own food, and rehearsed for days. The philharmonic quickly slid into the background of my musical world. In fact, it was difficult to concentrate on the philharmonic while the quintet was in town.

In June of 1987, Esa-Pekka Salonen—who was appearing as guest conductor with the Los Angeles Philharmonic for the week—invited me to Finland. I just happened to ask him in casual conversation about what happened musically in Finland during the summer. He told me that many music festivals sprang up all over Finland in the summer. He said he was from Helsinki and invited me to his summer music festival outside Helsinki. The festival performed chamber music in the little town of Porvoo.

That year, my yearly European adventure began with a philharmonic concert tour in May. By and by, the philharmonic tour made its way to Monte Carlo.

To my great surprise, at the intermission of that concert, a middle-aged woman approached me, grabbed my arm, and said tenderly, "You were in the orchestra, am I correct? You know, you rather stood out from the others." She said this with a strong French accent.

I told her that I had no doubt.

She smiled and said, "So, tell me, young man, do you play golf? I ask you this because I live in Cannes and tomorrow we are all playing eighteen holes. Would you care to join us? It's only a little ways from here. I could send a car for you in the morning. Oh! Please say yes, young man."

I said yes, with great enthusiasm.

"Bon, merci," she said and kissed me on both cheeks and then introduced herself.

I said yes, because it dawned on me that the next day was a free day for the orchestra and I'd be stuck with my colleagues all day doing mostly nothing. I was rather curious why that woman picked me, but on the other hand I didn't care. It was *manna from tour heaven*, so to speak. I couldn't wait till morning.

At 6:00 a.m. I was awakened by the hotel reception telling me that there was a car waiting for me. I quickly dressed and went down to the lobby. I could barely make out a silver-colored sedan in the dawn light. The whole experience was beginning to appear quite surreal. The driver was dressed in a dark blue uniformish type of suit, complete with cap.

He said in a French accent, "When you are ready, monsieur."

I got in the back seat of the exquisite-looking car and the driver took off. I thought for a moment that this might be a kidnapping, but I didn't care. I was just happy to be away from the orchestra tour element. In about twenty-five minutes to half an hour, we arrived in Cannes. I had dozed off for a few minutes and woke up as the car slowed and pulled into the driveway of a large, almost castle-like house.

The driver told me, "Please wait here, monsieur, Madame will join you shortly."

Madame? *What had I gotten myself into?* Soon "Madame" appeared looking very dapper in pleated golf pants, fancy golf cleats, and an elegant scarf.

As the driver loaded the golf clubs and a pair of golf cleats for me, Madame greeted me in a robust voice. "Hello, young man, glad you could come. We are going to have a wonderful time, I promise you."

When she said that—the way she said it—told me that something special was in the air, given the intense and pleasurable look in her eyes. I must say she looked pretty good in the morning for a woman her age. Standing about five foot nine, she had black hair with quasi-Asiatic features. She was well preserved with an interesting regal swagger in her walk, sporting full kissable lips, nice smooth skin on her neck leading down to an ample chest, flat midsection, great butt, and long legs. I was forced to admit that even though she had ten to fifteen years on me, she was a fine feminine piece of work.

We arrived at the golf course twenty minutes later and I couldn't believe how beautiful the grounds were. I forgot the name of the golf club, but from that moment on we were treated like royalty. The doors to the elegant car were opened by uniformed footmen and we were escorted into an elegant restaurant for breakfast. I couldn't believe all of this was happening to me based on my looks or the fact that I "rather stood out in the orchestra." I kept thinking to myself, *It's amazing what can happen at the intermission of a concert.*

Madame called out to me, "Come, Robert, meet my golfing friends." There stood in front of me several posh-looking couples dressed in the same elegant manner as Madame. I took a deep breath and spoke loudly and clearly, just like my father had told me when meeting new people. I could still hear him inside my head, "Just say, how do you do," except this time I added my own confident, "So nice to meet you." After all, I was in my own world and my father's rules no longer applied. I felt very comfortable being with Madame, so I just sat back and enjoyed the journey.

As we walked towards the clubhouse, the footmen began taking our breakfast orders. We took our table and the club began to serve breakfast—the best coffee I'd ever tasted followed by croissants, stinky Limburger cheese with jam, followed by bacon and eggs touched off with caviar. I was starving. I could feel Madame staring at me as I ate. I looked confidently into her eyes and smiled. Then she began to tell her friends how we met.

"You know, I must say, I found that he rather stood out from the other musicians. I thought to myself . . ." She mumbled something in French and they all laughed, I missed it, something about my face and color. She immediately turned to me and translated her comment, while warmly touching my face.

As the breakfast conversation went on, I thought I heard someone address Madame as "doctor." I turned towards her.

As if reading my mind, she responded, "Yes, Robert?"

I asked if she was a doctor.

"Ah! Yes, Robert, forgive me for not telling you. I am a doctor of acupuncture and Eastern medicine. Have you ever had acupuncture, young man?"

I told her that I had, several times, and really liked it.

"Ah, wonderful then, we shall talk more on that later," she said with a tone of great interest. "*Nous allez*, it's time to *tee off*, do you say that in America, Robert?"

I couldn't believe how green the course was as we started to do warm-up swings. I told Madame that it had been a long time since I'd played golf and that I had taken several lessons from my cousin Nick in Los Angeles.

"Oh Robert, don't worry about a thing, just have a good time today and I will be very happy. You see, it's the company that makes an event what it is and not how well we play golf."

The golf carts came complete with caddies and we were off to the first hole. I had never had so much fun with people who were almost complete strangers. We laughed as we tried to play our best and I must say I wasn't the worst golfer in the group by any means.

After the first nine holes we took a lunch break and another small royal feast. More caviar, grappa, champagne, and whisky. I don't know how people still played golf after such consumption.

Madame touched me on my thigh and said, "Are you ready, big beautiful man"—followed by another aside in French to her friends—"for more golf?"

I said something in French that got a surprised laugh from everyone. I was having a great time.

The second nine holes went quickly and before long we were back in that regal car headed for Madame's house. I think the car was a vintage Bentley. Madame asked if I liked the car.

I said "Yes, and I like you also."

She instantly softened and cuddled up closer, grasping my inner thigh. "I'm so glad to hear that, Robert. When we get back to the house . . . if you don't have any pressing engagements, I would like to treat you to a little acupuncture. Nothing serious, just some points to relax you from our long wonderful day."

I asked her, "What part of the body would that involve?"

She whispered, "Whatever part I want it to involve, Robert—are you nervous, shy?"

She hugged me again while still grasping my inner thigh. She was all over me and I loved it. Then as natural as breathing, we started kissing. I thought, *Here I am with an older wealthy woman, something I had never really done before, and I am loving it.*

Madam started talking, "My God, Robert, you are so sexy and romantic! I'm so glad I *stole* you from the concert last night. Oops—I did steal you, you know—I hope you don't mind. Show me, Robert, how do you make that sound with the lips when we kiss? It's so sexy. Oh! Do it again . . . and again." Then she said, *sotto voce,* "I think I would like to give you a *very special* acupuncture treatment this evening—do you have the time, Robert?"

I told her I wouldn't miss it for the world. We both had a hearty laugh.

"You know Robert, I have some very special equipment in my office I hope you will really enjoy."

When we arrived at Madame's castle, the driver helped us out of the car and said good night. Then she actually said, "That will be all for the evening, Henri."

I couldn't believe she actually said, "That will be all." It was like something out of a Basil Rathbone movie.

Madame pulled me out of my awe by walking me inside her house with her hand firmly on my buttocks. "Hmmm! You are so very nice back here," she said, as she slapped my ass hard. By then I was ready for anything. It had been such an incredible day.

"So, Robert, shall we have a bath? Yes, Robert, together, if you don't mind. Are you sure you're not shy?"

She always seemed to be reading my mind.

"Now, off with our clothes," she said warmly. Then suddenly she ripped open her blouse and threw it on the floor, pulled my shirt off, pulled me close, and kissed my chest.

"You know that I'm a widow, Robert?"

I said, "No, no, I didn't know."

"So, Robert, big colorful man, I'm as free as the wind. So please help me with my bra, won't you?" She threw it on the floor as well, as we walked to another area of the house that had a bathtub the size of a swimming pool. "Please continue to undress and touch me, Robert."

Her body was amazing for fifty-five and I did have my way touching her.

She undressed me, stripping me down quickly with sensual ease, and said, "I'm glad to see that you are becoming excited, Robert."

That whole experience was so amazing that I had almost forgotten about my own body. We slowly walked into the enormous bathtub. She gave special attention to my male hood and said, "I want to clean this especially well—I have special plans for it later. . . . Oh! I'm sorry to be so forward, Robert—what must you think of me?"

I told her that I thought she was just fabulous. I especially liked washing her long shapely legs. I told her that I was having such an incredible day and loved being with her this way.

"I'm so glad, Robert—and again, I really hope you don't mind that I stole you from your orchestra. I couldn't help myself, you know," she mused, as we sipped chilled glasses of fine grappa taken from her bathside bar.

Then she said we should get out and dry off and prepare for the special part of the evening. She gave me a little tour of her acupuncture studio—or, should I say, laboratory? She said she sometimes did a little bit of chiropractic work with special patients and for that she had some very special equipment.

We were still wearing only bath towels around our waists. She looked incredible with her wet shiny black hair streaming straight down to her shoulders. She took my towel and told me to grab hold of two arm straps that were suspended from the ceiling. I put my wrists into the straps and she pulled me up so my arms were above my head. It felt really good to be stretched like that.

She said, "I know this appears somewhat gruesome, Robert, but it really helps my chiropractic patients. Do you like it?" Madame kissed me long and hard as I hung there like a piece of meat totally at her sensual mercy.

Smiling, she asked if it was all right if she rubbed me down with some Swedish oil as I hung there. While applying the oil, her breathing got stronger and she kept telling me how beautiful my color was and that she could not understand for the life of her why black people had such a difficult time in America. "You are such a beautiful people! How could they stand not being around you, touching you, making love to you? Ah! So sexy."

When Madame finished, I was oiled from head to toe. She had wonderful powerful hands. Next she rolled an upright table behind me and pushed it right up against my body. As I stepped onto the footrest, she electronically reclined the table until I was lying down with my arms still suspended above my head in the wrist straps. It felt good, like being stretched and massaged at the same time.

She asked me how I liked her little chamber of horrors.

I said it was very impressive.

She said, "Great, because we are just getting started, my dear Robert, so please continue to relax."

Madame began to place acupuncture needles at certain points on my naked oiled body.

"Robert, this will help you relax even more." She stimulated each needle by slightly turning it with her fingers. She removed the needles one by one and said she wanted to do some acupressure points as well with her hands.

I realized then what she was doing. She was stimulating me sexually. I hadn't known that was possible, but I loved the way it felt.

Kissing me, she asked me how I was doing.

I was speechless. She raised the table again to the standing position and attached my ankles to straps that were mounted on the floor. Madame adjusted the arm straps so that I was completely suspended, arms over my head and stretched from the ankles, totally nude and oiled. It was the most wonderful feeling being stretched that way. Next she began to explore me with her mouth and hands.

"Oh! Robert, you look wonderful this way to me, a sexy shiny black man with a beautiful body and beautiful color. I just want to have my way with you, if you don't mind."

I wasn't sure what she was going to do next. I couldn't believe how great it all felt after being stretched, stimulated by acupuncture and then by a woman.

Then she said she just had to do one more thing. I thought for sure we were finally going all the way.

"Robert, if you don't mind . . . I mean, this is really a turn-on for me, I'm not sure if you will like it . . . well, oh Robert, I want to spank you while you are stretched out like this, looking so beautiful and sexy."

To my amazement, she turned me over and began slapping my ass, and hard!

"Oh! Robert, such a nice one you have. I love to slap a man here—it makes such a sexy sound—don't you think? I hope it doesn't hurt too much. Tell me if it does and I will stop . . . maybe."

She kept slapping my buttocks until she almost collapsed into a trance, leaning against me, when she was finished with her flogging.

She took me in her arms and said, "Oh! Robert, I'm so excited, but I must tell you that I can't take a man inside of me at the moment due to a recent injury, but I really get turned on by a man's body this way. I hope you're not disappointed and forgive me if you think this is all too bizarre. I do find you so insanely attractive." I was somewhat disappointed, but didn't want to force the issue with her—I had such fondness for her.

She unhooked me and took me back to the wonderful bathtub. We again washed each other while looking into each other's eyes with strong curiosity. This was a great woman, a deeply interesting woman. We fed each other Italian *panini* and grappa until we nearly fell asleep while sitting at the bath tub bar.

"Would you like to sleep with me, Robert?"

I said, "Of course, I don't have to leave until—"

She put her index finger over my lips, cutting me off. "Shhhh. I know you told me. I don't want to hear of your leaving—it's a pity you have to leave at all."

I told her that it was the first time I had ever felt like *defecting from my entire life* and staying with her forever. I had never felt that way with anyone before.

"Ah, promises, promises—well—I dare you, Robert."

We slowly walked arm and arm—well, Madame had her hand on my ass again—to her bedroom. It was a giant fairy-tale canopy bed with curtains. We talked about her husband and early life, as she held my head in her lap doing pressure points on my scalp with her magic fingers. She had Henri take me back to my hotel early the next morning.

While boarding the orchestra bus, one of the brass players approached me very excited, asking in a whisper if I had spent any time at the hotel pool observing the topless sights. My mind flashed on Madame for a second and I just smiled and said no.

Then he asked, "So what *did* you do on your day off, Bob?"

# CHAPTER FORTY-FIVE

~

# More European Adventures

The next interesting city, on that long relentless philharmonic tour, was the great German city of Munich. When we arrived at the hotel, only half of the rooms were ready. I ended up sitting with the interim music director. We made lots of small talk, but what I really wanted to talk about never came up until I broached the subject.

As a lead-in, I asked him if he was happy with the horn section.

He said, "I'm very happy with most of what I hear, although I must say that I'm not completely happy with both of my principals." Then he asked, "The question is, Bob, are *you* happy? You know, I want you to be happy back there."

I told him that I didn't think I could ever be happy in a horn section where the music director verbally promised a nonorchestra member a permanent position, completely negating our system of auditions and renewals.

He asked, "Well, look, we can talk about this at another time—but things are going all right for now in the section, are they not?"

I looked at him like he was crazy and said, "No."

In general, I found myself very unhappy with the quality of the orchestra performances on that tour. I was ready to leave the tour, leave the orchestra, leave my life, and go back and live with Madame.

*Finally* the orchestra tour ended and I was off to the fun part of my trip. I thought about going back to see Madame, but I had things to do in Scandinavia.

Once on the train, I fell quickly off and slept for hours. However, when I woke up I was looking into the face of a rather darling blonde woman who appeared to be waiting for me to open my eyes. Somewhat disoriented, I asked if I was still on the train.

She laughed, and said, "Yes, silly, of course you're still on the train. Hello, I am Ann-Sophie, from Finland. What's your name, Mr. Sleepy? And what have you been doing in Germany to make you so tired?"

I told her that I had just finished a month-long European tour with the Los Angeles Philharmonic.

She sat up straighter in her seat and said, "The Los Angeles Philharmonic? Then you know Esa-Pekka Salonen, our most famous conductor from Finland—we love him so much. We have heard he is conducting your philharmonic."

I told her that he had conducted the philharmonic a few times and that I was meeting up with him in Finland at a music festival.

She almost jumped out of her seat, "Oh! You're coming to Finland! *Huuvaa!* [Good!] You can come visit me, I live in Turku, I am painter. What is your name again, Mr. Sleepy?"

She said that I would be very popular in her country because there was a shortage of men and that the women love foreign men, especially men with color. She smiled and started writing out her address for me. "Well, Bob, Mr. Sleepy—(still laughing) you have quite a long ways to go as yet."

I asked her how the train crossed the water from Germany to Denmark. Was there a tunnel or bridge?

She said, "No, no, silly, the train rides onto the bottom of the ferry and the ferry carries the train, the people, the cars, and trucks over the water to the tracks on the other side. While we are on the ferry, everyone goes from the train to the deck of the ferry for some drink, to see the water and to walk around—some people even kiss." She was laughing as she said this.

I looked at her long and hard.

She said, "What is it, Mr. Sleepy—Mr. Bob?"

I told her that she had wonderful kissable lips.

She became very quiet and said, "Oh, a romantic too, Mr. Bob—I mean, Mr. Sleepy."

After a long pause looking out of the window at the passing northern German countryside, I finally asked Ann-Sophie what she was doing in that part of Europe.

She had just come off of a backpacking tour of Austria and Germany and parts of Italy. She sounded very excited when she described how she and her German friends had walked for miles in the country on well-traveled and well-marked trails, which always led to beautiful country inns at the end of the day. These hiking trails ran throughout Europe connecting countries and all one needed was their passport.

I told her that her hiking trip sounded like the journeys of a wayfarer—a traveler on foot. It made me think of the wonderful musical work by Gustav Mahler, Lieder Eines Fahrenden Gesellen [Songs of a Wayfarer]. "In the music, a traveler tells of his lost loves, happiness, and pains in life. He has traveled all day like you did and he talked late into the night with the other travelers in the inns across Europe."

Looking at me through squinted eyes, she asked me where I was originally from in the States and what was it like living there. She thought she would like to visit, but that it seemed like it might be a dangerous place for a foreign girl, because of what she had seen on television. She wanted to know if there was a big difference in the East Coast and the West Coast. We talked until we both got drowsy and soon fell off into a restful train sleep.

When we arrived in Copenhagen, Ann-Sophie was in a deep sleep. I had to shake her hard to wake her up.

She asked where we were.

I told her, "Copenhagen, my stop."

"Oh! Mr. Sleepy Bob, you're leaving?" She yawned, reached out her arms, and hugged me. She just smiled at me ever so warmly and said, "Bye, Mr. Sleepy Bob."

I quickly departed the train. My reason for stopping in Copenhagen was to set up a concert at Tivoli Gardens for the brass quintet. I had an appointment with the head of Tivoli Festival, Per Holst, which I had set up from Los Angeles. The Tivoli Festival didn't pan out, so I was off to the next place. I took a night train across Sweden to Stockholm to meet up with Ann-Charlotte, a Swedish Ballet dancer whom I had met in a coffee shop in West Los Angeles.

I arrived in Stockholm at noontime. During lunch, Ann-Charlotte said it was nice to see me and that she was preparing to have a midsummer dinner at her house that night. Back at Ann-Charlotte's apartment, she said if I needed a shower I was welcome and by no means should I be afraid to be naked around her.

She said as a dancer she was used to nude males. So I took a shower as Ann-Charlotte was preparing for a rather involved Swedish midsummer feast. She was cooking all sorts of fish and had bought many serious-looking bottles of schnapps, wine, and vodka.

Later that evening, guests started arriving early and the drinking started straight away. Some of the most beautiful Swedish women arrived, talking loudly and excited about the evening. When one thinks of Swedish women, it's always the blondes that come to mind, but there were redheads, auburns, strawberry blondes, platinum blondes, crew cuts, and some were almost bald. I was kind of hoping at least one of the beautiful black women I'd seen earlier in the city would show up, but it didn't happen.

It seemed there was a different drink for each stage of the dinner. A drink with the appetizer, a drink after the appetizer, a drink for the first course, a toast for the second course, and it went on like that for hours. I was so ripped I couldn't see straight and it was at that moment that Ann-Charlotte asked if I might play my horn for her guests.

At first, I laughed in disbelief and then Ann-Charlotte whispered in my ear. "It would mean so much to me, Bob, and to all the women, of course."

She had me. My entire face was numb. However, I managed to play some fast things for the party. After the deep breathing that it took to play, along with all I had to drink, I became quite dizzy and swooned into the guests. They caught me and pushed me to my feet with another loud Swedish cheer and, of course, that called for another toast. The Swedish mid-summer party went well into the morning. I had breakfast with Ann-Charlotte and was off to board the boat to Finland.

~

# CHAPTER FORTY-SIX

# A Black Brass Quintet in Finland?

I arrived at the dock and was amazed at the size of the ship taking me from Stockholm to Helsinki, Finland. It was like a small city with many decks, restaurants, nightclubs, and shops. They called it "The Party Boat." I got onboard and wondered how the trip was going to go. While I was thinking that, I noticed that the boat had already started out to sea. I went into the bar and was shocked by the number of women sitting alone and in groups. Yes, there were men, but we were seriously outnumbered.

A tall blonde woman sitting alone motioned to me to come join her. She removed her thick glasses as she spoke, "Welcome to the Party Boat."

"Is it really?" I asked.

"Ah, you will see very soon, especially after the dinner. I am Eria. Can you dance, Mr. Big Brown Man?" She told me stories about the ferry and how crazy the party activity became at times. She said that some of the passengers actually got so drunk that they fell off the boat and drowned.

"So, Robert if you drink a lot tonight, you may use my cabin to pee if you wish, but," she laughed, "please, don't pee off the deck."

The next morning I was awakened by waves thrashing against the side of the boat, and then it suddenly stopped. I was finally in Finland. At first glance it looked very gray and gloomy. As I left the ship, I was motioned by Customs to proceed straight through.

"No need to show the passport," the officer said. "Welcome to Finland."

I took a cab to a hotel somewhere in the middle of Helsinki. I called Jukka, a friend of Ann-Charlotte's who was a photographer for the Helsinki *Sanomat* newspaper.

When I reached him on the phone, Ann-Charlotte had already spoken to him about me. He invited me to dinner and I believe we ate Russian bear meat that night. While at dinner, Jukka called Esa-Pekka and told him that I was in Finland. Esa-Pekka said that I should go to another festival on the west coast of Finland, because the Helsinki festival was not ready.

Naantali was a famous classical music festival in a beautiful coastal town near the city of Turku. Jukka said he was going there anyway and perhaps I could go with him and his family.

After dinner, Jukka reminded me that it never really gets dark in Finland during midsummer and perhaps we could go see the Sibelius house, which was not very far from Helsinki. As we left the restaurant, I was amazed at how light it was at 10:00 p.m.

It was in an area called Ainola. As we approached the large house of the famous Finnish composer, I couldn't help thinking about all the music I had played by him. I looked around at the countryside that must have been much of the inspiration for his music. Just then, I was jolted out of my thoughts by the loud roaring bark of a Great Dane, who was on the other side of the gate. I suggested to Jukka that perhaps the spirit of Sibelius would rather we leave.

Jukka seemed a little distracted for a moment. He said, "Yes, we can come back here another time—but there is another place I would like to show you from my childhood, not too far from here."

We left the Sibelius house and walked across the road to a wooded area. Jukka was searching in his mind which way to turn.

I could see he was confused as we reentered the woods.

"Ah! Just around this rock, I remember," he said.

As we got deeper into the woods, Jukka became more and more confused. At that point, I took note of where the sun was in relation to us. I didn't really want to get lost in the Finnish woods wearing tight jeans and wobbly cowboy boots. Jukka smoked a cigarette and then announced that he was completely lost. I told him that we were walking east if that was any help. He kept stopping on the trail trying to recall the special place.

Then we found a rather uncomfortable cue that things were not going well: a nice round mound of "moose droppings" lay directly in front of us on the trail.

Jukka verified, "Ah, there is a moose nearby."

We continued on our unsure hike, walking for another ten minutes, when we came upon another pile of moose droppings.

Jukka verified, "A moose has come this way."

I agreed, as Jukka became more and more unsure of where we were.

"Ah! Bob, I am so sorry, now I am completely lost."

I asked him in which direction Helsinki was from our position, and then a third mound of moose droppings appeared. This one was steaming.

"Soon there is a moose," Jukka started to say.

Before the words left his mouth, a hundred yards away stood the biggest damn moose I'd ever seen in my life. I had visions of Jukka and me being thrown around like rag dolls when the animal made its attack. I had seen it on a film when a moose thought a man was threatening his young calf. As the moose started in our direction, I spotted the road through the trees. We ran for our lives towards the road.

Once back on the road, like something out of a dream, a taxi appeared. We flagged it down and asked him to take us back to Ainola. We were only 500 yards from the Sibelius house. We drove back to Helsinki and went directly to a bar for a strong drink. Koskenkorva! [Finnish wheat vodka.]

The next evening I ventured out after a long practice session and found The Metropol nightclub, a large busy place with dancing and lots of smoking Finns. I went to the bar for a drink and as I raised my arm to flag down the waiter, I felt someone draw very near. I turned and there was an extremely young and extremely blonde woman almost under my armpit looking up at me smiling. She was very cute with very healthy-looking skin wearing a white T-shirt, perfect fitting jeans, and clogs.

She smiled and said, "I'm sorry to crowd you, sir, but if you want a table I have one over there. You are welcome to bring your drink there."

I took her up on her offer and sat down with her.

The young lady looked at me in awe and asked, "Why are you so thirsty, what have you been doing? You drank the whole pint before I could make a toast with you. In Finland we say, 'Kippis,' so now I must buy you another beer."

She returned with an even larger beer for me and said, "Here, thirsty man, drink deep, but this time wait for me—Kippis!"

We smashed glasses together and drank. She was no drinker, almost choking on her first sip.

I smiled and she said, "I am Anna . . . how tall are you?"

She said that was what she liked about me when she saw me standing at the bar.

"I have never seen black men anywhere as beautiful as the ones we have seen in the television from America. And now that you are here in Finland having a drink with me, it is a little bit exciting."

I thanked her, we introduced ourselves, and I asked how old she was.

"Oh, I'm eighteen and what about you, Mr. Bob?" When I told her thirty-nine, she didn't believe me at first, but then she asked if I liked younger women.

I told her she was quite the woman regardless of her age.

"So then you'll dance with me, Mr. Bob?" She jumped up, grabbed my arm, and led me to the dance floor. After the dance, she actually curtsied.

I walked her to the train station where she had her bike parked. She said she lived on a farm a few kilometers away and rode her bike everywhere.

The next day I contacted Nina Talburg, a dancer friend of Ann-Charlotte's who owned a dance studio in Helsinki. Ann-Charlotte told me to contact Nina if I needed a place to practice. Nina sounded great over the telephone and we agreed to meet at her studio in the center of Helsinki. As it turned out, she owned the whole building. Nina was from one of the wealthiest families in Finland. Her family name, Talburg, was in lighted signs on several buildings in downtown Helsinki. She said it was almost embarrassing to see the name on all the buildings, especially since the family had sold the business years earlier.

After meeting with Nina, I felt that I had really arrived in Helsinki. I went back to my hotel for lunch. While I was in my room, reception called and told me I had a visitor. I couldn't imagine who would be visiting me in the afternoon. It was Anna, the eighteen-year-old from the night before. She said she was in town and wanted to stop by and say hello. We talked for a while and I told her to wait while I took a shower. She said she would wait and if I wanted she would give me a massage afterwards. I thought, "God, what a great idea." When I returned from the shower she had removed her jacket and was standing there with her more than ample chest stuck out, suggestively covered by a T-shirt, and wearing tight-fitting jeans. She invited me to stretch out on the bed and she would give me a rubdown. She started at my feet, alternately massaging and kissing them as she worked her way up my entire body in that manner. She pulled the towel away and elbowed my buttocks.

After about half an hour, she said she was finished and that it was my turn to do something nice for her. Before I could speak, she ripped off her T-shirt and my heart skipped two beats. She was looking right into my eyes, daring me to negotiate her bare charms, and I did so, in a most honorable and gracious manner.

That evening I decided to take Nina up on her generous offer and went to her dance studio to practice. The name of the studio was Tansiiviitii. I had an entire dance studio to practice my horn whenever I needed. I really felt like playing and quickly pulled out my horn, but when my lips touched the mouthpiece, I felt a sharp pain in my jaw. I slowly opened and closed my mouth several times and realized that my jaw was dislocated. Then it dawned on me that I had done that to myself while having my way with

Anna's ample chest that afternoon. I would be out of commission for a few days. Perhaps I could ask Nina the next day what to do for this problem, but then how could I explain such a situation to her? I wanted to laugh, but it hurt too much.

The next morning I left for Naantali with Jukka at 10:00. The drive was beautiful with spectacular views of the ocean and the rocky west coast of Finland. When we arrived in Naantali, the festival had been going on for a week and the little town was bustling with musicians and tourists. Jukka took me to the housing office to find me a room. The women in the office took one look at me and started whispering among themselves. I knew something was up by the way the woman was talking on the phone and glancing back at me. I didn't understand her, but I knew she was talking about me. Jukka said I was very lucky to get a room so quickly in the middle of the festival.

When I arrived at my living quarters, it was not a room but a large old-fashioned house. It belonged to a very famous artist in the town of Naantali, Helga, who welcomed me warmly and said that I was going to have a good time there. She said that no one sleeps in Finland during the summer, so I was welcome sit up with her in the evenings and perhaps have a drink and watch old movies of Naantali. She told me that the house was totally occupied by women and she hoped I didn't have a problem with that. I told her that I would never have a problem with such a wonderful situation.

Suddenly, she called all the women from their rooms to meet me. There were about twenty young Finnish women of all types making their way down the stairs. One very young and strikingly beautiful woman who was drunk out of her mind started feeling my arms, touching my face and hair, and whispering naughty things in my ear. She planted a wet juicy kiss on my lips and embraced me. The other women quickly pulled the woman off me, placing their hands over her mouth. They were obviously embarrassed by what she was saying, but I was none the wiser.

I walked over to the performance hall, which was a large church from the sixteenth century. It sounded beautiful inside. There was a chamber orchestra rehearsing and everyone was standing, except for the cellos, old European style. There were two horns in the orchestra also standing. After the rehearsal, I started to leave when I noticed the two horn players approaching me.

They asked, "Are you Bob Watt, horn player? Because Esa-Pekka has told us that you are here in Finland. Would you like some drink, we are going to a pub here in the town? Welcome to Finland, we are the horn players here."

I asked Olli and Passi if they wanted to play trios for the many women who were staying in the large house with me. Helga called all the women out of their rooms. They came out into the hallway—and oh, how they came out. Some were only half-dressed and still half-drunk, wearing only underwear, one stocking, some were topless, some wrapped only in sheets. They all sat on the floor of the large upstairs hallway and we played horn trios for almost thirty minutes. My damaged jaw had snapped back to normal I was happy to find.

After the impromptu concert, several of the women had fallen asleep on each other. The ones who were awake asked me if I would like to go to the *kokko*, a type of bonfire that celebrates Juhannus in Finland on midsummer—the longest day of the year. They asked me if it was all right if we had to climb up some rocky trails to reach the top of a famous hill to view the large *kokko*, which burned in the middle of a lake. I told them it was no problem. Of course, I wondered how some of them were going to make it since they were still drinking that strong Finnish vodka, Koskenkorva.

It was early evening. The sun had gone down, but it was by no means dark, and there was the most indescribable reddish-orange light remaining—something the Germans call *Abendrot* [evening's red]. The young women filed out of their rooms one by one and gathered on the front porch of the old House-of-the-Seven-Gables type of structure. There were about sixteen of us making our way through what seemed like hiking trails that led to the top of a rocky ledge overlooking a large lake in the distance. We saw and heard fireworks and lots of yelling from across the lake. Suddenly, without warning, an enormous fire ignited in the middle of the lake. Cheers from miles around could be heard as the *juhannuskokko* [midsummer bonfire] blazed and roared even brighter. The bonfire was supposed to chase away evil spirits with help from the loud noises made by the many vodka-drinking Finns.

When we arrived back at the house, the owner invited me into the living room to watch videos about Naantali and to have some vodka.

When I said good night to the owner and returned to my room, there came a timid knock on my door. One of the much younger Finnish women wanted to talk to me.

She said, first, that she was a little bit embarrassed by the way some of the women were acting. She said, "This was not the typical way women act in Finland, this fighting over men and all is crazy. In Finland, especially in this western part of Finland, we are not used to seeing a handsome black American man like you in real life—we have only seen in the TV. We are sorry if we are always staring and acting like childish girls. This special time of midsummer makes all Finnish people a little bit crazy, because it's not getting dark so we don't sleep well and some people in Finland, like those girls, are drinking too much. I would like to apologize for them. Oh . . . and can I ask that I kiss your mouth and touch the hair? Is it OK—my English?"

# CHAPTER FORTY-SEVEN

~

# Enchanting Encounters

I got up early the next morning for a side trip to Turku. Olli, one of the horn players, was staying there for the summer and said he would help me find Ann-Sophie, the Finnish woman I had met on my train ride from Vienna to Copenhagen. Olli and I took a taxi to her address. Ah! She wasn't home. Olli said we could come back at a later time. We took the bus back to Naantali where Olli had a rehearsal with the Slovak Chamber Orchestra.

I was amazed to find the celebrated German violinist Anne-Sophie Mutter leading the orchestra. They were playing the Mozart A-major Violin Concerto. Now I understood why Olli seemed a little nervous about getting back to warm up his horn. That A-major concerto is a little bit touchy for French horn. It was written for horn in A, which means the modern horn player has to mentally transpose every note up a third, pushing the horn into the high register.

Olli nailed all the high notes, even though they were standing throughout the entire rehearsal. I was very impressed. I was even more impressed with Anne-Sophie Mutter. I had played that very concerto with her earlier in the year with the philharmonic in Los Angeles. I wanted to meet her then, but there were just too many people around her. I thought this was a perfect setting to meet and have time to talk.

She was quite beautiful in the way that only a German woman can be—strong bone structure and a nice solid body. When she played, she always held the most sensitive expression on her face, almost pouting.

When the rehearsal was over, I found her alone back stage. I introduced myself and we started talking about the concerto. I told her I had just played it with her in Los Angeles some months earlier. She remembered and asked if she had met me there. I told her that I knew I would meet her in another place—in another capacity.

She smiled and asked, "Are you flirting with me?"

I said, "Absolutely." I asked if she rode a horse.

She shook her head in disbelief, "Oh, no, no, I don't ride." She asked if I was a rider.

I told her that I had a German horse.

She smiled, "Oh, really, which breed?"

I answered proudly, "*Hanovarana.*"

"Oh, *Dressurreiten.* You ride that way?"

I told her I did and loved it.

She asked what instrument I played. "I don't remember seeing you, but I do remember that you got all the high notes." Anne-Sophie frowned a little, saying, "Ah, the horn is frightfully difficult, isn't it?" Then she asked me how she sounded with the Slovak Chamber Orchestra. She thought there was a slight intonation problem. In Germany the pitch is quite high—a lot higher than in the United States.

I told her that she sounded marvelous and that she played Mozart as though she knew him personally. She smiled and thanked me.

Then I actually heard myself asking her to dinner.

She said perhaps, if she could find the time before she left. Then she smiled again and said, "You're . . . asking me out?" Then she said in German, "*Vielleicht*, Robert, *vielleicht*" [perhaps].

I asked her if she would mind talking to me about Herbert von Karajan.

She said, "Of course, I have known him since I was a little girl. We should talk tomorrow after the concert about dinner."

The next morning I had a meeting with the head of Naantali festival, Arto Noras. I talked to him about the brass quintet performing next year at Naantali festival and he was very agreeable to have me as a soloist as well as the quintet, but nothing ever happened.

The very next day, I called Esa-Pekka to tell him that I was on my way to Porvoo. When I arrived, the festival people helped me out of the taxi as if I were some kind of celebrity. They took me to where Esa-Pekka was sitting, but it was a very cool reception. I think it's just the style of Scandinavian men that can sometimes be confusing to others. They are so reserved that it could sometimes cause one to think that they are cold and indifferent.

One of the conductors upon seeing me yelled out, "Hey, you're a horn player, will you play with us? Would you like to do a concerto?"

That was exactly what I wanted to do, exactly why I had come to Europe, to play concerti and chamber music. Esa-Pekka agreed on a Mozart concerto and it was settled. We would rehearse it the next day at the church.

The next morning back in Helsinki while checking out of my room, the female manager said to me, "We are sad to see you go, you are a glory to our eyes!" I blushed.

Arriving back in Porvoo, I was told that we would rehearse the Mozart Concerto No. 1 in one hour at the church. It was a beautiful medieval church that had the most wonderful acoustics. I was hoping the concert would be there; however, I found out later that it would be held in a park up the hill.

Esa-Pekka arrived with a small entourage of other conductors, greeted me, and then introduced me to the orchestra. The orchestra was chamber size, about twenty or thirty players. There were many beautiful women, with wonderful, innocent baby faces all looking at me in the most curious way. We rehearsed the concerto for half an hour and then Esa-Pekka rehearsed a string work by Sibelius. I was moved to tears by the way they played Sibelius. He was *their* composer and it was something to behold. They played with such intensity and depth of feeling. I was amazed at how much sound Esa-Pekka got out of that small string section. I was convinced that in order to fully understand Sibelius, one must go to Finland and hear Finnish musicians play his music.

After the Sibelius, there was a break and a chance for me to meet the musicians. Everyone was very complimentary of my playing. I could see on many of their faces the novelty of my presence. However, none of them made the same blatant statements that other Finns made about liking to see me or that they only saw black men on TV. They did, however, make me feel welcome. Some of the women took hold of my arm and led me around, introducing me to other people and claiming me as their own.

The next question they asked was, "Are you married, Mr. Bob?"

I said, "I'm afraid to answer that."

They laughed.

Esa-Pekka gave the order for the orchestra to head to the park for the concert. I just followed everyone and five minutes later we were all in a small park where people were waiting, as well as TV, radio, and media. Esa-Pekka ordered the orchestra, "Set up right in here near the trees and bushes." The ground was still wet from a morning shower and everything was lush, green, and fresh smelling. I was wearing a black T-shirt with the word "Avanti" in white letters on the back, jeans, and a natural haircut. Esa-Pekka made a rather long announcement about the Avanti Festival as he introduced me to the enthusiastic audience bustling with midsummer energy.

The concert started with the Sibelius string piece and then my concerto. I got a nice applause and Esa-Pekka started the concerto. About halfway through the first movement, I noticed some movement to my right. It wasn't just movement, it was uncomfortably close. Out of the corner of my eye, I saw a drunken Finnish man illustrating to me where he had seen a black man before. First he pointed his finger at me, then he actually started going through the motions of dribbling a basketball and shooting it. I was trying to get Esa-Pekka's attention to get rid of the guy, but he whispered to me to keep playing and finally some Finnish women discreetly pulled the drunken man away.

When I finished the concerto, I noticed that the crowd had grown larger. I was very satisfied that I had played a concerto in Europe with a very fine conductor who had appeared with the Los Angeles Philharmonic as a guest. I knew then that he would have some kind of future with the Los Angeles Philharmonic, either as a principal guest conductor or as music director.

The next day the local newspaper raved about my performance and described me as "coming seemingly from out of nowhere, looking like an Archangel (the large one, a messenger) descending on Finland and playing like a God."

After the concert in the park, there was another chamber music concert that evening. The other horn players were involved and they invited me for a drink before their concert. Just before I was about to leave with them, I noticed a beautiful, young, delicate-looking Finnish woman who was eyeing me and perhaps wanting to join us, but she just waved shyly to me and walked away.

The horn players snapped me out of my drooling trance, saying "Bob, Bob, come, come, you can see her later for sure. We are all kind of prisoners here in this festival."

I loved drinking with those guys, because they drank for all the right reasons—good conversation and good laughs.

They assured me that the lovely curly-headed woman with freckles was interested in me. They said, "Bob, it is known fact that Finnish women go a little bit crazy over foreign men."

Everyone played like gods at the chamber concert and again, I especially loved the sound Esa-Pekka got from the strings. The horn players found me and said we should go back to the medieval house and eat a real Finnish dinner of codfish and vegetables. I talked for some hours with them about studio playing and how music was recorded and put into the films in Los Angeles.

After several drinks and good conversation, they suggested we go to the sauna. As we slowly stood up, I felt the many drinks traveling through my body. At the sauna, we were to quickly undress and head for the showers. But before I could undress, the other horn players were already in the pre-sauna showers. I looked to my left and there were two more women coming, undressing as they approached. They were already topless as they reached me.

They asked if I was going in the sauna.

I said yes and they said, "Great, we will come with you."

For a moment, I thought they wanted to go into the sauna with just me. So, I said, "Fine, let me get rid of the horn players who are already in the sauna."

They looked at me quite puzzled and laughed, "Ah! No, we won't be alone, everyone is coming, Esa-Pekka, Jukka-Pekka, . . . everyone."

The next thing I knew, everyone was squeezed into a very large sauna that was almost boiling hot. Then someone asked me how I liked the Finnish custom.

I said, "You guys sure are pale."

They all laughed and then Esa-Pekka said, "Now, let us see how many scoops the American can take."

Before I could react, they were counting in Finnish as Esa-Pekka threw scoops of water onto the sauna rocks. It made a giant steam cloud that filled the entire sauna with an extra rush of heat. It caused me to gag and eventually bolt out of the sauna. They all cheered as I dashed out the door and ran for the "cold dip." The cold dip had tiny little steps to the lower pool, step by step into the icy splendor. I screamed as that cold water reached my midsection.

Then everyone came bursting out of the sauna and jumped into the giant swimming pool. After the cold dip, the swimming pool felt heated. I jumped in with all the other naked bodies and swam to the other end.

As I reached the other end of the pool, I was shocked to see Anna, the lovely curly headed violinist with freckles, for whom I had been waiting all evening, swimming towards me naked.

She spoke to me, "Hi, Bobby. How did you like the sauna?"

The sauna . . . the sauna? She was in the sauna, with me and all the others? I guess I didn't notice her because there were so many other wet white bodies and I was too busy surviving the sauna steam game. Of course, she looked magnificent wet and naked. Her perfect classic body was glistening from the water. As we talked and treaded water we held hands to stay afloat.

She asked, "So, Bobby, I feel you wanted to be with me . . . is this OK? Or do you want to go to the woods and see the midnight sun? It's very nice in here, don't you think? Can we just talk here like this, is it OK?"

I could barely speak trying to grasp that surreal experience. I thought for sure that I was aroused by the presence of Anna's beautiful naked body holding on to me in the pool. I thought, *I'll just stay in the water until I calm down,* but at that very moment, Esa-Pekka called out to us from the other side of the pool.

"Bob, Anna, please come join us inside. Everyone is sitting by the fire." There was no way I was getting out of that pool in my compromised condition. Anna decided we should go sit by the fire because she was getting cold. God! I didn't want to let go of her, she looked so wonderful in the water. I leaned on my back and towed Anna to the edge of the pool lifeguard style.

Climbing out of the pool, I was prepared for an embarrassing moment, which didn't occur. Once out of the water, Anna and I simultaneously looked each other up and down and smiled.

She said, "Bob, you look very nice." I told her the same, as we walked inside holding hands, in wet naked splendor.

Once inside we wrapped a towel around our midsections and joined the others who were drinking vodka and roasting sausages in front of a large blazing fireplace. The room was full of orchestra men and women with only towels wrapped around their waists. It was all innocently sensual.

The next morning, after I had warmed up, one of the secretaries came running frantically into the room. There was a cancellation of a string quartet for a concert that was to start in a half-hour. The secretary asked if I could play for an hour or so by myself, because the people were already waiting. "The radio and TV are already set up and waiting and there is no one to play."

She grabbed my arm and pulled me into a Range Rover. Then she asked, "Is there a pianist here who can play with you?"

I saw Ari, who could sight-read fly shit on toilet paper. I grabbed him, my music, and we all headed for the seaside. The secretary said that the place where I was going to play was on a cliff high above the sea. Soon we were driving quite briskly through the Finnish woods. It was dark with trees, but the road was straight and solid. After about twenty minutes, the solid asphalt turned to a dirt road; however, the driver never changed speed to compensate.

After a while, I could see far in the distance a beautiful house high on a cliff. It looked like something from *Wuthering Heights*: a lone house on a seaside cliff. Soon, a rough Finnish sea came into the picture and I could see exactly where the dirt road led. After about ten more minutes, we arrived. There were people outside as if a wedding or funeral were going to occur. But no, it was just going to be me playing, with Ari on piano—two people who had never played together and less than an hour ago had no idea they were going to entertain a houseful of people. It was going to be a fascinating leap of faith—a huge adrenalin rush for the insanely adventurous.

# CHAPTER FORTY-EIGHT

~

# What I Live For

When Ari and I emerged from the Range Rover, we were welcomed like celebrities. TV and radio crews were following us as we entered the spectacular seaside house. We looked at each other laughing, because we knew we were going to have to wing it, since we had never played together—but I knew he was a fantastic sight-reader who would enjoy the adventure.

As we entered, there were even more people comfortably seated around a large room with a panoramic view of the ocean. When I saw the piano, I knew we were in for a *real* adventure. It was an old upright with antique woodwork covering it. It was out of tune, and when Ari gave me the A, I knew I had to make a sizable adjustment to the tuning slide on my horn. The A was flat, but for French horn that was better than being sharp.

When we walked out to play, the entire audience stood and applauded. It was almost humorous, since all of this was completely impromptu. Ari had never played or heard any of the music that I was going to perform. As he started the first movement, I knew then that I might be facing another disaster. He started the introduction twice as slow and I couldn't get his attention, because he had his head down almost touching his knuckles. He was totally into the music. I figured I would just *up the tempo* when I came in with my part.

There were scores of beautiful women sitting around the large beer-hall-size room. They looked at me with such delightfully curious expressions, as if they were thinking, "Hmm? A live black man from America, that we normally only see on the TV." Or, "How will he play?" However, all such thoughts vanished when it came time to play. I started the Franz Strauss at my chosen tempo to indicate to Ari that he was much too slow. He quickly took my cue and was right there with me until the end of the piece. A big applause—I even heard a few, "*Huuvaa . . . huuvaa!* [Bravo!] from the back of the room. After the Franz Strauss, Ari filled in the first half with a new work he had written.

When Ari finished, there was an intermission and everyone headed for the large dining room where a table was set with all sorts of Finnish delights. There were glasses of Koskenkorva lined up on the table along with red and black caviar, salmon on black bread, and fish stews. People came running up to me asking where I was from. Was I American? African? When I said Los Angeles, most of them asked if I knew Esa-Pekka. Someone hidden in the crowd asked if I was married. Some people asked who managed me and was I a soloist in America. I wanted to yell to the top of my voice that I just found out about this concert an hour ago, but I was having too much fun letting the people imagine things about me. As I answered all the questions, the TV cameras pushed in to interview me and several radio stations were holding their mikes over my head. I kept thinking how this was more than I could have ever wished for. I had wanted to come to Europe and play as a soloist and here I was on Finnish TV and radio doing just that.

Hearing my mentor, Jones, in my head, I couldn't help but reflect on what a wonderful thing it was to be a black man in this world—having everyone curious about me or, if not curious, still holding in their minds some form of exaggerated mythos. All the staring was enough to make one's head swell way out of proportion. At the end of the interviews, someone handed me a glass of vodka and said loudly, "*Kiipis.*"

On the second half of my impromptu recital, I played the C. D. Lorenz, an arrangement of arias from Bellini's opera *I Puritani*. I really had fun with that piece and everyone seemed to enjoy the playful humor in the work, especially the coloratura sections. Ari played like a god. I even think I heard him singing *sotto voce* [under his voice] sometimes. I loved playing with him. For an encore, I played some of the variations from the *Carnival of Venice* and the day was mine.

After the concert, several of the children, dressed in traditional Finnish folk dress, wanted to take a photograph with me. I said my goodbyes and was briskly driven back through the Finnish woods feeling like Robin Hood. It was early evening when we arrived back at Porvoo. The secretary from the Avanti Festival thanked Ari and me for filling in on such short notice.

The final event of the Avanti Festival was a sit-down dinner for everyone. When I sat down with the horn players, they were already ripped and asked me to join them in some vodka. I didn't want to leave the Avanti Festival, but it was over.

# CHAPTER FORTY-NINE

~

# "It's Good to Be Negro!"

During my time in Europe, I made a few contacts for the engagement of the quintet. Finland, by far, was the best prospect. I contacted the people at the famous Lieksa Brass Week in northern Finland. After hearing our tape, they invited us to the festival and paid us a nice fee in advance to perform during their brass week.

The group was very excited. I was very excited, because I had an ensemble to play with that really challenged me as a player. It was something that was mine—something I started with several black men—and The New Brass Ensemble was working very well.

Finally the time came to take the quintet to Finland. Our first meeting in Helsinki was quite funny and just plain "black male craziness." We adopted "Attack of the Killer Pimps" from the movie *Hollywood Shuffle* as our greeting ritual when we met at an airport—that crazy scene of a dozen pimps all grouped together walking like zombies, shaking, trembling, and foaming at the mouth.

I had been up late many a night on the phone with the festival. They were looking forward to having the group at their brass week. We were all to meet in Helsinki and take a train up north to Finland. The Lieksa Brass Week had arranged for the quintet to play in several towns on our way up to Lieksa. One of the first towns was Kuusankoski. We spent several days there rehearsing, played one concert, and went to Lappeenranta for another few days, played a rehearsal and concert, and finally arriving in Lieksa where we stayed for about ten days.

The festival in Finland had booked our train for us as a group with a private compartment. It looked like we were going to receive the red carpet treatment all the way. When we arrived at our first stop in the town of Kuu-sankoski, there was a group of Finnish men and women waiting to greet us. They came with taxis and a warm "Welcome to Finland." We were driven to our hotel and told to relax by having a Finnish sauna.

Therein came the first cultural clash. Our female hosts came to our rooms and escorted us to the hotel sauna. They told us, as I was told on my first visit to Finland, "Gentlemen, in Finland we don't wear clothes in the sauna, so please don't be afraid to be naked. It is our custom. No bathing suits, please."

The entire group turned and looked at me and asked, "Really? No clothes . . . you mean 'neckit'?"

Everyone began to strip down, laughing wildly as we ran naked into the very hot sauna. I could see the restrained delight on the faces of our female Finnish hosts as their eyes feasted on the naked black men. Once in the sauna, the women poured water on the rocks, creating that wonderful steam surge that took everyone's breath away.

Then they began showing everyone the way to use *vasta* (birch leaves tied together to stimulate the blood circulation by flogging the body). The group loved that concept. "Whoooo! This is kinky, I like it!" someone yelled. Then the hotel sent in some Finnish vodka for us.

There was such a sense of cultural shock, yet a great sense of freedom being naked with those lovely Finnish women showing us their customs. I was glad to have had that experience under my belt from the previous summer in Finland.

At the concerts, we had an interpreter for our musical commentary. There always seemed to be one person from the community who spoke English well. The audiences were large and very receptive. I always looked forward to the events after the concerts, mainly because I knew from the previous year that the Finnish people knew how to party. Our hosts always had things arranged and there was a reception after the concert in Kuusankoski. Little did we know that half the town would show up. Women of every size and age seemed to show up, whether they had attended the concert or not.

The quintet always seemed to be surrounded by lovely ladies buying us drinks, feeding us like Greek gods, hugging and kissing, or just *making over* us in general. It was always in the heat of such high times that we toasted each other, saying, "It's good to be Negro, except in America!" And as always before concerts we formed a circle, put our trembling "jazz hands" together, looking each other in the eyes while making our trademark sound, a quiet

"Woooooooooooooooo." This always made the Finns laugh because it was our private brand of silliness, our black maleness, and our good luck ritual.

Our group played well and I felt proud to be on stage with them. Our tours took us to venues like the Kennedy Center in Washington, D.C.; Severance Hall in Cleveland; The Harlem School for the Arts; and once again we were invited back to Finland for the Lieksa Brass Week. Unfortunately, the group ended its short, five-year run because of personal conflicts.

# CHAPTER FIFTY

~

# Missing Miles

In 1991, Mr. Willis Edwards—an extraordinary man, whom I always dubbed the Cardinal Woolsey of black politicians—introduced me to Barbara, an extraordinary black Canadian woman who was a wardrobe stylist and clothing entrepreneur in Los Angeles.

A short time after we began dating, she told me that she thought I should meet Miles Davis, the celebrated, Grammy-award-winning, legendary jazz trumpet player, who ushered in the bebop era of jazz and the cool jazz period, in which he used nontraditional jazz instruments for the recording *Birth of the Cool*.

She said she was friends with his wife and consequently had known Miles for many years. I asked her why she thought *I* should meet him. Granted, I had always been very impressed with him, but I was also content to know him from afar, based on the negative public relations hype that had always been associated with him. He was said to be volatile, moody, and just mean.

However, Barbara said that, unlike most people, I would more than likely get along with him, because she felt that we had some similar personality traits. I had mixed feelings about what she was saying. On the one hand, I was curious to know just what it was she saw in me that made her think I would get along with Miles Davis. Still, I couldn't help but feel excited by the idea of meeting the famous jazz trumpeter, if only to find out if my bias was even remotely accurate. Miles Davis, my friend? *A real stretch*, I thought.

My dressage horse, Mandela, was boarded just one mile south of the Miles Davis house on Pacific Coast Highway at the Malibu Riding and Tennis

Club where I was a member. As time went by, Barbara continued to bring up the idea of my meeting Miles. She had gone so far as to tell him about me and, since she was a very close friend of his, he became curious. She told him that I played French horn with the Los Angeles Philharmonic and that I had a dressage horse boarded just a mile from his house.

According to Barbara, Miles asked, in his raspy voice, "You say he plays French horn in the LA Philharmonic and the nigger rides a horse too? I gotta see this shit, damn! If he plays in the philharmonic I *know* he caught hell, 'cause there are some sorry motherfuckers in that brass section. You think he'd mind coming over here after he rides his horse one of these days so I can check him out—I mean, meet him? Going out with my fine friend, shit."

All the discussion about my meeting him so he could check me out finally evolved into a day and a time.

Barbara had promised Miles that she would come up to Malibu and cook collard greens and her special cornbread with the whole kernels of corn mixed throughout, which Miles just craved.

"Goddamn, I'd walk forty miles for a piece of that cornbread. That shit's so good it makes your dick hard . . . and she don't be talkin' all loud and shit like most of these black bitches . . . all she says is, '*Hey*' in that real quiet soothing tone. . . . I like that shit."

Unfortunately, it turned out that Barbara had to go to traffic school on the chosen day and after some discussion with the "Chief" (as he was called by his musicians), Barbara broke the news to him that she would not be able to come there and introduce me as planned. Miles, somewhat disappointed, asked Barbara if she thought I would mind bringing the collard greens and smoked turkey wings for him to cook and at which time he could check me out thoroughly. "He *should* be afraid, motherfucker."

The next time I saw Barbara, she told me all the things she had discussed with Miles and that it turned out that he actually wanted to meet me.

"He *wants* to meet me?"

"Yes," Barbara replied. "I think that I might have gotten a little carried away describing you to him, now he's really curious and wants to know if you could come by after you ride on Saturday and bring the collard greens and smoked turkey wings with you?"

I suppose I looked somewhat incredulous to Barbara and she added, "I know how you're feeling, but you two should do fine. However, I must warn you, Bob, when you meet him . . . if he *doesn't like you* for some reason, you will know instantly. In that case, just hand him the collard greens and leave. Don't try to fix it."

The very next day, Barbara came to my house with the collard greens and smoked turkey wings. Now I was committed. I had to go see Miles in the next few days or the celebrated "soul food" would surely spoil. I chose the next day, which was Saturday. I went up early morning to work my Dutch Warmblood dressage horse. It was a task I managed four to five times a week. I had to ride him, especially since I was just getting used to him. He was trained to the highest level in dressage and I had to learn how to ride him. He was a hundred times more sensitive than my previous horses.

Finally the day had come. It was the kind of stuff that invaded your entire body until it was over. Even the night before, I could feel that nagging anticipation while sleeping. While I was working my horse, I felt extra tension in my body and so did my horse. I cut my riding session short and proceeded up the coast to the Miles Davis house. My curiosity was screaming inside of me. Here I was on my way to the home of Miles Davis with smoked turkey wings and collard greens and I didn't even know the man.

At that moment, I concentrated hard on clearing my mind of all preconceived notions about him that had seeped into my belief system over the years. I just got into the moment of what was about to happen in the next ten minutes and programmed myself. Whatever happened would be a positive and memorable experience.

Suddenly I was snapped out of my daydreaming by my arrival at his house, which was on the west side of the Pacific Coast Highway just a hundred yards from the ocean. What a spectacular location—and a fabulous house.

I was getting a little nervous as I approached. I pulled my graphite-colored Volvo next to a sleek gray Ferrari. Now I was scared. I took a deep breath, opened my car door, and headed up his walkway. There before me stood a twelve-foot-high wooden door, which looked like it was made from petrified wood. I found a string of rusty bells hanging next to the door. There was no doorbell so I shook the rusty string of bells, which didn't make a hell of a lot of noise. Then I knocked on the extremely hard, grooved wooden door with my fist and it didn't make any sound at all, but it really hurt my hand.

Suddenly the huge "Great Gate of Kiev"–sized door slowly opened, revealing the pint-size head of a teenager. It was Erin, the youngest son of Miles. He was wearing a wetsuit and peering around the door as if he couldn't wait to get a look at me, as if he'd be sitting in on all the conversations about me. As the door opened wider, there, in all that is regal about splendor, stood the great Miles Dewey Davis. He glared right through my being as if we were engaged in a laser-beam battle of the eyes. His eyes were large and bright white against his rich black skin, making him appear like an African teak statue with diamond eyes that had suddenly come alive. Never moving a muscle, he just stood there with two large paintbrushes crisscrossing his chest, like the crook and flail of an Egyptian pharaoh.

He quietly looked me up and down and finally said, "Big motherfucker . . . Barbara's just a little thing." Pausing, he motioned me into the living room, never taking his eyes off of my face. He said, "I can see you play that horn, you got that ring around your upper lip. You practice a lot—or just eat a lot of pussy?" Chuckling, he broke down and said, "Aw shit—I'm sorry, man. I'm Miles Davis. Please have a seat." Never taking his large, bright white eyes off of me, he thanked me for bringing the collard greens and smoked turkey wings. "Where's Barbara?" he blurted out. "Oh yeah, shit, she had to go to traffic school?"

Miles took the greens and dumped them into a large pot that was already boiling. Then he shouted, "Greens, greens, the way to a motherfucker's soul!" Then I noticed that he forgot to remove the hemp string wrapped around the greens. I said, "Miles, take the string off." He said, "Fuck it, fuck it. . . . It'll all cook up. . . . Fuck it."

He got a phone call. Someone was coming over to photograph one of his paintings. While on the phone, he lowered his voice and looked around to see if anyone else was listening besides me. Then with a guilty expression, whispered to the person on the phone, "And bring some glazed donuts . . . yeah, a dozen." He looked at me as if it mattered to me what he was asking. He hung up the phone and looked around as if he had gotten away with murder.

He jumped up from the telephone and went to check on the boiling caldron of collard greens. He opened the pot and let out a big "Ahhhh! That shit smells good . . . but you know . . . I think they still need something. I can't put my finger on it. So, Bob, who do you know that knows how to cook these motherfuckin' greens? Where's Barbara? Oh shit . . . that's right, she can't come."

I told Miles that the only person I knew that could tighten-up his greens was my mother.

"Your mother . . . shit, OK, where's your mother?"

I told him New Jersey.

He said, "Fuck it, fuck it, call her up—use my phone, go ahead."

I called my mother, telling her that I had a man here who needed help cooking some collard greens.

Miles got on the phone with my mother and he suddenly took on a totally different demeanor. He sounded like a little kid talking to his grandmother. "Hello, Bob's mother, this is Miles Davis. Can you please help me with these collard greens? I already have them boiling, but there's something missing." He started making a list of ingredients.

I could hear my mother rattling off her recipe from the top of her head. Miles was very attentive. "Yes, ma'am, one whole potato, garlic, two tablespoons of sugar or cloves. . . ." When Miles was finished, he handed me the phone.

My mother was quite curious. "Was that really him?" she asked.

I told her yes and that I would call her later.

Miles began to lecture me about how lucky I was to have a mother like her. "I'm going to tell you something, Bob. You are one lucky motherfucker. Your mother taught you how to hold your head up as a black man, you know that? You should be thankful you had a person like that in your corner."

I asked him, "How is it possible that you know that?"

He said, "I just talked to her."

I said, "But you talked about—collard greens and cloves, whole potatoes, garlic—"

Miles interjected, "I know, I know, I can do that . . . that's ma' shit."

There was one thing I noticed about him. He had little quiet spells where he wouldn't say anything, but I knew instinctively not to invade those moments by talking. I always let him break that unique silence. It always seemed to work and it was always worth the wait.

Miles's silence was broken by the doorbell ringing. Well, there was no doorbell, but someone was at the door. I was amazed that I could hear someone knocking on that giant wooden door that had hurt my hand so much. It was the person he had talked to on the phone.

The young man entered with camera equipment and lights. He was also carrying a medium-sized brown paper bag that had large grease spots all over it from the glazed donuts inside.

When his son Erin saw that greasy bag, he started in on Miles. "Dad, you know you can't eat those, now come on—"

Miles lashed back at him, "I'll eat what I motherfuckin' please."

Erin quickly came into the kitchen and pleaded with me and the photographer to eat as many of the glazed donuts as we could, because his father was diabetic and sweets like that were deadly for him.

Miles checked on the greens again, "Ahhhh, shit, these motherfuckers are ready. Here, Bob, try some."

Soon I found myself eating a small plate of collard greens with hot sauce, a large funky glazed donut, and a beer that Miles gave me.

After that wonderful snack, Miles blurted out, "Let's go see your horse, Bob! I'll get dressed." While still talking to me, Miles proceeded to put on an outfit that was more than a fashion statement. He looked like the cover of any major fashion magazine. He shook his hair with all of its braided extensions like a dog shaking water off its coat and we were off.

Once in his driveway, I opened my car door, which was dusty and dirty from being around the barn and dust from the schooling ring.

Miles looked at me before I was about to start my car and said, "You want to zip up there in the Ferrari?"

I said, "Yes, sir, I would."

As we drove to the Malibu Riding and Tennis Club to see my horse, I told him that his car was much faster than mine.

Miles, looking surprised, said, "No shit, Bob, I'm glad we cleared that up."

Arriving at the stable, Miles asked if he could pull my horse out and have a look at him. I opened the stall door and Mandela was still enjoying his lunch. He was not happy to be disturbed.

"He's beautiful, Bob, but he ain't happy to see nobody. . . . I can see that." Miles put the halter around my horse and led him out. He looked him in the eyes and said, "You a big pretty motherfucker . . . and you need to be this size to carry Bob's big ass. What's your name?"

I interjected, "His name is Mandela."

Miles snapped, "I ain't asking you, Bob, I'm asking the horse . . . are you black?"

Mandela got a little uncomfortable and pulled back from Miles and reared up slightly.

Miles decided, "OK, big pretty boy, I'll let you finish your lunch." As Miles walked my horse back into his stall, I saw a nightmare approaching.

Heather, one of the riders and a rather proper but delightful British woman, was coming to give her horse some grain. When she reached us carrying her brown bag of Pride Mix, she noticed the jet black cross Miles was wearing, awarded to him by the Knights of Malta. She stopped and said, "Well, hello, Bob," and to Miles she said, "My dear sir, that's a lovely cross you're wearing."

Miles looked sternly and said, "Thank you, I'm a knight."

Heather replied, "Well, I'm British."

And Miles said, "So what?"

Returning to his house, he asked me if I had my horn with me. I told him I wasn't sure, I had to check my car. I looked in my trunk and sure enough, I had brought my horn.

"Bring it in," he ordered.

Suddenly I got a little nervous. What if he asked me to play the blues, a ballad? Would he laugh at my jazz playing?

As I entered the house, I kept thinking to myself about how this was more than I had expected from our first meeting. I guess I had passed the test. It was 4:00 p.m. and I had been with him for several hours and was forced to the conclusion that he must have liked me.

Erin held the door open as we entered the living room.

Miles said, "Go ahead, warm up. I'm going to have some more greens."

As I started my warm-up, Miles began to comment. "Ah huh! Listen to that shit, Erin, a nigger playing a French horn like that . . . ah huh!"

As I started to play faster and faster figures in my warm-up, Miles blurted out, "All right, Bob, don't get cute now . . . playing all that fast-fancy shit."

He came back into the living room and sat down in front of me eating a plate of greens, making a smacking sound as he chewed on his home-cooked favorite. Then he said, "I make you nervous sitting here staring at you like this?" He laughed and said, "Bob, play that solo that makes them white boys turn red. It's a nice solo, but why they turn so red when they play it?"

I asked him which solo was that.

"Oh, Stravinsky, Firebird, at the very end of the suite there's a real quiet French horn solo and the motherfuckers turn red as a beet, Goddamn . . . play that shit for me."

I knew then that he meant the Berceuse in the finale of the *Firebird Suite*. I took a deep breath and played the solo. While I was playing, Miles was making comments: "That's some pretty shit, Bob. Erin, you hear that mother—I mean, Bob—playin' that shit? What's so hard about that solo, Bob?"

I told him that it wasn't hard. It was just that it contained a lot of the worst notes on the horn and you have to make sure they're in tune.

"So when you gone turn red, Bob?" Miles laughed so loud, I could see the greens still stuck in his teeth. "I guess a nigger can't turn no color except blue," he said, still laughing.

The phone rang. It was Barbara. Miles was talking very softly and looking back at me every so often. I heard him say, "Yeah, yeah, he's a nice guy . . . a little strange." He looked back at me to see if I'd heard what he said. It was very funny the way his large white eyes revealed his guilt. He hung up the phone and said, "That was Barbara. Oh, I didn't say nothin' bad about you."

As I drove home after that amazing experience, I was wondering how I was going to concentrate and play the concert that night after meeting Miles Davis.

The next time I saw Barbara, she said "Well, I guess you two hit it off OK. Miles said that he approved of our relationship and that we could continue on as far as he was concerned, but to tell you that you are 'one lucky motherfucker to be dating me.'"

# CHAPTER FIFTY-ONE

~

# Salzburg Festival

It was 1992 and the Los Angeles Philharmonic was invited to Salzburg Festival, the oldest and most prestigious classical music festival in the world.

When the philharmonic arrived in Salzburg for a month-long residency, I was experiencing the height of my career as assistant principal French horn of the Los Angeles Philharmonic. I had been in the orchestra for twenty-two years and playing a good amount of principal horn, which was well beyond my contracted duties.

I was in my prime as a brass player, and my playing situation in the French horn section was as good as it was ever going to be when the Salzburg residency came along.

The Salzburg residency was far superior to being on tour. It was more like a month-long "one-nighter."

Once I got to my hotel, Hotel Byricherhof, I showered and went for a walk around the beautiful city. I remembered well how the Austrians stare at people of color from my past visits to the old city. It never really bothered me much. Sometimes for fun I would lash out at them in German, *"Warum starrin Sie so viel."* [Why do you stare so much?] They always looked very surprised and replied, *"Oh, es tut mir leid."* [Sorry.]

When I got back to my hotel, I decided to ask the concierge about the constant staring I always received when in Austria. He said that he understood my concern and that people in Salzburg do stare, but that it wasn't a bad thing really. I asked him to explain.

"Well, you see, here in Austria, as far as black people are concerned, we have many Africans whom to us look quite normal, but you African Americans are looking so different. You are so striking looking and I might add quite beautiful as a people. You are larger and grander in stature than the Africans here, you dress better, your color is more interesting—more beautiful, making you really stand out. Therefore, when we are staring at you here in Salzburg, especially being such a small town *mentalität*, you must understand that it is not that we have any bad feelings against you because you are black, in the racist way, like you have in the United States. It's just that we really find you quite interesting and, may I say, just plain fun to look at. I hope that you now understand this staring problem."

During the Salzburg residency, the workload of the French horn section was quite heavy and the principal horns were both worried about the major works they had to play and were fighting over which one of them would play the famous Emperor's Waltz by Johann Strauss. It was an unwritten rule in the section that when this happened they ended up asking *me* to play the extra works. So they offered me the Emperor's Waltz—not a problem, by any means, except that we were playing at *Salzburg* Festival and this was *their* music. As I said, this was the oldest and most prestigious classical musical festival in the world.

In spite of my exuberance about playing in Salzburg, I could see that the playing conditions at the festival were going to be physically uncomfortable. The orchestra had just changed back to wearing full dress, so the outfits were therefore brand new. The concert was going to be televised using extremely hot lights with cameramen flying all over the stage and, of course, with the heat wave of 100 degrees, it was in a concert hall built without air conditioning, because in Salzburg they never had the need for it, so it was certainly going to heat up the playing experience.

The first rehearsal of the Emperor's Waltz was a clear indication of what was to come. There was a large gap the size of a small road for the TV cameras that ran through the middle of the orchestra, dividing the string section from the winds and brass.

When we started to rehearse, the TV crew began their rehearsal right along with us. It was always a busy task for the TV control room to keep up with the music and for the camera crew to focus on instruments that had a big solo and move on to the next instrument with a solo or an instrument section and then to the conductor with wide-angle shots, always creating distractions for the orchestra.

The evening performance was buzzing with excitement. As I entered the Grosse Konzerte Halle, I noticed across the street hundreds of locals standing in a roped-off section on both sides of the entrance waiting to see the parade of people who attended every year from all over the world—the rich and famous, heads of state, and American high society arriving in their limousines, the women with their jewelry and beautiful gowns. However, I couldn't shake the feeling of snobbery that I got from the high-end Salzburg audience. It was as if they were saying, "Let's hear this American orchestra play *our* music in *our* house, in the presence of *our* world-class prestige."

I was a little nervous as the lights dimmed for the beginning of the concert, but mostly uncomfortable wearing the brand new cotton shirt and tail coat that made it seem even warmer. I knew I would be all right once Esa-Pekka came out and started. The music always calmed my nerves; it had a power over me that demanded my full concentration and focus.

As the music director made his entrance and took his bows, I recognized the people in the front row: all the celebrated maestros that I had played under for so many years.

Once the music started, I relaxed and even the busy TV cameras didn't bother me any more.

My mouth was watering for my first big moment when I got to play the famous main melody. Finally, from what seemed like half a mile away, Esa-Pekka looked right at me and cued my solo entrance with the largest arm-stretching gesture possible. I was so excited that I could actually feel myself wanting to smile as I took a really deep breath pushing any hint of tension out of my body and sang out the wonderful tune on my horn. Esa-Pekka kept his eyes glued on me as he playfully stretched and shaped the famous waltz melody.

Once the first big solo was over, I relaxed and paced myself like a long-distance runner, playing the many waltz off-beats light and easy. I wanted to save my lip for the many repeats of the famous waltz melody and for the next big moment at the end of the piece.

The orchestra was playing very well in spite of the TV cameras and the sheer weight of the event that was Salzburg Festival.

During my rests in the music, I noticed the TV lights reflecting off some of the sweating faces in the audience. They were feeling the heat like everyone else.

Towards the end of the piece, I took several deep breaths and got ready for the wonderful ending where the horn and cello play the main theme together in harmony. The cello plays the main melody and the horn plays the harmony. It was such a beautiful moment and I always loved playing it. When that moment came, I forgot that I had my own cameraman for that particular passage. He dropped down on me like a giant python from out of nowhere, whipping his camera into position just eight inches from my jaw. I noticed that the cello had a camera on him in the same manner. On the TV monitor, I could see the shot they had created. It was a split-screen effect between the cello and horn. Such a magical event—I couldn't miss a note—it had to be perfect.

After the concert, as I walked into my hotel lobby feeling very relieved, the whole staff applauded me. They said, in German, "We saw you playing in the TV and you looked very serious. The music was quite beautiful and we are proud to have you staying here at our Hotel Byricherhof."

~

# Finale

The saddest and most difficult time in my musical career was losing my dear friend Jerome Ashby to cancer in 2007. He was indeed my only true peer. I have many great memories of him, but most enjoyable was performing the Bach Brandenburg Concerto with him at Gateways Music Festival, an all-black music festival that took place at the Eastman School of Music every fall.

When I arrived at the festival, I went to my hotel room to freshen up and then to the lobby to meet Ashby and the rest of the black French horn section. Before they arrived, I sat in the lobby and watched as the all-black orchestra members arrived. It was something I never thought I would ever experience in my lifetime. They kept coming, especially the black women, scores of them carrying cello, viola, and violin cases one after another, smiling and greeting each other, creating a scene I had only witnessed with white orchestra players.

It was a new day, the early 1990s, and all the black women in classical music that Ashby and I never got to experience when we were coming up were now on the planet.

The Gateway concerts were great, but the "after the concert hang" was even better. Everyone was excited to be together and of course they would be, because all of those black classical players were coming from situations where they were always the lone black person.

The thing that really surprised me was the fact that every one of those players knew about me. Of course, I was one of the oldest players there and since there are so few black players in major orchestras, I suppose I had become a rather visible icon.

As time went on, I realized that I was not going to get married in the Bel-Air house, that I miraculously ended up with, nor was I going to die there. I actually grew tired of the downtown commute to my job and wanted to start mapping out my exit strategy from the Los Angeles Philharmonic.

I was not happy with my work situation in the horn section; in fact, it was getting worse as each year passed. Therefore, I moved downtown across the street from my workplace. It was a very heady time in my life. I paid off every bill I ever had and started thinking about writing this book as part of that exit strategy.

I decided to write an article, "Come Hear Me Play," written mainly to black people who thought it was so great that I was playing in the philharmonic but never came to hear me play. That was also my personal demographic poll to see if anyone was interested in a person like me at all.

The article was first published in a small throwaway newspaper, *Accent LA*, published in the black community. The philharmonic was first to reprint it in their concert program, and the article got published and reprinted almost ten more times. With help from close friends, I started to write my book.

My last concert with the Los Angeles Philharmonic was with the very fine and celebrated maestro Lorin Maazel. We played the Benjamin Britten *War Requiem*. At the end of the concert, the maestro gave me my final bow. It was a sweet moment, with my older brother Ronnie and many dear friends in the audience. That moment, that final bow, I thought would live only in my memory for the rest of my life. However, I found out later that a friend of mine was able to get a photo of it.

A few hours later, I was no longer a member of the Los Angeles Philharmonic. It was a departure with a deep sense of completeness. I had played a lot of music in those thirty-seven years and I was ready for a change. I was satisfied and happy to move on to the next wave in life. Many people in the orchestra thought I was too young to retire. I had a wonderful philharmonic departure party and my life was mine.

I departed the philharmonic, yes, but my pension I saw as a wonderful gift that would cover my basics until I could move on to the next station in life. So to me it was more of a commencement—a beginning.

My first new engagement was a teaching job at UC Berkeley. I got a call one day from a woman who ran a program called "Young Musicians Program." She asked me if I could teach beginning students and create a French horn section for their symphony orchestra. I took the position and I fly every Saturday to Berkeley, California, to teach my students, which has become very gratifying, because the students are very fast learners with first-rate minds.

After a few years into my new free life, I found a new house in Baldwin Hills Estates. I moved from my downtown, walk-to-work environment and rejoined middle-class America. However, in contrast to my other homes, Baldwin Hills Estates is an upscale black community, a concept to which I'm joyfully adjusting.

After a life spent largely in a white working world, living in an upscale black community gives an added sense of gratification.

I've yet to experience all the treasures of living here, but again it was an early lecture from my high school mentor Jones, who said I should always embrace being a black man, that set me on the right path, and I certainly have. He was right, it has given me a lifetime of rich experiences and I couldn't imagine being anything else. And for all the things ever said about black people—good and bad—they are, with all praise to God, my piece of humanity.

Being in good health, I'm still looking forward to new adventures. I still wonder sometimes how I was able to endure all the strife and stress of playing in a symphony orchestra for so many years. But strife and stress are part of the yin and yang of life. One could never have a rich life such as I had without the ingredients of both the positive and the negative. Even God will tell you that she needs both elements to do what she does.

I also realize that I am a beneficiary of what my black forefathers achieved and carved out for me in these United States. They have been a large part of my inspiration, along with my family, to achieve what I have. They have passed me the torch and now I know beyond a doubt that my calling in life is to initiate, open doors, and engage the impossible.

~

# List of Negro Musicians Compiled by the New York Philharmonic (April 1969)

## Violin

Elwyn Adams—Concertmaster, Bordeaux Symphony, Boredeaux, France (NEC)

Sandford Allen—New York Philharmonic

John Blair—c/o San Diego Symphony

Augustus Braithwalte—Peabody Conservatory, Baltimore

Valerie Bynum

Doreen Calender

Charlene Clark—St. Louis Symphony

Winston Collymore

Noel DaCosta

Corinne Davis—New England Conservatory

Gail Dixon—Mannes

Marie Hence

Stephanie Lee—Cleveland

Sylvia Medford

Thomas H. Poindexter—Roxbury, Massachussetts

Howard Rollock

Paul Ross—Pittsburgh Symphony

Booker T. Rowe

Barbara Saxton—Cleveland

Joseph Striplin—St. Louis Symphony

## Viola

Julien Barber
Ada Boyston—New England Conservatory
Alfred Brown
Selwart Clarke
Rollice Dale—Los Angeles
Denis De Cateau—Faculty, College of San Mateo, San Mateo, California
Renard Edwards—New School, Philadelphia
Marilyn Gates—Manhattan
David Johnson
Julius Miller
Ashley Richardson—Manhattan School (Lilian Fuchs)
Melvyn Roundtree—Philadelphia
Marcas Thompson—Juilliard School

## Violincello

William Brent—Portland Symphony (Oregon)
Ronal Cooper—UCLA (Piatagorsky pupil)
Edward Culbreath
Marion Cumbo
Bernard Fennell—Manhattan School
Carlotta Gary
Norman John—Philadelphia
Ronald Lipscomb—New York City (Marlboro, summer)
Earl Madison—Pittsburgh Symphony
Jo Anne Minnis—Cleveland
Kermit Moore
Stephen Peirson—Juilliard
Ronald Sanders
Patrick Smith—Hartford Symphony
Anne Taylor—Manhattan School
Charles Turner—Cleveland
Donald White—Cleveland Orchestra
Edith Wint

## Bass

Philip Bowler—Hartt College (Double Bass)
Charles Burrell—Denver Symphony

Ron Carter
Arthur Davis—New York City
Richard Davis—New York City
William Davis
Lucille Dixon
Guillermo Edghill—Juilliard
Eustis Guillemet
Dennis James—Juilliard
Bruce Lawrence—Seattle Symphony
William Love—Manhattan (ex-New Orleans Philharmonic)
Wendell Marshall
David Moore—New York City
Donald Pate—New England Conservatory
Benjamin Patterson
Warren Petty
Walter Robinson—New England Conservatory
Henry Scott—Baltimore Symphony
Clarence Stephens—North Carolina
James Tranks
Lewis Worrell

## Flute

Carl Atkins—Faculty, New England Conservatory
Hal Archer—Manhattan
Antoinette Handy
Kenneth Harris—Manhattan
John Jackson—New York City
Joyce Jackson—San Francisco Conservatory
Harold Jones—New York City
Hubert Laws—New York City
Cleophas Lyons—In Europe
James Mack—Chicago Civic College, Music Department Head
Richard Smith

## Oboe

Ralph Flanagan—Chicago
Joseph Haygood—UCLA
Robert Joelle—Philadelphia, Settlement Music School
Ernest Simms—Allston, Massachussetts

Harry Smyles—Personnel Manager, Symphony of the New World

## Clarinet

Kenneth Adams
Weldon Berry—Curtis (American Symphony)
James Cutliff—San Francisco Conservatory
William Draper
Roderick Loney—Henry Street Settlement Music School
Michael Pierce—Juilliard

## Trumpet

Robert Agnew—Berklee
Benjamin Forney—University of Kansas
Leonard Goines
Renauld Jones Jr.
John Mosley—Manhattan
Jimmy Owens
James Tinsley—New England Conservatory
Joseph Wilder
Wilmer Wise—Baltimore Symphony

## French Horn

Clarence Cooper—Denver Symphony
Vincent Griffin—Henry Street
Sharon Johnson
Robert Northern
Edward Perry
Julius Watkins
Robert Watt—New England Conservatory

## Horn

Clarence Cooper—Denver Symphony (also listed under French horn)
Charles V. Cornish—Halifax, Nova Scotia
Charles Darden—San Francisco Conservatory
Bill Wilder—ABC Staff Orch.
Aaron Wyatt—San Francisco Conservatory

## Trombone

George Jeffers
Porter Poindexter—New York City
Alvin Thomas

## Bassoon

Fred Allston—Curtis
Kenneth Alston
Cedric Coleman—New England Conservatory
Dennis Milner—Hartford Conservatory
Karl Porter—New York City

## Tuba

John Buckingham
Joseph Daley—Manhattan

## Percussion

Dolphy Abrahams—Hartford Conservatory
Matthew Hopkins—Settlement Music School, Philadelphia
James Lattimer—Madison, Wisconsin (University of Wisconsin)
Harvey Mason—New England Conservatory
Mark Sunkett—Curtis, Philadelphia
Carl Thompson—Boston

# Index

~

# About the Author

**Robert Lee Watt** is the first African American French horn player to be hired by a major symphony orchestra in the United States. He attended the New England Conservatory of Music, where he studied French horn with Harry Shapiro of the Boston Symphony. In 1970, at age twenty-two, he was hired by the Los Angeles Philharmonic as assistant first French horn under maestro Zubin Mehta. He held this position until 2008. This is his first book on a rarely written about topic—the experience of African American classical musicians playing in symphony orchestras. Mr. Watt has written several articles on classical and jazz musicians. He was a staff writer for *Brass Bulletin*, a brass trade magazine published in Switzerland.